# The Grunt

# 2

### The Lonely Heart Series

*Latrivia S. Nelson*

**RiverHouse PUBLISHING**

**The Grunt**
RiverHouse Publishing, LLC
1509 Madison Avenue
Memphis, TN 38104

All **RiverHouse, LLC** Titles, Imprints and Distributed Lines are available at special quantity discounts for bulk purchases for sales promotions, premiums, fund-raising and educational or institutional use.

First RiverHouse, LLC Trade Paperback Printing:  05/30/16

ISBN:   978-0-9962725-8-2

www.riverhousepublishingllc.com

This book is dedicated to all the service members of every branch of the United States Military who have served this country with pride, honor and dignity. Your work will never be forgotten. *Thank you.*

# Acknowledgments

I would like to acknowledge four very important people for helping me complete this project. To my husband, Bruce Welch, thank you for reading my work, critiquing conversations and allowing me to see things through a man's eyes. To my editing team, Miranda Howell, Michelle Jackson and Karen Moss, who are very much my friends, thank you for encouraging me and combing through each detail of this final work that culminates my career as Latrivia Nelson and starts my career as Latrivia Welch. I appreciate all three of you so much for your own service to this country, both foreign and domestic, and the sacrifices that all three of you have made for us. It is an honor to call you friend, colleague and in my case, husband.

Dear Friend,

This is it! My last book under the name Latrivia S. Nelson. As I think back on all the wonderful memories that you've given me through your unwavering support over the last six years, it truly brings tears to my eyes. I've connected with you all on a level that I never knew was possible through the power of storytelling.

It's only fitting that the last book in this chapter of my life be The Grunt 2 from the Lonely Heart Series. This series is truly about love saving people from heartbreak and restoring their faith not only in man but also in themselves. Each of the characters is seeking something different and they find it in the person that they fall in love with. And in each story, the African-American woman is always the hero. Regardless of what race you are as my reader, you have to admit that's pretty awesome. We're breaking barriers with our books and exploring new perceptions of the interracial romance experience. And with your support, we will continue to push the envelope and challenge the norm.

Now, I start a new journey. Same great stories. Same sincere passion. New name. Latrivia Welch is the beginning of a new life with new experiences that I hope to share with you for many years to come.

I hope that you enjoy my last book as Latrivia S. Nelson, but I hope you'll be geared up and ready to buy everything new from Latrivia Welch. And don't worry. All the other stories that we've been working toward will still be completed.

Till the next time...

Your friend and author,
Latrivia
www.latriviawelch.com

# Chapter 1

**Camp Leatherneck**
**Helmand Province**
**Afghanistan**

Brett Black wished for winter. In his mind, he literally pondered what snow would feel like hitting his skin in the middle of a white *bitching* blizzard, just so he could mentally cool his body down from the scorching summer heat that was tipping just over 120 degrees today.

He had learned the trick of mind-over-matter a few tours ago. It didn't *just* take lots of water and a little shade to keep the body from over-heating. It took a steel-trap mind that was determined not to falter in order to fight Middle Eastern summers, *unless you wanted to be one of the poor bastards that got a silver bullet up the ass by a less than gentle Corpsman.* He had experienced that back in Recon training many years ago. It had not been pleasant or forgetta-ble, which was why now, he drank more water than probably half of the men in his unit com-bined....no way was he getting power drilled by the silver bullet ever again.

Today, the sun blazed down on his body like hell's fury, nearly singeing his retinas even though he had on his favorite Ray-Ban shades. Everything on him was sunburned, a true testament to a deteriorating ozone layer that no one wanted to talk about. Plus, he started to chafe in very intimate areas, despite the use of baby powder, and his farmer's tan had to be the most pronounced he had ever experienced.

God, he hated this place. He hated the heat. He hated the smell. He hated the irritation. But war was like that, never easy or pleasant, even in the smallest of ways.

Brett took a deep breath and looked out over the camp as he quietly gathered his thoughts. He had spent all day mulling over briefing materials, cleaning up strategy and looking at satellite photos. And before he began his descent into his necessary evil and purpose for existence, he just wanted to look out over this shithole and take it all in exactly as it was one last time.

The hot wind was coarse and thick with the distinct smell of burning waste from the open-air burn pits. The hellfire wind carried with it little bits of sand that stuck to the body and slowly dug its way into pores, which always made him itch. And when he wasn't itching and sweating, he was chaffing.

He had been here in the armpits of the Earth for seven months. One more month and he'd be back at home. Back stateside. Out of the shit. It was the second most pleasant thought he could conjure. But for the moment, number one was snow. Lots of snow.

Spitting dip down on the sand beside his dirty boots, he glanced at his watch and realized it was his favorite time of the day. *Finally.*

Walking back into the barracks, he headed to his room to make his call. It was the one call he looked forward to, that thing nothing – no matter what – got in the way of him making this call. Hell, this special part of his day was the only reason he was still sane.

"Evening, Staff Sergeant," one of his men said, walking past him in a purposeful stride.

Brett's head inclined. "Corporal," Brett said in a scratchy deep baritone with an authoritative nod. He saw the man's eyes, wanting to ask if he was going to be present at the briefing. "I'll be there in 10 mikes, Corporal," he said, even though the man wouldn't dare ask it.

As a rule of thumb, a Corporal never asked his Staff Sergeant much, but never did he ask about his whereabouts. Still, the men in his unit were a little more relaxed, a little more like family, especially as the months rolled on and the missions had become more dangerous.

"Yes, Staff Sergeant," the Corporal replied, disappearing down the hall toward the war room. Everyone knew Corporals had to arrive early. They had something to prove. He, on the other hand, would make them all wait a minute.

Arriving to his room, he closed the door quietly, grabbed his laptop to log on and pulled off his cover. Immediately, his heart sped up a few beats. Sand fell to his wide muscular shoulders. A dirty blonde perfect high-and-tight haircut emerged, tanned around the edges from the sun. He could smell sweat and Axe body spray seeping from the opening of his blouse, and he was soaking wet from the heat. How he wanted to take a shower right then and rid himself of the long day. Just another thought of what he'd do when he got home. *Multiple showers in a day.*

The musical hum of Skype connecting him to his little family back at Camp Lejeune made him as giddy as a kid on Christmas. Only three things made him flutter: Courtney, Bella and Cameron. Two rings into the call, his wife, Courtney, answered, just as eager to talk to him as he was to her.

"Hey, baby," Courtney said, gazing into her monitor with a bright smile. The glow from the monitor on her face made her look like an angel. Her hazel brown eyes sparkled with excitement. It was literally the best thing that he'd seen all morning.

"Hey, baby," Brett said back. Just the sight of her eased his spirit. He pulled the monitor as close to his face as he could, wanting to reach out and kiss her heart-shaped lips. "Whatcha doing?" he asked, hoping she had on something sexy so he could sneak a peek at what he was missing before he logged off. *A man had to have something to do when he was in the shower.*

Her voice was low and seductive. She looked around the room as if someone would hear her. "Just put Bella back down to sleep for her morning nap," she whispered. "She's right beside me, instead of the crib. I think she likes our bed more. I had to pull the curtains to make it dark in here so she could sleep better."

Brett had other thoughts about his bed, and it didn't involve his daughter. Another thing he'd do when he got home. *Bang his wife multiple times a day.*

Scratching his nose, he sneezed. "How's her schedule doing?" he asked, imagining his brand new baby girl curled up with a teddy bear in her crib. God, he wanted to see her for himself. He had memorized her perfect face, every single solitary feature. However, he wanted to hold her in his arms and kiss her adorable little cheeks. He wanted to see her smile for himself, instead of always gawking at her photos.

"She's getting there," Courtney said, moving her long black hair out of her face. "How are you, baby? You look so tired." She studied his aquamarine blue eyes and dark circles under them. Without being there, she knew that he wasn't sleeping. He never slept.

"I'm bored," he lied. "We're not doing shit here. *Hurry up and wait.* Same old thing, just a different day. Trust me. There is nothing going on here." He quickly changed the subject. "How's my son?" Brett hated talking about himself. He hated being the center of attention and abhorred having people worry about him, especially Courtney. She had enough on her plate taking care of both kids alone. Thank God for Diane, her mother, who made the effort to help them out.

"*My* son is doing fine," she corrected with a giggle. "He misses you. We all do."

Brett tried to ignore the obvious sadness in her voice. Every time, she became sadder still. He knew that descent; he had experienced the same with Amy, which made him even more eager to get home. "Has he been doing his homework?" he asked, resting back in his bunk. He kicked his feet up for the moment and rested his head back on his pillow. "Tell him no PlayStation® if he doesn't get it done on time. Kindergarten is the real deal. It's the start of his career as a student."

Courtney laughed at his seriousness. No matter what it was, he was always 100 percent dedicated to success. She chuckled at him. "He's doing his work and watching the calendar daily. He knows you'll be home in a month. So, I think he's starting to clean up shop."

Brett couldn't hide his pride. A small smile tugged at his wide lips. "Smart guy."

"Are you still not smoking?" she probed. They had agreed that he would quit his worst habit at the birth of Bella. Courtney wanted to make sure that he was around for his daughter as long as possible, and she also didn't want either child suffering from second hand smoke.

Brett smiled bigger. He didn't have to lie *this time*. "Yep. I haven't smoked once." He did avoid, however, telling her that he'd taken up chewing tobacco, but he was pretty sure he could kick that too before he headed home. "So where you wanna go when I get home?" They had been talking about vacationing for months but had yet to come to a conclusion, mostly because they both felt it bad luck to plan so far in advance.

"Since you're taking 30 days' leave, I was hoping we could go to two places," she said, sitting up in the bed. As she moved the monitor, he got a glimpse of her pink lace nighty.

"Damn," he said, forgetting what they were talking about. His eyes narrowed on her dark brown skin and the contrast of it against the pink lace. He licked his lips. "What do you have on, girl?"

Courtney grinned; glad she had his full attention now. "Just a little something I threw on for the call." She moved the monitor where he could get a better view of it. Her voluptuous frame quickly came into view. "Do you like?" she teased.

"Pregnancy does the body well," he said, biting his lip. What he wouldn't give to taste her right now. An image of her hoisted up on his desk across the room came to mind, but as quickly as he had thought about it, he had to suppress it. Couldn't go into the briefing with a glaring hard on. "Did you send me the pictures I asked for of you in the shower?"

"I sent them five minutes ago," she said, raising her cell phone. "You better not let anyone else see them. I'm not playing."

"Are you kidding me? I'll be guarding those pictures like they are the President," he said, licking his lips again. "I want you so bad." His voice was husky now. "It's been fucking forever. I'm dying over here."

Courtney adjusted the monitor where she could see his face again. Her eyes flashed with sincerity. "I want you too," she said, biting her lip. "One more month and I'm all yours."

"Just thirty days," Brett said, taking a deep breath. "Shit," he adjusted himself. "You might want to get that birth control you were talking about before I get home. We've had seven months and thousands of miles between us. I'm not standing for anything else between us when I get home. No condoms. No bullshit."

Courtney laughed. "I'm already on it," she said yawning. "The doctor says that I could be very fertile right now. So, I don't want to take any chances. Don't get me wrong. I love having your children. I just would like to space them out enough to have some time for myself."

"I hear ya." Brett had to change the subject or he'd be walking around with full wood for the rest of the night, even talking about getting her pregnant turned him on. "So what two places do you want to go to?"

"The Bahamas and to New Orleans," she said, pulling something off the bed. Waving papers into the monitor, her voice pitched high. "I've already been researching traveling options. I found some great deals that won't break the bank. Plus, there is a military discount for both."

"I guess I'm good for something," he joked.

"Sometimes."

"Whatever you want, baby," Brett said, looking at his watch. *Damn it. It was time to go.* "I hate to cut us short," he said apologetically.

Courtney tilted her head. "But you've got to go because you're bored and you have nothing to do," she finished his sentence condescendingly. "Just sitting around doing nothing, eh?"

"Yep," Brett said with a huff. "You know the drill."

"Just be careful doing nothing and being bored," she said with sarcasm lacing her voice. Touching the screen, she pursed her lips together. *How she missed him.*

"I will."

Not as an afterthought, but almost, she inserted, "And tell my big brother to be careful too."

Brett laughed. "He's always the most careful asshole on the Base."

Courtney couldn't help but laugh. "He loves you now. You're his brother-in-law."

Brett shrugged. "Love is such a strong word. I think he tolerates me. But I'm okay with being tolerated...it requires less attention than love. And no one wants the Captain's attention."

Courtney grinned, even though her eyes were a bit wet. "Well, I love you."

He paused and drank her face in. It was amazing that he was still so smitten with her. "I love you, too," he said, kissing his fingers and putting them to the screen. "Kiss my babies. Tell them Daddy will be home real soon."

"Bye," she said, hating to have him go so soon.

"Bye, baby." Logging off, he closed his computer and placed it back on his desk.

Yep, he'd rather be anywhere but here most days. The heat. The stench. The sand spiders. The occasional dysentery. The insurgents. The food. He spent so much time reflecting on what other things that he could have done with his life. Only he loved the Marine Corps, and he loved his wife and they intersected dead smack into one another to make his life more complete. So, this must have been where he was supposed to be. There was very little argument to make about that. But at this very moment, it wasn't just anywhere he was thinking about. He knew exactly where he wanted to be...home with his family.

# Chapter 2

"The art of coalition command - whether it is here in Afghanistan, whether it was in Iraq or in Bosnia or in Haiti - is to take the resources you are provided with, understand what the strengths and weaknesses are and to employ them to the best overall effect."
– Gen. David Petraeus

Brett stalked into the dimmed war room, refreshed and newly groomed, just in time to rush to the front to begin Force Recon's confidential briefing. Sitting around him were 10 of the smartest and deadliest men that he'd ever known, and they all had the distinct pleasure of serving in the same platoon under the direct supervision of Captain David Lawless, the pristine African-American man in the corner watching everyone quietly with his arms folded across his chest. He had a hawk-like glare, dark smooth skin, piercing brown eyes hidden under jet black lashes, bold carved features and a screaming high and tight. In essence, he was a walking, talking poster child for the Corps.

Brett and Captain Lawless had a sordid past that left them with several things in common. First, the unwavering love for the Marine Corps; second, elite training under pressure; third, a deep love and admiration for retired Colonel Jeffery Lawless; and lastly, familial ties. In short, his Captain was also his brother-in-law and for the longest time, his most vocal adversary. He was also his superior officer. The combination had proven to be a bleeding ulcer for Brett during the first part of their relationship.

Married into the family only a year ago by way of Courtney Lawless, the feelings of admiration that often came with nuptials were substituted with tempered mutual respect, which in Brett's mind was a step up from where he had first been relegated to – the live-in boyfriend that everyone hated. In his defense, he didn't know he was courting and employing the Colonel's daughter. However, reality dictated that no one gave a damn what he didn't know.

A million evolutions of life had happened since then.

A new marriage. A new baby. A new tour of duty. A new opportunity to get it right. And he intended to do just that. He wanted nothing more than to prove to his wife that he would always be the man for her and he wanted to prove to her family that she had chosen someone worthy of her, especially since he had such bad blood with his late wife's family. Lord in heaven knew that he was glad to be moderately rid of them and all their racist right-wing rhetoric. But the Lawless family was something different. He really cared to be accepted by them. After all, they were all the family he had left. For him, such a large task started with the simplest step – doing his job. And he was good at that. In fact, he prided himself on it. He was a lifer in the Marine Corps, destined to retire after 25 years and spend his days tinkering on his truck and making love to his wife.

"Good evening, Marines," Brett said, scanning the room to make sure everyone was present. His authoritative, scratchy baritone echoed and boomed, waking up nodding men who slouched over in their seats, from a long day in the exhausting heat.

In that exhilarating moment, he transformed from father and husband Brett Black to Marine Corps Staff Sergeant Brett Black. They were two very distinct personas of the same man. One was designed to love and protect his family. The other designed to be the swift and accurate arm of the military.

"Good evening, Staff Sergeant," the men answered nearly in unison. Everyone snapped to immediate attention. Heads shot up. Backs went erect. All eyes faced forward.

Something that never changed - not in 244 years, not in a million men, not on seven continents - was the sounding off of well-bred, elite, human killing machines. It was the first thing that was taught in boot camp, one of the main things that Marines carried with them to military occupational specialty or MOS school, and it was the thing that bonded them during grueling trainings – *cadence*. He loved the sound - could never get enough of it. It motivated him, mobilized him, and reminded him yet again, why he loved the Marine Corps.

Sergeant Morales, aka Rusty, a 23-year-old baby faced Latino in charge of all things technical, turned on the PowerPoint presentation on cue as the men picked up and opened their dossiers to follow along with the mission briefing.

A satellite photo popped up on the projector screen of a white stone house in the Helmand River Valley. As Rusty zoomed in on the house sitting along the waterway, near a mix of patchy grass, rocks and sand, Brett rubbed his temples and cleared his throat. He could feel a headache coming on. They had become more frequent lately and lasted longer and longer, but for the moment, he had to ignore it.

His rasping voice carried across the room without effort. "At o-8 hundred hours, we received orders to raid this location exactly 250 miles due North from our base. Intel has indicated that this location is of key importance to our boys who are taking the fight a little closer to the locals than we have to." He paused to give Rusty time to move to a ground view of the house. "As you can see, the home appears a little more modern than homes in this region, *so you can't miss it*. It was built with the sole purpose of housing computer servers that feed intelligence and funds to local and regional cells of the Jihadists." His eyes widened slightly, mostly due to dull pain starting in his left temple. "We believe this house holds over 20 computers, stores, bank account numbers, files on real property in the area, contacts within the Afghanistan government who are providing protection and aid to cells both in this region and throughout the country, locations of munitions and other very important counterintelligence. Our goal is to acquire that information tonight at 2200 hours. This is a last minute operation, but we have painstakingly prepared the most optimal strategy we can in the short period of time given."

Captain Lawless finally stepped out of the shadows and unfolded his veiny muscular arms. He was a man of few words, and a serious and pragmatic planner.   Therefore, it went unsaid that he was unhappy with the impromptu mission, but as a servant to his country, unwilling to raise concerns with upper brass, he had worked with his team to create the most viable plan of action.

Moving into the view of his men, he turned toward the PowerPoint and slipped his hands into his pockets.   "Word from the top brass is that this information is central to our success in the Helmand Valley.  It would have been ideal to conduct this mission when the property was vacant or less heavily armed. However, in the last 48 hours, our satellites indicate that there has been a constant presence at the home, which is abnormal. Armed presence has tripled and so has overall activity in the neighboring city, which is also indicative of insurgents preparing for an attack."

Rusty clicked to another photo showing thermal infrared images of bodies outside of the home over a 48-hour time-span.

Captain Lawless sucked his teeth and talked calm and clear, standing like a statue in front of the image. "Our Intelligence close to the home has informed us that Mohammad Nabi, the British-educated Jihadist responsible for running the house and computers, may be at this location during the time the mission is carried out." His voice projected louder. "If he is, this mission becomes a snatch and grab spec op. If not, then we'll get him soon enough. Our sources indicate that he has not left the country in over four years. We don't expect him to go anywhere anytime soon. Our priority remains to collect the data, extract the target and evac so that air support can destroy the house. This will be our one and only opportunity, gentlemen." He turned his attention back to the men and glared at Brett. "I cannot stress the precision in which this mission must be carried out. Nabi is arranging to transfer millions of dollars and priceless information to another facility *permanently*. We have tonight and tonight only to get that information."

Brett didn't beat around the bush. This was not his idea of an optimal operation. There were too many variables and not enough planning. "There will be casualties," he said in a matter-of-fact tone. Scanning the room, he looked at each of his men. "It is my goal to ensure that those casualties are not American ones. Rules of engagement dictate this mission is deadly force authorized. Kill anything that moves. If they are there, they are a threat."

Captain Lawless quickly jumped in. Brett's form of communication was a bit crass for his tastes. Some things needn't be said, just understood. "Over 30 men are posted at the house. But because we need the information, any ideas about using strike drones are out. We have to physically enter the home, take the motherboards and jump drives, download the desktops, grab any documents that are visible and easily accessible and then get out. From the time boots land on the ground to the time that you are picked up a click from the home on the river bend, the operation in whole will be 20 minutes."

"What about logging in remotely?" Hound, one of the men on the team, asked from the back of the room. He scratched at his curly, dirty blonde ponytail and squinted at the screen. "Just in case we miss some information, how are we to ensure that it won't land back into the wrong hands? That's a lot to get in a short period of time. If this stuff is as important as you say, *and I don't doubt that it is*, overlooking something could cost additional lives down the road."

"We've already tried. It's not possible." Captain Lawless answered honestly. "This is our only recourse. What we don't collect during the mission will be destroyed by air support during the fly over. This is a time-sensitive target."

"Alright men. Let's go over to the planning table and walk through this mission one last time," Brett said as one the men hit the lights and Rusty turned off the projector. "Put on your thinking hats. We have to consider every possible threat and prepare."

His gut knotted every time he thought about tonight. He hated last-minute shit, and the idea of putting his men at risk was always daunting. He knew the wives, children, mothers and fathers of each of his men. Even losing one of them would be like losing all. Plus, this wasn't his first mission. Hell, it wasn't his 20th mission. With so much experience behind him, he knew that they were walking into a fucking mess. There was no doubt, however, that he could get the Intel. That was not the concern. These guys were.

Many years ago, a wiser, older Gunnery Sergeant had warned him what getting too close to men in an outfit could do, but he hadn't listened. Over time, he had gotten close to each and every one of his men. They were all family now. Hell, his best friend and godfather to his children, Staff Sergeant Joe Mabry, was across the room about to go under the wire with him.

*** 

Immediately after the briefing, all the men headed from the war room to dress out and prep for the mission. As they filed quietly out of the room, Brett caught a glimpse of his best friend, Joe, lingering back intentionally to have a few words with Brett alone. He stopped at the table and waited.

"Talk to the wife?" Brett asked when everyone else had left the room. Looking at the small figures on the table, he studied the plan in his mind again.

"Yep," Joe said, tugging at his dog chains. "She's suspicious as usual. You talk to Courtney?"

Just hearing her name sent a zinger up Brett's spine. "Yeah, just before I came in here. She's suspicious too. She knows something's up...always does. She makes these little digs about it, trying to fish out information. Hell, I might as well tell her I'm going on an operation instead of keeping it from her. I have no poker face when it comes to that woman."

"You know what?  The military actively recruits the wrong sex.  From across the ocean, these nosey ass women know everything.  Do you know the wife had the nerve to ask me if I had gotten new boot straps this morning?" Joe chuckled with pride. "I'm telling you, the entire female race is comprised of well-trained, natural spies."

Brett looked down at Joe's boots. "Well...have you purchased new boot straps?"

"Went as soon as I got off the phone," Joe said, pulling out his wallet. "Got a new photo today too.  The kids are growing fast, man. I need to hurry and get home to see the new little guy.  He's going to be shaving by the time I hit stateside."

Brett looked at the photo of Joe and Judy's newest creation.  He was a big healthy boy with his father's smile and his mother's Irish complexion. "Nice looking kid, man.  Too nice looking. You sure he's yours?"

Joe laughed. "Oh, I'm sure.  You sure about yours?"

Brett didn't let on to the fact that the joke rerouted to his end carried a different type of brevity.  Changing the subject, he shook his head.  His voice was ominous. "Just between the two of us...I got that feeling again."

Joe rolled his eyes. "You and your superstition. Man, your gut don't mean anything. It's just a stomach. It doesn't have supernatural powers."

"I know you say that, but, dude, my gut is never wrong," Brett said, walking out of the room with Joe into the empty hallway. Their voices echoed down the narrow strait.

"You and your gut can keep your bad luck over there," Joe said, forming a cross with his index fingers towards Brett to ward him off. "I'm covered by the blood. I ain't got time for your shit."

Brett pulled down Joe's fingers playfully. "I can't believe that you're saved now. You were already a mother hen, now it's like living with Madea in uniform."

"Going on 10 months with the Lord," Joe said, proudly. "I feel sober."

"You were never a hard-core drinker," Brett laughed.

Joe shook his head as if he was ready to explode into a fiery sermon. "No, sober in another kind of way." A broad smile crossed his brown lips and his eyes sparkled. "I feel free...refreshed. I feel like everything is going to be fine no matter what. Have you ever had that feeling, bruh?"

Brett pursed his lips together and considered the feeling. "When I'm with Courtney."

Joe leaned into Brett like he was telling him a huge secret. "What if I told you that you could have it all the time?"

"What if I told you that a couple hours before the op is not the time to try to save my soul," Brett said with a wink.

Joe's response was immediate, like a used car salesman. "It's the perfect time if you ask me."

"I got baptized when I was a teenager. You know that."

"Then all you're doing is returning back to the fold," Joe said as they walked.

"I tell you what, if I ever decided to get all churchy, then I'll come and see you first."

"Deal," Joe said, serious but playing.

Brett had known Joe for many years. He had been his confidant and often his big brother in times of despair. Over the course of their careers, Joe had been faithful to his wife, who was a white woman while he was a black man. He had persevered in the face of adversity and racism in the Marine Corps. In all, he was an honorable man before he was saved, but shortly before their last tour to Afghanistan, Joe had gone with the family, as he did every Sunday, to church and really found God. He hadn't been the same since. He was a better version of Joe and everyone around him knew it. Brett preferred it, although he also enjoyed giving him shit about it.

Brett patted his best friend on the back. "Think about what you're turning from," he joked. "No more titty bars, no more shots at the bar..."

Joe raised his hand to clarify. "No titty bars, but a few shots at the house will work. Drinking is fine, just gotta know my limits. I don't drink to get drunk anymore."

"Well, no more shots at the bar then. Just living your life on the straight and narrow. I can respect that. Hell, I'm so deep in love with Cort, until I can't see past her, so I know. I guess we've both just finally grown up and found a better life."

Joe huffed. "I want you to get saved so that you don't crumble if something were to ever go haywire in your life. Right now, you got it all figured out, *but in this life* we have to prepare for bigger trials. That preparation comes in the form of prayer and meditation. Think of it as Recon training on a spiritual level."

"You think Courtney is going to run off and leave me too?" It felt like a million years ago, but not even two years ago, his late wife had died in an airplane crash trying to ditch him to run to Japan to be with a higher-ranking Marine.

"I don't think Courtney is going anywhere," Joe clarified.

Brett stopped at the door of his room and looked his friend in the eye. "So why do I still have this gut thing, man? If everything in the world is fine, why is my gut going crazy?"

Joe laughed and walked off. "You need Jesus, man."

"Why don't you want to talk about the gut?" Brett said, shrugging his shoulders and laughing as he disappeared into his room.

# Chapter 3

"If in order to kill the enemy you have to kill an innocent, don't take the shot. Don't create more enemies than you take out by some immoral act."

-        General James "Mad Dog" Mattis

Dressed out in full tactical uniforms, camouflage, aviator gloves, go-packs and parachutes, the Recon Unit assembled quietly inside of the HH-60 Pave Hawk in preparation for their HALO (high-altitude, low-opening or HALO) parachute insertion jump.

It was everything that kids across the country dreamt of as they played their life-like video games, and everything wannabes lied about when trying to impress women in bars. However, this was the real thing; there were no video cameras for reality TV, no theme music for an action movie, no updates every minute on Facebook and most of all, no turning back for the sake of life over country.

Standing by the hatch already let down for their departure, Brett looked down the line at his men standing at the ready. Each one of these men were brave and had shown valor in the face of death a hundred times. Joe, Bear, Rusty, Geek and Hound. He would die for any of them, *all of them*, if needed. But he hoped that their training would prevent the need to ever make that decision.

Right before the team reached their mark, Brett stepped out where he could see his men and made his normal speech. It was the same one every time, but each time it was warranted, *needed in fact*, to remind each man of why he was there.

His voice thundered, "No one on this plane rang that bell three times in training. No one gave up *then*. No one gives up *now*. Do you know why they send us, Devil Dogs? It's because we're the baddest motherfuckers they could find!"

"Oorah!" the men replied in cadence. Their voices boomed like lightning against the black night as the wind from the open hatch beat across their camouflaged faces.

Bear, the six-foot six Irish ginger good ole boy from Alabama, spit his brown snuff out on the floor beside his boot and tugged at his Kevlar. It was his normal routine and Bear's way of saying that he was ready to earn his paycheck.

Joe made the sign of the cross and rolled his neck. *He was ready.*

Rusty kissed the picture of his son.

Hound scratched his balls.

Geek stood stoically focused on the hatch, ready to wig out on as many insurgents as possible as soon as his feet hit the ground.

Each man had a thing, and now was the time to do it.

Brett's square jaw clenched tight as he moved to the open hatch; the wind pushing and pulling at him like a rag doll. Anticipation coursed through his veins like a synthetic drug. The veins in his muscular neck protruded as he screamed, "Let's go to work!"

If one had never thought about their mortality before, they thought about it then, being as small as ants in a world so vast that it could suck them up before anyone could notice. The twinkling stars and the full moon in the sky looked close enough for the men to reach out and touch, and the ground so infinite below looked like it was a million miles away while they dwelled somewhere in the middle of this world and the next.

Brett stood by the opening, hitting each man on his back as they plunged out into the night in a free fall.

They looked angelic as they fell from the heavens under the moonlight, but in fact, they were trained killers, *the whole lot of them*, going to do the government's bidding.

With a nod toward the Birdman, Brett prepared in his own way. Checking his gear and his lucky watch, he clasped the sides of the entryway with his gloved fingers, looked out at the vast world below him, imagined his family back home, and made the unreturnable leap toward danger.

With his arms splayed wide, he cut through the thin clouds in a perfect arc, feeling his body become one with the air. His massive, brawny frame, while formidable on land, dropped through the atmosphere like penny off a tower.

Balancing himself out, he fell hundreds of feet before he checked his wrist detector and pulled the rip cord on his parachute when he had reached the right altitude.

The parachute exploded open violently, giving him a small familiar jolt as he navigated it down into darkness.

Brett bent his knees before his boots hit the ground. Dust billowed up around him while his feet crunched dry soil below. The sound of a perfect landing was always a welcomed one.

Releasing himself from the parachute, he pulled his earpieces from inside of his tactical gear and knelt in a crouched position to look around.

It was dead silent around him. No motion. No lights. No people.

"Check in Bulldog Team," he said, listening as all the men sounded off on their tactical communications equipment. All five men were right around him, but with no light, they were nearly impossible to see, save the light coming off some of the men's tactical watches. He waited while his eyes naturally adjusted to the night.

As soon as his voice registered on the radio, the Command Center back at the base went live. Captain Lawless, who had been leaning on his desk, glaring impatiently at the blank wall of monitors, popped up and put his coffee mug down.

"Bulldog Four to Nest, we are live. I repeat, Bulldog Team is live," Brett said, just below a whisper as the men gathered closely; ready to move on the Captain's command.

"Do we have eyes on our men yet?" Captain Lawless asked, glaring at his Comms Specialist.

The young Specialist quickly averted his eyes to the monitor while the screen in front of them linked to the satellite and produced a night vision picture. "We are live, sir," the young man said, typing into his computer.

Captain Lawless turned to his second-in-command but did not bother to look him in the eye. "Get the General now," he ordered, taking a wide stance in the middle of the floor and watching the operation from the body cameras installed on each man.

This was what Captain Lawless did best. In this command room, he was a warrior, a strategist and a swift hand for the U. S. Marine Corps. The sudden pride that always overcame him made him want to sing *God Bless America*, but for now, he would just settle for kicking some ass.

"Zoom into Bulldog Four," Captain Lawless said flatly. He slipped on his earpiece to communicate with the team. "Bulldog Four, we have eyes. Satellite says you're good to go. Proceed."

Slipping on his night vision goggles, Brett wiped sweat from his brow. "Copy that," he said, making a knife hand motion for the men to advance toward the house.

They humped fast and low, but still paying attention the entire time to the ground, making sure to avoid possible land mines.

When they arrived to the house, which sat down in the valley, they surveilled their surroundings. The back of the house was surrounded by an elevated hill with a steep incline. It was perfect for them to take initial cover and monitor the surroundings. Plus, the view spanned out at least a mile out down the dirt road.

Exactly 10 under-trained insurgents were guarding the perimeter, all carrying AK-47s. None of them looked too formidable, a possible walk in the park for the sniper, Bear, who had already taken his position.

Each one of Brett's men had a specific talent, but Rusty was special at crawling fast. His tall lean body could slide against any surface like a snake. Moving toward the two-story white-washed house as soon as the guards had moved out sight, Rusty made his way to the side of the house and stuck a listening device on the exterior wall.

As Rusty made it back to his position up on the hill, Captain Lawless tapped his ear and raised a brow. "We have sound, Bulldog Four," he confirmed to Brett.

The Marine Corps Farsi translator listened in through the device and typed the conversation going on in the house into a system that showed up on one of the large monitors in front of Captain Lawless in English, *although the Captain prided himself in reading Farsi just fine.*

Evidently based upon the insurgents' conversation between each other, they were exhausted and hungry from packing all day and were anxious to move to their new location tonight. The Intel had been correct. This was the team's last chance to get life-saving information.

With his sniper rifle pointed directly at three men congregating on the opposite corner of the house, Bear slipped his finger carefully near the trigger and locked in on them.

Captain Lawless watched on from the men's body cameras as well as the satellite above the house. "Wait," he said abruptly. The cameras zoomed in to the moving object coming toward the op. "You've got a vehicle approaching. It's about two miles from you."

One of Captain Lawless' men passed him a large black and white picture in a file. He quickly scanned it and looked back at the monitor translating the men as they talked inside of the house.

Throwing the file down on the desk, Captain Lawless licked his lips and cracked his fingers. "The vehicle approaching may be Nabi. Don't move in until you have a visual confirmation that it is, and he is inside of the house."

"Check," Brett responded.

The tension intensified immediately. They all knew that it was a possibility that the target could show, but now the second layer of the mission rolled out in front of them. Nabi was a target that the Marine Corps wanted alive. This meant this just elevated to a snatch-and-grab operation.

Brett took a deep breath and leaned his body against the hill. "Bulldog Three get closer to the road to give me a visual on just how many people are in that vehicle," he said calmly.

"Copy," a voice said.

Not even a minute later, a tattered off-road Range Rover came down the dirt road blasting high-beam lights. As it passed, Joe radioed in. "It appears to be a man and a boy. I repeat - we have a civilian."

"Motherfucker!" Brett snarled.

Taking out his binoculars, Brett zoomed in on the truck as it pulled toward the front of the house. A man in his mid-to-late 30s with a short beard and traditional Afghan dress stepped out of the truck. Guards met him and helped bring empty crates into the house from the back of the truck. A young boy barely seven years old jumped out of the passenger seat and followed his father.

Captain Lawless didn't blink. Watching the monitors carefully, he read the conversation between the men as the translator relayed it to the monitor.

A tall, stately graying General walked into the war room and strode over to Captain Lawless' side. With a nod to acknowledge the General's presence, Captain Lawless focused in on his men. Now was not the time for ass-kissing. He had lives to protect and a mission to complete.

"What's the status?" the General asked, taking a file passed to him by the First Lieutenant.

"We are active on the site. Nabi has just arrived with his son," Captain Lawless reported.

The General's eye twitched. "Good. Well, let's get him back to the base and get some answers."

"Yes, sir," Captain Lawless answered, rolling his shoulders.

On the other end of the radio, Brett waited patiently. He knew that with additional people involved, especially a child, the Command Center would want to weigh their options before moving forward.

Crossing his arms across his wide chest, Captain Lawless released a deep breath. "Move in."

As soon as Brett heard Captain Lawless' voice, he was up on the hill. "Move, move," he said quietly over the radio.

On cue, Bear took a deep breath and as he exhaled, pulled the trigger three times. Each man standing outside fell, knees buckling under them, into the dirt before they knew what hit him. As far as Bear was concerned, it was the most painless way to go.

Another unsuspecting insurgent moved out of the darkness into the light when he heard the thud of bodies dropping and was hit dead between the eyes by one of Bear's bullets before he could even process that they were being attacked. His blood splattered against the wall as he fell backward without dropping his gun.

"I could do this shit all day," Bear said to himself. He scanned the perimeter for other possible threats as the men moved in.

Brett and his team advanced down the hill swiftly in a two-by-two formation. Muzzles up, they surrounded the house while Bear picked off more men from his position.

Kicking open the front door, Rusty threw a flash grenade into the house and moved back to the side with his team to take cover. "Fire in the hole!" he screamed.

The explosion was instant and effective. The men inside, completely disoriented, grabbed their ears, ran into the walls due to temporary blindness or dropped to the ground to take cover.

"Bulldog Four, take Nabi alive," Captain Lawless reminded them with his hands planted on his hips. He had to will himself not to show the emotion that was overwhelming him at that moment. Since Brett had married his sister, the relationship between him and his brother-in-law had become more complicated, especially ever since the baby had been born. It wasn't enough for him to be responsible for six military men; he was also responsible for his sister's entire family, including his new little niece, who was ever-present in the back of his mind.

"Copy that," Brett said as his men rushed the house from both the front and back.

Their voices boomed with anger and urgency as they gave direct orders to the captured.

"Hands up!" Joe screamed at one of the men trying to bolt out of the back door. "Drop to your knees! On your fucking knees!" he ordered, motioning downward with the muzzle of his gun. He bit his lip as he cursed, feeling the old Joe coming out.

"Hands behind your back!" Geek screamed to another man.

"Clear!" Hound said, clearing the adjoining room.

"Don't fuck with me," Rusty snarled. "You're not necessary to the completion of this mission. I will blow your fucking head off if you give me one reason!"

It was a fact. Even if a man did not speak a certain language, he always spoke *weapons*. No matter what, a gun in the face made any man comply.

Stepping over the broken down wooden door, Brett walked into the house with two of his men on his flank. They stopped and assessed the damage and gave a visual confirmation that it was Nabi, who was now being held at gunpoint. He looked around the makeshift computer room and motioned for his men to start taking the information that they came for.

Immediately, each man's Comms earpiece splintered off to specialist back at the command post responsible for assisting with securing all digital evidence.

Brett sized the target up. "Let's get this straight before we even start. You're coming with us," Brett said, looking Nabi in his eyes. His voice was firm and calm. "This isn't a request. This isn't a negotiation."

Nabi swallowed hard as he looked down at his son, and then said something in Farsi.

"Hey!" Brett yelled, making everyone in the room snap to attention. "You don't look at him! You look at me! And speak fucking English. I know you can, Mohammad Nabi. It's too late to play the concerned father. You brought your son into some pretty illegal fucking shit. That's on you – not us."

Nabi's eyes rolled and cut to Brett. "I'm not afraid of you," Nabi said, spitting on the ground beside Brett's boot. "American terrorists have been invading our country, desecrating our land for..."

"Save your recruitment pitch; I've already got a job, fucker." Brett spat on Nabi's shirt, gun pointed directly at the man's forehead. "One way to keep your kid alive is to not show up to do illegal activity with him in tow. And we know that you're responsible for over 15 linguists murdered on their doorsteps among other things, you flaming piece of dog shit."

Brett watched Nabi carefully. Nothing about him, despite the fact that he was surrounded, said that he was willing to give up. His posture was off; he was not sweating and despite the grenade blast; he seemed more in control of his own body than the others did. This was the sign of a man still on a mission, and Brett didn't like it one bit.

Brett scanned the room carefully, looking for booby traps. The men swiftly packed up and bagged everything while Rusty pulled out the zip ties to take Nabi into custody.

Still, Brett had that bad feeling in his gut, and it was only growing more noticeable by the minute.

"You, come here," Brett said, motioning for Nabi's son. "With me."

The boy looked back at his father first for permission. He was visibly shaking, face covered in tears and pant leg covered in piss.

Brett motioned again; this time with a louder voice, he said, "Come here now!" He knew the boy was deaf from the grenade and possibly injured. He touched his earpiece. "Advise as to how we handle the civilian," Brett said as he kept his eye on the boy and Nabi.

Captain Lawless' eye twitched. This was quite a call to make. Anyone left in the house would be a victim of the airstrike that would happen in 15 minutes, but on the flip side, there was no way that the USMC wanted an insurgent's kid on the base. He carried no political power and at his age, he had no intelligence to offer.

Captain Lawless rubbed the bottom of his chin and pursed his lips together, knowing every decision that he made was being logged for review. "Bulldog Four, this snatch-and-grab is about Mohammad Nabi. This is not a field trip. Proceed as previously discussed. The civilian is not our concern."

"Copy that," Brett said, rolling the dip in his mouth. "Watch him," he ordered one of his men. He turned his attention to the boy. "You know how to get back home from here?" Brett asked with his back to Nabi.

The boy shook his head *yes*.

Brett wiped the tears from the child's face. "Think you could make it home or at least back to the city by yourself on foot?"

The boy shook his head *yes* again without saying a word.

"Give me my son!" Nabi demanded, struggling against the wrist ties. "You have no right to speak with him!"

Normally, this would have been the point where Brett would have used his K-bar to plant into Nabi's hand to encourage his complete compliance, but with the cameras back at the Command Center live, he had to behave himself.

Brett talked calmly to the scared child. "Here is what you're going to do, boy. You're going to walk, and walk and then walk some more until you get to someone who can help you. Do you understand that?"

"Yes, sir," the boy finally answered, looking back at his father.

It was a relief that the boy spoke English. "Don't look at him. *Listen* to me," Brett said, grabbing the child's face by his chin. "You have to get as far as you can from this place when I tell you to. You don't stick around. If you do, you will die."

"I think that's quite enough Intel," Captain Lawless interrupted.

Nabi's nostrils flared. "My son doesn't have a mother because of you *Americans*." He said the word, Americans, as if it was a curse. His teeth showed as he roared. "My town is destroyed and my country. Our women are widows. How would you feel if I killed your wife, blew her into little pieces, so small you can't even bury her?"

In one quick turn, Brett pressed the muzzle of his weapon to the man's forehead, fighting every urge to pull the trigger and end him there. This guy was up to something; he could feel it. "One more word, Nabi, and you'll no longer be in the land of the living."

That was no threat. It was a promise. Brett's right index finger stroked the trigger.

"Remember your objective," Captain Lawless said into Brett's earpiece as the situation became more heated.

"I have already given my life to Allah," Nabi said, hands still behind his head. His fingers twisted around the gold chain at the nape of his sweaty neck. "I am not afraid."

Instinctively, Brett bent to Nabi's gold necklace and pulled it closer to see that it was a beacon.

"He's transmitting," Brett warned, snatching the necklace off his neck. He stumped it with his boot. "Let's move. I repeat. Bulldog Team is departing." Brett ordered his other men out of the house. "Secure the perimeter."

Immediately, they turned and headed out, leaving him alone in the house with the boy, Nabi and Rusty.

Tired of being even remotely civil, Rusty yanked Nabi roughly up to his feet. He pushed him on the back of the head. "Walk," he ordered.

Nabi stumbled forward and fell awkwardly on the ground toward the wooden desk, then used the tip of his nose to press a button embedded into the leg. He looked up at Brett with a smirk on his face.

*Checkmate.*

Brett knew it was an intentional move before the man could hit the ground. "Move! Move! Take cover!" he said, pushing the boy back through the doorway.

The explosion was instantaneous, and while contained to the computer room, it did the damage of destroying the remaining equipment, injuring but not killing Nabi and throwing Rusty several feet into the opposite corner.

The power of the blast blew Brett and child completely out of the room into the common area. Landing on his back, weapon still in hand, Brett rolled over on his side and coughed up blood.

"Son of a bitch," Brett muttered, trying to get his breath. His ears rang as he tried to get his bearings.

Stumbling to his feet, Brett found the boy in the corner of the room, bleeding badly from his head from an obvious skull fracture and unconscious. He quickly checked the boy's pulse and then ran into the burning computer room to get Rusty.

Throwing his team member over his aching possibly dislocated shoulder and at the same time dragging Nabi's broken body out of the rubble by his arm, Brett headed in the direction of the front door toward the boy when suddenly another explosion happened. The second bomb was on a relay, designed to detonate right behind the first one.

This explosion was bigger and more powerful. It rocked the entire house, causing the second floor to partially collapse.

The men outside turned in dismay, but quickly sprang to action.

"What the hell?" Hound asked, getting on his radio to let the Command Center know that they had additional trouble.

"Get eyes on him," Joe said, seconds after the smoke cleared from the rubble. "Black!" Joe screamed. "Black!" Joe threw debris, drywall and furniture out his way, frantically looking for his friend.

"Here," Brett said, pushing his hand out from under the pile of rubble that covered him.

"We've got company! We're either going to stay and play or get the fuck out of here," Joe screamed, grabbing Brett's hand and at the same time, pulling the debris off of him as he yanked him out with all of his strength. Rusty lay beside him, completely out. They were a mangled pair, covered in blood, heads covered in white dry-wall.

"Help *him*," Brett said, pointing at Rusty. His chest wheezed like he had possibly broken his ribs.

Joe picked up Rusty and threw him over his shoulder. "Can you walk?" Joe asked Brett, helping him through the ruins.

"I'll be fine." Pulling a long shard of wood out of his neck, Brett spit blood. "I've lost my ears," he said of his earpiece. "I'm running blind. You'll have to lead me."

"Got your back," Joe said, helping him still, even though his friend insisted that he was okay.

Brett forced himself to perk up. "I can make it." He picked up his weapon and scanned through the rubble. "Where is the boy?" he asked, wincing in pain. His eyes were blanketed in a sheet of blood.

Joe shook his head. *Now was not the time.* "We have to move."

"Get the boy!" Brett ordered, looking franti-cally around the destroyed house for any sign of the child. However, due to the explosion and the collapse of the parts of the second floor, any hope of finding him was lost. His heart sank.

"Move, Marine," Captain Lawless said into Joe's earpiece. "That's an order. You have the payload, and you have company coming your way." He knew that Brett couldn't hear him and while he admired his heroics, the boy was not the Marine Corps' priority.

"Where is that fucking drone?" David screamed, leaning against the desk.

"Coming now, sir," the Specialist answered.

"Now! Damn it!" Captain Lawless screamed as his fists hit the table. "I want some cover for my men right fucking now!"

As Bulldog Team exited the home, they heard enemy gunfire on the horizon. Evidently, the signal from Nabi's necklace had transmitted to a nearby faction of insurgents and the cavalry was on the way.

The other two men on the team, Hound and Geek, were posted up, returning fire when Bear pulled up in Nabi's Land Rover. The steering wheel had been jimmied and hotwired.

"Let's move! They are hot on our asses, Marines!" Bear screamed.

"Drone approaching," the Specialist relayed to Captain Lawless at the Command Center.

Captain Lawless raised his attention back to the monitors. "Give me a count. How many inbound enemy hostiles do we have approaching and in what position?"

"Four vehicles, sir. Present count is 16 men, headed northbound," the specialist answered.

Captain Lawless was quick to relay. "Nest to Bulldog. You have 16 armed enemy hostiles approaching in four vehicles. They will be pulling up on you shortly. Engage enemy hostiles as they appear."

"Copy that," Hound answered.

"Shotgun," Geek called, diving into the passenger seat of the SUV. Quickly, he checked his magazine and popped it back inside of his weapon. There was a little smirk on his face, having never been able to show nervousness even under duress, even as the enemy approached. Holding his rifle at the ready, he winked at Bear. "Holy shit! It's about to get real, huh?" He rolled his neck. "Motherfuckers getting ready to wet their shorts!"

"Boy, you stuck on stupid," Bear said, knitting his bushy brows into a frown.

In a calm, almost soothing voice, the Command Center radioed over to the men. "Be advised. Air support is on the way," Captain Lawless said, pacing the room. "ETA five mikes. *Move your asses*," he enunciated with a little more urgency.

The General kept quiet but smirked. He liked the way that this Captain did business.

"Five mikes is a long fucking time, man," Joe said sweating his ass off and helping Brett into the back of the SUV.

"Get my fucking ass in this damn car!" Brett yelled, throwing his weapon over his shoulder. He hated himself for being injured. Now was not the time to be the weak link in the chain. His men needed him.

A single bullet flew from over the hill and tore straight through Brett's leg. He dropped to the ground, but was quickly caught by Joe, who returned fire while shoving Brett on top of Nabi inside the SUV.

"Move faster! We're taking fire!" someone yelled.

"No shit!" Joe said, slamming the door behind him.

Now packed liked sardines inside of the run-down SUV, the six men pulled off, headed as fast as they could toward the riverbank.

The night sky lit up with gunfire. The sound of bullets whizzing past the vehicle sounded like snaps and firecrackers in the wind.

"Bulldog Four is hit!" Geek sounded off to the Command Center as Joe checked Brett's wound. "I repeat. Bulldog Four is hit."

"The shot is bad. We have to get to the extraction point before you bleed out." Pulling out his medic pack, Joe prepared to dress the gaping wound. "Can you shoot?" Joe asked Brett while he propped up his leg and pulled out the quick clot.

"Argh!! I hate that shit!" Brett said, screaming out in pain.

"Focus on something else then," Joe said calmly.

"Break out that back window. Let's return some of this fucking gun fire!" Brett ordered, angling his body where he could shoot his weapon, despite his blurred vision and aching leg. "Joe, I need you to work on me, while I work on them."

"Gotcha," Joe said, glad that Brett could focus. They couldn't afford to be down three men, counting him as he worked on his best friend.

Dirt billowed up in the air as Bear burned rubber and tore past the house, away from the oncoming convoy of trucks, toward the river. The low-lying ditches, trees and rocks made the midnight drive even more chaotic with sudden jolts and bumps as he mowed down sparse undergrowth and rocky terrain. "Hold on to your asses, gentlemen!"

The pain of the bumps in the road shot through Brett's body, but he continued to send back rounds at the incoming convoy.

A barrage of loud blaring shots rang through the vehicle while each man dedicated himself to doing his part in securing their safety, but only muzzle fire could be seen from afar lighting up the atmosphere.

Letting back the sunroof, Geek popped out, adjusted his feet into the leather seats and started to return fire with his rifle. "They are gaining on us!" he screamed down to Bear.

Frustrated but maintaining his cool, Bear drove faster. Dirt and grime flew up against the windshield and the shitty wipers weren't doing a thing to clean them. "I'm going as fast as I can in this broke down piece of shit! Just pray it doesn't stop all together. You gotta get us some distance!" he yelled. "Get in the game. Slow their asses down!"

"On it," Geek said, pulling a M67 grenade from his chest pocket. The wind beat against his face as he glared down at the incoming fire. "Come just a little closer," he begged, measuring their distance from the insurgents. When he was certain that they were within 40 feet, he pulled the pin and deployed the grenade, launching it toward the Jeep full of men behind them.

A new transmission came in. "Bulldog Team, ETA is three mikes on that air support. Repeat, three mikes," Captain Lawless said over the radio. "Paint your targets now!"

"Copy that," Hound said, lighting up the trucks behind him with his red tracer laser. "Be advised, these motherfuckers are painted."

"Grenade out!" Geek shouted, getting back on target at the lead vehicle.

The leading Jeep, gaining with every second, exploded behind them, illuminating the night sky as it tilted over and erupted in fire.

"One down, three to go," Geek confirmed to both the Command Center and Bear.

"No fucking shit! Tell me when they're all dead!" Bear screamed sarcastically, accelerating down the bend, splashing through the dirt, sand and water. He prayed quietly for the car not to give out, even though he could feel the engine lagging.

"Everybody, pass all of your grenades to Geek!" Brett screamed, shooting out of the back window and taking cover as bullets whizzed past them. "Geek, you keep lighting their asses up! Men, give him cover!" He wiped blood from his cut brow and slipped his sticky finger back over the trigger after he passed his team all of his grenades.

"Be advised. We have got a visual on you, Bulldog. Eagle Six is inbound." Captain Lawless said as air support arrived on the scene.

Geek threw another grenade toward the three jeeps still following. In the distance, he saw air support release a strike on the house.

"They're finally fucking here," Geek screamed as the fighter jet advanced from the house toward them.

"Adios, motherfuckers," Brett said, watching from the back seat as the fighter jet descended just below the back of the convoy of Jeeps.

The fighter jet deployed heavy guns, plowing through the Jeeps like paper. The vehicles exploded behind them as bodies blew out of the top of the Jeeps and into the shallow river bend.

Bulldog Team moved as fast as they could out of the way. Bear pushed down on the gas until he reached max speed with Geek still wedged in the sunroof with his weapon, screaming to the top of his lungs.

"I can't understand shit you're saying!" Bear screamed to Geek.

"Bulldog, this is Eagle Six. We have finished our gun run. Threat neutralized. Helo inbound to extraction point. Confirm with command on ETA. Eagle Six out," the pilot said, flying over them.

"God bless America!" Geek screamed out as he saluted the fighter jet.

The elation in the SUV was unmatched until Nabi came to. As he groggily gazed over at Brett, clueless as to what had just happened, Brett reached back with his last bit of his strength and punched him right in the mouth, breaking Nabi's nose and knocking out his tooth. He grinned confidently. "Like I said, you're coming with me, motherfucker." With that last word, Brett fainted and fell into his friend.

Joe caught him and looked down at the pool of blood between them. Quickly, he got on the radio. "Bulldog to Nest! Bulldog Four is bleeding out! Expedite that extraction over! I've got a man seriously injured."

David swallowed down his own personal concern as best he could, but suddenly, he felt a little nauseous. "Copy that," he said over the radio. "We're headed to you. ETA two minutes." He got off the radio and wiped his face. "Get that fucking chopper there, right now," he said, snatching off his earpiece.

# Chapter 4

"For our present troubles are small and won't last very long. Yet they produce for us a glory that vastly outweighs them and will last forever. So we don't look at the troubles we can see now; rather, we fix our gaze on things that cannot be seen. For the things we see now will soon be gone, but the things we cannot see will last forever."

-2 Corinthians 4: 17-18 (NLT)

Nestled under an oversized beach umbrella, Courtney Black relaxed and basked in the mid-day sun with her brand new little baby, Bella. The cool wind coming in off the Atlantic Ocean felt sublime, and the tranquility of watching breathtaking emerald green waves roll into the sandy white beach below clear blue skies was both therapeutic and hypnotizing. *Such colors, such life.* She could have sat and took in God's beauty for hours...just drifting off to a place where she didn't have to think.

Think...think....All she did was think. The pursuit had become utterly exhausting.

Since Courtney had not heard from Brett in two days, she had to do something to take her mind off what could have been happening to him halfway across the world. Sure, he had gone under the wire before and not been able to call her for a few days after an operation, and nothing about this time was any less routine than the times before. Still, for the last two days, she had not been able to sleep, and when she did, she had visions of him crying and alone.

In her dream, she would always reach out and try to help him, but she could never reach him, never touch him, and never make him hear her voice. Every night, the same dream. Every time, she'd wake up frantic, heart beating fast and sweating through her nightclothes. It was not a positive image to fixate on; and this beach was the only place in the world that seemed to drive away all of her bad thoughts.

So, she stayed here as much as possible, instead of lingering in her house, where she seemed to stalk her own phone, waiting for it to ring or staring at her computer praying for a Skype call.

With her small portable radio playing "Imagine Dragons," she slowly read the latest edition of The Medlov Crime Family: *Gabriel's Revenge*, while the baby sipped on her juice bottle and fell off into a peaceful sleep.

A sigh escaped her involuntarily.  Mmm. This was pleasant enough.

True, she really wished she could catch some waves on her surfboard, but she'd get some surfing time in when her mother watched the baby tomorrow.  For now, she was in a place of Zen.

Courtney had made coming down to Emerald Isle Beach part of their daily adventures. She'd always packed them lunch, books, sunblock and music to past the time away until her stepson, Cameron, got out of pre-school.  To get a workout in, she'd strap Bella in a harness when the sun was hidden behind the clouds and get a brisk walk in to cut back on the baby fat she'd acquired with Bella's birth.

She really wanted to be in top shape when Brett got home, considering he had never seen her so "chunky." When he left, she was cut like a diamond with sinewy muscle and marble curves. Now, after nine months and a nine-pound baby, she was more water weight than anything. Plus, she had stretch marks.  But that was another thought for another time.

There were other good points of Emerald Isle. The beach was also good for her *mini-me*.  Bella didn't seem to mind the sun or the waves. Courtney occasionally took her out in the water to introduce her to aquatic life. She would always giggle and wade in the water trying to pounce on the foam. Considering Courtney had been raised on beaches, she wanted her daughter to have the same empowering and exhilarating experiences. There was nothing like hunting for shells and building sand castles for little people. It was a place where children could let their imaginations soar – for that matter, it was a place that big people could enjoy as well.

The golden soft sand snuggled between her toes while she rocked Bella in her bouncy swing with one hand and held on to her book with the other.

They were nearly alone today. Off in the distance a few couples hung out under umbrellas or caught some sun, but for a mid-afternoon in the middle of the week, most people were at work, which was perfect for Courtney. She hated crowds almost as much as Brett and she didn't have PTSD.

Just as she was about to set down her book and dig into the cooler for a Gatorade, she noticed a familiar figure coming her way. It was in his cool, confident stride and the way that his body angled dominantly in the sun's glow that caught her attention. Linen shorts and a white cotton shirt clung to his meaty body. The formidable figure in the distance, with the shiny ball head, the six-foot four stature of muscle and brawn was her father.

Straining, she sat straight up and pulled off her shades. The sun made her eyes squint and water, but she was 99 percent sure that it was him.

"Daddy," she said, loud enough for him to hear her. His head popped up at the sound of her voice. As soon as she spoke, Bella's eyes shot open and she was fully awake. Giving a little cry, she threw down her bottle in the sand below.

Courtney's heart sank down in her chest. Her heart began to beat rapidly. For as long as she had been coming to this beach, which far exceeded the time that she had been with Brett, her father had never shown his face here, and he lived right down the street in one of the posh luxury homes behind the infamous private gate.

She picked up the baby and cupped her in her arms as she walked toward him, unable to take another moment of the anticipation of why he was there.

"Do my eyes deceive me," she said, bouncing Bella. "Are you finally deciding that fresh air and sun will do you some good or did Mom kick you out?" She tried to smile despite her worries.

Her father, retired Colonel Jeffery Lynn Lawless, was not one for theatrics. He raised his cell phone in his large right hand. "Found you on the Find My Phone App," he explained, reaching for Bella. The baby instinctively cuddled herself in her grandfather's warm embrace, melting his heart as she did so. "There's my girl." He kissed his granddaughter on her fat little rosy cheeks. "There's my princess."

Courtney frowned. "Daddy, how long have you been tracking me on that thing?"

"Since your husband left for Afghanistan," Colonel Lawless answered without hesitation. "A man should always know where two of the three most important women in his life are." He had that look as if he didn't owe her much of an explanation, considering she was his daughter. Moreover, his inability to show an ounce of humility let her know that he still felt comfortable taking certain liberties when it came to her, regardless of how grown she was.

After years of living with him, Courtney knew that her father tracking her was the least of her worries. He didn't go out of the way to leave his house unless there was a problem. *Thus, there had to be a problem.*

"Ok, stalker.  Why are you tracking me *is more to the point*?" she asked, walking behind him as he led them back to their umbrella and began to gather her things with one hand and hold the baby in his giant grip in the other.

"I can take her," she said, reaching for Bella.

"Oh, I've got her," he said, kissing the baby's forehead.

"What's going on, Daddy?" Courtney swallowed down a tight lump of air.

He released a sigh and looked up the beach away from his daughter's worried glare. "Baby, I just got a call.  Brett's been injured."  He picked up her small pink tote bag and turned to hand it to her gently.  His eyes lowered from her pained face.  "We need to get you to Bethesda immediately."

Suddenly, Courtney's senses turned against her.  The sun was too hot and the scent of salt water turned sour in her nose.  She felt faint. *Oh God!  Was she going to faint?*  Her legs began to give way, but her father quickly caught her.

"Cort," he said, wrapping his free arm around her waist.  "Baby girl, it's going to be okay."  He gave her a minute to get herself together, although now he wasn't quite sure how he was going to get her, the baby and all of her things to the car at one time. He might have to come back.

"Wait." She put her hands over her mouth, fingers twitching. Her diamond wedding ring sparkled in the sunlight. "It might be a mix up. No one...no one has called me. Why didn't they call me, if he's hurt?" Courtney asked, hot tears pouring down her cheeks immediately.

Her father gave her a look that let her know there was no mix up.

"God." She gazed up at the sky and ran both hands through her hair. "Is he okay?" Suddenly, her husband's handsome face flashed in her mind, and all she wanted to do was go to him.

Colonel Lawless rubbed the tears from his daughter's face. With a reassuring smile, he nodded. "He'll be okay. Brett's tough. I'll give him that. He's one of the toughest I know outside of your brother." He had done this a 100 times, but never for his own family. It was more difficult than he imagined, even though the call had come from his son, instead of a Family Readiness Officer. He knew his daughter wanted more of an explanation, even in her state. "They didn't call you because Brett listed me as his next of kin. He didn't want you to get that call in the middle of the night while you were alone taking care of the kids. Thinking that such a thing would be cruel for you to endure, he asked me to handle the responsibility of getting that information to you."

Courtney stood in a trance for a moment. The words that her father had just spoken were not translating well. *Injured* could mean a lot of things, but from her time volunteering at the Wounded Warrior barracks, she'd not seen much of the mild kind. Most of the men she'd seen where faceless, fingerless, legless... She stopped herself before she went down the rabbit hole of possibilities.

Wrapping her arms around her, she began to cry. "Brett..." she sobbed.

Colonel Lawless patted her on the back and gave a soft, soothing voice as only a father could provide. "Now, now. Everything is going to be okay. Your mother has gone to get Cameron from school, and I'm going to help you to the house to get packed, then we're on the first flight out."

It was killing him to see his baby girl like this, and he only prayed his words provided the comfort that his son-in-law intended. "Walk with me now. We need to go."

"Where are they taking him?" Courtney asked, trembling. "Is he okay? What happened? Where are they taking him?" She became more frantic by the moment, not realizing that she was asking the same questions repeatedly.

Colonel Lawless knew that she was headed toward some version of shock and decided that the beach was not the place for it. "We can talk about it in the car," he said, passing her the cooler. It wasn't that he couldn't hold the cooler; he just wanted to give her something to do with her hands, something to focus on besides fainting. "I know it's hard, but I need you to hold it together and trust me. He's safe. The military will do everything that they can to make sure he's recovering well." He lifted her chin. "You'll be fine. You'll get through this and so will he."

Courtney looked dead into her father's eyes and suddenly felt the world stop turning so fast. The way that he assured her gave her some comfort. After all, if he said it was okay, maybe it was.

She walked closely beside Lawless, hidden from the sun by his massive shadow. In a daze, she stumbled through the sand. Quietly, she shook her head as her thoughts assailed her. "Daddy, I'm not going to make it," she said, stopping for a minute.

"We can stop, if you need to. There is no rush," Lawless said, halting in his tracks.

She rolled her head and then whispered as she reached out for his arm, "I feel..."

Suddenly, she fell down to her knees, hands planted in front of her, and vomited in the sand. Her body violently convulsed as she threw up her lunch and breakfast. Tears mixed with thick spit. Wiping sand on her face, she began to cry.

Kneeling down with her, but still holding Bella carefully, he rubbed her small back. "Let it out," he said, moving her hair out of her way. "Just let it all out."

"I'm sorry," she apologized, feeling embarrassed. Confusion overcame her. "I don't know why that happened." She looked out across the beach, but only saw stars.

"That's just nerves. It happens to the best of us," her father assured. "Want to try to walk again or do you feel like more can come up?"

Courtney propped one knee up, and then pushed herself to her feet. "No, I'll make it," she said, wiping her mouth again. "I don't want to waste time. I need to get to him."

All her father could think was at the moment Courtney didn't look like a strong mother of two, but like a scared little girl lost on the beach in her swimming suit, and he was glad that he was here to comfort her as only a father could. No family deserved this, but it didn't stop it from happening every day, all across the world. This was a part of war that people didn't see and didn't care to know about.

He still remembered each man injured under his command, and each man killed. Their faces never left him. He had gone to each funeral and stood with each family visited each hospital bed and never did the job get any damn easier. Human loss and suffering was dirty business.

In that moment, another thought came flooding to mind, washing over him and bringing brilliantly raw clarity. What about his own wife? How must she have felt when the news had come back to her many times before about his injuries down through the years? Who had comforted her? At times, he was certain that no one was there with her. No one gave her reassurance or even an explanation. But still, in her unwavering strength, she had prevailed...endured for their family, for him.

*Damn*, he owed Diane his life for all she had gone through. It was a pity that he had to realize it through the pain of his own child. He only wished that it didn't have to be Courtney going through this.

As they walked, Courtney looked up at him, her red hazel eyes nearly stopping his heart as she tried to smile. "Thank you for coming, Daddy," she whispered.  She and her father had experienced some dark moments in their lives. He wasn't always in approval of her choices and she wasn't always in approval of his.  Yet, at that moment, all of the bumpy spots in their relationship were made smooth.  He was there for her when she needed him...there to comfort her, to hold her up, to walk beside her.  Even in her grief, she had to recognize that.

"There is no other place in the world that I'm supposed to be right now," he said with his arm wrapped around her.  His heart swelled and he had to fight his own tears back.  "I never wished for this life for you, mostly because I know how hard it can be.  But you picked a good man and sometimes you just have to play with the cards you're dealt.  Your mother and I will be right here for whatever you need, whenever you need it.  But trust me, you will get through this."

She nodded at him.  "I know," she said honestly.  "I love you.  I know I don't say it all the time, but I do.  And..." she swallowed salty tears. "And I would never trade you, never in a million years."

"I love you too."  He smiled and kissed her sand-covered hand.  "Let's get you home.

# Chapter 5

**"I have not yet begun to fight!"**
**-John Paul Jones**

Within 44 hours after being injured, Brett was asleep in the safe, clean, cool confines of Walter Reed National Military Medical Center. He had been treated in theatre and transported immediately to Joint Base Andrews by the Medical Evacuation and Critical Air Transport Team. It had been, without a doubt, a painful journey, but one that reassured him that there was no place like home. He knew that more than ever when as he arrived on campus and passed an American flag waving high above them, a rush of tears burned his eyes and cascaded like a waterfall down his bruised face.

He remembered feeling embarrassed about his tears, when everyone around him kept calling him a hero and a warrior. *If they look closer*, he thought quietly to himself, *they'd see that I'm not*. But before he could get the thought processed in his head, he was suddenly reassured by one of the team members who slipped her hand into his and smiled at him. "Sometimes I cry when I pass it too. It's a beautiful sight to be-hold," she said, turning from his misty blue eyes to look out of the window. Still, she had not let go of his hand and he had not let go of hers. It had not been some ridiculous attempt at flirting; it had been one military personnel giving anoth-er comfort when they needed it the most, and he appreciated that.

When he had gotten to Bethesda, he had re-quested a phone several times, but his vitals were not doing well; the drugs had him loopy and the pain was excruciating. Brett had been injured before. A scrape here, a break there. But this time had been different. He had nearly lost Rusty. Joe had nearly given up his entire family to save him from incoming fire. And well, he had been popped by an insurgent with an AK-47 in his dominant leg. What good was a Force Recon Marine without a leg?

While they admitted him to the hospital, counseled him and saw after him, he kept won-dering when someone was going to tell him that he was going to lose his valued limb, but no one was saying anything to him, or at least, he didn't quite hear them. They had him on so many drugs, he could barely focus. And if he focused too long, he seemed to pass out completely.

However, in his sleep, he had never truly left Afghanistan. In the dark hospital room, only illuminated by monitors and equipment, blinking and buzzing, he sweated through his gown, moaned in his sleep and relived the pain of being shot.

Stuck in a state of panic, Brett gripped the covers and screamed out, veins protruding in his neck, bloodshot eyes popping open. "INCOMING!" he yelled, voice echoing down the hall.

His own screams jolted him awake. Frantically, he looked around for his men, but no one was there.

When he realized where he was – not in a war zone but safe in a hospital bed - he rested his head back on the sweat-soaked pillow and felt a sharp pain shoot through his leg up to his waist. At the same time that he tried to adjust, another pain shot through his chest from his dislocated arm. The frustration of all of it was too much. Croaking out a curse, he began to cry.

"Fuck you," he sobbed. "Fuck *all* of you," he said, thinking of Nabi's dead son.

The door to the hospital room flew open and a small, heavyset nurse in pink scrubs, and graying blonde bob flipped on the lights. With a smile, she walked up to his bedside, pulled out her stethoscope and began to check his vitals.

"How are you doing, Staff Sergeant Black?" she asked in a Bostonian accent. She looked him dead in the eyes as if to say, *I'm talking to you.*

Brett tried to speak but his throat was sore from the tubes they had used earlier. "I'm fine," he lied. "It was just a nightmare." *Another nightmare.* He tried quickly to wipe his face of the tears. He was tired of crying in front of these people. Looking over to the clock on the table, he licked his cracked lips. "I need to call my wife," he said as another pain hit him. He winced in pain.

"Alright, let's get you some pain meds, first." She picked up his chart and flipped through the pages. "Looks like you're due some pain management in less than 15 minutes, so I'm going to give it to you early."

He tried to catch his breath. "If I take the meds, it makes it hard for me to control what I say," Brett explained as he balled up his fists. "I have a low tolerance for drugs. I have since I was a kid." He thought back to when he had busted his knee in high school football and had been placed on pain meds. It had been a nightmare when he accidentally cursed at his mother. He can still remember her tears...right before she slapped him.

The nurse chuckled. "Which is why you want to talk to your wife first..." she assumed as she put the chart down. "Don't want to say the wrong thing?"

"Yes ma'am." Brett wiped his eyes again. The tears wouldn't stop despite the fact that he now knew where he was. "I just think if I hear her voice, I'll feel better. Maybe I'll be able to get some rest."

There were no other words that needed to be exchanged as far as the nurse was concerned. Pulling her cell phone from her pocket, she passed it to him. "The phones shut off here at a certain time. You can use mine, if you make it quick. I have a few errands to run. I'll just leave you to it, and I'll come back when I'm done."

Brett was grateful. "Thank you...very much." He struggled to pull himself up in the bed. There had to be a comfortable place in this bed where he could get some relief.

"I've got two boys over there in Afghanistan," she winked. "We're all family as far as I'm concerned." Leaving him alone in the room, she closed the door quietly.

As soon as the phone rang, Courtney answered.

"Hello," she said voice groggy. Looking at the alarm clock on the night stand, she raised up in the bed.

Brett paused. She sounded beautiful, even at two in the morning. Salty tears began to form again. "It's me, baby," he said, mouth quivering.

Courtney's voice sounded strained. "Brett," she paused. "Is that you?" He sounded so funny over the phone.

He smiled despite the pain. Releasing a sigh, he wiped his head. "It's me. Did I wake you?"

"No," Courtney lied. She jumped up in the bed and pushed the covers off her body. Her heart began to flutter.

"I just wanted to hear your voice. I thought maybe it'd help me sleep."

Diane, Courtney's mother, was lying beside her. They had fallen asleep together with the kids between them. She rose up on one elbow and smiled at her daughter, knowing how good that first call always was.

"I'm here," Courtney said, standing up carefully to keep from stirring the babies. She wiped tears.

"Where?" Brett asked.

"I'm at Walter Reed. Well, we're at Fisher House. They were nice enough to put us up for a few days to come and see you. We were going to surprise you in the morning," Courtney said, walking over to the window. She peeked out the blinds at the streetlights and the hospital in the distance. Although he was closer than he had been over the last few months, he still seemed so far away over there in that tall building.

"You're in Bethesda?" Brett asked, more alert.

"Yep. Mom, Dad, the babies and me. Not far from you at all," she said in a soothing voice. Her smile lit up the conversation. "Does that help you sleep?"

Brett chuckled for the first time since he had been injured. "No," he said, looking down at his leg. "It makes me wish you could come over."

Courtney's brain began to spin. *Could she get over there tonight?* If she could find a way, there was no way that she wouldn't. "I think visiting hours are over."

Brett thought of his nurse and her son. Surely, she'd help him out. "I think I can get you in. Turns out, I've got some family here."

"Family?" Courtney said confused.

"Just a figure of speech. I'll call you back in a few minutes with directions. Just get dressed." He paused for a moment. He sounded like he was giving orders to one of his subordinates, not his wife. "I mean, if you'd like to come over..."

Courtney cut him off. "Call me back in five," she said, hanging up the phone.

Turning back to her mother, she smiled. "He wants to see me *right now*," she whispered, jumping up and down. "What am I going to wear? He hasn't seen me in months." Suddenly, she was frantic. "I don't want to look fat."

"You don't look fat." Diane pulled herself out of the bed and slugged over to her Louis-Vuitton over-night bag. "Go take a shower quickly. I'll help you get ready. Do you have a sun dress or something to slip on?"

Courtney shrugged her shoulders. "I'm sure that I do, but do you think a dress is appropriate for the middle of the night?"

Diane gave a sinister smile to her daughter. "You haven't seen your husband in eight months. You're going to see him at two in the morning. Do you really want to have on something as constricting as pants that makes it difficult to pull up or down when the nurse isn't looking?"

Courtney's mouth fell open. "Mom, I doubt he'll want to make out. He was just shot, re-member." She blushed as she opened her dress bag, but inside, she knew that her mother was right.

"You could show up in a pair pajama pants with your hair on fire, and he'd still want to see you. I've been married to your father for a *long time*. And he's been injured quite a few times over the years. Let me tell you, men never change. If there is an opportunity, they'll find it. You just need to be ready." She pulled a box perfume out of her bag and tossed it across the room to her. "I was saving that for a date with your father while we were here, but you should use it tonight, and if he really likes it, I'll give it to you. And every time he smells it, he'll think of tonight."

Courtney caught the box and gaffed. "Mom, this is Chanel No. 5. This is really expensive...like $2,000 a bottle."

Diane winked. "Well, dear, when you're my age, you only wear the best. Now, put a little behind the ears, wrists and knees...or the most likely places he'll put his nose."

Courtney shook her head. "You and dad are some real freaks, aren't you?"

"A woman should never tell," her mother said, patting the rollers in her hair.

"Will you be fine with the babies?" Courtney asked looking over at the children curled up quietly in the bed sleeping peacefully.

"I'll be just fine.  Now hurry, girl. Your husband is waiting," Diane said, getting back in the bed, "and I'm exhausted."

***

Dressed in a blood red, ankle-length t-shirt dress that showed off her voluptuous shape and engorged breasts, paired with yellow sandals and yellow earrings to mirror the colors of the Marine Corps, Courtney quietly followed Brett's nurse up a back staircase to the floor where Brett was being treated.

"Are you going to stay all night?" the nurse asked, looking back at Courtney as she opened the door for her to the unit. Cool air hit both of their faces from the climate-controlled building, which was a drastic change from the heat outside.  The nurse hated to stare, but Mrs. Black was very pretty, not to mention in that killer dress, she stuck out like a sore thumb. It's no wonder the man couldn't sleep.  She wouldn't have minded her son bringing home a pretty girl like that – polished, pretty, presentable even in the middle of the night.

"Can I stay all night?" Courtney asked, pulling her small Coach purse up on her shoulder.

"You're his wife.  Sure, you can. I'm his nurse for tonight. I'll come by and check on him as needed, but if the doctor should make his rounds, just tell him that you've already checked in. Trust me. He won't make a fuss. It happens all the time." She stopped abruptly at door 415, turned and smiled. "He's right inside waiting for you." The nurse wouldn't get into all the prep work he had put her through, including helping him clean his undercarriage, teeth and ears, like he was preparing for an inspection.

Courtney looked at the door and then back at the nurse. She shrugged. "I'm nervous."

"So is he," the nurse reassured, grabbing Courtney's hand. "You both will be fine."

Courtney nodded and then reached out and hugged her. She knew it wasn't exactly PC, but neither was sneaking in a woman in the middle of the night into a secure Naval facility. "I can't thank you enough. I know that you didn't have to do this. You don't even know us."

The nurse patted Courtney's back. "Just take care of him." Grabbing the door handle, she looked around. "Hurry inside before someone sees you."

The room was dark when Courtney stepped inside with only the lights from above Brett's bed to illuminate it. Closing the door behind her, she cleared her throat. "Brett, are you in here, baby?" Her voice carried in the small room. She hoped that she wasn't waking anyone up. *Did he have a roommate? Had he fallen back to sleep?*

"Yeah," he said quickly, pulling his gown down over his bruised knees. "I'm here," he answered.

She poked her head around the corner hesitantly and gazed intently across the room at the man she called her husband. So close, yet so unrecognizable. He left a whole man; he returned something else – not necessarily something less, but definitely something different.

Brett watched her emerge slowly into view. Could it be that she had gotten more beautiful since the last time that he saw her? He blinked hard and tried to push himself up.

Walking slowly, almost staggering to the bed, she pulled off her purse and set it on the nightstand without thought. Her eyes slowly trailed up his body, accessing his physical state. Shaking her head finally, she lifted a brow and locked eyes on him. "Wow," she said in a low, solemn voice.

"I know," Brett said, feeling worse. God, what she must think of how he looked all hooked up to monitors, and black and blue. It was at that moment that he knew that he had not given up. Seeing his wife, his future, and his life right in front of him made him know that there was so much of life left to live, and it was his duty to live it. It was his duty to provide her with everything that he always promised himself that he would. His precious angel...his Courtney. It all became clear what he was fighting for, not for king or country, but just to get back home to her.

Courtney swallowed down her growing nervousness. Being *Captain Obvious* right now would add no levity to the situation, so she opted for something a little less expected. Twisting up her lip, she narrowed her eyes and clucked her tongue against the roof of her mouth. "Guess, I'm going to have to cancel those salsa lessons I signed us up for, huh? You sort of need two legs to do that, and by the looks of it, you're short one."

Brett was taken aback. With his mouth gaped wide open, he looked up at her in total bafflement having first expected her to be melancholy and possibly dramatic about the entire situation, then he began to laugh. Despite the pain and emotional agony, he laughed. Despite his broken ribs, fractured leg and concussion, he just kept laughing, and she laughed with him until she couldn't laugh anymore.

"Owww," he said, grabbing his ribs as he chuckled and holding up a finger toward her.

"Don't make me laugh...it hurts," he said, breathing deep for air.  Still, he laughed.

Everyone on the base had been so serious, so attentive, and so professional.  No one had cracked a joke or even thought about making fun of him.  Her attempt at humor was a breath of fresh air and a much needed change from the last couple of days.

Courtney laughed too, until she began to cry. She tried to hide her tears, but they rushed over her face like a waterfall.  It wasn't that she wasn't happy to see him.  Words could not express her elation to actually know that he was alive. However, his physical state was another discussion all together. He was all rigged up on the bed with monitors and cords attached to his body. His face was black and blue, swollen and scarred, as were his hands, and a cast was on his right leg.  His head was bandaged as well as his shoulder.  She had to stop assessing the damage in order to stop the tears.

She had tried to be funny, and it had worked, but the more that she laughed, the more that she realized that it was only through God that he had returned to her and his wounds were evidence of that fact. She wasn't sure if the tears were joy or sorrow, but either way, she couldn't stop them.

"Baby," Brett said, reaching for her with his good left hand. "Don't do that, now."

"I'm sorry," she said, covering her mouth with her hands as she shook her head emphatically. "I just..." She stopped and tried to take a deep breath. The words left her, even though she wanted to reassure him. It was just so hard to do at that moment.

"It's okay," Brett said, pulling her closer to him. His long eyelashes flapped like wings against his piercing blue eyes. "Hey," he cooed at her, tickling her side with his fingers. "Hey, Cort. I'm okay. I promise."

She gripped the cool rail of the bed and leaned over near him. Her long brown hair fell down on his shoulder, as they looked each other in the eyes. It was then that she noticed he had a deep, dark tan from being in the sun for long months. Despite his injuries, he was still ruggedly beautiful. His dusty blonde hair, his full, wide heart-shaped lips and ice white teeth, the strength of his square jaw and thick intense brows, the way he bit his lip when he was emotional and swallowed hard when he wanted to kiss her.

"I'm going to take care of you," Courtney whispered, inches from his face. Her sweet tears fell down in between her bosom. "Everything you need to get better, I'll provide. You are not alone." She hated to sound like words ripped out of a poorly formed poem, but as clumsy as they were, there were no truer words spoken.

Brett pushed back his own tears by blinking quickly, causing the chain reaction of lower-lip biting. He knew his telltale sign was giving him away. Through a nasally sigh, he tapped her hand. "And I'm going to take care of you *back*," Brett whispered.

They rested their foreheads against each other and took in the moment.

Courtney had seen her husband vulnerable before – when he found out his late wife left him, when he found out his late wife died in a plane crash, when he found out Cameron was not his biological son, when her father and brother chose not to accept him as her lover because he was a white non-commissioned officer – but never had she seen him *this vulnerable*. Maybe it was the hospital gown, or the injuries or just the idea that he would have to depend on someone else for a while until he got on his feet, but she could feel his sudden helplessness and she wanted nothing more than make him feel protected.

"I feel like I'm seeing you for the first time," he said, touching her face. Courtney was absolutely breathtaking. Dark perfect skin. Dimples in her cheeks. Heart shaped chocolate lips. Natural, thick curly hair. Hazel eyes. A body to die for. He could go on and on about how beautiful she was. He loved that she didn't let her beauty define who she was and that was even sexier.

"You know, I think the scars actually make you look even sexier," she flirted with pouty lips, tracing his face with her fingers. The touch of her skin against his made his eyes close.

"Do you know how long I've waited to feel those fingers on me?" he asked.

"On your face?" Her cheekiness starting to show its edges.

Brett's eyes flashed open and rolled. "Other places too."

Courtney giggled. He had to be okay; he still had his sense of humor.

"I love to see you smile," he said, shaking his head. "There is nothing like it."

Moving her hair out of her face, he slipped his fingers behind her neck and pulled her carefully into him. "Can I kiss you?" he asked.

Courtney wasn't used to such a humble request. Brett always took what he wanted, especially in *that* department. "What makes you think you have to ask?" as her heart lurched for him. *Please kiss me*, she thought.

He raised a brow and shrugged. "I sort of look like the elephant man right now, so it's more like a pity kiss anyway."

"You look amazing," Courtney reassured. Dipping into him, she kissed his lips slowly, tasting the mint of newly brushed teeth and tingling mouthwash. His lips were sweet to the taste, soft and fleshy.

Slowly, they fell into their rhythm, a synchronic flow of give and take.

He inhaled her scent, feeling himself forgetting his injuries and moving toward that rampant sexual need that had long gone unsated inside of him. If he could have, he would have pulled her over onto the bed and slipped that sexy little t-shirt dress right up past her shapely hips. *Mmm.* How he wanted to be inside of his wife again, to feel her body tighten around his as he entered her.

Their kisses became heavier, longer, filled with more passion. The echo of their lips against each other filled the dim room. Carefully, she ran her fingers down the front of his gown and slipped them in between his legs.

Pulling back a minute, Brett exhaled. "I want you so fucking bad."

Courtney licked her lips and ran a finger behind her ear to push back wild strands of hair. She was desperate for him, aching in fact, just because of one little kiss. Brett bit his lip and slipped a hand over her breast, teasing her rigid nipple. He amused himself with the fact that she wasn't wearing a bra.

"Does *all* of you hurt?" she asked, looking down at his mighty steel erection pushing up his nightgown like a tent.

Brett looked down at his hard-on and back at Courtney. "Feel like getting a little creative?" he asked, ignoring the low throbbing pain in his leg. *Screw his leg*. They could cut it off right now if they needed to, he just wanted some *alone time* with his wife.

"I thought you'd never ask," Courtney said, reaching over him to turn off the light.

Not even 30 seconds later, Brett let out a painful groan.

"What's wrong?" Courtney asked, reaching above him to flick the light back on.

Brett moved her head and mocked a cry. "It hurts," he said, completely defeated.

Courtney chuckled. Her mother was right. All he needed was one opportunity. "Oh, baby. We don't have to do anything tonight."

"I want to," Brett huffed. "I really, really want to." Nevertheless, in his mind, he knew it was a bad idea. Sure, his body said yes and was definitely responding to his drop-dead gorgeous wife, but his wounds were singing a different song. He had to heal first before he could do *extracurricular* activities. Still, he had to try. He had to say at least that he had attempted, otherwise, what kind of man would he be? There was a half-naked woman in his hospital room ready to pleasure him and all he could do was talk to her? What a crock!

"There will be other nights," she explained, pulling down his gown and trying very hard to ignore his erection. It seemed even bigger now that it had been months since they had been together. Her eyes shifted up to his face. "In fact, there will be a lifetime of other nights."

Brett was glad for her. He was glad that Courtney was his wife and not Amy. He was glad to have someone really give a damn about him, even if he was in the worst shape ever. With her, no matter what, there was no pressure...ever. She simply allowed him to be, and he knew what an unbelievable find she was. Strangely enough, it only made him want her even more.

*Down boy.*

Growling, he looked over at the window seat and smacked his lips. "Will you at least stay with me tonight? I don't want you to leave me."

Courtney pulled up a chair right beside his bed and sat down in it. "I'll be here until they send you home," she promised.

# Chapter 6

"The lie is a condition of life."

- Friedrich Nietzsch

At dawn, Jeffery Lynn Lawless' eyes flashed open abruptly. Lying on his back with the covers tucked perfectly around him, his arms flat beside him like anchors, and his head planted in the middle of his crisp white pillow, he looked up at the ceiling and began to count back from 60. *Always 60.*

He needed at least one minute to adequately adjust from the dark, murky abyss of his past - painted in hauntingly realistic nightmares so vivid that he couldn't tell the difference from dream state and reality - back to the normalcy of his current otherwise peaceful life. That one minute of brief mediation kept him from moving from a ghoulish nightmare to an embarrassing conscious flashback.

Unfortunately, that kind of episode happened even more now that he was newly retired. The shrink said that it was because he had more time to think back on his life. He, however, felt that it was because he needed more to do than just mill around his house with his hands idle.

Even after 30 damn years, the nightmares didn't just stop the way that many had claimed they would. It was as if miraculously because of retirement he was supposed to get better, no matter the emotional wounds, no matter the young lives lost, no matter the time that could not be purchased or begged back. *Lying naïve bastards.* He still had evocative images that flooded his mind from the war back in Vietnam. Sometimes, he swore that he was right back in the country again as a young man with his friends and his enemies piled together in one big heaping shit storm. He wasn't even going to get into all the things he had seen since then. It was enough to make a grown man cry. And sometimes, he did. But he refused to just give in.

Giving in was a sign of weakness.

Weakness was not a sign of valor.

Valor was something that he held on to regardless of retirement. Otherwise, what would all the years that he had dedicated to something other than his family have been worth? That was a question for the ages, and he was too smart of a man to go looking for answers. He was too old and too tired. Besides, one thing he was not was a philosopher. He was no Gandhi, no Aristotle, and no Garvey. He was a Marine.

He had, however, learned how to handle the dreams, instead of the other way around. Strangely enough, he had picked up this meditation method from some highly educated hippie on a plane once, when he was headed to Camp Pendleton to see his son, using a commercial airline. The hippie, who was no more than 30, was also some new-age doctor who probably only ate organic and shopped at one of those frou-frou grocery stores that Diane always wanted to go to.

On the plane ride, Jeffery had fallen off to sleep and was experiencing a nightmare when the hippie doctor woke him up by placing his hand on his. At first touch, he was awake. Then he looked down at the man's hand and then back at him to give him the "Don't touch, don't lose your hand" face when the man quickly explained that he recognized Jeffery's symptoms.

"All you need is 60 seconds after you wake to process what you have just experienced and move back into a calmer reality. But you have to give yourself at least 60 seconds," the bearded man with a man-bun and glasses had explained.

So, Jeffery did what the man suggested. Despite his feelings about hippies and their love-the-world theory on life, he tried the exercise and he's been doing it ever since.

*And five, four, three, two, and one.*

He rose slowly from his slumber and stretched out his long body, relaxing tense muscles as felt the smoothness of the sheets covering him. Rolling his neck, he took a deep breath and centered himself. Alas, he was back into his calm reality.

It was a new day, plenty to...

Wait. His head turned on a swivel. Where in the hell was Diane? She had promised him that she was going to come back after the kids had fallen off to sleep for a little alone time. Evidently, she had fallen off to sleep instead.

Sitting on the side of the bed, he planted his feet on the floor and curled up his lips. The room was nice enough, but he was spoiled and wanted to be back at home where he woke up to the smell of coffee and Diane cooking breakfast. He missed the view from his bed of the vast Atlantic Ocean in the distance and sailboats peacefully passing back on greenish blue water under puffy clouds. Even being away for a day was...burdensome.

As he stood to make his way to the bathroom, he heard a key jam into the lock and the knob twist to the door. In came Diane with Bella in her arms. She looked like she had been up for at least an hour, all bright-eyed and full of life. But that was always Diane. She was always up at the crack of dawn and the last one to fall asleep; still she always looked like a million bucks.

"Morning sleepyhead," Diane said throwing her overnight bag on the end of the bed like it weighed 1,000 pounds. She gave him a look as if he was supposed to immediately take it off her hand as soon as she entered the door.

He ignored, but completely comprehended the look. "Morning," he said, yawning. "Where is Cameron?"

"Still asleep next door. I didn't want to wake him until the last minute. It took forever for him to fall asleep last night. He's dying to see his Daddy. Bless his soul."

"*Dying* is probably not the best word, right now," he quipped. His eyes were deadlocked on Bella's. She was eyeballing him as she always did. "You're going to spoil her holding her all the time. A child shouldn't be coddled every moment that she is awake. It makes her dependent upon human touch...makes her vulnerable."

Diane put Bella on the bed beside the bag in a matter-of-fact way and raised a brow at him. "There. You happy now, Colonel?" She rolled her eyes. "I mean it's not like I've raised two of my own, absent mostly of their father's presence."

"Mostly absent still means *some of the time*," he reminded his wife with a wink.

Bella looked up at her grandfather and giggled, showing gums and dimples. She instantly reminded him of Courtney when she was little – always grinning. He grinned back at her and then reached down and picked her up.

He sighed. "But then, Bella is special...smarter than most children her age and being reared properly so a little affection won't hurt."

Diane knew that was coming. Jeffery could never deny a beautiful baby, and in truth, she loved that about him. Turning from both of them, she walked over to the mirror above the desk and started to take out her rollers. "We're going to meet Courtney and Brett over at the hospital this morning."

Bouncing Bella in his arms, Jeffery shook his head at Bella. "She's already over there?"

Diane grinned as she pulled the pins out of her hair and looked at her husband through the reflection in the mirror. "He called her last night on her cell phone and asked her to come over. I told her to go. I mean, it was so romantic. You'd have to be there to appreciate it."

Jeffery huffed. *Romantic, my ass. It's unsafe to be out at all hours,* he thought to himself. Anything could happen, even on a base.

Diane continued despite his grimace, "I tried to call her on her cell phone this morning, but it's dead. So, I figured we can grab breakfast and meet them afterwards."

Jeffery kissed Bella on her cheek. "It's a good thing you're moving fast. Your mother is probably already pregnant again."

"JEFFERY!" Diane admonished while holding back a laugh.

"What?" Jeffery said with a devious frown; he knew exactly *what*, but he didn't care. It was the truth. "You know I'm right," he pushed. "Those two screw like rabbits, Diane. We could never get them to dinner on time once they were married. And it was so damned obvious what they had been up to." The idea of his precious little girl being deflowered by a Devil Dog still made him nauseous if he were honest. However, the idea that she was married to a man who was loyal to her made swallowing crow a little more bearable.

Bella cooed innocently while pawing at his chin and warmed Jeffery's heart, making him forget his thoughts. She hit his cheek with her small hand and giggled.

Looking down at her, he gave her an Eskimo kiss. "But you'd never do that, would you, my little princess," Jeffery said, smiling at Bella. *God, he loved this little girl so.* It was absolutely bizarre what a connection the two of them had made in such a short period of time.

Diane turned to Jeffery and leaned on the desk. Even in her night get-up, she was still sexy. Throwing a shoulder and kiss his way, she flirted. "Well, I'd like to think that you and I are still vigorous when it comes to our intimacy despite our ages, but my calculations could be off."

With a Denzel-like sway, Jeffery walked up behind Diane and kissed her on her neck. "You owe me for missing our appointment last night. I took that little blue pill and fell asleep. I'm surprised it didn't fall off in the middle of the night."

Diane couldn't help but laugh. "Oh, I'll make up for it, just as soon as we're alone."

"You better," he said, passing Bella back to Diane. Lovingly, he kissed his wife again – softly and slowly, to make sure that she felt his passion before breaking into a statement that would end their sexual tension until the evening was theirs. "I have to shit, shower and shave, my dear. Hold our little bundle for me."

***

When the Lawlesses arrived at Brett's hospital room a little after eight, he and Courtney were still peacefully asleep. So grateful to finally be in each other's company again, they had stayed up most of the night talking and staring into each other's eyes, whispering sweet nothings and planning their future.

Finally able to sleep since he arrived back stateside, Brett rested in the bed while Courtney rested on the reclining chair right beside him with her feet propped up and her body curled into the fetal position under a thin sheet. It looked as though they had both pushed as far as they could toward each other, him nearly at the edge of the bed and her hanging off the side of the chair.

"Look at them," Diane said with a smile. "Back together again."

"Like magnets," Jeffery said, quietly proud.

"Grandma Lawless," Cameron said, hugging tight to her side. His little fingers pinched the fabric of her St. John's pants suit. "Is Daddy okay?" The little boy was scared at the sight of his father. With tears welling at the sides of his big brown eyes, he looked up at Diane for an explanation. "He doesn't look okay."

"He's just fine, baby," Diane said, rubbing Cameron's head. "Don't you be afraid."

Brett heard his son's little bell of a voice even in his deep sleep and stirred awake. He raised his head and looked across at his family. They were truly a sight to behold.

"Hello, son," Jeffery said, setting down the baby bag on the chair across the room. In his arms, he held Bella, all dressed up in a pink lace dress with little pink lace socks and a pink headband.

"Hello, sir," Brett said, pushing himself all the way up. "Is it Christmas? Sure looks like it." The pain had begun to set in again in both his leg and arm, but he didn't let on to anyone.

Cameron inched up to his father with his Thomas the Train clutched in his hand. "Daddy." His words trailed off.

Despite his busted up face, Brett smiled brightly. "Come here, little man, let me see you," he said, reaching for him. Without asking, he knew that Cameron was afraid.

Cameron did as his father said. He walked all the way over to him and tried to smile.

Courtney stirred slowly awake. "Baby, do you need anything?" she asked groggily, pulling the covers over her. Suddenly, she got a glimpse of Cameron beside her and sat up. Glancing over at her mother, she checked her watch. "Oh, no.

I'm so sorry. I overslept." She reached for her phone and saw it was dead.

"Girl, you're fine," her mother said, sitting down in the chair that Jeffery pulled out for her at the foot of the bed. "I've got your charger." Reaching into her purse, she pulled it out and threw it over to Courtney.

"Thanks, Ma," Courtney said, catching it and immediately plugging it into the socket.

"Daddy," Cameron said, touching his father's face with a frown. In a way, the little boy couldn't believe that his father was actually here with him.

"What's up, little man?" Brett asked, wanting to know everything that was on his son's mind.

"Did you get beat up?" His small fingers trailed over his father's stubbly beard.

Brett missed his son's little fingers. Even in the morning, they smelled like bubble gum and dirt. "You could say that," Brett winked and rose up a little. "But you should see the other guy." He nodded to the little tyke.

Even Jeffery had to chuckle. At least those bastards hadn't broken the man's spirit over there. That was always a good sign.

"Is he as bad off as you?" Cameron probed. His fingers lingered near Brett's bandaged neck.

"Oh yeah," Brett said, pitching false bravado for the young boy. Normally, he would have never gloated about a kill, but he needed his son to feel better about what had happened to him. And to do that, he'd say anything right now, including a lie.

"Are you going to be okay?"

"I'm better now that I see your face, son," he assured Cameron. "Everything is going to be much better now."

"Can you come home with us then?" Cameron asked, looking at Courtney for an answer.

"When he's better," she promised. A beep of her phone turning on startled her. Evidently, she had missed more than a few texts and calls, some of which had come from Mrs. Riley, Cameron's biological grandmother, wanting to know why she hadn't been at the mall yesterday to exchange Cameron for the weekend. She looked at her husband and decided not to bring it up. Brett had very strong feelings toward the Rileys and she didn't want to spoil his reunion by discussing such a touchy subject or by calling her back in his presence. When time permitted, she'd reach out and schedule for sometime in the future. She put the phone on vibrate and set to "Do Not Disturb." After all, she had everyone she wanted to talk to right here in this room.

"I'll be home before you know it. It's not as bad as it looks," Brett jested as a pain hit him. He pursed his lips together and breathed through the pain. "They are just going to patch me up and then I'll be coming home. You and I will be out in the backyard, playing catch again in a month."

"I'm getting good, Daddy," Cameron said with a bright smile. "Mommy goes out and plays with me every day...except when it rains, and then we practice in the den."

"You're lucky to have such a good mother," Brett said, looking over at Courtney.

She'd never know how much he appreciated her and all that she'd done for them – how she'd swooped into their lives and saved them from having to be alone. Now, she had taken on the job of motherhood again as not only a mother to his son but also to his new little daughter.

Brett tried to focus, but his eyes kept wandering over to the little bundle of joy in the Colonel's arms. She peered at him quietly, watching his every move and clinging to her grandfather. He felt a sudden envy of the old man for being able to hold her so close and for building a bond that was obvious to anyone around, including him.

"Is that who I think it is?" Brett asked, looking over at Courtney. He couldn't explain it but nervous butterflies erupted in his stomach to meet the two-month old.

*Would she like him? Would she cry?* His mind rambled.

By now, Courtney was sitting up in her chair, watching on quietly as her son acclimated to the man he had loved his entire life and watching his daughter for the first time be introduced to him. "That's your little Bella," she said, putting her hand over Brett's.

Jeffery approached slowly. "This is your father, Bella," he said in a soothing voice to the little girl. "Go say hi to your Daddy."

Brett reached out for her, although his arm was in pain. He had had many dreams over the last few months about seeing her and holding her for himself, and now that it was finally possible despite the many obstacles that had been thrown before him, there was no way that he was going to miss this opportunity.

"Can you get her?" Jeffery asked, concerned about Brett's injury.

"I'll make do," Brett said, his eyes welling with tears again.

"Bella is my little sister, Daddy." Cameron said, stepping out of the way so that Jeffery could pass. "She likes me," he said shyly. "Sometimes, she lets me hold her."

"Let's hope she likes me too," Brett said, taking a deep breath.

From one set of arms to the other, Bella was passed. She hesitated to leave her grandfather's embrace, clinging tightly to his shirt, but finally, she let go and went to Brett.

"Sorry that you had to see me like this on our first meeting," Brett said, wiping his face as he held her, "but I've been waiting a long time to see your face."

Bella looked into her father's eyes for a moment as if she was processing his words and then smiled, revealing huge dimples and gums.

"I think she likes you," Courtney said, standing up and kissing Brett's head. Tears fell from her cheeks onto the top of his head.

Brett was speechless. Bella was absolutely the most breathtaking little girl he had ever laid eyes on. Just as he had always wanted, she had her mother's features, hazel brown eyes, beautiful pink lips, soft skin. Still, she looked a lot like him, especially her wide-set mouth and the shape of her eyes.

He rubbed her face. "I don't deserve something so special," he said, kissing Bella's cheeks.

Courtney raised a brow. "Oh, I know." She smiled at him. "She's a big responsibility, much bigger than the Corps."

"And when she's a teenager, much more trouble," Jeffery quipped.

Brett chuckled. "Oh, I think I'm up for the task."

"That's what I said," Jeffery rubbing Diane's shoulders said. "But nothing ever prepares you for Daddy's little girl."

Courtney looked over at her father and felt a swelling of pride inside of her. "Yeah, but you did a good job, Daddy."

Diane's eyes started to get teary. "My goodness," she said, wiping her face. "All we're missing is David."

\*\*\*

An hour and a half drive from Wilmington, NC to the sleepy Army town, Fayetteville, NC was not enough time for Leo Tabor to get his story right. He had practiced it repeatedly as he listened to talk radio, but he still wasn't sure if he sounded sincere and convincing enough to win over his needed allies. However, considering recent events, there was no more time to waste. He had to act faster than the original timeline he set out for himself.

In truth, he hated coming back to this place, because it brought back so many nauseating memories, but hopefully there was a pot of gold waiting on the other side.

Glancing over at the passenger seat toward the yellow file folder protecting the only evidence that he had of his confession, he pulled onto the tranquil cove of the Reverend and Mrs. Riley.

The suburban neighborhood of Willow Landing was an enclave of middle income white Southern Baptists with conservative ideals and controversial views of everyone who didn't fit into their boorish views, so he had chosen his dress carefully.

As he turned off the engine, he took a deep breath, checked his teeth in the rearview mirror, popped a mint into his mouth and slipped on his shades to cover his dilated eyes.

Stepping out of his rented Ford Escape, he straightened his navy blue polo shirt and smoothed his hands down his crisp khaki pants. With the file in his hand, he strode up the front walkway of concrete platform steps amid a perfectly edged, well-sodded lawn to the porch and rang the doorbell.

A white-haired woman in her 60s opened the door and peered up at him suspiciously through the storm door. "Yes?" she said, a hand on the doorknob.

"Good morning, ma'am," Leo said in his kindest Southern gentleman's voice. "My name is Leo Tabor. Are you Amy Black's mother?"

There was hesitation in the woman. No one had referred to her daughter as Amy *Black* in quite some time. Her eyes narrowed on the folder in the stranger's hand. Could he be from the airlines? "I am Sharon Riley, Amy's mother," she confirmed, pulling at the lapel of her pink cardigan. "How can I help you?"

That was a fluid question. It depended. Leo raised a brow and smacked his lips, as though what he was about to say wouldn't be handled well. "I don't know how to quite say this, so I'm just going to say it. I'm the biological father of Cameron Black." His dark brown eyes didn't blink even though the shades covered his eyes. Swallowing hard, he waited for an explosive response.

Sharon, however, didn't seem as surprised as he expected. Unlocking the storm door, she pushed it open to get a better look at the man as he removed his sunglasses. He had the same chocolate curls as her grandson and the exact same eyes and narrow boney nose.

"And you are here to do what, may I ask?" she said, as her husband, hearing the conversation, approached from the study with his Bible gripped in his hand.

Leo looked over her shoulder at Rev. Riley and then back at the small woman. "Well, I want my son, ma'am."

Sharon couldn't hold back her smile. Opening the door, she dipped her head to greet him. "Come on in, Mr. Tabor. It sounds like we have a lot to discuss."

# Chapter 7

"Sometime they'll give a war and nobody will come."

~Carl Sandburg

Kevin Daugherty only had a handful of families of the deceased passengers from Flight 3245 that had not devoted time and money to suing Southern Atlantic Airlines (SAA) under a class action lawsuit set to go to the State Supreme Court in a month. In addition, he had to begin immediately catering to them to ensure that they didn't become the elephant in the courtroom.

The debacle happened two years ago when one of SAA's planes crashed and every single passenger aboard was killed. SAA's situation had only been made more difficult when the FAA concluded after a lengthy investigation that the crash was due to faulty wiring on the plane, making the case one of negligence, thus the company was liable for considerable payouts.

The ensuing public relations fallout had been one big clusterfuck. All crisis-communications tactics were blown out the window.

Prior to the crash, millions of dollars had been spent on multi-pronged marketing campaigns, media training and brand awareness to get the newer airline noticed; but the thing that puts Southern Atlantic Airlines on the map was not their savvy marketing, it was the infamous crash.

For months after the incident, every major media outlet in the country interviewed families of victims, who were primarily families of military personnel with deeply moving stories. On top of that, social media took on the second wave of the PR nightmare, reminding those who might have otherwise forgotten the crash and that the culprit was SAA.

The stories and photos that circulated resonated with millions of viewers and increased any potential compensation that the company would be forced to pay along with hampering their ability to successfully compete in the airline marketplace.

It seemed that potential passengers were more willing to take a bus across the Atlantic before riding on their planes, even with the jaw dropping deals and lower pricing schedules.

Southern Atlantic Airlines was screwed, at least according to quarterly stock reports, weekly media stories and potential investors.

After 18 months of lengthy bills and failed negotiations, lawyers for SAA had made the contingency plan simple. Settle with as many as
possible for undisclosed amounts as soon as
possible. The clock was ticking and every signa-
ture counted. When they got to court, if the
airline only had a few people trying to sue for the
maximum amount, they could potentially avoid
bankruptcy.

Kevin was exhausted. On top of a recent divorce and a less-than-promising parental plan
for his 4-year old son, he was fighting to stay
afloat with this lawsuit. He had spent long hours
in closed-door meetings with lawyers coming up
with offers. He had spent even more time nego-
tiating with some of those who were named in
the lawsuit to accept the payout instead of
moving forward. Plus, in just the last few weeks
in an attempt to shore up money, many employees had taken a pay cut.

*So with all that, why hadn't he left?* Because
Southern Atlantic Airlines was a family business
that his father had put everything in to and
neither he nor his four brothers could just walk
away from this without giving it everything that
they had first.

Now, he had arrived at the Amy Black case.

Brett Black had been continuously unavailable for meetings over the past last two years, but had named his new wife the executor over the negotiations through a power of attorney. Oddly enough, Black had been the least emotional out of all the families of the deceased. He had taken the news quietly. He had refused interviews quietly; he had refused first offers from their lawyers quietly and hopefully he would finally agree to this more generous offer *quietly*.

If more people had been the caliber of Brett Black, maybe their business wouldn't be sinking.

Looking at the live check lying in front of him on his smooth sandalwood desk named out to Courtney Black, he picked up the phone in his little box of an office on the 15th floor of SAA's Raleigh, NC headquarters and dialed her number.

"Hello," Courtney answered, unloading off the plane from Baltimore to Jacksonville. She moved as quickly as she could with the crowd of people exiting the terminal.

"Mrs. Black, its Kevin Daugherty. I'm glad that I finally reached you." He touched the check. "You're quite a hard woman to get in touch with these days."

Pushing her shades up on her head, she rolled her tired neck. "Sorry," Courtney said, pulling her small luggage with Brett trailing closely behind. "I've been *really* busy."

"Baby, can I help you with anything?" Brett asked, moving slowly on his crutches.

"No, honey. I've got it," Courtney said emphatically for the 50th time. She appreciated Brett's desire not to be helpless, but he really needed to understand that what she needed from him was just to follow the flow of the crowd. He had already turned down a wheelchair, not because he didn't need it, but because he was too proud. Now, she worried about him falling or being bumped into.

Kevin inhaled and raised his voice a little so that she could hear him better over the noise in the background. "Well, ma'am, I'd like to drive down to Swansboro and talk to you this week, if I can."

Courtney frowned, not another appointment. She had to take Brett to the Naval Hospital for follow-up for his injuries, meet with the pre-school teacher, and meet with the Claims Adjuster about the roof. "This week really isn't good," she said apologetically.

Kevin wasn't taking *no* for an answer. "We'd like to make you a final offer," he said, hoping she might change her mind. "I can tell you it's significantly larger than the first three. I won't waste a moment of your time, and there will be no double talk. I promise you."

*Double talk seemed to be all that these people could do,* Courtney thought to herself. She turned to her husband and adjusted the heavy bag on her shoulder. "It's Southern Atlantic." Her voice had a hint of sarcasm in it that she wanted Daugherty to hear. "They want to drive down and make us a final offer," she said, hoping that Brett would weigh in and tell them to wait until they were settled back at home.

Brett had nearly forgotten about life stateside with all that happened, especially regarding Amy. For nearly eight months, the only types of choices he had to make were ones of life and death. There were no meetings over there that were not about Ops or calls that were not about strategy.

Sweat rolled down his face as he fought the pain throbbing in his cast. *Maybe what he needed to feel normal was to start doing normal things again.* In all honesty, he welcomed shaking up the pace a little. Plus, he was certain that Courtney could use some help with everything she had been left to take care of. It was better to just dive back in. "Okay, well, we'll be there," he said, wiping his brow. "Tell him to come on down."

Courtney smacked her lips. "This week is fine," she said, turning back around with the bags. She rolled her eyes. "What day?"

"Today's Monday," Kevin said, scanning his desk calendar. "I can be there tomorrow at 11:00 A.M." In truth, he'd cancel everything set up for the entire week if he had to.

"We'll see you then." Courtney said, hanging up the phone. *Great, one more meeting.*

Brett stopped after they finally entered into the luggage claim of the airport and took a breath. It was a long haul for him from the plane and he needed a second. "What did he say?"

Courtney walked up to him, pulled a wet-wipe from her purse and wiped the sweat from her husband's flushed face. Looking up into his eyes, she kissed his lips and lingered there for a minute. "He said no double talk and he's ready to make an offer."

Brett gripped the handles of his crutches. "Better than the previous offers?"

"Better than the previous ones," Courtney answered as she turned on a swivel and saw her father waiting for them in a chair near the door. "Good. Dad is here." She waved toward her Dad and smiled. "The one thing I love about that man is that he knows nothing if not how to be on time."

"We could have taken a cab. I mean, they've watched the kids for two weeks; they've taken Cameron to school for two weeks. We could have done this, at least, for ourselves." Brett could feel himself getting upset. Colonel Lawless had to feel as though Brett was behaving a little less than chivalrous with his daughter lugging around her own luggage. It took a stab at his manhood.

Courtney put her hand over his as if to hush his thoughts. "Hey, that's what family is for, Marine. Dad and Mom don't mind. They volunteered. They want to help."

"Yeah, but I feel as though we're taking advantage of them."

"That's because you don't ever ask anyone for help," Courtney said, releasing him. Her smile made her words easier to take. "Don't internalize this; be grateful for it." Her naturally arched brow rose.

Brett couldn't look her directly in the eye; it was like being hypnotized by one of those mythical sea sirens. "Don't *shrink talk* me," he huffed. "Just because you're in school for it, doesn't mean that you get to use it on me." He glared down at her with mock disgust and a bit of playful banter.

Courtney grinned. "Oh, I'm going to shrink talk you...as soon as we get home."

Brett couldn't help but grin then. They had not been able to get as intimate as he would have liked in the hospital, but his pain management had gotten better and his hopes were high for a little more privacy when they arrived at the house. Plus, that kiss, while short and sweet, woke up something in him that was anything but innocent.

*** 

The devil was busy, and Jeffery Lawless just couldn't catch a break from him. First, he had to break the news to Courtney that her husband had been injured and now this news to Brett.

He had been at the airport for nearly an hour waiting by the window looking at all the happy people as they passed in and out of the doors with bags of clothes and bright smiles. The sun was out, shining bright. The weather was unseasonably nice. And he was left with this fresh hell to yet again wade through, all while promising to someone that things would get better.

Pinching the bridge of his nose, he fought the anxiety building up at him with each passing second.

He had received the call the night before from his son. David had called on his private line around three a.m. and had been a complete mess. The boy had cried on the phone for hours trying to find a way for this to be his fault, but the simple truth of it was that this was war. Death was a very nasty part of a very nasty business, and if he ever wanted to ascend further up the ranks in the Marine Corps, he had had to learn to deal with it as quietly and discreetly as he could, while they did their jobs.

David had first wanted word to be sent to Brett at the Naval Hospital, but Jeffery had warned him against it. He promised his son that he would personally deliver the message to Brett as soon as he arrived back to Jacksonville.

But now that task felt nearly too hard to bear.

He watched the young couple come out of the terminal bright with hope renewed and encouraged from being with each other, which was a long way from when he had first seen Brett back at the hospital just two weeks ago. Now, he'd have to suck the life out of the man one more time.

"Daddy," Courtney said, walking up and giving him a big hug. She embraced him tightly. "How are you?"

There was no point in starting the conversation off with a lie. So it was better not to answer. "How are *you*?" Jeffery asked, redirecting his question.

She appraised him suspiciously. "Good. The flight was *okay*, not too bad on Brett," Courtney answered, seeing stress in his face and the twitch in his eye. "Everything okay?" She stepped back a little.

"How are you, sir?" Brett said, offering his hand as he approached.

"Good to see you, son," Jeffery said, holding his hand for a second. "Let me get your bags and get you loaded."

"I can help," Courtney said, setting down her bag on the chair. "Baby, can you watch the luggage while I get our other stuff?" she asked Brett.

"Sure," Brett said, noticing Lawless' weird mood also. Something about him seemed off.

Jeffery and Courtney walked over to the baggage area and waited for their things to come around on the carousel. Brett decided to take a second and have a seat. Resting on the bench, he watched from afar, as Jeffery leaned into his daughter and whispered something to her. She looked up abruptly and paused, then looked over at Brett.

"What in the hell is going on now?" Brett asked under his breath. Pulling nicotine gum from his pocket, he popped one in his mouth and looked at his watch. Not being able to smoke was driving him insane and with Courtney not knowing about the snuff thing, it forced him to really quit. Maybe he could find a way to send her out of the house on an errand so that he could bum a smoke from the neighbor. It would be just his luck that Joe had quit while he was away also.

As they brought the luggage back with them, Brett got up and balanced himself on his crutches. "Let's get this show on the road," he said as Courtney walked back up to him.

"Ready?" she asked, eyes wet from impending tears.

"What's wrong?" he asked, looking back at Jeffery.

"We should go home first," Courtney said, looking down at the floor.

"No, I want to know what's going on *now*!" Brett said, waiting for Jeffery to tell him. "Are the babies okay?" His first mind went to his children. Had something happened to them? Had something happened to Diane?

Jeffery twisted up his lip and stood up straighter. "The kids are fine."

"Then who isn't?" Brett asked. He knew that look. Something horrible had happened...again.

"I was hoping we could discuss this once I got you home," Jeffery said, looking around.

"And I respect you for your dignity, sir, but I insist," Brett said, swallowing hard. "Tell me now...whatever it is."

Jeffery couldn't say no. Had he been in Brett's shoes, he would have insisted on the same in a lot less respectful way.

Courtney's eyes overflowed with tears. With her hands balled up beside her, she waited for Brett to explode, to make some scene in this place.

"Son, I am sorry to relay this message," Jeffery said, shaking his head. He stepped up closer to the young man. "Your entire team expired last evening at around 2300 hours our time while in the Zabul Province on an Op."

Brett bit down on his lip and tears welled up in his eyes. Gripping the sides of his crutches tighter, his entire body began to tremble.

"Everyone?" he asked, blinking fast as the hot tears dropped down on to his cheeks.

"Everyone," Colonel Lawless answered regrettably. "We found out last night. David called, wanted to call you at the hospital but I advised against it. Considering that you had to make the flight from Baltimore back here; I felt it best to tell you now." He put his hand on his shoulder. "But I still didn't want to tell you like this...out in public. I was hoping to wait until you got home...seemed like the most decent thing to do."

"Doesn't really matter, does it, sir?" Brett's Adam's apple bobbed in his muscular neck. "They're still dead." Even as he said the words, he simply could not believe it.

"They died bravely serving their country," Jeffery said, stepping back.

"How did they die? What killed them?" Joe's face flashed through Brett's mind.

"An IED," Jeffery said, shoving his fists down into his pants pockets. "They completed the operation successfully. However, the extraction was ambushed."

Brett shook his head and took in a deep breath as the tears rolled. Courtney stood beside them, looking at her husband in complete sympathy. She was angry that he had been injured, angry that his team had been killed, angry that the war had not ended after all this time but so thankful to God that Brett had been spared.

The men whispered something between them and then Jeffery wrapped his arms around Brett and held him for a minute, seeing that Brett couldn't keep his tears and sobs at bay. When

Jeffery was certain that he could stand alone, he picked up the bags and escorted them to the car.

"I'm so sorry." Courtney said while rubbing Brett's back.

"I just want to get home," Brett said, barely above a whisper. "Take me home, baby."

# Chapter 8

"Homecoming means coming home to what's in your heart." - Anonymous

It was near dusk when the car pulled up to Brett's house, he looked at it from the driveway as if it were completely foreign to him – not because it had been run down since he was gone, but because it was so very picturesque.

Courtney had been up to her normal over-hauls – a continual process to make their home better, more comfortable and more inviting. She was like her mother in that respect, always preparing for the night that she would be called on to be the hostess. And she played her role well. Every single detail of their home was full of love and thought, a thing that he had become accustomed to with her around but still appreciated.

The yard was well-manicured, the garden tended to and filled with plants, flowers, bushes, rambling purple Clematis vines and red mulch; new sparkly butterfly stickers were on the mail-box, and a crisp United States flag flew patrioti-cally on a pole attached to the front of their home.  It was peaceful and beautiful and yet another reminder of why men happily went to their deaths over there, so that no one would ruin the lives that they have here.

The sprinkler was out in the middle of the lawn, rotating its flow of fresh water into the earth right beside the red-hatted gnome that he and Courtney noticed on a day trip to Morehead. Newly cleaned windows gleamed in front of white plantation shutters around the house. Track lights lined the perfectly edged corners of the lawn leading up to the front steps.  On the porch, the two rocking chairs sat with yellow pillows on their seats and in between the chairs was a large tin canister filled with vibrant yellow sunflowers.

Parked in front of the garage was his beloved black F-150 truck, clean as a whistle and waiting for him. Beside it was Courtney's new little red supercharged Fiat.  The vehicles made a hand-some pair, just like them.

Alas, everything was in order.  Everything was well taken care of - a thing that he could not have expected if his late wife had been here. Amy was a woman of waste, and where she was not lazy, she was selfish, a combination that did not bode well for housework, yardwork or *work* in general.  He saw that even more now being married to Courtney – oh what world he nearly missed.

Pulling himself from his thoughts, he slowly stepped out of Colonel Lawless' immaculate Lincoln Navigator with his crutches leading him and closed the door.

"Welcome home," Courtney said, leaning in and giving him a kiss.

Brett rubbed her back as he looked at his house. "It's good to be home." He looked down into her hazel eyes. "You kept the place real nice, baby." His southern Texas drawl seemed to come out most when he was emotional. And today he was a basket case, though he tried desperately to keep it together.

"I do what I can," she said with a wink. "Now come inside. I'm going to fix a big dinner for you; run you a bath and we're going to relax."

"Actually, I had hoped to go in and get settled, and then see what Judy and the kids need. Word got to her, right?" Brett asked, looking over at Jeffery.

"Yes, she's been notified." Jeffery popped the back of the SUV open, grabbed their bags, and carried them up to the porch before Brett could protest.

"Do you think now is a good..." Courtney was cut off right before she asked the most obvious question of the day.

"Well, I'll be damned," a female voice said from the house next door.

Brett looked over to see their neighbor, Allison, as she stepped out of the front door of her home and made her way over to them. "Is that really you?" she asked, throwing her checkered hand towel over her shoulder.

"It's me," Brett said with a painted on grin. Although he wanted to rush right into the house, Allison was a friend and considering how scarce those were getting for him; he needed to be as amicable as possible.

Allison and Terry were the neighbors who moved into the rental home beside them. They were a military family, where Allison took on the role as the stay-at-home wife who took care of all things domestic and Terry took on all things foreign as a Naval Intelligence Officer.

However, *don't ask-don't tell* didn't stop them from keeping their marriage as quiet as possible. Being a lesbian still wasn't widely accepted on or off military installations in North Carolina. But the way that Brett saw it, neither was being an interracial couple. They both got dirty looks and quiet whispers, so he was in good company.

With a bright smile, Allison quickly skipped through the wet grass with bare feet exposing hot pink, freshly painted toenails and rolled up Ralph Lauren khaki pants, looking like a Stepford wife.   Chipper and grinning, she wrapped her arms around him and gave him a big hug. "Mmm.  Good to have you back, Marine."

"Good to be back," he answered, wondering when she was going to ask what happened to him. "You're in a great mood."

Allison rose on up her tiptoes.  "It's the Xanax," she confessed.

"Hey, girl," Courtney said, kissing her cheek.

"Hey *yourself*," Allison said, kissing her back. She adjusted her turquoise Tiffany eyeglasses and smoothed her blonde bob.  "I told Diane that I'd keep an eye on the house. She stopped by and told me what happened." Making an *ouch* noise, she glanced down at Brett's leg. "I've just been going in and watering the plants, changing the lights from room to room each night, picking up your mail and watching porn on your computer. You know *nothing big*.  I'll bill you later for my services."

Brett chuckled under his breath.

"You're a lifesaver," Courtney said gratefully.

"No worries. We have to look out for each other." Glancing over at Mr. Lawless as he stepped inside with the bags, she whispered. "Some guy and an old lady came looking for you. They seemed really..." She searched her mind for the right words. "Really right wing conservative nut bags."

That got Brett's attention. "Who was it?" he asked.

Allison bucked her eyes as she tried to accurately recall. "Said that she was your late wife's mother, the guy didn't say who he was. He looked suspect."

Brett couldn't take any worse or big news. He'd figure it all out later. Plus, the mention of the Rileys made his blood boil with anger. Both of those old Bible-thumping racists were shit starters and always looking for a way to insert themselves into Cameron's life. So if they were showing up here, then it wasn't good.

He scratched the back of his neck and debated if he should ask Allison for one of her happy pills. *Naw, better not.* "You girls can gab if you want. I know that's what you do, and I don't want to stop you. But I need to get in here off this foot for a minute. Allison," Brett said, leaning over and kissing her cheek, "it's good to see your face, darling. I'll buy some beer and we can catch up soon with you and Terry."

"We'd both like that," Allison said, rubbing Courtney's shoulder. "We'll do our normal coffee in a couple days. I'll give you a minute to settle down first. Then, I want to know *everything*."

"It's a lot worse than the leg," Courtney said, as Brett walked off.

Allison frowned. "What happened?"

"Joe and the whole team..." Courtney tried to say the words, but they just brought tears to her eyes. Even she couldn't quite process yet what had happened to their friends. "No one made it."

Allison's mood suddenly perked out. Dropping her shoulders, she looked at Brett as he made his way up the porch and shook her head. "Damn, girl. How is he handling it?"

Courtney looked back at her husband and shrugged her shoulders. "I honestly don't know."

*** 

As soon as Jeffery set the bags down in the den, he turned and headed straight for the front door. He had been home from deployment before, so he knew that the two of them just wanted to be alone, but more than that, he understood that Brett needed time to decompress. Right now, Brett was still trying to process all that had happened around him and to him, but eventually, he was going to have to let the anger out, and that would require or should require utter privacy.

Courtney came through the front door shortly after Brett. Wiping a tear before Brett could turn around and see, she cleared her throat and smiled. "Dad, I'll be on my way in a little bit to pick up the kids."

Jeffery raised a hand in protest. "The kids are fine. They are keeping Diane entertained. Leave them there tonight and just be with your husband."

"I don't mind, sir," Brett interjected quickly.

Jeffery wasn't hearing it. "You kids can pick them up in the morning, if you like." His voice boomed with the kind of authority that dared to be questioned.

And that was that.

Courtney kissed her father's cheek and Brett shook his hand before he made a very neat and quick exit out the front door.

Alone at last, Brett looked around the house at the updates. New hardwood dark cedar floors had been put in the entryway foyer. New drapes for the living and dining room. New paintings.

Fresh paint of a neutral but very warming color connected the front rooms with a splash of bright yellow in the hall leading upstairs.

"Impressive," he said as she circled in front of him.

"You like?" she asked, voice slightly flat.

"Yeah, it looks like something out of Southern Living," he noticed her mood change. "Did I say something?"

Courtney was used to being alone after eight months. It caught her off guard that he was actually physically there and recognized the slightest of her emotions. She tried to look up with a smile, but it was lost on him. Why bother? *Be honest*, she thought to herself. "I don't think you should go to Judy's tonight."

"I'm sure that they need me. This isn't the kind of news that you need to hear alone."

"I need you," she insisted. "And I'm not being selfish." Her inner voice laughed at her. Of course she was being selfish. "Plus, maybe what she needs is a moment to be alone." She stammered over herself. "I know how I would feel."

Brett smacked his lips and looked off but didn't argue. He didn't want to be difficult with her. But that was just the point...she didn't have to know how it felt to have her husband dead, because he was right in front of her. No one could say the same for Judy.

Unable to read his face, she sucked in a slightly irritated breath. "So are you going to go?" Courtney followed up after a long silence.

Brett ducked his head. "Yes." He braced himself for a barrage of reasons why he shouldn't.

But Courtney didn't give him the response he was expecting.

"Okay," she said, moving her hair out of her face and taking a deep breath. "Well, we should pick up some food to go with."

"Sounds good. I'll call her now and see what she'd like."

Before he could reach for his phone, Courtney had already pulled out hers. She passed it to him without showing the attitude hiding behind her eyes. "Here, use mine."

He took it and smiled gratefully. "Thank you."

"No problem," Courtney said, walking off. "I'm going to put away our things. You make your call." *That last part had two meanings.*

Brett knew that she was upset. In fact, he knew that she was right. He needed to be home with her right now, but he couldn't deny the push inside of him to keep going. Joe was gone. His best friend was dead, and now he had to be there not only for his family but also for Judy and the kids.  He just hoped that Courtney would eventually understand and work with him on it, instead of fight him.

Dialing Judy's number, he went to the dining room and sat at the tall table.  Getting the weight off his foot felt good.

On the second ring, Judy answered, voice slightly nasally from crying. "Hello."

"Judy, its Brett."

"Brett," Judy paused. "I'm sorry that I didn't call you up at the hospital.  Joe told me about a week ago what happened." She sniffled.

"No worries," he said, running his finger down the table to make a streak.  "I just got home and was just told what happened. Damn, Judy. I'm so sorry." He wanted to tell her how he really felt; that it was his fault.  If he hadn't been injured, none of this might have ever happened.  But he decided not to make this about him.

"Nothing you could have done, Brett. Don't apologize."  She looked at the picture of her husband she was holding as she sat alone in the dark den.  "I'm just glad one of you made it."

Brett sucked his teeth and hunkered down on the words that wanted to badly to sneak from his tongue. "I was going to come over and bring you and the kids something to eat."

"No, Brett. Thank you, but I just want to be alone."

Brett nodded and pushed back in the seat.

"How about tomorrow or the next day even? I need some time," Judy tried to explain.

"Whenever you want, Judy," Brett said, hearing Courtney dragging the luggage from the den toward the foyer. "I just want you to know that I'm here for you."

"I appreciate you," Judy said, sobbing a little. "I just...I need to be alone for now."

"Well, you just say the word and I'll be there." He looked up to see Courtney pass by the doorway.

"I will. Thanks, Brett," Judy said, hanging up the phone.

Brett hung up and stood quickly. "Is there any way at all that I can help you?" He felt like a piece of shit with her having to do the work.

"I'm fine," Courtney said voice lighter than her mood. "Just give me a minute and we can head out."

"We don't have to." He scratched his ear. "She wants to be alone."

Courtney lifted a brow but refused to say, "I told you so." With a nod, she threw the bags over her shoulder and hiked upstairs.

# Chapter 9

"Rain, rain go away.  Come again another day."

The sun had not even broken the horizon and Courtney was already awake.  Unable to sleep a second longer, her eyes flashed open, and she realized that her husband - after eight months of being away - was lying right beside her in their marital bed.

She had grown used to the bed being cold and lonely on his side, but his body heat radiated over to her now. She prayed a grateful and heartfelt prayer to God for that blessing considering how differently things could have played out for their family.  Brett could have never been injured on that fateful day, and then he would have been dead too, never to return home to her, never to have met Bella.

Turning slowly over on her side to face him, she studied the mysterious Brett Black as he lay in peaceful slumber.   It was funny. He had been her husband for over a year, but she was still smitten with him like she was the first day that they met in the Swansboro library.

She remembered thinking that day how he looked like the poster boy for the Marine Corps, even before she knew what he did for a living – well dressed, well groomed, well spoken. Yet, he was human, clinging to his son, looking for answers and scared to death of an impending divorce. Even then, he was honorable and gentle with her.

Now that she knew him better than she knew anyone else, she knew that he was so much more than a poster boy – he was a hero.

Sometime during the night, Brett had kicked the covers off, like he always did. Despite Courtney dropping the air down to a crisp 65 degrees, he was still sweating and probably in pain even in his dreams.

Completely naked, he rested flat on his back with his hands curled under his head and his bad leg propped up on pillows.

She scooted a little closer to smell his masculine musk, a fragrance of sandalwood, soap and deodorant. *Mmm, she had missed that smell.* The pinkness of his lush, sweet lips teased her with memories of their first kiss and their last. She inhaled him, madly wanting to reach over and kiss his heart-shaped and wide-set mouth.

Hungrily, her eyes cascaded down his long tanned body assessing his every asset. His six-foot two inches Michelangelo-like wide, muscular frame. Veiny, brawny tattooed arms. His beautiful marble-like face. The long thick column of his neck with that teasing mole near his Adam's apple. A mountainous wide chest. Carved, sinewy muscles rippling down his elongated torso. A rock-hard eight pack. Sleeved colorful tattoos that ran down the length of both forearms to his large hands. Scars from multiple tours of duty. The cut of lean muscle between his legs and thighs that curved down into a perfect V-shape. Curly blonde hair that started at his wide upper thighs and ran down his legs past his bulging deltoids to his huge tattooed calves. The deep dip of his innie belly button. Lastly, another trail of blonde hair nestled around his thick penis, lying lazily over on his leg.

The sight of it all made her want him inside of her.

How she longed for him to take her the way he once did when he used to command her body as soon as he laid eyes on her. How he tasted her, kissed her, licked her into an oblivion of ecstasy. Did he even desire her anymore? Recent events clouded the truth from fiction. He could potentially be overwhelmed with all that had happened to him, but she still couldn't fight the tiny voice in the back of her head that brought marital doubt.

"It's you," *It* whispered like a cunning snake to Eve in the Garden. "He doesn't want you."

They couldn't make love at the hospital, and to make thing worse, they hadn't made love last night. It had been their first night alone, and he had fallen asleep on the sofa in the den looking at photos of his team members. She had so much planned, but none of that mattered. The sight of him lost in agony had hurt her to her heart, but when she had told him to come to bed – so that she could try to make the pain go away – he had turned her down.

Somewhere in the night, he had finally come to bed, but only after she was asleep. *Had that been intentional?* A way to avoid her and her desperate advances.

Courtney was starting to think that the extra baby fat she still carried had ruined things between them. When he met her, she had been fit from swimming and unscarred from carrying a nine-pound baby. Now she was 15 pounds heavier and a lot less toned.

Another thought bothered her even more. Maybe, just *maybe*, life married to her wasn't what he had expected. Was she different to him now as a wife instead of a girlfriend? Was she not as much fun? Had her mystery disappeared? The thought made her even sadder.

She loved him so much, and yet she felt like she was losing him, as if she was being ejected from his life by life. The idea of such a thing troubled her immensely, because she had always been sure of herself both emotionally and physically. However, motherhood was a different concept all together. It had caused her to second-guess everything that she had once believed about life.

Without thought, her little fingers found their way to his meaty chest. She laid her small hand over his heart and listened to the beat. Strong and fast, it boomed.

"I love you," she whispered, fighting back tears.

Brett's crystal blue eyes flashed open and stared at her, although his stoic face did not change. "I love you too," he said, moving his left hand over hers.

She looked over at his wedding ring and fought back sobs.

Nestling his head down in his pillow, he blinked slowly. In a deep southern Texas baritone soft as silk, he asked, "Why are you crying, baby?"

Courtney sniffled and wiped her nose. "I don't want to say." *She really didn't.* It was one thing to be quiet, and unsure of yourself. It was a total different thing to admit it to someone else.

He shifted a little to the side without moving his leg. Muscles flexed in his wide chest with every movement. "Say anyway." He swallowed hard. *Had he done something? Had he not done something?* His face finally lit up with concern as he became more coherent.

Courtney bit her lip in nervousness. "I miss you," she confessed innocently.

He frowned, blonde eyebrows furrowing. Suddenly, he was confused. "I miss you too, but I'm right here."

"No," Courtney said, moving her wild hair from her face. She looked up at the ceiling to avoid his eyes. *How did she say this without sounding ridiculous?* "I miss you...*intimately*," she said, blowing out a breath. *Okay. There it was. Out in the open.*

Without a word, Brett trailed an intense sensual gaze from her angelic brown face ripe with expression down her long swan neck to her large breasts. Her nipples were hardened under her soft cotton USMC t-shirt. His mouth parted involuntarily as his groin began to swell. Just looking at her turned him on. He finally spoke, "And that made you cry? Not being intimate?" His gaze continued down to her long, muscular thighs and the tight little spot hidden by hot pink lace panties.

She knew that look of lust. It caused her heart to flutter. "I thought maybe you didn't want me; you know that you didn't find me attractive anymore since the baby." Hence the big t-shirt to cover up the little after-baby bulge.

His eyes darted back to hers. Then suddenly he chuckled and then sighed. *If she only knew.* "Baby," he said, shaking his head and pulling her closer with an iron grip. "I *want* you." Sliding his hand down her back to her small waist as she crawled on top of him, he looked up at her. He needed her to understand what he had to say, because it was the truest thing that he could explain. "I want you so bad until it literally hurts inside. If you think for a moment that *baby fat* of any kind on you is going to turn me off, you're crazy. You gave me my daughter. You've raised our son." He shook his head emphatically and tried to find the words. "Woman, I'm crazy about you. And I'm attracted to you, more than you know. And you look amazing." He scanned her body. "Every sensual curve. Every little mole. Your skin color. Your eyes. Your lips.

Every single part of you is beautiful just the way it is. You're the woman that I fell in love with. Nothing has changed."

Courtney wiped another tear. "It feels good to hear you say that." A smile curled her lips.

That's what he wanted to see. A smile. Everything in his life up to this point had been shit...everything except her. If she was okay, then maybe he would be too.

He smiled back playfully. "Yeah?" Pulling her down closer to his face, he looked at her plump lips. "It feels good to hear me say that I want you?" he asked in a near whisper. He could feel himself coming alive at just the thought of taking her.

His smooth voice sent zingers up her spine and goose bumps over her body. Straddling him, she bent to him and kissed his lips. "Yes," she whispered into his mouth. The first kiss was quick and playful.

"I want you," he said with finality.

As he uttered the words, everything changed. The room suddenly became electrically charged and what started out as caring and gentle was slowly becoming carnal and visceral.

The second kiss was slow and passionate. His velvety tongue slipped into her mouth and tasted her hidden desires. Her fingers lingered on his chest, clawing at him as she kissed him deeper.

His warm hands felt so good on her skin, finding their way under her shirt and up her torso. Massaging her aching muscles, caressing her skin, he relished in the sight of her. Her silky skin. Her tempting curves.

*How in the hell could she think that he didn't want all of this? Hell, he'd kill for it. He had killed for it.*

She looked so vulnerable right now, so in need of being taken care of. He had been away an incredibly long time from his new wife, and she had been so alone. Now, it was up to him to make up for all the time that had been missed, and it was a job that he would do with all the passion that he could muster.

"Come here." Brett slowly sucked on her bottom lip and pressed his fingers down into her skin. "Can you feel me?" he asked, thrusting upward and at the same time cupping her round breasts and pinching her nipples.

Courtney sucked in a ragged breath. It had been such a long time, but his touch was so familiar. "Yes. I can feel you. You're getting harder." Her hair fell over on his shoulder. Closing her eyes, she opened her legs wider, aching to have him inside of her.

He inhaled her perfume. "You're making me harder," he said, clenching his square jaw. He undulated under her, watching her face. "You do this to me. You make me so hard until it hurts." His hot breath singed her skin.

"I need you," she begged.

"I need you more." Brett slipped both hands around her waist and grabbed the sides of her lace panties. He liked these. *Pity*.

Ripping them off, he grunted and flung them across the room. "I've thought about you every day since I left." His heart raced in his chest. Sliding a digit over her tender clitoris, he watched her body blossom. If her pheromones had been visible, they would have lit up the room like embers from a fire. "Every single day, I dreamt of you." Her wetness slipped over his hands. Pulling his fingers away from her, he slipped them inside of his mouth and made her watch him taste her essence.

Courtney's sex instantly clenched tight. She missed his lips there. Just the thought made her even wetter, and the sound of her rubbing against him became more audible as her sex became slicker.

"The taste of you," he whispered as he sucked his fingers. "The feel of you."

Moving her hips downward with his grip, he pushed the tip of his engorged penis inside of her. "Coming inside of my wife."

Courtney's head flung back and her eyes closed tight. Heat burned through her body into his as she waited for the connection to be made. Legs trembling with desire, she felt her breath get caught in her throat.

"Take me," she muttered.

"*Take* this off," he ordered, pulling her shirt off. "Don't ever be ashamed around me. You're beautiful."

Bobbing full breasts emerged; nipples erect and begging to be tasted. The sight of her long torso, her wide hips and thick thighs drove him insane. Turning to steel, he moved his veiny shaft between her legs, teasing her.

"I don't want to hurt you," he said, knowing it had been a long time since he had been inside of her. He had to remember to be gentle, if not a gentleman.

"You won't," she bit out. "Do it!"

Courtney planted her hands firmly on the broad caps of his shoulders. Taking in a deep breath, she adjusted to the sudden thrill of him entering her body, one slow, tortuous inch at a time until he was buried to the hip. Her body pulsated around him, tightening around his throbbing shaft. It was pleasurable pain and she welcomed it gladly.

He hissed, muscles tightening all over his body. "Slow," he said, holding her down. His nostrils flared. "It's been a long, long time and you feel so good." He would have to walk himself through this first session, lest he make a fool of himself. She had been waiting nine months; surely he could give her more than nine minutes.

"You feel so good too," Courtney said, moving her hips and keeping her eyes on his.

He watched her torment him with slow pumps for a moment. Trailing his hands all over her body, he finally gave in and clasped her perfect ass. The need inside of him began to build to a thunderous level and he could feel himself giving in to her pleas. "Fuck it," he said, thrusting harder inside of her. "I. Can't. Stop."

Courtney moaned aloud. Her voice, audible and sexy, turned him on even more.

His back arched as he pushed deep into his wife over and over again, making her his once again. Moving his hips in circles, he made sure to feel every single part of her soft brown temple. The motions became mindless and they melted into each other. Slow then fast, hard and then soft. In and out. He focused, eyes narrowed on her body.

Courtney bucked against him. Skin against skin, her nails dug into his chest as he held on to her by her hips. He watched himself slip in and out of her as she rose up off of him and then plummeted back down to his hips.

Grabbing her by the back of her head, he pulled her down into his eager kiss and then trailed his lips down her neck to her breasts. Sucking on her nipples, he speared into her, feeling himself moved from one wave to another of complete bliss.

Releasing her mouth, he let out a sigh. "Damn," he said as sweat rolling down his chest. He had forgotten how *good* it was.

"Harder," she screamed, grinding her hips. "Harder!"

"Not yet," he said to himself. But just the sight of her pushed him to the brink.

He ground harder like she commanded. Their bodies slapped against each other madly. Taking deep breaths and closing his eyes, he let out a growl. Wet sex pooled between them as she came hard with her body going rigid as her eyes flashed open and her mouth parted.

"Brett!!" she screamed as her orgasm exploded, releasing her from the bondage of her first concerns. He did want her!

Forgetting about his leg, he pushed up in the bed, back arched, slamming into her over and over until finally, heart pounding, he felt himself release. The veins in his neck protruded as he let out a loud unmistakable moan. Alas, he emptied himself inside of her ounce by ounce until he was left twitching and weak under her.

Collapsing on top of him, Courtney's heartbeat against his own. Sweat dripped from her forehead onto his neck.

"Was it good for you, baby?" he asked, out of breath. He wiped the sweat off his wet marble face and rubbed it on the bed.

"Yes," she mumbled. Rising up, she looked him in the eye. "You?"

"Oh yeah," he said, feeling his leg throb. "But can you...get off me? My leg is killing me," he said mock crying and tapping her bare bottom.

Courtney's head snapped toward his leg and then rolled off of him. "I'm sorry, baby."

"It's okay," he said, laughing and out of breath. "Just for a minute."

"And then?" she asked, lying on the pillow beside him.

"And then, I want you again," he said, reaching for the glass of water on the nightstand. Glancing over again, he grabbed his bottle of pain pills. He was definitely going to need those.

# Chapter 10

**And the winner is...**

After weeks of being around each other with no intimacy, it seemed that all they could do when they finally touched each other was make love. Hours of endless, mindless sex had left the pair exhausted, naked and wrapped in each other's embrace well past the alarms that sounded, the blaring sun shining in on them from the bay windows or even the constant phone calls.

Courtney hadn't slept so well since before Brett had gone to Afghanistan. In a near coma, she nuzzled in the middle of her husband's chest, between his legs, and melted into him.

Somewhere in the morning, Brett had found a comfortable spot in the middle of the bed and dug in there to sleep. He had drifted away feeling Courtney's heartbeat against his own. It hypnotized him along with her enchanting smell. With his hands planted on her firm, round behind, he slept without a care in the world. No dreams of war. No dreams of death. No dreams at all.

At 11:00 on the dot, Kevin Daugherty and his team of two lawyers pulled up in the driveway of the Black family home as promised. Armed with pens, documents and laptop, they moved with a purpose up to the front door and rang the door-bell.

As soon as the doorbell sounded, Courtney's head popped up from Brett's chest. She looked around in a daze, trying to figure out what time it was. Wiping her mouth, she slowly tried to ease off of Brett, but his strong hands grabbed her and pushed her back down against his bare penis.

"Where are you going?" he asked without opening his eyes.

"I heard the door," she said, narrowing her gaze on the alarm clock.

"Whoever it is can go away," he said, rubbing her back. "Come back to bed."

"It might be Mom," she knew it was not, but what if it were.

Brett knew better. "It's not your mom. She wouldn't come over without calling."

She looked over at her cell phone on the nightstand. "She probably did call. We just didn't hear it." Then it hit her. "Shit!" she exclaimed, heart racing.

"What?" he said, now fully awake.

His eyes batted quickly as he adjusted to the sun. With a groan, he pulled himself up as he watched her leap off the bed and run to the bathroom.

"Who is it?" he asked.

"It's the Airlines people!" she screamed from the bathroom. Slipping on her pajamas, she pawed at her hair as she made a quick exit out of the bedroom.

Brett laid his head back down on the pillow and blew out a breath. Hearing her feet halt on the hard wood floors in the hallway, he sat up as she ran back toward the bedroom. "Get dressed," she ordered, sticking her head back into the door.

"You first," he said, looking at her attire.

Snatching the front door open moment later, Courtney looked at the well-dressed group of men from Southern Atlantic and gave a side-smile. "Gentlemen," she said, stepping to the side so that they could enter her home. "Sorry to keep you waiting." *Oh God, I forgot my bra,* she thought to herself as she tried to smile.

"Mrs. Black, how are you?" Kevin asked, re-moving his shades as he walked past her. He knew better than to comment on her afternoon wardrobe. Evidently, she had overslept.

Courtney couldn't even muster a lie. "I'm well...actually," she said, closing the door and leading them to the dining room table. "We'll be ready in a minute. I'm just going to go up and change really quickly. I do apologize."

"Don't apologize, ma'am. Take your time. Thank you for seeing us on such short notice," Kevin said, looking around the table at the men. It was show time. There was no way in hell that they weren't going to do this deal today.

When Courtney arrived back at the bedroom door, she saw Brett still lying in bed, naked and groggy. She came in and closed the door loud enough to wake him. "Rise and shine, *sleepy head*. I need you dressed in like five minutes."

Brett grunted. "Like five minutes, which could be more like 10 minutes, or exactly 300 seconds."

"Three hundred seconds," Courtney answered, slipping out of her pajamas. They dropped to the floor, and Brett's eyes popped open. Her brown temple had him immediately transfixed.

"Now we're talking." He stroked his penis. "A little early morning incentive."

She couldn't help but blush. Moving her hair out of her face, she pointed at the door. "Those men are downstairs waiting. So, no sex. Not until you've taken care of this."

He rolled his eyes. "Don't they know how early it is?"

"It's 11:00," she said, pulling her top dresser drawer open. Fishing through her folded panties, she sighed. "God, I smell just like sex."

"What do you think we did all morning? Take a shower. Make them wait."

She snapped around and looked at him with her most serious glare. "Two hundred and forty seconds, now Marine. So move your ass." Slipping on her panties while she looked at him, she raised a brow. "And I won't take a shower and leave them down there. That's rude. Plus, you said that you wanted them to come. *So get dressed.*"

Brett finally pushed up out of the bed and grabbed his crutches off the floor. "I hate these things."

"Well, you can't walk without them," she said, pulling a pair of his PT jogging pants out and throwing them on the bed.

"Shit, if I can't." He popped his neck. "I've been shot before. I'll be on my feet in no time." As he tried to stand up, a pain ripped through his broken ribs. Sitting back down, he grinned.

"Okay, maybe it'll take a little longer than normal."

Courtney quickly wiggled her jeans up her legs by bouncing up and down and then grabbed her soft white lace bra off the top of the dresser. Slipping it on, she grabbed a cotton white t-shirt and her thong sandals from beside the dresser. "See, it didn't take that long," she quipped while pulling her hair up in a ponytail.

Brett frowned. "Why don't you ever get that dressed that fast when we have somewhere to go?"

"Because it doesn't involve a few hundred *thousand* dollars," she said, walking over to the bed. She picked up his pants and then bent in front of him.

"I can't get those over my cast. I'll need shorts." He rubbed his hand over his five-o'clock shadow. "Just give me a shirt, baby."

She did as he instructed and in a few minutes she had him dressed in black Nike basketball shorts and a black USMC t-shirt.

"Do you think that they will at least offer us $500,000?" she asked hopefully.

"If they offer us half a million dollars, then we'll accept it," he said, walking with her to the bedroom door.

"Promise me," she said, stopping in her tracks. She turned and looked up at him with her arms wandering around his waist. Her voice was pouty. "I'm tired of haggling with these people."

He made a cross over his heart. "I promise. Half of a million dollars, we agree, but not a penny less," he said, stomach growling.

"You sure? Because you sound like you'd settle for a cheeseburger right now." Winking at him, she turned and took a deep breath. "Okay, baby. Get your game face on."

As the lawyers sat down at the table, Courtney and Brett slowly made their way down the staircase. It looked trickier than it actually was for Brett, but he took it slow as to not worry *the wife*.

"Good morning, Mr. Black," Kevin said, popping up. He immediately glanced down at Brett's leg in a cast and noticed the bruising still visible on his face and neck. "Welcome back, sir."

"Thank you." Brett shook his hand and the hands of the other men as they neatly filed in line to do the same. "But we can leave the *sir* off. I work for a living."

*Not for long*, Kevin thought to himself. He gave a clever smile. "I brought our best lawyers. This is Trey Donovan and Mike Dell," Kevin introduced them quickly before taking a seat again. They couldn't waste any more time. There were still other families that they needed to see.

Both men nodded and greeted Brett as he sat down at the head of the table with Courtney at his side.

"Thank you so much for seeing us. Mrs. Black told us about your injuries sustained while in the line of duty. Your service is truly appreciated." Kevin made his introduction to the conversation as amicable as possible.

No matter how many times he heard it, Brett always shied away from being thanked. "No problem," he said, darting his eyes over at Courtney.

She raised a brow at her husband and then shifted her focus on Kevin.

"I know in the past, we've haggled about the final benefit amount that Southern Atlantic was willing to pay you for your loss," Kevin said, looking over at Brett. "But we finally feel that we have something to offer that you'll be more comfortable accepting. We want to offer with this, our truest and sincerest condolences. And while we know that this won't take away your pain, we hope that it can provide you some closure."

Without looking at the check, Brett sucked in a breath. This whole fake sorrow thing was really getting to him. How could he pretend that he was all broken into pieces about Amy's cheating ass with Courtney sitting right beside him? It was rude, condescending, and complete bullshit. Clearing the air, he held up a hand. "Let's be real, gentleman. I'm sitting here with the woman of my dreams. I don't need any closure from the act of God that took place two years ago. I need some financial benefit."

*Ouch*, Courtney said to herself. *That was harsh...but true.* She covered her face slightly and tried not to look at the reaction of the men.

Kevin hesitated and nodded his head. "Yes, sir. I mean, yes Mr. Black. We understand." *In truth, he didn't give a flying shit.* He had memorized the lines that were given to him by their PR person. That was it.

Brett smacked his lips. "Alright. Well, now that that's out of the way, we can move on with a certain amount of transparency."

The other men smirked as Brett finally looked down at the check.

Trey Donovan, the young, eager, attractive dark haired attorney put his elbows on the table. "Keep in mind that this agreement will be executed and finalized today. We'll sign all the necessary documents here and immediately provide you with this live check."

For a moment, Brett did not blink. Finally making himself breathe, he passed it to Courtney. "Sorry baby. It's not $500,000." He winked at Kevin. "That was her dream number."

Rolling her eyes, she took the check in her hand and then let out a small whimper. "$2,600,000.00," she said in disbelief. She dropped the check on the table and put her hands over her mouth. Could this be? Was this real? Did this just happen? Darting her confused look between Brett and the men, she let out a laugh, followed by tears.

"Right here, today," Kevin said with a smile. "I told you we'd come back with an offer that was more *respectable*."

"Well," Brett wiped his hand down his mouth and chin. "I can respect the hell out of that." He finally laughed aloud.

There was a sigh of relief around the table. The lawyers immediately began to pull out their paperwork to be signed, and Kevin pulled out his shiny executive pen – the one he only used when he closed deals.

"Let's make you a millionaire, Mr. Black," Trey said with a wide grin.

Brett had never signed his name so fast.

Within 10 minutes, they were all done. He had signed over 30 pieces of paper and would have given them a blood sample if they liked. When it was all done, he looked over at Courtney in complete shock. What a fucking twist?

Passing the check to Courtney, he rose up out of his chair and kissed her lips. "Hold on to that for me, will you, baby?"

"You bet," she giggled. "All the way to the bank."

The men laughed and stood. As they were about to shake Brett's hand the doorbell rang.

"Who is that?" Courtney said, getting up from the table. She turned and looked at the figure at the door. "If you would excuse me, just one moment."

She walked a few feet to the door and opened it to find a Sheriff's Deputy waiting.

"What's wrong?" she asked, tears still in her eyes. "What happened?"

The look on her face made the Deputy stutter. "Ma'am, I'm sorry. I know how this looks." He raised his hands so that she could see them. "No one's hurt and no one's dead." Looking in the door at the men around the table, he smiled. "Is one of those men in there Brett Black?"

Brett walked to the door on his crutches. "I'm Brett Black," he said, the smile still permanently on his face. "What can I do for you, deputy?"

The Deputy pulled a summons from his back pocket and slapped into Brett's hand. "Sir, you've been served." Walking away, he left Brett to open the paper and look at it more closely.

"What is it?" Courtney asked, looking over his shoulder.

Brett opened the paper and stared at it. "It's a fucking paternity hearing for Cameron," he said, dropping the paper on the floor. He rubbed a hand through his hair and laughed cynically. "That fucking bitch! Even in death, she's still ruining my life."

# Chapter 11

**Four Years Ago**

Checking her rear view mirror every few minutes to make sure that she wasn't being followed, a paranoid Amy Black hightailed it into the small coastal port town of Wilmington, North Carolina for a clandestine appointment near noon on a blistering hot Wednesday.

Only, this wasn't one of her normal afternoon trysts with some no-name officer in a seedy hotel. Today was all business, and she only had a short window of time before Brett came home from the base and wondered where the hell she had run off to.

"Turn right at the next light," the female voice programmed into the GPS system instructed over her sound system.

"Move out of my way!" Amy yelled in a high-pitched Southern accent at the car blocking her from entering the right lane.

She snatched her BeBe shades off and rolled down her window to flip the honking car off as she darted in front of it just in time to make her turn.

"Fuck you, asshole," she sneered, not bothering to look back as car horns blared behind her.

That one singular moment in time summed up most of Amy Black's short, complicated life. She was the type of woman who always made selfish choices at someone else's expense, but she never looked back to see how those decisions affected people who happened to fall into her path.

However, she had not always been this way.

***

When she first married Brett, she was head over heels in love with him as much as he was in love with her. They had big dreams and were happy to be in each other's life. Everyone thought they were the perfect couple – attractive, young and full of hope.

Then it all changed.

They moved onto the Camp Lejeune military base housing for a short stint while Brett worked and saved his money for the down payment on their house in Swansboro, and during that time, Amy experienced what it was like to have raw, unadulterated ambition.

On base, she saw a completely new world of status where polished men with emblazoned insignias on their chests were treated dramatically different from the men who reported to them, and so were their families. These officers were saluted, respected, and revered, much more so *in her eyes* than *the grunts*. They even had their own clubs and their own facilities, which were much nicer than the ones for enlisted personnel.

Everywhere that they went, their presence commanded attention - attention that she wanted.

As the only child of her parents, Amy was used to attention. She had gotten it all her life from her family, her friends, her peers and her suitors. Except, when she married Brett, she expected a lot more from him than she received. She had pushed him to become a Recon Marine, because of the kind of prestige that came with the title, especially when she had found out he wasn't interested in going to college and becoming an officer. The only problem was that once he became a part of a special operations team, he was never there. He was always training, always deploying, always somewhere else with someone else and not keeping his promise to always keep her first.

Thus started her love story with *the other man*. Only, the other man was no particular man to speak of. He was more of a rank of a man. She wanted an officer instead of an enlisted man.

She wanted a better quality of life. She wanted a better quality of man. She wanted the house with the white picket fence, and to be a part of the officers' wives club and to be catered to by everyone else because she was part of an elite society, and she couldn't get that with her absentee grunt husband.

At first it was just a fantasy that she cuddled in her mind, especially at the Commissary or the gym, where officers normally were, *simply out of sheer necessity*. Then she started to pick them out in town, based on their clothes and demeanor. She became a pro at identifying places that officers frequented in Jacksonville. Then she branched out and find out where they liked to hang out in neighboring cities, especially the coastal town of Wilmington.

The next transition was an internal one. She started to dress like an officer's wife, although it cut heavily into the family budget. She got her hair done at the same salons as the officers' wives, even though they snickered at her behind her back. And she went to the gym religiously, so that when one of those wives was slipping, she'd be ready to catch *his* eye.

After a complete overhaul of her outer appearance, she was invited by girls from the gym to several wild parties while Brett was away training, giving her a chance to be the center of attention by horny officers looking for a good time. They spoke better, came from better families and were destined to have better futures. Everything about them turned her on and suddenly a whimsical fantasy became a lifelong goal.

However, any officer - on his way to be a U.S. Senator or even better President - would never take her seriously if she met him at a wild party with trashy women.

So again, she had to change her plan.

The spider needed a web. The web needed a fly. It was just that simple.

Brett had been a good stepping stone, but she'd have to ditch him as soon as she had secured *said officer*. She'd have to woo the mark with charm and sex, before making him fall head over heels in love with her. When he was so in love that he couldn't see straight, she'd have to tell him she was married to make sure that he was knowledgeable of the fact, and she'd have to do it via text, so she would have tangible proof of her confession. Then, once she'd gotten him over that hump, she would lock him down by telling him that she was pregnant with his illegitimate child and that her husband would bring it before his superiors, if he found out.

Everyone knew that adultery was an offense punishable by the Uniform Code of Military Justice under Article 134 and led to a dishonorable discharge, forfeiture of pay and allowances, and confinement for one year. Basically, the military didn't like it when people screwed their wives. So, if the mark wanted to protect his skin, his career and his future, he'd have to insist on her leaving Brett, marrying him and legitimizing the baby.

With Brett's schedule, he'd just sign the divorce papers and move on without questioning a thing. And although she knew that he'd never tell his superior officers even if he did find out that she was cheating with another Marine, she definitely wouldn't paint him that way to her mark.

It was the perfect ploy, guaranteed to snare some poor schmuck into giving her everything that her heart desired.

So, the plan was hatched and carried out, but then as life would have it, Amy hit a snag.

The mark officer she thought she had trapped had other plans.

***

Pulling up to a small Mexican restaurant off of Front Street, Amy parked her car under a tall palm tree to shield it from the hot sun, grabbed the paperwork on the passenger seat and jumped out on the gravel parking lot. Why in the hell did he want to meet here was beyond her, but desperate for things to be finalized, she had agreed.

*Shit, she was late!* But it wasn't her fault. The drive from Swansboro to Wilmington had been a daunting one today with roadwork being done for half the trip. *Plus, it took longer to get ready when her boobs were still leaking milk.*

Pulling down her shirt and hiking her shorts up her toned thighs, she sashayed across the parking lot and up to the front door.

Then it hit her just as she made her way inside of the shabby, dark Los Cabos Diner.

"Shit," she said, stomping her feet. Turning on a swivel, she pushed the doors back open, marched back across the parking lot to her car, snatched open the back door and unsnapped the baby, who had fallen off to sleep on the hour and a half drive.

This had been the third time she had forgotten this kid. Hopefully, eventually, she would remember that she was a mother.

Cameron's dark brown eyes popped open as soon as she scooped him up. With a small cry, he reached for her and nuzzled his small body into the curve of her embrace.

"Don't cry little fella," Amy said, closing the door behind her. She felt his diaper and cursed. He was bound to overflow at any minute, but hopefully, he could hold on just a little longer.

Kissing his forehead, she headed back to the front door with the little bundle wrapped in her arms. "Mama's going to get you taken care of in just a minute, little man."

\*\*\*

In the very back of the seedy restaurant tucked into one of the worn, red leather booths, Lieutenant Leo Tabor sipped on a Jack and Coke and texted his wife. He needed to make this meeting quick and get back to base, but he had to pick a place where no one in the world knew him.

After all, it was a little hard to explain meeting a woman and a freaking baby without looking highly suspicious. Plus, he got the feeling that it wouldn't take too much probing for Amy to proudly tell everyone whose baby she had given birth to. It was not a proud moment in his life.

*I'll call you in a few. I'm busy*, he texted. Rubbing his thumb over the screen, he quickly checked to make sure that the "Find My Phone" app was off. The last thing he needed was his nosy wife showing up and confronting the mistress.

*Where are you?* She texted right back.

*In a meeting. I'll call you in just a little bit.* He texted.

*You're a lying piece of shit.* End of text.

Leo rolled his eyes, but he knew his wife was right. He was a lying, *cheating* piece of shit, which was why today was so important. It was bad enough that he had a thing on the side, but what made matters worse was that the affair hadn't even been with the caliber of woman that his life-sucking lawyer wife was. So a transition, while welcomed under the right circumstances, could not happen because of the sheer financial implications.

Wow, had he fucked up.

Over a year ago, on a hot Saturday night, Leo met the short, blonde bombshell Amy Riley at an upscale bar off the pier in Wilmington. It was a little after midnight and his friends had left already to get home to their wives, but he had stayed to prowl.

Surprisingly, Amy was alone and seemed to be interested in what he had to say, even though he was noticeably drunk. She laughed at his jokes, bought him a few rounds. She even blew off the fact that he was an officer, which most girls went for immediately.

After a few more shots and some serious heavy petting, they went back to a hotel, had rough, dirty sex and parted ways early the next morning after a complimentary continental breakfast.

What he had liked about Amy was that she didn't seem clingy or the least bit interested in a long-term relationship. She didn't call much. She didn't want to meet all the time. She didn't mention meeting her folks or her dreams in life. Plus, she had an amazing body and loved anal, so the relationship naturally flourished.

On a few occasions, they went off on the weekend together. Occasionally, they'd have dinner together. And nearly every day, they talked or texted on the phone for a quick, non-evasive check-up. It was easy and a break from his normal grind. He liked her conversation and he loved her body. He'd even said he loved her a few times, but that was when he really wanted to do something freaky in bed.

Overall, things were going good.

Then, one evening after a show and dinner, while they were lying in bed together, Amy broke the news.

She was married to a fucking Marine. *Great.* Then she dropped the bomb on him that he was a Recon Marine. *Wonderful.*

It explained a lot in terms of her sometimes erratic behavior, but it also made things easier on him. He knew that Amy wouldn't risk getting caught. He knew that their time together was precious. And he knew that it would never go anywhere. So, things actually were perfect for him. Unlike other previous situations, he was in no risk of getting found out by his wife. So, he didn't mention her.

Conversely, after her heartfelt confession about her failing marriage and her unwillingness to leave it, the sex got even crazier. She met him in hotels with just her coat on; she went down in him in parking lots; she sent him porno via email; she talked about threesomes and hinted at wanting to go to private sex parties with him. She would let him do anything to her, and she never protested, no matter how degrading, no matter how painful. It was completely different from his conservative home life, and he loved it. Finally, he was in control, not his wife, not her money, not the Navy.

A couple of months later, the entire little arrangement went to shit.

He remembered the news feeling like a ton of bricks falling on his universe. She had texted him a picture of the ultrasound, then told him that she didn't believe in abortion. "What are we going to do?" she'd asked, like it was his responsibility to tell her what to do with her body.

He felt like texting her back, *I'm going to run*.

Of course, he had thought about changing the number to his cell phone and forgetting all about her, but while she didn't know he was married, she did know his full name and rank, and would have easily tracked him down.

So, in the spirit of not giving up, he had pushed again for an abortion, but she had stalled him with verses from the Bible.

The Bible!

Based upon their sexual activities, he was not even aware that she was a Christian.

The only good news was that she hadn't been stingy with sharing her goods with her *hubby*, so he had no idea yet that his cheating whore of a wife was carrying another man's child. Only, Amy said that if her Marine did find out about the affair, he'd have him personally brought up on charges; especially considering he out ranked him.

"What do you expect me to do?" he remembered asking her over the phone.

She mock cried as she stared at herself in the bathroom mirror. "Well, you said that you love me. Let's just run off and get married. I'll divorce him immediately."

This was a clusterfuck and he had no choice but to drop a bomb of his own.

"I still can't marry you," he said, sliding his back down the office wall to the floor.

"Why?" she sniffled.

"Because I'm married."

There was silence as Amy tried to process what he had just said.

"You're married?"

"Yes. I'm a married man with two kids."

"Well, divorce her," Amy said in a matter of fact tone.

And honestly, Leo would have, until he found out that Amy was unemployed, she was the daughter of a Baptist preacher and she didn't even have a junior-college education.

Unfortunately, Leo Tabor was fucking broke. Student loans. Spoiled wife. Mortgage. Couple car note payments and a two and four year old made his money short.

But Amy, in her plan for world domination, had thought that the silver bars on his shiny white uniform meant that he was liquid. She also thought that because he didn't wear a wedding ring, he was available. She was wrong on both counts. And even if he had been available, Amy wasn't exactly his family's type, even if she was his. True, she was good for a romp in the sheets, but she wasn't the kind of woman he would introduce at the Officer's Ball or to his blue blood, conservative East Coast parents, who were pressuring him to make something of himself.

So over a few desperate phone calls after the baby was born and paternity was proven, they had come to another more *doable* agreement.

\*\*\*

In a pair of extremely short cut-off denim shorts and a bedazzled Victoria Secret tank top, Amy flounced down in the booth seat in front of Leo and threw down her baby bag. "Why in the hell did you pick this shitty little place," she said, pushing the papers across the table for him to review.

Small talk between the two of them had ended with the birth of Cameron and they were left in a constant state of conflict.

Leo remembered when the sound of her voice got him a little excited, but now it was like nails on a chalkboard. "I picked this place because nobody that I know frequents here."

"And you couldn't have found a place closer to Camp Lejeune?" Cameron began to cry and she stopped her rant for a moment to pull out a baby bottle and slip it in his mouth.

"No, I couldn't." He barely looked across at the baby. Cameron was too much of a painful reminder of how stupid he had been. "Is this it?" he asked, picking the papers up. Today, he wore his wedding ring for good measure. He wanted Amy to see it and remember it always, because he would never take it off again.

She saw the ring immediately, and it was the painful reminder he intended it to be. He sat there all smug and proper, dark brown eyes glaring under heavy, thick black brows and tanned skin with a scowl on his face, ignoring her.

"Yep, that's it, lover boy. Now, where's mine?" Amy asked, nauseated by his faux-arrogance.

Without taking his eyes off the paper, Leo pushed the envelope across to her. "There it is," he said, prickly exterior slightly showing. Reading through the paperwork carefully, he finally made eye contact. Clenching the papers in his hand, his mouth curled at the corners. "This says $750,000. I told you $1 million," he bit out. "And it says that the payment goes to a lawyer's office?"

Amy cut her eyes at him. *The nerve of his broke ass to question her.* "You don't have to pay child support, because I'm married. You don't have to shell out medical insurance, because I'm married. You don't have to get caught by your wife, because I'm married. And on top of that, I've got to chip a little more off the poor bastard's pay to cover your son's policy. So, don't be greedy. I could get this policy without him noticing. The other one was more expensive."

Leo exhaled his anger. "You're a real piece of work, you know that?"

Amy read his papers quickly. "How so?"

"First, you go and get pregnant and blame me for it. Then you demand a paternity test that I have to pay for. Then you demand a life insurance policy in the event of my death to help you take care of a kid that no one will even know is mine."

Amy's little southern voice was dripping with contempt. "I should be demanding a little some extra," she snapped. "It's not my fault that the DNA test came back with you as the father. It's yours. It's not all my fault that I got pregnant. It's half yours. It's not my fault that you're broke and can't provide for the baby that you knocked me up with. It's yours."

Her nagging was starting to remind him of his wife. "Well, I don't have extra to give. My wife is too much of a succubus for me to have anything more than gas money when I'm done paying bills. Guess you should have picked some other asshole to scam."

Amy didn't really care for his whining. Waving her acrylic nails in his face, she cut him off. "Stop your bellyaching. If all goes as planned, you never have to see me and I never have to see you again. But this policy ensures that if one of us dies, then the baby will be taken care of by the biological parent. It's only fair."

Leo didn't really feel like getting into what was fair.

His eye twitched. "Don't you feel morally bankrupt about letting this man raise the kid knowing that one day he might find out he's not his." He eyed Cameron for a minute. Pity. He had two girls at home, even though he and his wife had tried for boys. Now, the only son he had was going to be raised by a viper.

"So make Brett the beneficiary of your death benefit then," Amy snapped. "It's up to you."

"Hey, I don't know the guy." But he sure felt sorry for him. "I made sure your name is on this, but keep in mind, if I find out you're lurking around, planning my demise, I'll end you first." He pointed his long finger in her direction.

Amy chuckled at Leo's paranoia. "Look Lieutenant, you aren't that important. I just want to make sure Cameron's got some security, if anything should ever happen to you or me. I don't have time to be plotting no one's death."

"Anyone's," Leo corrected her language. God, had she dropped a few IQ points since the birth?

"What?" Amy asked.

He dismissed it. "Nothing," he said, rolling his tongue over his gums. "It's not important."

Even though Leo was an asshole, he had to admit that the policy was the honorable thing to do. Plus, he knew that he was getting off scot-free with no child support, no medical insurance and no acknowledgement of Cameron's birth. Also, she must have trusted him just a little because he could have easily dropped the policy next month, but he'd do the right thing and keep it paid up for 18 years as they had agreed.

Stuffing the paperwork into his back pocket, he picked up his drink and scoffed the rest of it down as the waitress approached. Throwing his finger up to order another one, he looked over at Cameron again. Strangely, he couldn't stop eyeing the boy now, even though he wanted to.

"So let's just say that something does happen to you. We won't be in touch. How will I know that you've died?"

Amy's eyes sparkled with mischief. "That's what the lawyer is for dumb shit. He's in Jacksonville and his information is on the paper I just gave you. He's got your number and your name and your rank. If anything happens to me, he'll get in touch with you. And more to your previous point, if I'm murdered, he'll implicate you."

Leo smacked his lips together and pushed back in the booth. "Well, I guess that plan is out."

Amy ignored his quip. "Anyway, he'll let you know that something has happened to me. Then you'll get a check for $750,000, but there is a cavat."

"A *what*?" Leo asked, nearly spitting across the table.

"A catch," she explained.

"You mean a *caveat*?" Leo asked, wiping his mouth and raising his brows.

"Yes, that's what I mean," Amy said, irritated. He was such a smart ass now. "The lawyer will receive my death benefit directly from the insurance agency. He will serve as the trustee over my little estate. The money will be signed over to you only after you have been given paternal rights through the courts for Cameron. You don't get to just collect your money and run off with your wife, leaving him behind with Brett. If you want the money, you have to take him too."

"If you die, you want me to adopt your son?" Leo asked, frowning. *Was she kidding? Not even $750,000 was worth that.*

"How can you adopt your own son?" Amy sneered. *Was he stupid or something?*

*How can you not understand how this works?* Leo thought to himself. He ran a hand through his jet black hair and scanned the room again for safe measure. "Because you're married. Because he's legally Brett's son." Leo let out a sigh and gave up on explaining himself. "Just do us a favor and don't die," he said, standing up to leave.

"There's more," Amy said, pointing at the chair. "Have a seat."

Leo plopped back down. "Make it quick. I'm late."

"You only have 30 months, or two and half years from the date of my death to collect the money. After that, it goes to someone else."

"What?" Leo said, louder.

"You can't just decide to collect out of the blue one day. You have to do it in two and a half years or the deal is off." She sucked her teeth, proud of herself at that moment.

"What if the paternity case takes longer than that in the courts?" Leo pointed out. "Sometimes, these things take years."

Amy rocked the baby and smirked. "Well, I guess you better not let that happen."

# Chapter 12

"Never trust a person who throws a stone and hides their hand. It means that they are a smart coward."

- Anonymous

Being one of those *glass-half-full* types of people when it came to life in general, Courtney walked into the front entrance of the Jacksonville Mall and felt suddenly like a kid in a candy store. A rush of endorphins released into her system, and she suddenly felt like a thousand-pound weight had been lifted off of her shoulders. This was a dramatic environmental change from the last two weeks of pain and sorrow at the Naval Hospital. People here seemed happy. Life here seemed simple. And although she knew it was strictly cosmetic, she rather liked the change of pace.

Immediately, she could smell the expensive perfumes, see the brilliant diamonds glittering in the windows, feel the new clothes she'd always wanted on against her skin, and it was all calling her name at the same time, *begging to be taken home*.

For the first time ever, she could buy anything in this place that she wanted. *Anything.* There wasn't a piece of jewelry, an appliance, an electronic or even a car that she couldn't swipe on her bank card, when just a few years ago, she was hustling between jobs just to make rent. It almost didn't seem real.

She was rich!

That idea was exhilarating and frightening at the same time. To think that there were some people in this world who had felt this type of power since the day that they were born. And to think there was an even larger population that would never know how it felt, even until the day that they died.

But swoosh...

Everything had changed in their lives overnight. She had gone from a military wife with a moderate little nest egg in savings, mostly from the insurance benefit from the military when Brett's late wife passed, to being a certifiable millionaire.

A millionaire!

She had said the word repeatedly to herself in the last twenty-four hours, but it still didn't feel real – not even when she held the check in her own two hands and counted the zeros.

Brett didn't help with grounding her in reality. There was no talk of what dreams were going to be fulfilled or what good he was going to do with his newfound fortune. He hadn't put the money away in a private account yesterday when the airline gave him the check. He hadn't sat her down and given her a heavy-handed *talking to* about what the money was going to be designated for or what they were not going spend it on. He hadn't even looked at the check more than a couple of times before handing it off to her and offering to "ride up to the bank and deposit it." *Which by the way*, stunned the poor bank clerk speechless, and having the branch manager leap out of his chair getting to offer coffee and snacks while the bank called the check in to make sure it was legit.

It was then in Navy Bank eating lemon cookies and drinking lukewarm coffee, that she knew her life had changed.

Conversely, it was as if it had not computed in Brett's head at all that suddenly things had changed for them, *for him*. After all of his hard work and sacrifice, she thought he would have been absolutely elated by the news, but he had barely blinked.

But it had resonated for her.

That check was the promise of security for their financial future.

And it was a very distinct possibility that this chance would never happen again in their lives. This was their one opportunity to get it right – to live a good life and leave something for their babies.

But they had to be smart. They would have to resist temptation on every level and think about their future. She had read a good blog entry about it just this morning – stay away from impulse buys.

*Tough but doable.*

So as she gazed around at all the *stuff* that she could have purchased, she finally adjusted her purse on her shoulder and made a B-line to Foot Locker to buy what she had set out to get in the first place – comfortable shorts for her husband to relax in around the house – and nothing else.

Determined not to even look at the hot pretzels that were tempting her from behind their glass encasing, she headed through the food court and the crowd of military wives as they sat around on the benches tending to their kids and texting on their cell phones.

As she rounded the corner headed toward the sports store in view, she felt the distinct buzzing of her cell phone in the bottom of her less-than-organized purse. Her first thought was that Brett had gotten overwhelmed at home with the kids and needed her to come back. Earlier, he had insisted that she get out and go do something *normal*, while he spent some quality time with the babies alone.

Digging down past the wallet, keys, make-up and assortment of peppermints, she pulled out her I-Phone and felt herself get a little queasy when she saw the number.

Her lungs drug in a deep breath as she answered. "Hello." Exhale.

"Courtney," the woman said in a shrill voice, "it's Sharon Riley."

Courtney rolled her eyes in irritation. "I know it's you, Sharon."

"Well, I've been trying to reach you non-stop for two weeks to see my grandson." The arrogance and entitlement in her tone radiated across the phone lines like toxic waste.

It was enough to make Courtney gag. They did this little song and dance way too often for her taste. Plus, the exaggeration of two weeks was a lie, but she didn't bother to address it. *What was the point?*

Courtney bit her tongue. "I left a message on your home phone *two weeks ago* that we were away due to a family emergency. I also said that we'd have to reschedule a time for you to see Cameron after we got back home and settled."

Sharon pounced immediately. "Well, you could have left him with me," she snapped, "if you were having a family emergency."

Courtney noticed the "*if*", *as if she were lying*, and let out an audible sigh. Lord in heaven knew that she was in no mood to deal with this wretched woman today. "I appreciate the offer, Sharon, but it wasn't necessary. Thank you. Now, what can I help you with?" There was no question that it was to start shit, but Courtney just wanted to see how much.

"Is it not clear how you can help me? I want to see my grandson."

Courtney raised a brow. *Was this where she was supposed to be the angry black woman, because she could do that?* A tickle pricked the back of her throat. "It's not possible to see him right now. I'm sorry. We have a lot going on, but I will let you know when in the next couple of days when we can get together and set a date." She hated herself for being remotely respectful at that moment, because Sharon deserved everything but that.

In general she prided herself on poise and elegance, but it was really hard for Courtney to keep her cool, especially with a woman who purposefully tried to bait her with passive aggressive bullshit. However, a voice that was not her own slipped into the back of her mind. *Patience is a virtue.* Her mother had taught her better than to be quick at the tongue, *although she was good at it*. And her mother was a far more refined human being that Sharon Riley.

Contrariwise, Courtney's answer was not to Sharon's liking either, especially considering that the girl sounded so smug about it. *How she hated that woman!* Just the sight of her made Sharon ill. "I think we've waited perfectly long enough to see Cameron. This is getting ridiculous," Sharon snarled.

Courtney took another deep breath. "Well, I'm sorry that our lives *inconvenience* you, Sharon, but that's not my problem. I will, however, call you when I can and give you a firm date." She assumed that the old woman would take that as the last word on the matter, but she was sorely mistaken.

Sharon closed her leather-bound book and set it on the stand beside her wingback chair. "Now you listen to me. We had an agreement with Brett Black that twice a month we could spend time with *our* grandson. He needs to be with his biological grandparents some of the time, considering that he spends all that time with *your* parents."

Courtney smiled with thoughts of choking the old bitch with her bare hands. "When have we ever *not* allowed you to see Cameron?" she asked then quickly answered for Sharon. "Never. We've always made good on the agreement that my husband made with you, when it was doable. Right now, it's not doable. So, we'll call you as soon as it is possible, and you can pick Cameron up then."

She thought about telling her that Brett was back at home, maybe that would help her understand why Cameron couldn't come over, but Brett had explicitly said not to tell the Rileys one part of his business. *Not one part.*

She could hear his voice on the matter. "I explained enough to them when I was married to Amy. Now that that's over, I don't owe them shit," Brett had said a hundred times over. She couldn't go against him now.

*His son. His rules. His way*, as far as Courtney was concerned. The Rileys would just have to make do until Brett was ready to let Cameron visit.

"I know what you're trying to do," Sharon erupted. "You're trying to take Cameron away from us! You want to fill him with those liberal thoughts of yours and turn him into one of those gay marriage sympathizing race mixers."

Courtney had had enough. Now, the old biddy was just being mean. "You're an idiot," she said flatly. The words just leaped from her mouth before she had time to say anything. Sharon had been rude in the past, but not this blatant. Evidently, something was way up her ass today.

Sharon's mouth popped open. *That bitch!* "Well, I'll be glad when the paternity case is heard in a court of law." A smile curved her lips as she prepared to drop the bomb on Courtney. "After that, we'll be doing the deciding on when you see him and not the other way around," she said with malice in her voice. "If you get a chance to see him at all," she added. "I don't see why you would be considering it since he's not biologically either one of yours."

*So that was this was all about.* Sharon was finally showing her hand because of Leo Tabor. *Didn't take her long.* Courtney knew that Sharon was in Fayetteville just relishing in the thought of taking Cameron away from Brett, but that was not going to happen.

"That's it," Courtney finally said after a brief pause. Now was not the time to have loose lips. "You can stop your silent gloating."

Courtney realized that it was Leo who accompanied Sharon to her home while they were away. The nerve of that woman!

"Who's gloating silently?" Sharon asked. "I have no intention of throwing a rock and hiding my hand. You people have no business with my blood in your house."

Courtney stepped out of the flow of traffic and stood beside an ATM, taking her voice down a few notches. Her fingers trembled as she clutched the phone to her ear, she was so angry. "My husband and I have been nothing but good to you two."

"Says who?" Sharon taunted.

"Says anyone. Says me. But mark my words; you won't get away with this." Courtney clutched her small cross necklace as she said the words, praying for Him to back her up.

"We have a good lawyer who says otherwise," Sharon quipped pivoting to blame. "Maybe things wouldn't have come to this if Brett had been more amenable in the first place."

Placing the culpability of the situation on Brett was a big mistake. Courtney shook her head in utter disbelief. "People like you don't even understand the meaning of the word amenable. That would require you to give something. All you do is take. Just like your daughter. Just like you. You know, Amy was an apple who didn't fall far from the tree. You people have no honor at all, but don't expect me to trade in my honor to roll around in the mud with you."

Sharon was pleased that she had finally gotten under Courtney's skin. "The likes of you referring to me as *you people* is laughable."

Courtney found it odd that that was all that Sharon heard. "What is laughable is how much control you think you have in this situation. What's laughable is the idea that you think you'll see Cameron a day before the judge says that you are allowed, and trust me, it will take a judge to order that you're allowed to see him before you do."

Sharon sat back in her seat a little deflated. "You don't have the authority to make that call." *Did she?*

"Oh, I'm making the call, Sharon. Because you see, I'm the one doing homework, giving baths, teaching numbers and running away the boogey man, *not you*. I'm the one fixing dinner, and taking him to doctor's appointments and trying to fill the void that your worthless, whoring daughter left when she hopped on a plane and left this child behind to run off with another man, *not you*. And I'm the one making the call on who he can see and who he can't see, *not you*." There was more that she could list, but Courtney had been taught by her father to never show all of her cards.

A man passing by as Courtney shouted into the phone shook his head. Stunned, she tried to bring it down a notch. *Was she talking loud? Was she making a fool out of herself?* She was so angry she hadn't noticed.

Sharon didn't like the confidence that Courtney was exhibiting. She was expecting something else – something more pliable. So she did the only thing she could do, she stabbed at a point that was fact. Much calmer, she flipped her hair back and curled her lips. "No matter what you do, he'll never be your son."

Courtney smiled. This woman was not about to steal her joy, hard as she might try. "That's where you're wrong, Sharon. No matter what you do, he'll never stop being my son. He knows that I love him. He can feel it, and you can't take that away." She cleared her throat. "We're done here. Don't dare show up on my doorstep, or it'll be the last door you ever knock on."

Sharon perked up. "Is that a threat?"

"No, it is not," Courtney stilled her shaking hands. "That's a promise. And Sharon, I always stand by my promise." Hanging up the phone, she slipped it back in her purse.

Looking around to see who had seen the argument, she was relieved that no one was gawking at her or even concerned by her existence. As far as she was concerned, that was a good thing at the moment.

\*\*\*

Even though she'd never admit it, Sharon Riley was fit to be tied. *To think that that woman had the nerve to tell her off.* She looked down at her cell phone in shock and then slid it on to the table. She hadn't been talked to like that since she had become a minister's wife. Of course, she wouldn't tell her husband everything that was said by Courtney - just the juicy parts- otherwise, she'd be made to look a fool by that second-class citizen.

Heart still racing, she glanced over at her husband, sitting across from her in his chair reading the Bible in preparation for Sunday's sermon and tapped her long manicured nails against the table. She knew he had been listening the whole time, at least to her side of the conversation. So he had to be expecting some sort of reply. "Well, I was just threatened." Her voice resembled more of a *tattle* than a report.

Licking his fingers and flipping the page, he uncrossed his long legs. "How so?" Reverend William asked dryly.

Not the response she expected. *Where was the damned urgency?*

"Courtney Black says that if *we* show up to her door before a court date, it will be the last door that we ever see. I think she meant that she'd kill me. That's a reportable offense." She paused for a minute to let that sink in to the good Reverend's head before proceeding with her call-to-action. "We should file charges with the authorities immediately. I do believe that I fear for my life."

The Reverend, a man of great contempt for black people dating back to the civil rights movement but not one who was foreign to the judicial system because of his own run-ins when he was more friendly with the local Klan, begged to differ. He knew beforehand that his reply would cause an argument, but after 35 years of marriage to an only child, what more could he expect? "I know that you're not going to like this, so let me go on and preface my statement by getting this out of the way." He huffed and scratched the side of his mouth with his finger. "You called her. She didn't call you. Plus, you threatened to take away Cameron. No police officer in the world could do a thing about what she said to you. She has the right to tell you not to come on to her property. She has the right to tell you what will happen if you do, and you'd better listen, because if anyone else was witness to that exchange, they'll testify on her behalf."

Sharon was not pleased at all. She gripped the arm of the chair and glared at her husband as though her evil stare might change the very laws of government. "There is nothing that can be done?" Grit and growl filled her voice. "This woman threatened my life for wanting to see my grandson, and you're telling me that there is nothing at all that can be done?"

He huffed.

William knew his wife. She was the world's biggest instigator, which was great during church fundraisers and tea party political campaigns, but not so great in day-to-day life. "If there were anything to be done about it, *as your husband,* I'd be the first to tell you." He closed his Bible with a thud. There was no point in expecting to finish his sermon anytime soon with this brouhaha. "I told you to stop calling them. I told you to just let the lawyers handle things, *but no,* you wanted to rub it in." He shrugged his bony wide shoulders. "Well, now it's rubbed." He raised a brow. "You have to be more strategic in your thinking instead of letting emotions get in the way, Sharon." *The Good Lord knew that it had kept him out of jail throughout his life.*

Accusatorily, she pointed across the room as though Courtney was present. "They are keeping us away from our only grandchild," she said with the intention of firing up his fragile sensibilities. "Your grandson is being raised with those people." She blinked slowly and watched his eyes as they averted to her – right where she wanted them. "He's the only one that we have now that Amy is dead, and Jimmy, bless his soul, left us as a baby. Cameron is our only legacy. If we lose him, then all of this will be for nothing, because I'm far too old to try again." She tugged at his heart strings as she began to cry. "Don't you care about that at all?"

"You think that I don't know that my only living child is now dead? You think that I don't remember burying Jimmy, my only son, because of crib death?" He eyed her sternly as if to say that she had gone too far. He sat up in his chair. "If I were a young stupid man, then I might have grabbed a shotgun and headed to Jacksonville after she threatened you, but age gives you wisdom, *if you're lucky*. And wisdom dictates we handle things better than a couple of bumbling teenagers who got hold of a phone while their parents were away."

She ducked her head and wiped a tear. "I feel like I'm in this all alone. I was finally given hope the day that Leo showed up on our doorstep. I don't want to lose it again. I don't want another circumstance to keep us from our family."

"No one is losing hope. I'm simply asking that you not allow your emotions to mess things up for us." Sympathy crept into his tone. "Sharon, we will get him," he assured, putting his hand on her leg. "Harold Murphy is one the best lawyers in all of North Carolina, in my opinion. Thank God, he's also a member of our church. He's already told us what to do. We need to follow his direction."

"I'm trying. It's just," she wiped her tears and sniffled. "That woman is so wretched." More than anything, she wanted her husband to hate Courtney as much as she did, but evidently that pursuit would have to take time.

"Harold is a fine man. Make sure that you tell him what the incomparable *Mrs. Black* said to you today. That should go over real nice at the hearing, telling a preacher's wife that kind of foolishness."

Sharon nodded her head emphatically. "Oh, I won't forget. I'm going to make her eat her words." Suddenly, she was starting to feel upbeat again.

Her sudden voice pitch made William relax a little more. "Trust me, Sharon. This is going to be a short fight. Cameron will be with us in no time. Marines don't make much money, and I'm pretty sure he's run through all of that insurance money he got spoiling his new wife."

"Just the thought makes me sick. I'm just glad that Leo came forward. As complicated as their story is, the point is that he and Amy loved each other dearly, and he's determined to be a good father to their son."

William held his reservations on that subject. There was no point in knocking the wind out of Sharon's sails further.

# Chapter 13

"Watch out for false prophets. They come to you in sheep's clothing, but inwardly they are ferocious wolves."

**Matthew 7:15 (NIV)**

Contrary to Sharon Riley's belief, Leo Tabor was anything but a good man. God had blessed him with amazingly good looks. His family had blessed him with a good strong name. He was also good at covering his ass; good at making women believe that he was dependable; good at sex and even better *at leaving after sex*. But in the truest sense of being a *good* man, Leo Tabor fell ridiculously short of the definition. Always had. Always would...and he didn't give a damn.

What he did give a damn about was money. Pure, green, in-his-hands money. And he had a plan to get all of it. It was just a damn shame that he had put a young, innocent boy into the middle of it, but in this life, a man was bound to regret his actions one way or another. So why pass up an opportunity to be regretfully wealthy?

Sitting at the dimly lit bar in the back of The Hellhound, a local Wilmington strip club with notoriously high-end clientele, Leo watched from across the room as a petite topless blonde in a purple glitter G-string with extremely large augmented breasts gave an older male patron a vigorous lap dance to the song, *"Pipe It Up."*

*Strange choice of music to Leo, but it wasn't his dance or his money.*

Pulling his intense gaze away from her momentarily, he tapped his empty glass and motioned for the young bartender, who was engrossed in the sports recaps, only a few feet away. "Another whiskey sour," he said, eyes locked on her naturally large breasts pushed up in a low-cut V-neck shirt tied in a knot just above her belly button. *That sight whet his appetite.*

"Sure thing," she said, taking her eyes off the television. Prancing over to him, she made sure to bend forward for more ice so that he could get a better look at her assets.

*He noticed.* Leo had a knack for noticing everything about women – their strengths, their weaknesses and most of all their insecurities, because the insecurities were what he used to get what he wanted. *And he always got what he wanted.*

"Hell of a hot day outside, huh?" she said, making small talk.

Leo shrugged. "I've been in hotter."

"Middle East?" she asked, drawing him in with her big brown eyes.

Leo left something to mystery. It was part of his illusive charm. Flatly, he replied, "Military life takes you to a lot of places." He knew the drill. Women always wanted to find out what a man did within five minutes of meeting him, whether they were CEOs or bar flies. It was part of their genetic makeup to identify the alphas, the money makers, the heroes, especially in these parts. So, he gave them just enough to want more.

"What branch?" she asked, more intrigued.

His brow lifted as though hadn't expected that to be her next question. "Navy."

"Really?" she said, voice pitched high. Her eyes were bright with new ambition.

He knew the second question too.

"Enlisted man or officer?" she paused.

"Officer." He bit his wide-set bottom lip. "That's all past me now." Putting both elbows on the bar, so that she could better inspect his large muscular arms in his polo, he twirled his straw in his empty glass, clanking it against the ice. "You gonna hook me up, or what?" His words were intentionally suggestive. "Just because you're beautiful, doesn't mean you get to make me wait all day."

The bartender read between the lines enough to make her swallow hard.  Moving her long bangs from her face, she blushed. "Coming right up."

Turning his head back toward the dancer, he narrowed his gaze, wondering if the stripper was enjoying the extensive dry hump she was giving the old bastard. If not, she pretended damn well. Rubbing her small hands over her nipples, the dancer pushed back on the crotch of the old man's khakis until he grabbed her by the waist and adjusted her.

Leo snickered.  *Couldn't last one dance. Pathetic.  He deserves to pay for it.*

The bartender quickly refilled Leo's glass and followed his glance across the room to the dancer.  A smile crept across her glossed lips. "She's working real hard over there on that guy, huh?" she said, wiping the water marks from the bar in front of him.  She angled her breasts so that they would be in full view when he turned around; reminding him of what he was missing.

Leo took a sip of his drink. Not too strong, not too weak...just right. He nodded in approval. "That is a bona fide, professional dry fuck, my dear." He stretched his arms out and cracked his neck. "But I'm sure he'll give her one hell of a tip for it."

Flipping her long brown ponytail off her shoulder, she frowned. "And that doesn't bother you?" Considering the preppy clothes and the classic good looks, she figured him to be a gentleman.

He was anything but. "I'm not her daddy," Leo quipped.

Her head tilted in confusion. "But you *are* her boyfriend," she said in a matter-of-fact tone. "At least, that's what *she* says."

Leo knew what she was getting at. Demeaning the stripper allowed the bartender to be elevated. The female persuasion had been playing this game since they were competing in the sandbox as babies. But he wouldn't let her elevate herself too quickly above the working girl across the room. "Women have to eat, just like men. What she does is just a job. It's not who she is as a person."

The stripper's phony giggle echoed across the room as the old man grunted in enjoyment.

The bartender had a dumbfounded look on her face. "You really believe that bullshit or do you just say it to keep from feeling like shit when she's 20 feet away from you making some old fart cum in his pants?" She thought she had him dead to rights.

Leo had to admit, he liked her sassiness, even though it was misplaced considering she worked here too. But he was certain that under her bimbo-exterior there was a woman with a brain, and that was dangerous. He glanced at her name tag for a long minute and the rigid nipple a few inches under it. She was mad for the moment, but still incredibly turned on by him. He bet if he reached over and pinched that angry little nipple, she wouldn't even slap him. *Tempting.* "Daisy, you're young, but you're not slow. If you want to say something, just say it. Don't mince words with me. You have no reason to. I'm just a guy at your bar..."

"You could do better," she blurted out, cutting him off. There, she had finally said it. Amber Valentine was a bleached-blonde, big-boobed, dumb slut.

"I can do better than Amber?" Leo repeated as though he felt he couldn't. With a wicked grin, he leaned closer. "Because she's a stripper?" he whispered condescendingly.

"No, there are a couple of good women in here that happen to be strippers. Because Amber is a bad person," Daisy emphasized, furrowing her brow.

Leo calculated in the young woman's facial expression, tense with emotion, she knew more about Amber than she was willing to say on their first meeting. But she was young and vulnerable and Amber Valentine...well, she was a viper, just like him. Still, the thing that made him good at what he did was that no one knew he was a viper until they had already been bitten.

He ran his finger over the bar gently as though he was running them over the smooth curves of her voluptuous young frame. My, how he loved young meat. The only problem with it was that they were full of piss and vinegar. "Amber's okay once you get to know her." He wouldn't say one bad word about his meal ticket to anyone, especially someone looking to replace her. But he would toy with her. "You interested in the job?"

She clucked her tongue against the roof of her mouth and then smiled. "I might be," she said, pushing her elbows up on the bar. She gazed into his dreamy green eyes, the color of US currency, and took in his expensive cologne. "You thinking about changing the scenery?" Glancing down at his vintage Rolex, she guessed he must be rolling in dough. Why else would Amber be with him?

He laughed at her question, considering his current circumstance. If only she knew how badly he wanted a change of fucking scenery, it might scare her. Only, he wasn't interested in taking sand to the beach.

She coiled back. "Are you laughing at me?"

"No," he said, stopping his laugh long enough to put his hand over hers. "Laughing with you, because yes, I do want a change in scenery. What can I say? You see right through me."

"Or maybe I don't see you at all?" she said seriously.

He shook his head and sighed. "Well, I do believe you are... dangerous." And he knew that she was. She was probably some pre-law, college girl working here to pay the bills with dreams of burning her bra and running for public office one day. He had fallen for her type once. Married her too. That didn't work out well. He had the divorce papers to prove it.

"Well, I wouldn't say that I'm dangerous," she said, turning up her lips. "But I do believe in going after what I want."

Leo *wanted* to kiss her right then and there. Her luscious glossy lips. Her minty fresh breath. Her natural skin, no sign of makeup. Just fresh face and transparent honesty. In fact, his could feel the ache rising up in his balls at just the idea of throwing her over the side of that bar and fucking her independent brain out right in front of Amber and that fucking idiot john.

But Leo wasn't a stupid man. Daisy was broke. The chipped nails, lackluster dead-ends in her hair, her mere presence in this place, alluded to the fact that she was a worker. And he had no space in his life for workers, no matter how good they were.

"What's wrong? Are you silently debating it in your head?" she teased. "You can't depend on the woman who only eats what you bring to the table," she joked. "Gotta have someone who brings the whole damn table."

That snapped Leo back into reality. His eyes grew dark, but he quickly hid his jaded inner monster. "A man can't eat a table, lovely."

Daisy's body language suggested that she took that as a rejection.

The alarm went off in Leo's sick twisted head. After all, *he knew women*.

She was new to the club and green as grandma's grip – the combination was good for club Intel, his second-string team and free drinks. His face warmed like sun coming across a dark horizon. Instantly the mood changed. He was back to being the gentleman that Southern women responded to. "I'm always interested,

Daisy, especially in a woman as *special* as you."
He made sure to use the word woman instead of
girl. Being as privy to bullshit as she was, she
would have noticed that little slip. "I mean,
hell's bells, even in this place, your light shines
bright. You're different from these girls. You're
going places."

"Going to Duke University's School of Law in
a year, if I can just keep my head above water
with the bills," she said, allowing her own pride
to expose the truth about her. She wasn't a
bimbo. She wasn't a slut. She didn't see how
these women allowed themselves to fall so short
of such a simple standard.

*Bingo*, Leo thought to himself. He knew he
recognized the *bitch* trait. When women had it,
it was hard to cloak. Trying not to blatantly
patronize her, he finally winked at her and
rested his back against his bar seat, throwing one
arm over the side. "Soon as I laid eyes on you, I
knew it. I gotta admit, you're tempting the hell
out of me. But my weakness is that I'm a one-
woman-man. Always have been. But if I weren't
already with Amber, I'd be picking you up and
carrying you out of here, right now." The lie
oozed out of his mouth with such finesse that it
sounded like pure sincerity.

Foolishly, Daisy believed him. She took her rejection without offense, not realizing that she had just dodged a huge, life-changing bullet. He was already with a woman, despite her infinite shortcomings – that was the reality of the situation. "Well, you know where I am, when that doesn't work out."

"Oh, I'm making a mental note," he said, tapping the side of his head.

The conversation had taken too long. He looked back over at Amber, who was eyeing him now even as the old man behind her lost control in his pants, loudly gasping as he jerked against her backside. Leo was surprised the john had lasted that long.

"That's my cue. Looks like I better get back to work," Daisy said, winking back at Leo before she went over to the other side of the bar to clean up.

"Sounds like it's closing time," Leo said, watching Amber stand up and pass the old man a baby wipe. Covertly, she took the large wad of money from him and kissed his cheek. Now done with the woman, he patted her on the ass and rested back in his seat.

Without missing a beat, she pounced in her stilettos over to him. "What the fuck?" she said, sitting down in the seat beside him.

"What the fuck what?" Leo asked innocently.

"Are you over here flirting with this bitch in my face?" Amber snarled over at Daisy.

Leo turned slowly to Amber, pulled her seat to him so that she was in between his legs and cupped her face in his large hands. "Baby, she was just talking about how pretty you are." His voice lowered to almost a whisper. "Be nice, baby. She's just a young girl. And...I think she's got the hots for you."

Amber's face changed. That idea had not crossed her mind as she watched the two of them talk from across the room. Amber was a conceited, self-centered woman and the idea of another woman wanting her, especially in this place, was a good possibility.

"Oh," she said, shoulders relaxing. "Well, why didn't you say so?"

He smiled at her. "I just did."

Wiping the sweat from her brow, she smiled. "Have you been studying the stuff the lawyer gave you?"

Leo ran his hands over the papers. "Got it all right here. I'm going over everything with a fine-tooth comb."

"Good. We need that money. I can't keep supporting you. It's breaking my back," she said, keeping her voice low so that no one would hear her real plight.

"Baby, just hold on with me for just a little while longer and we'll have plenty of money."

"And a new kid," she lamented.

"No," he said, holding up a finger. "I figured that out too. See, I told Mrs. Riley that I was accepting an offer to do contract work in Afghanistan and I'd be gone for about a year after the case ended."

"She bought that?" Amber asked, picking up his glass and taking a sip of his drink.

"Yeah," he laughed. "I'm a convincing man. Once I get legal and physical custody of the kid, I'll march him right over to his grandparents, where he belongs, and then I'll collect the check from the lawyer. I'll be able to pay you back what I owe you and we can head down to Miami, like we always planned."

The idea made Amber giddy. "We're so close to being millionaires."

Leo smiled big at the thought. "Baby, I'm going to take such good care of you. You just wait and see. The best clothes, cars, and a condo off the beach. You never have to worry about anything again."

Leo's promises nearly made Amber forget that she was footing the entire $5,000 a month bill for his expensive lifestyle as she thought about how life in Miami was going to be. She's always wanted to live there, ever since she was a little girl growing up in the trailer park. But all that was behind her now. She'd found a real live Naval officer and she was on her way to a good life.

She leaned in and kissed him. "Get back to studying. I've got about an hour left and you and I can get out of here and go get something to eat."

"I'm in the mood for lobster. How about you?" Leo said much louder than the previous more clandestine parts of their conversation. He knew that she could afford it. She'd amassed a little fortune today dry humping the elderly.

"Lobster sounds delicious," she said, kissing him again. Slipping down off the bar stool, she looked across at Daisy and winked at her.

Leo watched as Amber frolicked happily back across the floor, just in time to snag a gray-haired gentleman walking through the front door. *Pay dirt.*

"Work it, baby!" he said, shimmying a little for her to see.

Amber laughed and grabbed the man by his tie to lead him to the back room, where the more expensive favors were given.

When she was out of sight, Leo looked back over at the curious little Daisy, who was watching them just out of earshot, and grinned.

# Chapter 14

"There is a time for everything, and a season for every activity under the heavens: a time to be born and a time to die, a time to plant and a time to uproot, a time to kill and a time to heal, a time to tear down and a time to build..."          -Ecclesiastes 3:1-15 (NIV)

Amidst a collection of over 200 Crayola® crayons and markers, Brett rested flat on the floor of the den in front of his coveted 60" curved television and a room full of toys, while he colored in a very brilliant, extremely large Star Wars coloring book with Cameron.

Oddly enough, it had been the first coloring book he had used since he was a boy; but somehow, just freeing his mind and doing something simple yet creative with his son was actually calming. Go figure. *Therapy was as simple as returning to his childhood.* He almost laughed. If only he had known this years ago, he could have cured himself of PTSD.

Right after breakfast, he sent Courtney away to get some fresh air and not be at his every beck and call for once. He had figured out early in their relationship that his wife was like a sun-flower - in the sunlight, she flourished but in the dark, she wilted. No matter the situation, the result was always the same. And considering this was without a doubt one of the darkest moments of their life together, he knew that he needed to tend to her needs now more than ever.

Plus, Cort had been working her ass off since they got back from Bethesda. *Cleaning. Cooking. Washing. Making calls. Emailing. Taking care of the kids. Taking care of him. Running errands.* Just watching her made him tired, and worse, it made him feel guilty. She was supposed to be enjoying a fruitful marriage where she was catered to, yet it seemed that all he had brought back home from Afghanistan, despite his prom-ises, was a shit ton of problems.

*Stop feeling sorry for yourself*, a voice whis-pered in the back of his head.

"Darth Vader is not red," Cameron said, pointing a short, stubby finger at his father's work, like a teacher to a student.

Brett paused, crayon still against the paper. "Says who?" he asked, repressing his grin.

"Says me," Cameron answered flippantly. Af-ter all, if anyone in this house was an authority on coloring books, it was him.

At that moment, Cameron reminded Brett so much of Courtney. He could tell that his wife was rubbing off on his son - picking up her sayings and her quick wit, having an answer for everything.

Tousling the little man's mop of brown locks, he went back to coloring Darth Vader red to make a point. "Well, I like him red. So, that's what I'm coloring him."

Cameron was dumbfounded. *Red? Really?* "Have you ever *seen* the movie?" Cameron asked, waiting for an answer from his father.

"Before you were even born," Brett snickered.

Unexpectedly, Bella giggled as if she were following the conversation. Resting in the swinging chair beside them in a pink jumper, she beat her yellow rattle against the front tray and flashed her gummy smile.

"Bella thinks he's not supposed to be red, too," Cameron argued.

"Do you speak *baby*?" Brett joked.

"No one speaks *baby*, Daddy," Cameron said seriously.

"So, you guys are just gonna gang up on poor dad, huh?" Brett said, picking up the black crayon. If they wanted Darth Vader to be colored black, then damn it, he'd color him black.

Cameron giggled too. He thought Daddy was funny. "It's fun having you back home," he said, leaning over to kiss his father's head.

Brett's heart instantly warmed. *If this guy still loved him, maybe everything was going to be alright.* He glanced at the boy's brown eyes, blush red chubby cheeks and his frumpy brown locks with pure admiration. Cameron had been his saving grace through all of this.

Propping himself up on his elbows, Brett looked at his two kids, feeling undeservedly blessed. "You know I love you, right?" Brett asked Cameron. "No matter what."

There was no question for Cameron. "I love you too," he said, coloring his picture again. He didn't look up from the paper. "Is something wrong, Daddy?"

"Why do you say that?" Brett asked heart lurching at what the boy might already know.

"You seem *sad*," Cameron huffed. For a little guy with a tiny vocabulary, the word *sad* would have to suffice to articulate all of the emotions that he had felt since he was told that his Daddy had been injured. There was so much more there, so much he didn't know how to explain.

However, with all of his experience in life, Brett also found it difficult to find the words to express to a four-year old what was going on. He blew a breath out of his mouth. "I'm having a hard time. Daddy got hurt real bad, and he lost his friends."

Cameron stiffened. "I know."

"How do you know?" Brett asked.

"I heard you and Mommy talking about it in the kitchen last night. Uncle Joe is dead. The men from your unit are dead." Cameron swallowed hard. Even as a child, he understood the weight of the circumstance. "I'm just glad you didn't die."

Brett pursed his lips together.

Cameron's voice pitched high. "Are you glad, Daddy?" he probed innocently.

"Glad of what?" Brett realized he had been gone too long. His son had grown up...a lot. These were not the type of questions his son would have asked eight months ago.

The little boy felt like it was obvious what his question was. "Are you glad that you didn't die?"

Brett looked over at the clock on the entertainment center. *What time was it?* He needed a damn beer, but Courtney would kill him, if she came in and he had one in his hand before noon, especially around the kids.

Rubbing a hand over his head, he looked away and nodded. "Yeah, I'm glad that I didn't die." His voice sank. *Why did he feel bad about admitting that?*

"Momma Amy died," Cameron continued.

*God, kid. You are killing me*, Brett thought to himself. But he would never cut his son off from expressing his emotions. After all, he was the one who had left the boy alone to figure things out while he was off fighting a war. It was only fair that Cameron have an opportunity to talk about his feelings.

"Yes, Amy died, too," Brett said. "It was an air plane crash that took your mom." He wanted to make it clear that while his men died valiantly in war, Amy's death was more of a freak accident and nothing commendable.

Cameron put down his crayon and tilted his little head up to look at his father. His little nose wrinkled. "Where was she going when the plane crashed?"

*Really?* Brett bucked his eyes. *Wow.* "Hey, do you remember Mommy Amy?" he asked, changing the subject slightly. *How could he tell his son that his mother was leaving them for good for another man*? That was a conversation he could avoid for the rest of his life, if possible.

"Yes," Cameron said with a not-so-readable look on his face. "Mommy gave me a picture of her to keep, because sometimes it's hard to remember her in my mind. She told me to never lose it, and that way I won't ever forget her."

*That was more than Amy deserved*, Brett thought to himself. But that small omission made him want to know more. What else had Courtney said while he was gone? What other morals was she instilling in the little guy that he had forgotten to focus on as a somewhat absentee parent?

"What was it like here with Mommy by yourself? Brett asked.

Cameron smiled big. "I don't know. It was...happy. She bakes cookies. She lets me splash in the tub and play with my boats and rubber duckies. She reads to me a lot and kisses me before bedtime. And when I'm sick she rubs my tummy."

Brett was relieved at Cameron's response, but what did he expect? Courtney was the same no matter what. "You like that, huh?" Brett asked.

"Yeah, especially the cookies."

Brett chuckled. He liked Court's cookies too. "Do you like..." He cut himself off. How did he ask this? "Do you like Mommy being here more than..." Then it hit him. He didn't need to ask that question. Of course the boy did.

Cameron was curious now that his father had stopped mid-sentence. "Do I like it more than when we were alone?" he asked his father.

That wasn't what Brett was going to ask, but he nodded. "Yeah."

"I do like it. She's the best mommy in the whole world."

Cameron's conviction was without bias. He had no reason to choose one woman over the other. He had loved both, but he loved Courtney more, because she actually gave a damn about him. And without knowing it, Cameron had answered Brett's unspoken questions.

"I think we're pretty lucky to have her," Brett said to Cameron.

The alarm on Brett's phone that Courtney had set sounded, which meant it was time for both children's naps. He reached over on the table and turned it off. "You know what that means?"

"It's time to take our nap so that we can grow big and strong," Cameron answered, standing up.

"Alright, let's do this." Brett struggled to raise himself from the floor. Working with one leg wasn't exactly easy, but he tried not to make a big deal about it, especially in front of his son.

"Don't get up," Cameron said, putting his hand on his father's shoulder before he could get up off his knees. "I can go upstairs by myself. Mommy taught me what to do.  Take off my socks, turn off the light and get under the covers and go to sleep."

Brett used the table and sofa to prop himself up and stand all the way up, just to show Cameron that he could.  He looked down at the three-foot terror. "You sure you're good to go?" he asked, his deep Texas baritone echoing around the room.

"I'm sure," Cameron said, walking to the door.

Brett remembered a time not long ago when the mention of a nap would have immediately been met with crocodile tears and a tantrum. Now, Cameron did so without the slightest argument. Impressive. "Hey, how did you get so grown up?" Brett asked proudly.

Cameron smiled as though the answer was simple. He shrugged his paper thin shoulders and lifted his little hands.  "I take my naps."

Disappearing down the hallway with little footsteps echoing against the hardwood floors, Cameron headed to his bedroom for his afternoon nap.

Brett dragged a silent, deep breath into his lungs. If he lost Cameron, it would kill him. And more than that, it would kill Cameron. That boy would feel abandoned and alone. Cameron would think that he had failed him, that he didn't love him. So no matter what, Brett couldn't lose him. He would fight this custody case with everything and every dime that he had, but he would not lose another person that he loved.

Looking down at his hands, he realized that in his rabid thoughts of what he'd do to this Leo Tabor person if he got a hold of him, he had balled up his fists to the point of his knuckles turning sheet white. The large veins in his arms and neck protruded. His heart was racing, booming in his chest like an angry drum, and heat was starting to form at the tip of his ears, turning his face beet red. Trembling uncontrollably, he stood staring blankly through the doorway, body stiff as a board, blinking hard and ready to scream.

*God, he just wanted to scream!*

But he couldn't...or maybe it wasn't that he couldn't. It was more that he shouldn't.

*Calm down*, he spoke to himself barely above a whisper. He couldn't lose his cool...ever. It was apparent to him, though maybe not to everyone else because of his sheer will and determination not to show emotion, that he was Mount St. Helens on the verge of violent eruption, but if he did erupt, he would annihilate everyone and everything around him. So, he had to *just* calm down.

In jerky movements, he turned from the door way and quieted the rage boiling inside. The sounds of the television re-entered the atmosphere, and he could finally breathe through his rock-hard chest, knotted up with tension and hurting from an impending panic attack.

Brett caught a disturbing glimpse of himself in the mirror on the wall as he went back to check on the baby. His face was dark and twisted in the anger that had accidentally found its way to the surface. Pushing it back down as far as he could into his subconscious, he focused on releasing the emotions for the time being.

Alone with Bella, Brett sat on the sofa and carefully pulled the chubby little baby out of the swing. She was so warm and soft until just being close to her was like a mild sedative, one that he badly needed. Wrapping her in his embrace, he picked up her bottle off the coffee table and slipped it into her mouth.

Keeping her eyes on her father, she lifted her small hands and ran them over his dog tags and then cradled them around his large hand and the bottle. Sucking quickly and breathing heavily out of her nose, she scarfed the bottle down.

Brett got tickled, forgetting his anger all to-gether. "I guess you know what to do during nap time, too?" He rocked back and forth with her, gazing into her eyes. "How did you get to be such a beautiful baby?"

As she suckled the bottle, he watched as her steady gaze began to drift and her hazel eyes began to close. She burrowed her head into his brawny chest just above his heart, where she could hear it beat. Rhythmic and strong, it put her to sleep like her own special melody.

*So this was love?* Brett stared at her trying to memorize every single feature. He wondered how many times her precious little face had changed since she was born? He wondered if she knew who he was, and if she liked him? Most of all, he wondered if he could live up to what she deserved in a father.

While on tour, he had never stopped thinking about her, but didn't expect to fall head over heels as soon as he saw her. She was so amazing, from her tiny little fingers to her fat little feet.

"Daddy loves you," Brett said, kissing her cheek.

Rocking slowly, they both finally drifted off into a peaceful sleep.

***

Brett had been resting for about an hour without even realizing it, not dreaming of war or even turmoil, when his phone rang interrupting an otherwise peaceful slumber. Eyes flashing open, he reached for his cell before it could wake up the baby.

*Sheesh*, he had to get used to cell phones again. In Afghanistan, there wasn't exactly this much communication with the outside world on a continual basis. One sort of got used to not being bothered but here, this phone never stopped ringing.

"Hello," he answered, putting the phone between his ear and his shoulder.

"Brett, how you doing man, it's Gavin," the man said in a Midwestern accent.

"James Gavin?" Brett asked. *What in the hell?*

Brett could hear the man smiling over the phone. "The one and only. Hey bro, you at home or what because I'm out in your driveway stalking you like a motherfucker."

Brett looked down at the baby sleeping. "Yeah, I'm here, but I'm holding the baby and on a bum leg. The extra key is in the flower pot by the door. Let yourself in while I try to put her down."

"Flower pot? Baby?" Gavin chuckled. "Shit, I've got to see this for myself."

"Well, what can I say? A lot has changed."

"Sounds like it. Alright. Be there in a second," Gavin said, hanging up the phone.

Brett slowly pulled himself off the sofa and hobbled over to the bassinet in the corner of the room, where he laid Bella down carefully on her back and pulled a small coverlet over her. As he leaned over, his dog tags loudly clinked together stirring her from her sleep and making his butt clench tight.

"Don't wake up," he begged, freezing in his tracks. Scared to take a breath, he waited until she fell back to sleep before he finally rose up. That was a close call. If she woke up now, she'd be up for the rest of the day with no reprieve for anyone in the house. Best to let her sleep as long as possible.

Making his way to the hallway, Brett heard the front door open and close. Heavy steps moved across the hardwood floors toward him.

Stepping out into the hallway, he saw his old friend. There standing like the cocky prick he had always been was the lost member of the once famous three amigos. He, Joe and Brett had served together for years before Gavin was shot in the knee by an AK-47, blowing off his lower right limb. The Marine Corps had medically discharged him after that and Gavin rode off in the sunset broken hearted about having to leave his dream job. Communication between the three friends became less and less common, until one day, Gavin was just a memory.

But he didn't look all broken up now. A solid six-feet four inches tall, Gavin had put on at least 30 more pounds of muscle and gotten a lot more ink tatted up and down his arms. Wearing dark jeans that fit his long legs, brown boots that gave him a few inches in height and a red USMC t-shirt that fit the defined muscles of his broad shoulders and herculean chest, Gavin stood before him now a picture of health.

"Damn, you look like dog shit," Gavin joked, radiating almost supernatural charm with his million-dollar smile, California tan, sun-drenched sandy brown hair and big brilliant brown eyes. Needless to say, he was a ladies' man.

Brett laughed. "Well, I got shot, you son of a bitch, what's your excuse?"

Grinning ear to ear, Gavin walked up and hugged his old friend, nearly picking him up off the ground. "Good to see you, bro. I feel like it's been fucking forever."

Brett couldn't believe his old friend was here, and still had the sewer mouth of the century. Gavin used the f-word like most people used the b-verbs.

"Good to see you, too," Brett said, truly surprised. He stepped back speechless. "What are you doing here? I thought you were off on the west coast somewhere riding your Harley and chasing ass."

Obviously, word had gotten around. "Normally, I am, when I'm not running my business, but I flew back in for the funeral." Gavin's face changed. No matter how long it had been since they had seen each other, Joe had been one of his dearest friends. It still didn't seem real to him. They had been the three fucking amigos. Now they were two gimp-legged veterans. "Went by to see Judy earlier today. Her folks are there; said she didn't feel like visiting with anyone just yet. So..." He shrugged it off. What else could he do?

"Yeah, I tried to go and see her too. She told me the same thing." Brett felt better knowing it wasn't just him that she had brushed off.

Pivoting from the obvious discussion, Gavin looked around the house. It was nice and warm, clean and welcoming. An extreme cry from the days of old when he was married to Amy's crazy ass. "So, I know you're all domesticated and everything now with the new wife and the new baby, but you must have a beer or some whiskey hidden around here somewhere."

"How did you know about Cort and Bella?" Brett asked.

"Last time I spoke with Joe he told me. He sent me a picture of the wedding to my cell." Gavin wished that he could have been there, but he was out of the country on business. Plus, he swore the only time that he'd ever come back to this place was if someone he really cared about died. "So you got something to drink or what?"

Brett shook his head. Gavin hadn't been here five minutes and already was working on getting him in trouble, but at least it was closer to noon than it was when he first thought about having something to drink.

"Yeah, I got something." He turned and headed toward the kitchen. "No whiskey but I got beer."

"Well, if we're going to get all caught on up on the last five years, then I'm going to need something. Beer will do," Gavin said, following behind Brett. "Lead the way."

# Chapter 15

"If you bungle raising your children, I don't think whatever else you do well matters very much."

- **Jacqueline Kennedy Onassis**

Courtney punched in the code to the security gate as if she was punching Sharon Riley right in the face. As the wrought-iron double gate swung open, she barreled up the long, paved driveway lined with palm trees and parked in front of her parents' house. Jumping out of her little car, she slipped on her shades to hide from the bright afternoon sun. A cool breeze from the coastline blew through her hair as she hiked up the stairs to the large porch and opened the front door.

"Hello," she said, wiping off her feet on the welcome mat.

"In here," her mother said, voice echoing through the foyer.

"In here where?" Courtney said, looking for the dog.

"The reading room," Diane answered.

Courtney found Diane in the study standing at the top of a ladder, cleaning the tall wooden bookshelves embedded into the wall. She looked down from her chores and smiled at her daughter. "What a surprise!" she said, glad to see her. "I figured you'd be holed up in the house for at least a few more days with Brett before you came up for air."

"He told me to get out and stretch my legs," Courtney said, leaning against the doorway.

Diane instantly heard something in her daughter's voice that didn't sound right. "What's wrong?" Putting down her duster, she held on to the sides of the ladder and made her way down.

Courtney rolled her eyes before stepping into the airy bright room. "Sharon Riley is behind the custody case."

"Why am I not surprised?" Diane pulled off her vintage polka dot apron and picked up the mint julep drink she had been nursing on the end table. Taking a sip, she wiped her brow. "Want one?"

"Sure," Courtney said, taking a seat on the white tufted leather sofa facing the large bay window overlooking the Bogue Sound waterway.

This room had always been so peaceful to her with its sea blue walls, expensive paintings, white crown molding, dark hardwood floors and maple ceiling-to-floor bookshelves. Her mother had turned the room into a reading haven with a perfect little bar in the corner and surround sound speakers to blast Cuban jazz and Al Green.

She stared at the blue water and boats sailing with envy. She'd much rather be out there catching a wave then dealing with real life right now. "Why are you cleaning so hard?" Turning from the picturesque view, she watched her mother tend bar like a professional.

"Your brother is due to arrive home tomorrow. I want the house spotless," Diane said with a spark of excitement.

Courtney was glad that David was coming home, but she also knew things would change dramatically when he got here. She couldn't explain why, it just always did. David had a knack for polarizing any situation.

"Don't take this the wrong way, but I doubt that he will notice the dust on the bookshelves," Courtney said, kicking off her loafers.

"He might not notice, but I will," Diane said quickly.

"You work too hard, Mom." Courtney knew before she said it that those words were lost on her mother, but she still had to say it.

Diane ignored her daughter's pleas. "You can only have one of these since you are driving home," she said, pouring the pre-made contents out of a pitcher into a crystal tumbler.

"In that case, please make it a big one."

"I made this pitcher of sunshine to get me through the day, especially with your father gone to play golf. I have the house all to myself." Diane threw a little mint on top just to make it pretty and then walked over to the sofa. "There you are, my lady."

"Thanks," Courtney said, folding her leg under her and taking the glass. "Dad finally got out and did something outside of tinkering in the shed like the Unabomber?"

Diane sat beside Courtney and decompressed after a long afternoon of deep cleaning. "Yeah, I know. It surprised me too. He got up, grabbed his golf clubs and said he was going to play 18 holes." She ran a hand over her side ponytail. "I did not protest."

Courtney noticed the sweat coming down her mother's forehead. "You need a maid," she joked. "It's not expensive to get a service. They can come in and do this for you once a week."

Diane wiped her head again. "Jeffery said the same thing. But you know, I would never feel comfortable with anyone else cleaning my house, and going through all my things." She dismissed the idea completely. "I've done it all these years. Why stop now?"

"Falling off that ladder and breaking your hip could be a reason. It's not like you don't have the money. And what if you did fall and no one was here?" Just the thought sent chills up Courtney's spine.

"Enough about my cleaning habits. Tell me what is going on with Sharon," Diane said, resting back on the large comfortable pillows. She would hear no more about this maid business. It was worth the risk of falling off a ladder to keep some woman away from her unmentionables.

"Well you know we were served with papers saying that we have to be in court to answer a paternity suit case by a man who claims to be Cameron's biological father, and then today, Sharon called throwing a fit about why she hadn't seen Cameron."

Diane eyed her daughter. "Why did she call you? Doesn't she know that Brett is home?"

"No, Brett doesn't like for me to tell her anything at all."

Diane pursed her lips together. "Well, it would not have been out of the question to tell her that, but never mind...go on."

"If you knew how Brett felt about them, you would understand. Anyway, we both had some choice words for each other as usual, but this time she really showed her butt. She said that she was not about to throw a rock and hide her hand. Then she said Cameron had no business in the house with us because he was her blood."

"Let me guess, she was implying that you being African-American were a bad influence on her poor grandson," Diane said, rolling her eyes.

"Exactly." Courtney shook her head in disgust. "She was overtly racist today and it took everything in me not to go off and curse her out. She said that she couldn't wait for this Leo guy to take Cameron away from us."

Diane rubbed her temples. "That woman is a bane to the human species. And there is no doubt that she is a racist hick from the back swamps of rural North Carolina, but you will not lower yourself to roll around in the mud with her. Trust me – that is what she wants."

"I know how you feel about that, but Mom, trust me, there is only so much that I can take."

Diane found the solution to be simple. "Block her number from your phone and ignore her."

"Ignore her for how long?" Courtney's impatience began to show.

Diane reached over and touched Courtney's hair. "Until the court appearance. Then you can paint her as the confederate flag that she is. You can explain to the courts why you will not put your son into a negative environment where his morals can be irreparably warped."

"I told her that she couldn't see Cameron now that she said all that until after a judge orders it. Do you think that was right? Can I do that?"

There was no question in Diane's mind. "Of course you were right. Of course, you can do that. Sharon should be kissing your ass for all that you do to make sure that Cameron still knows Amy's family, but make no mistake about it, they have no legal precedence." She took another sip of her drink casually as if all of Courtney's dramatics were for nothing. "Do you know how many grandparents would be in court if they knew that they could just demand through a judge to see their grandchildren?" The idea that Sharon had actually threatened with such a baseless threat was preposterous to her.

"Maybe you're right. I'm just worried. Brett hasn't left the house at all but to go to the bank and to go to have his cast checked at the Naval Hospital. He's turning into a hermit. Plus, we haven't even gotten a lawyer yet. You would have thought that he would have done that immediately. I mean, we're talking about our son." She clenched her jaw tight. "Something is wrong with him. He's so unresponsive."

Diane knew exactly what was wrong with him, the same thing that was wrong with Jeffery. "Give him time. He'll come around."

Courtney looked into her mother's eyes with a plea for help. "I don't have time to wait for him to come around. Things are happening now."

Diane put her hand on her daughter's hand and soothed her. "Things will always be *happening*," Diane said, nodding her head. "Trust that he will be there when you need him, but give him time to process everything in his own time. I know that you love Cameron but there is more going on in Brett's life than just this paternity case. Jeffery said that looking at the damage to his leg; he'll be moved out of Recon. Plus, he lost his entire unit. Now, this man wants to take his son away from him. Even $2,000,000 can't fix that." Diane truly felt for the young man, but more than that, she felt bad for her daughter. "I'm going to tell you something that you might not understand. Brett's unstable right now. Let him get settled and in control of the situation. Trust me, you don't want him to lose control and do something that he can't take back."

Courtney didn't like her mother's answer. It took too much control from her. "It's not like we can't afford a good lawyer now," she lamented. "I would feel better if we at least had that ironed out. The rest of it I can see giving him time on."

Diane could appreciate how Courtney was feeling inside but the truth of the matter was that it wasn't her daughter's call. "Brett will do what's best for you and Cameron. I promise you that. He always does." A question hit her. "Does Sharon know that you adopted Cameron before Brett left for Afghanistan this last time?"

"No, Brett said not to tell her."

"Good." Diane's smile became smug. "And no one outside of this family knows that Brett is not his biological father?"

"No, I've never said one word to anyone, not even to the pediatrician. It's such a sore subject for Brett. Even when he's alone with me and he brings something up about it, he whispers like the universe might hear him. Why do you ask?" Courtney hoped it was because that would carry some weight in the case.

"I read something interesting in the newspaper a few months ago about establishing parentage after being away from the child after a long period of time. It wasn't exactly your situation, but it was damn close."

"Was the person able to establish it?" Courtney asked hopeful again.

"No, the judge ruled against it, which is good for you."

"I can't even imagine us having to turn over Cameron to someone else after all this time." Courtney felt a headache coming on. "What if he's some undercover drunk, or a druggy or a pedophile?"

"You'll wear yourself out thinking like that. Right now, you just need to focus on winning the case. Who this man is will come out during the trial." Diane hated to admit it but she had had the exact conversation with Jeffery after Courtney had called her the other day. And he, in turn, had told her the exact same thing she was telling her daughter now.

"What if we lose?" Courtney's eyes began to water. "I can't even think of our lives without him."

"It's important that you start to speak victory over this situation now. There is no "what if we lose." You can only speak the positive. You have to stand in the gap and start to pray. You have to believe that God will deliver you from this." She rubbed her hand over the small golden cross on her neck. Lord in heaven only knew the number of times that she had had to do the same over the years.

"I'm trying Mom," Courtney said, wiping her eyes quickly. "It just seems so hard to do lately. Not just to pray, but to be positive. My husband is a mess. My son..." She swallowed down the doubt that she was about to speak.

Diane patted her daughter's hand. "In this day and time, anyone can take anyone to court over just about anything, but that doesn't mean that they will win. The laws are still written to protect the parents who are taking care of the child, not the parent who abandoned him. Brett will win the case. Your husband will be restored. You just have to believe that and stand on it like you believe it. You are the mother and wife of your home. It's up to you to stay strong, to help guide your family and rejuvenate them. You can't do that if you don't believe it in the first place. But I know that you can, Courtney, because you've always had that gift. God made you special, and He made you strong."

Courtney was amazed. She came here empty and she was suddenly full. "How do you do that?" she asked her mother sincerely.

"Do what?" Diane asked, putting the glass back up to her mouth to take a drink.

"Make everything sound like it's going to be okay?" She wiped another tear.

"Because it is going to be okay," Diane said lovingly. "I tell you what. Go home and tell Brett exactly what Sharon said, and then give him a day to get himself together. If he hasn't done anything in two days, then start to nag him about getting a lawyer. But I'm willing to bet that you won't have to do that. In fact, I'm willing to bet, he's already doing something about it."

"I hope you're right," Courtney said, gulping down the last of the mint julep. "Thanks for that." She put the glass down. "Thanks for everything. I really needed it today."

"That's what I'm here for. Where are you going? You just got here," Diane said, not bothering to get up now that she had finally gotten comfortable.

"I'm going to go and do what you said. I'm going to put some urgency in him," Courtney said, fired up.

"Not so fast. It's not just about picking a lawyer. It's about picking a good one," Diane reminded. "Interview at least three; pick one with an A-rating and an impeccable trial record with references out of the ass and a sensible retainer."

Courtney stopped at the door and turned around. "Do you want to help pick the lawyer, Mom?"

Diane smiled. "Well, if you need me to, I can send some people your way."

Courtney shook her head and smiled. "Thanks. I'll call you and let you know when to start looking."

"Well, I already have a few in mind," Diane said, raising a brow. "Just in case."

\*\*\*

While the kids slept peacefully, two old friends got reacquainted on the back deck under the large umbrellas. Today was unusually cool with a calm breeze and patchy clouds, so it was just right to enjoy a few beers. With the baby monitor beside him, Brett backtracked down memory lane with Gavin about all of their missions and the crazy things that had happened while they had been away from each other.

"So, after years of misfortune, you finally got lucky," Gavin laughed with his feet kicked up on the table. It was good to hear. Brett had been the example of "what not to marry" on the base for many years.

"Finally," Brett said, opening another beer. "Amy left me in the worst possible situation. Kid. No babysitter. Bills. No money. Marriage.

No wife." He was amazed how he could laugh about it all now. In truth, it felt like a lifetime ago. "She was leaving me for a Marine captain in Japan." He paused. "A Black Marine."

"Yeah, I know, Joe told me. I always thought she was racist from all the shit she used to say," Gavin said. Some of her quips had made him embarrassed to be in the same race as Amy.

Brett was still stunned by that one. "Me too. Go figure."

"Then the bitch goes down in flames literally," Gavin said, astounded by the chain of events. "And you end up with a fine, black surfer chick who loves your ugly ass and your bad ass kid not knowing she was Colonel Lawless's only baby girl. It's ironic, but also blind justice in my opinion." Gavin watched his friend's face twist into a smile.

"I wouldn't exactly put it that way but...yeah," Brett said, feeling good about the situation. "I am happy...about my wife." He couldn't say the same for everything else.

"So, what's next after this?" Gavin asked, looking down at Brett's leg. "You plan to get out and join the civilian work force or go to Admin and becoming an official person other than grunts (POG)?"

Brett frowned. "I plan to go back to Recon." That was a stupid question. It wasn't like his leg was blown off. It was just injured.

Gavin pursed his lips together. *And now for the bad news.* "Oh man, I was like you?"

"Like what?" Brett asked defensively.

"I thought that I could work my way back in. Go to physical therapy, get back in the game." He tapped his titanium leg hidden under his jeans. "But Recon doesn't have a prosthetic division. If they did, I'd be in it."

"My leg is still attached," Brett clarified.

"But it's fucked," Gavin added with a shrug. "They are not going to let you back in. Tell me you know that already."

"I don't know shit and neither do you," Brett said, looking down at his leg again. "You forget. I've been shot before, and it didn't stop me."

"You got clipped in the shoulder. The leg is sort of *required* in Recon." Gavin released a deep breath and pushed back in his chair. "It's easier to come to terms with it before they tell you that you're going to the wounded warrior battalion. The next thing you know, they're slapping medals on you and showing you the door. I wish someone had been there to tell me, but no one did and that's life. I'm not going to let you go through the same thing with blind ignorance. That would be on me."

"Look, I know it's a thankless job, but it's all I've got," Brett said, unwilling to accept his friend's advice. It was nothing personal. Gavin just didn't have a clue about what he was talking about.

Gavin didn't come all this way to argue with Brett and refused to let something he had no control over get in the way of the little time that they had together. It was better to just drop it for the moment. Besides, he knew that eventually, they would arrive back at the conversation once Brett was ready. "Well, you know better than me, man. I've never seen anyone with more dedication than you to the Corps. So, if you go back, just promise me you'll get the motherfucker who killed your men." Even though he said the words, he knew that Brett would never see Afghanistan again. However, he also knew, it never hurt to give another person hope.

"Damn right," Brett said, thinking of his friends. He had to go back an avenge them, but more than that, he didn't know how to be anything but a Marine.

"You know, my business is doing really well, but I don't have someone like you on my team. Private Security pays well. We get contracts all over the world, and most of the time, all you have to do is put on a suit and a gun. Beats carrying a 120 pound pack any day." Gavin's eyes gleamed as if he got a clever idea.

"Are you trying to recruit me?" Brett asked, putting down his beer.

"I may be," Gavin winked. *He was.*

Brett couldn't begin to talk about another job. It would mean that Gavin was right about him having to give up the one that he already had. "Hey, how long are you going to be here?"

"A week or so. Then I'm headed back to San Francisco."

Brett thought about his son. He had kept his secret from nearly everyone else in the world, but if he could trust anyone, he could trust Gavin. "If you're looking to make a little more cash while you here, I could really use your help."

"How so?" Gavin asked, sitting back in his chair. He didn't need the money at all, but if his friend needed him, he wanted to help.

Brett huffed. *This was embarrassing.* "I'm in the middle of a paternity suit. Turns out, Cameron isn't biologically mine. Courtney and I found out shortly after Amy died, but we didn't tell anyone. Now, this fucker I know absolutely nothing about is trying to take my son away from me."

Gavin's eyes bucked, but he tried really hard to hide his utter shock. "Sure thing. What do you need?"

"I need eyes in places I can't be. I want to find out who Leo Tabor is and what he really wants with my boy. It's hard for me to believe that after nearly five years, he suddenly wants to be in his life and play daddy. There has to be some other spin on this. I need to discredit him. You know," Brett paused. "But I don't want this to get out. Amy made a fool of me long enough while she was alive, dude. And I took the punches like a man is supposed to, but this is below the belt."

Gavin would never say a word. Hell, he felt embarrassed for even knowing about this. "Full confidentiality just like any other client." He made the sign of the cross over his heart. "You said that his name is Leo Tabor?" he asked, pulling out his cell phone to put his name into his notes.

"Yeah." Brett appreciated Gavin's help. It took a load off his mind not having to entrust this to a stranger. "Whatever you charge, I'll pay."

"Bro, don't offend me," Gavin said, sending a text. He looked up at Brett. "That name isn't common. Let me do some digging for you over the next couple of days and see where you want to go from there. I've got good resources though, what I can't get myself, my team back in San Francisco can."

"Thanks, man. I want to go to court and make a judge understand that taking my son out of his home for any reason and for any amount of time is not in his best interest, but right now, I don't know anything about this cat. He could be a fucking saint or he could be the biggest asshole that ever fell out of a woman's crotch."

Gavin curled his lips up. "We could do some investigating to see if he's worthy, or we could just kill the guy." He didn't smile.

Brett chuckled and scratched his eyebrow. Only Gavin. "I can't say that I haven't thought about it, but we live by a different code on this side of the fucking Atlantic, you psycho. Plus, I think I'd be the prime suspect."

Gavin laughed. "I'm just saying. There is always more than one way to skin a cat. And people die in car accidents all the time."

"Well, I think we should take the route that won't get me locked up and sent away for the rest of my natural life," Brett said, reaching down in the cooler for another beer. He knew that Gavin suggested it jokingly, but he was certain that he'd do it if he asked.

Looking at his watch, Gavin stood up. "Well, I don't want to stay too long. I just wanted to stop by on my way to Morehead. Gotta see a girl there about a *job*."

"A job?" Brett was confused. Gavin had spent an hour talking about his successful private security business.

Gavin grinned sheepishly and corrected himself. "A blow job."

Brett shook his head. *Lord knew that he didn't miss the single life.* Standing up, he gave his friend another hug. "Dude, you haven't changed."

"Never will," Gavin said, patting Brett on the back. "I gave you my number. Call me if you get any more information, and I'll do the same."

"I'll call you. After all, I have nothing to do right now. I'm on 30 days of mandatory leave. It's a perfect opportunity for me to get this taken care of once and for all."

*You've got a lot longer than that*, Gavin thought to himself. "Well, just heal up and get better. I'm sure all of this will work itself out."

"I plan to," Brett said, walking him back through the house. He was about to escort him out of the front door when Courtney walked in.

Halting in her tracks, she looked up stunned to see that they had company. Based upon his frame and his overall demeanor, he had to be a Marine.

"Hey baby, glad you made it back in time. I want to introduce you to an old friend of mine, James Gavin. We came in together, served together, and fought together...the whole nine. He was also close to Joe." Brett hit Gavin on his back. "Gavin, this is my lovely wife, Courtney."

"Nice to meet you," Courtney said, extending her small hand.

"The pleasure is truly all mine." Gavin shook her hand gently and looked over at Brett in astonishment. "Wow, she is even more beautiful in person," he said, nearly unable to take his eyes off of her.

"Yes, she is...amazing," Brett said, smiling at Courtney. "I don't know what I would do without her."

Gavin chuckled. "Well, you are about to find out, because I'm going to steal her and take her back to California with me."

"This is one time I'd come after you," Brett joked.

"I know you would," Gavin laughed.

Courtney blushed and took her hand back. "Are you here for the funeral?"

Gavin sighed. "Yeah, unfortunately."

"Well, before you go, you have to come by and let me fix you dinner. Brett rarely has friends that visit," she said, raising a brow at her husband. "I think it would do him some good." Walking up beside Brett, she rubbed his large arm and kissed his cheek.

"I'd be happy to. I think a home-cooked meal would do me good, if nothing else. I'll await a call from your husband on the date and time," Gavin said, continuing to be impressed. How in the hell did he get her?

"I'll call you," Brett said, stepping past Courtney to let Gavin out.

Gavin waved goodbye to Courtney and stepped out the door. Turning around, he slipped on his aviator shades. "Don't flake out on me about dinner. I want to see your smoking hot wife again."

"I won't flake out," Brett said, looking out at the driveway. "You've got to be kidding me."

Gavin turned on his heels and gave a big playboy grin. "I flew here, but this guy had it up for sale over in Sneed's Ferry, so it looks like I'm driving back, baby."

Brett stepped out on the porch for a better look at the candy red 1969 Chevy Camaro Z28 with black stripes, black leather bucket seats and radial tires. It was a classic American muscle car that boys and men alike dreamt of having as their own. "You really going to put that thing in the road and put all those miles on it?"

"Cars are meant to be driven my friend. It's in perfect condition. Only one owner. The guy who owned it passed away and the daughter put it up for sale in the front yard. She didn't have a clue what she had. I got it for a steal."

Brett shook his head. "You lucky son of bitch."

"Tell me about it," Gavin said, looking at the car. "Well, dude, I'm going to get out of here. Let's hook up for dinner and that beer at the bar. I'll pick you up and show you what kind of horse power she's working with."

"Sounds like a plan," Brett said, watching Gavin head down the walkway to his car.

Stepping back inside the house, Brett found Courtney in the kitchen pulling out steaks to cook for dinner later. Without seeing her face, he knew something was wrong by the way that she was slamming the spices down on the counter. He walked up behind her and put his arms around her waist.

"What is it?" he asked, smelling her hair.

Courtney could feel his manhood resting up against her backside with the thin Nike shorts he had on. "Sharon Riley," Courtney bit out. "She called me in the mall going off and wanting to know why she hadn't seen Cameron."

Brett sucked his teeth. "What do you mean that she went off on you?"

Courtney tensed. "She went off...clean off. She said that she didn't want her blood over at this house with the likes of us and that he spent far too much time with my mom, dad, and me instead of with his own family. Then she said that she'd be glad when Leo Tabor had full custody so that we'd be in her shoes, where she'd decide if or when we got a chance to see him."

Brett's eye twitched. "What?"

Courtney stopped setting out the food and turned to her husband. Looking up into his blazing blue eyes, she made it as clear as she could for Brett. "Sharon is behind the paternity suit." Leaning against the counter, she exhaled a breath. "Brett, we need a lawyer...a good lawyer."

Brett licked his lips and turned away from her. Putting his hand on his head, he gave a condescending laugh. "That no good, conniving, low-down, racist bitch."

Courtney didn't move. Instead, she let him get it all out.

Brett looked back at her. "She said that she's going to take my son?"

"That's what she said."

"Over my dead body," he said, pulling his phone out of his pocket.

"Wait, Brett. Don't," Courtney protested.

"Don't what?" Brett snapped.

"Don't call her. Not right now. I've already told her that she can't see Cameron until a judge says so. I also told her that if she came to this house, it would be the last house that she ever came to. I made myself extremely clear."

"Well, she should have never called you in the first place, harassing you and shit. If she wanted to throw her weight around, then she should have called me." Brett's chest expanded with anger. "I don't know who the fuck she thinks that she is, but it's time I put her in her place for good."

Courtney was glad to finally see him respond to something. "We need a lawyer. Mom says that she knows a few."

Brett put away his phone. "Tell her to send me the names tonight. But until I get this taken care of block that bitch's number from your phone. If she wants something, she'll have to come through me."

Brett needed some air. Realizing that he had raised his voice to the point of possibly waking up his kids, he headed back out to the patio. "I'm going outside for a minute. I need to clear my head and figure some things out."

Courtney nodded. "Okay, I'll fix dinner."

# Chapter 16

"Regard your soldiers as your children, and they will follow you into the deepest valleys. Look on them as your own beloved sons, and they will stand by you even unto death!"
— *Sun Tzu*

Arriving back to the infinite pine trees, freshly low-cut grass, and red-bricked, perfectly squared away buildings of Camp Lejeune was like landing back on Earth after a long stint on an intergalactic space station. Everything that was once so familiar was suddenly inexplicably foreign. The blinding splendor of blue water reflecting off the deep blue bay, the beginning of a yellow-gold sunset just off the mesmerizing horizon, the feel of a warm, fresh breeze caressing the skin. It was all so different now. So much more appreciated than before.

Loved ones lined up in the parking lot with balloons, signs and gifts, waiting on their husbands, sons and boyfriends as they loaded off the charter bus. Each of them eager to get a little distance and time between themselves and the Marine Corps after eight long months in the sandy hell of Afghanistan packed like sardines on a base doing the government's business.

This homecoming was glorious for others.

But for David Lawless, it was more than just a surreal experience to return back to the home-land, especially considering how unworthy he felt not only as an officer but also as a person. It was a sobering reminder.

*I'm not worthy*, he thought to himself.

Feeling less than triumphant, he stepped off the bus in his desert uniform adorned with rank and honors and planted his size 12 tan combat boots on the ground. *Home.* The word took on different meaning now – now that he had lost men – men who were depending on him to bring them home also. They would never again be able to capture the beauty that was America in their own eyes. They would never breathe free air or see the world that they had fought so valiantly to protect. They would never see their families waiting and happy to hold them in a joyous embrace. The thought emotionally impaled him.

*I don't deserve to feel any of this either*, he thought to himself.

Despite his inner feelings of inadequacy, his hawk-eyed gaze zeroed in on his family across the parking lot waving and smiling. In conflict with his emotions of grief, he couldn't help but feel excited to see them, after all, they were all that he had in the world; and they were waiting for him. As normal, his father was sitting relaxed inside of the car behind the cool vents of his air conditioner, while his mother and Courtney stood with his girlfriend, Kelly, at the front of the car in the heat like his very own stalker fan club.

*They are beautiful.*

With bright smiles, they spotted him as soon as he got off the bus. It wasn't hard though, considering that there were few African-American men in the battalion and only one officer. His mere presence here in this capacity was a testament to all that he owed his father and all the men of color who had come before him. They had paved the way for him to be regarded for his rank and his achievements, not the color of his skin.

So, why at this moment did he feel the pang of unworthiness? Had he let all of them down? Had they all felt the way that he was feeling right now? Was this some cruel rite of passage? So many questions. No way to get all the answers. So, he tried to shake off the feelings. If he didn't, his family would surely know something was wrong, then they would dissect and finally they would make him discuss his feelings.

*No*, he couldn't let them see. So he perked up. *Head up. Chin up.* Face as stoic as any other day of categorically being an asshole. Emotions were for someone else, anyone else but him, because he didn't do well with them. He waved their way, masking his contempt for his failure with an indignant haughty smile.

Funny. As he scanned, he didn't see Brett Black, although he wasn't sure why something in him led him to believe that his brother-in-law would be there. Surely, he was the most disappointed in him of them all.

With his sea bag and gear thrown over his back and his cover down low over his chiseled face and tired red eyes, David made his way through the thick crowd of people, squeezing past crying mothers, talkative babies and ecstatic wives.

"Need a hand with that, Captain?" a voice asked a few feet behind him.

David knew that distinctive Texas baritone. He turned to see Brett leaning on crutches, leg in a cast, wearing a USMC gray jogging suit.

*So he had come!* "I should be asking you that," David said, cracking a smile.

Walking back up to Brett, David stared the man who had started off as a stranger and ended up being his brother-in-law in the face. However, he didn't have his normal stance of authority and privilege that seemed to propel itself into every situation. Instead, David stood before him now almost as though he was reporting to a superior officer. Humble, regretful even.

"I'm sorry." David refused to look away although he wanted to. His lips straightened into a line as he pursed them together.

Brett frowned, the sun shining into his face, highlighting the healing bruises and cuts indelibly marked on his skin as a reminder of the war he had been forced to leave behind. Squinting, he could see their family waiting behind them, probably wondering what was taking them so long. "Sorry for what?" Brett asked honestly.

David's shoulder's squared. "I'm sorry that I didn't bring your men home with me, especially your best friend." David swallowed down his pride and stood a little straighter; bracing himself for whatever Brett might have to say or might have to do. No matter what, it was warranted.

Awash with emotion, Brett inclined his head. *Oh, that.* While David's confession was completely unexpected, it was completely understood, because he felt the same way. Only, in his own quiet hell, he had never imagined what David might have been going through. Maybe this was a glimpse into his own selfishness. Maybe this was what he needed to make him understand that other people had lost someone too.

With sincerity, Brett reached out and put his hand on David's shoulder.

There was no need for an overly ambitious response. "We both lost them," Brett said, nodding at David. "You don't owe me an apology. You don't owe *anyone* an apology." He only wished that he could take his own advice. It was the reason driving him to get to Judy. He wanted...needed to say the same thing to her.

David's eyes looked as though if he had not been so stubborn, they might have watered. Instead, his eye twitched as he quickly pushed passed the moment. "I wish that were true, but we both know it's not," he said honestly.

Brett knew what it was like to be the center of attention, even if it was only for an audience of one. These situations were never comfortable. He looked over again at their family waiting and growing impatient. "Let's get you over to the women folk before they lose their shit. We can catch up later over a beer or something."

"I think I'd like that," David said, recognizing that he'd never in the history of their relationship had such a "beer" with his brother-in-law. It was well overdue.

\*\*\*

A picture of elegance, Diane stood with her covered cup of lemonade under the shade of a large black beach hat and black Jackie O shades, looking as sophisticated as a cover model on a Southern Women magazine, but inside she was a nervous wreck.

She just needed to see David for herself to make sure that he was okay. Hearing his voice over the phone wasn't enough. Reports from the base weren't enough. She needed to look into her boy's eyes and touch him. Then she'd know that he was fine, and she'd be fine.

Standing up off the hood of the car as he approached, Diane walked over, meeting him half way, and wrapped her arms around him. Hugging him tight, she pulled back and slipped her manicured hands around his handsome face. Her diamond wedding band and tennis bracelet glimmered in the sun as she drank him in.

"Thank God in heaven, you're home," she said, tears slipping down her cheeks from under her shades.

David quickly wiped the tears away with his thumb. No reason was a good reason to ever see her cry. "Hello beautiful," he said to his mother, glad to be back in her presence once again. Everything about her was calming.

"Hello little boy," she whispered. Wiping more tears, she laughed and looked him up and down. "My God, you look skinny!"

He had shed nearly 20 pounds and was now all sinewy muscle, iron, brawn and smooth dark skin – a poster Marine. He reminded her so much of Jeffery when he was David's age.

"Well, they don't cook as well as you do over there, I'm afraid." David winked at her.

"Today, you're in luck. I've prepared a feast for you. Kelly and Courtney helped. We've been in the kitchen most of the morning fixing all your favorite dishes." Diane stepped to the side so he could see his girlfriend, who stood still by the car, waiting for him.

In a simple A-line black skirt and a black cotton shirt clinging to her well-defined form decorated with a single strand of pearls, Captain Kelly Jamison stood by. Her long narrow face, deep midnight skin, high cheekbones, wide-set nose, wide blazing, brown eyes and full lips were as captivating at that moment as the first time that he had laid eyes on her. *The blacker the* berry, *the sweeter the juice*. And Kelly got his juices flowing beyond measure. He knew that she would be the last person that he would greet and for the longest amount of time.

One cue, Jeffery stepped out of the car and closed the door. In his perfectly starched polo and khakis, he strode over to David and stuck out his hand. "Welcome home, son." His voice was formal and stout.

"Thank you, sir," David said, shaking his hand firmly.

Grinning, Jeffery pulled him in for a warm hug.

David embraced him happily, patting him on the back. Words could not express how good it was to be in his father's presence again.

"Leaving me here alone with the female persuasion isn't good for my heart," Jeffery joked. "I trust you'll give me a year before you do it again."

"War definitely isn't the same without you," David admitted. "If you ask me, they need a little more *Lawless* in their lives over there."

Jeffery appreciated the compliment. "My war days are over, but I left the Corps in good hands."

David avoided affirming that. He wondered if his father had been there with all of his years of experience, would his men even be dead right now. *Probably not.*

As if telepathic of his son's hidden woes, Jeffery gave a bit of much needed advice. "You'll get used to it...the war," he said, seeing something dark in his son's eyes. He twisted his lip up and inspected David closer. "It will take some time, of course, but each tour gets better. You become surer of your decisions and surer of what could happen, one way or another." Slipping his fists into his pockets, he waited for David to reply.

David blinked fast. What was he to say? How had he read him so quickly?

"Alright, you've hogged him long enough," Courtney said, pushing past her parents to hug her big brother's neck. Her intrusion was more than welcomed.

"Hey sis," David said, kissing her forehead. By all accounts, she was glowing and looked happier than he'd ever seen her.

"Hey yourself, Marine," Courtney quipped, hitting him across his broad chest. Blocking the sun from her eyes with her little hand, she complained. "It's melting out here. Hug your girlfriend and let's load up and go home. The food is getting cold, and we worked too hard to order out."

"Sounds like a plan," Brett chimed in, looking in on the kids who were still waiting in the back seat of Courtney's car. He slapped the top of the car like it was one of their Humvees. "Let's get this convoy moving, Marines."

Courtney looked over at Kelly, who was still waiting by the car. She smiled at David. "She already gave the order. You're riding back with her...alone," she said suggestively. "Do us a favor. Don't stop off anywhere between here and the house. I don't want to wait for you guys to get reacquainted."

"Don't count on it," David said, pulling his cover off. A man had to greet his lady properly. "Can you hold these for me, Pop?" Passing his sea bag to his father, he walked over to Kelly. Without saying a word, he slipped a hand behind the back of her head cupping her ponytail, pulled her statuesque body to him and kissed her plush mouth passionately for all the days that he had been gone.

"Oh my," Diane said, looking away. It was one thing to do it; it was another to see it done. She blushed immediately.

Jeffery grinned proudly, not taking his eyes off the young couple. "What did you expect? He is a Lawless."

***

Diane wasn't lying when she said that she had prepared a feast for David's welcome home party. In the formal dining room, among elegant oil paintings in opulent frames, rich upholstered chairs, fine Japanese bone china, gleaming antique cabinets holding sparkling crystal and an aromatic fragrance of lemon and honey, there was an extravagant spread of warm breads, sweet butters, an assortment of cheeses, succulent meats, steamed vegetables, decadent deserts, expensive wines and chilled bubbly champagne. And in the background, soft music played while the family dog sat by the door opening watching but knowing better than to enter.

With candles burning on the high on the vintage brass candelabras on both sides of an elegant flower arrangement, the family sat around the long table laughing and joking as the sun set in the distance. The French windows opened in the adjoining den to take in the breathtaking view of green foaming waves hitting against the white sandy beaches and to receive the breeze off the bay.

Alas, the celebration of life cast away the lingering stink of regret and loss for a few hours.

As customary in their family, Diane and Jeffery sat at the opposite ends of the dining table;

Kelly and David sat on one side together with David sitting closest to their father and Courtney and Brett sat beside each other on the other side with Courtney sitting closest to their mother, while Bella sat in the same wooden high chair that their mother had used on her when she was a little girl between her mother and grandmother and Cameron sat cattycorner between Brett and David.

Brett was quietly grateful as he followed the many gleeful conversations with a smile but in silence. In all of his adult life, he had never known family gatherings to be so warm and festive before marrying Courtney. And he definitely had never experienced such classic elegance. He was just a Texas boy at heart, straight from a little farm that his mother ran until the day that she died. They hadn't been big on formalities, just love and loyalty, which was what his family shared in common with his wife's family.

Diane played hostess better than anyone on Emerald Isle - tending to everyone's needs with a big, bright smile, pouring wine continuously, serving up more food and keeping the conversation light and engaging. And she did it all while dressed to kill.

Jeffery had earned his right to sit at the head of the table, and had a certain alpha dominance that radiated around the room. His deep baritone roared like a pride lion as he laughed and joked with everyone all while keeping his eye firm on his wife, whom he always looked like he was ready to sexually devour. Their insatiable appetite for each other was something that he hoped to continue to have with his own wife. Old Man Lawless was lucky; he had never lost sight of the ultimate goal of happiness. Brett envied him that, and he was sure that everyone else did also.

David was always the proper officer. He ate everything in small portions with the specified utensil all while ironically relaxing even with a stiff back and a mellow charm that spoke to his impeccable breeding. Brett imagined that David would eventually be a full bird before his career was over the Marine Corps, because he carried himself like one even now.

And although it had been said that opposites attract, he couldn't help but see how those similar to each other seemed to do well also. Kelly was a quiet, strong woman, a fellow officer of her boyfriend and highly educated at MIT. She sat beside him a picture of beauty and poise, enjoying him and his stuffiness as much as Brett seemed to enjoy the down-to-earth hearty banter that he shared with Courtney.

"Do you want more wine?" Courtney asked, looking over at his glass to find it nearly empty. Her hand was placed on his thigh, small and accurate; he could feel the heat coming from her palm even through his jogging pants. She was a little tipsy now from one glass too many of the expensive spirits and her face was flushed and full of life.

He turned from his observations of the Lawless family slowly, sweeping a look over her with his blue eyes that made her heart skip a beat. Moving his tattooed arms from the table, he cleared his throat. "Yes, please," he said, mouth curved for a kiss.

Courtney tightened her legs together. Was that admiration she saw in the twinkle of his enchanting gaze? Did she hear lust in his voice? It had been a while since she had experienced that, but even now she welcomed it. Not to mention, she had a serious thing for his bad boy exterior.

"Red or white?" her voice carried like a feather as she tried to calm her deepening blush.

"Red," he said, suddenly wanting her. Something about that moment amidst the candles, the aromas, the laughter and the fleeting sun made him feel alive again.

She rose up and grabbed the bottle of wine near her mother and then reached over him to pour it. It was a simple gesture of respect, but she knew that he would take it for what it was...her offering of herself and her submission to whatever was forming in the darkness of his thoughts.

He watched her every move. Eyeing her graceful body, the way that her sundress clung to her supple wide hips and small waist, the tendrils of soft hair flirting with the nape of her neck and the way that her still engorged breasts pushed up around her cleverly low cut ensemble. Suddenly, he felt the need to literally growl.

Courtney could feel his stare and his raw, unadulterated thoughts consuming her whole. She was swallowed by pheromones that seemed to be intoxicating in the room. Giggles. Laughter. Looks. Dancing candle light. Wine. Nearly stumbling, she put the bottle down and sat back down as her family continued to talk, not bothering to notice or acknowledge what was happening between Mr. and Mrs. Black. Perhaps it was happening to everyone else at the table.

Inexplicably to even himself, Brett wanted to slip his large hands between her thighs, sink his fingers into her soft warm center and then lick each finger clean. He felt his mouth watering at the thought and when she glanced over at him and smiled again, he quietly fought the need to reach out and suck on her velvety tongue and bury himself in her kiss.

The thought of what she tasted like nearly made him rise to a rock hard steely attention, but with mind bullets, he shot down his erection.

Courtney's hazel eyes rested on him for a minute. Long lashes flapped like wings. "You okay?" she asked, head tilted just enough for him to admire her swanlike neck.

He leaned in to her, slipping his arm behind her chair and resting only his thumb on the bare skin of her back. "I'm great," he said, making a mental note to fuck her mercilessly later.

*\*\**

They arrived at the house near 10:00 that night. Both children were exhausted and wanted nothing more than to be tucked in to their comfy little beds where they could properly dream of sugarplums and superheroes. Together Brett and Courtney put both children in their rooms, turning off the lights and quietly retreating into the hallway.

By now, Courtney was adorably drunk and in a blissful mood.  She giggled when he put his fingers over her mouth.

"Shh," he said, leaning in to finally kiss her. "You'll wake them."

She had been waiting all night, but not nearly as long as Brett.  Still kissing her mouth, he pushed her up against the wall hard, allowing his hands to roam all over her, groping her breasts, raking over her small adorable pooch of a stomach, cupping her wet aching sex and finally pulling her in by her large sexy ass into his erection.

"God, I want you," he bit out as he made her feel what she did to him. If he didn't get inside his wife right now, he was literally going to die.

Her skin was on fire; her vision a little blurry. "Brett," she whispered.  "I'm yours."

The recognition of possession sent Brett over the edge.  All night, all he could do was think of how lucky he was to have her, how he didn't deserve her, but to hear her say that she was his drove him insane.  Quiet hysteria rose over him.

Her enchanting eyes met his in the darkness. In silence and stillness, he looked down at her, finally lifting her chin with his index finger; he stared at her pouty mouth.

Courtney liked it when he looked at her mouth. He seemed transfixed by it and the more he stared, the more turned on she became. She bit her bottom lip, teasing him as she moved slowly down to her knees.

"What are you doing?" he whispered.

He watched, breathing hard as she grasped the sides and pulled his jogging pants and boxers down, and then slipped the head of his throbbing penis into her pouty little mouth. Clasping the shaft of his well-endowed member with both hands, she tasted the distinct, arousing taste of pre-ejaculation on her lips.

Balling his fist up, he hit the wall. FUCK! His shaky breaths were even more exasperated as she took all of him into her mouth in one fell swoop. He swallowed hard, not realizing she even knew how to do that. AND IT FELT SO GOOD. The warm soft orifice of her gentle little mouth felt like heaven. He grabbed her by the back of her head, fisting a handful of her feathery hair and guided himself in and out. The sound of suction echoed down the hall. Her saliva ran down his shaft and over his balls as they slapped against her face.

*Don't you dare blow your load,* he told himself quietly.

Her small fingers slipped under his shirt and moved up his cascading valley of deep muscles in his abdomen until she found his nipples. Then she pinched them.  Hard.

*Thank God for a kinky wife*, he said to himself.

Throwing his head back, he released a sigh, and then sucked in a breath.  HOLY SHIT!  She was going to make him do it, if she continued.

"Get to the bedroom," he ordered finally. There was only so much torture he could take in this hallway.

She pulled her lips away from him and looked up.  "Now?" she teased.

"Right fucking now," he ordered, following so fast on his crutches behind her until he wasn't sure that he needed them anymore.

*** 

Courtney couldn't breathe despite her many honest attempts.  She lay with her head over the side of the bed, hair in a sweaty nest, butt naked and covered in her husband's semen.  Looking out at a full moon beaming through the open window, she wiped a hand over her exposed breasts, surprised that they were still there after the sucking that they had endured from her husband.

"What was that?" she asked, as quakes of the last orgasm still rushed over her body.

A gleam shone in his menacing blue eyes. "That was," Brett tried to catch his breath as he rolled over beside her in the bed, naked also, except for the cast. "That was just a night cap," he said, coughing.

Courtney giggled again. "I like your night caps," she croaked.

In the last hour, Brett had taken her in every position possible, all with one functioning leg. Her skin glistened with sweat and welts from slaps and scratches and friction. He had pulled her hair and sucked her clit. He had licked her neck and kissed her feet. He had sucked her toes and every inch of her vagina.

In truth, she was spent and completely certain that no other man could ever satisfy her the way that her husband did.

"Mmm," she moaned in utter satisfaction.

"Want to do it again?" Brett asked, rising up.

Courtney shook her head emphatically. "I can't."

Normally, that kind of rejection might have tamped Brett's desire for her but tonight, it made him happy. He had fulfilled her. *Good.*

With her eyes still on the moon, she finally felt her heart start to calm. "David's different," she said flatly. "Can you tell?"

"We're all different after we come back from that place," Brett said, turning over on his side to run a finger down the length of her body. Damn, she was gorgeous.

Goose bumps formed on her skin, but she tried to stay focus on the conversation. "He seems humbler than before."

Brett raised a brow. "It is a humbling experience."

"What did you two talk about when he first got off the bus? It seemed intense from where I was standing." Her eyes locked on his.

Brett wasn't exactly the type to reveal such a thing. Plus, it wasn't like she'd understand if he told her anyway. "We just welcomed each other back. It wasn't a full conversation, per se."

Courtney figured that Brett wouldn't say, but at least she had tried. "I'm just glad that you never have to go back to Afghanistan," she said absently. "In truth, I wished that he never had to go back either. Mom is a wreck when he's gone."

Brett was taken aback. "Why wouldn't I go back to Afghanistan?" he asked, brows knitting together.

Courtney sat up. She thought it was obvious why. "Because you were injured. And because we have money now. You can find something else to do, and I can go back to school and have some help around here."

Brett wiped a hand over his face like she had just spit on him. "Baby, I'm glad we've got this money, but..."

"But what?" she pushed.

A frown creased across his beautiful face. "I'm going back," he said in a sorry-to-tell-you sort of way.

Courtney was lost for words. Her body language however was not. She pushed her back up against the headboard and curled her knees toward her. "Brett, you can't be serious?"

Brett didn't understand. "Why can't I be?" He asked in a sensible low voice.

"You almost died," she said, sternly. "You almost left your children fatherless and your wife without a husband. Thank God that you're here, but you can't possibly think of putting us in that situation again."

Brett let out an irritated sigh. So much for a peaceful night. He could hear it in her voice. He wasn't going to win this argument. It had boiled down to who would be right and who would be happy.

She looked at her husband, naked and stunning, and felt like slapping him right across his gorgeous face.

He could see her irritation, but after such a sensible night, he refused to jump head first down the rabbit hole of chaos she was inviting him into. "I don't want to fight," he said, demeanor soft. Maybe it was him and how he had presented it. Courtney was big on presentation.

Reaching for her arm, he pulled her to him, despite her quiet anger. "Come here. Don't be like that," he cooed. Pulling her into the curve of his body, he kissed the back of her head as he pushed his manhood up against her firm buttocks. "We don't have to talk about this tonight. We're both tired. We're both emotional."

Courtney took a deep breath. He was right. Today had been a good day. There was no reason to ruin it talking about hypotheticals. Whether he knew it or not, he was not going to be allowed to stay in Recon with a bum leg, her father had already told her so.

"I love you," Brett said, softly into her ear. "That is what is important."

She reached for his arm and pulled it around her waist. Nestling into his embrace, she quieted herself. "I love you too, baby."

# Chapter 17

"It is a pleasant world we live in, sir, a very pleasant world. There are bad people in it, Mr. Richard, but if there were no bad people, there would be no good lawyers."
                                    - Charles Dickens

Driving along the Crystal Coast of Carteret County would have been enough to take most people's breath away. The scenic route of Highway 24 was filled with palm trees, tropical summer beach houses on magnificent stilts, continual waterways, fishing boats, elegant roadside cafes and coastal charm, but in Brett and Courtney's emotional state, the tranquil beauty of their heavenly surroundings was lost on them.

Trapped in a private hell of worry, even in paradise, the entire morning had been spent in utter silence. They showered, got the kids dressed, fixed breakfast, read the paper - all in silence. They dropped the kids off with Diane silently, only making conversation because they had to, but not really wanting to talk, because what they wanted to talk about had already been discussed a thousand times with their parents.

With the radio playing low and the windows half-cracked to circulate fresh air, Courtney gripped the leather stitched steering wheel and stared blankly out onto the nearly empty road. Her wedge-sandaled foot pushed down on the accelerator headed east as fast as her little car would take her – not once thinking about being pulled over by cops for violating the limit as she normally would.

In a similar zombie-like state, Brett gazed out of the window of the passenger seat, shades covering his red, tired eyes from no sleep the night before, playing back moments in his previous marriage, trying to figure out how he had missed all the signs that Cameron wasn't his. *How had he missed it? How had he allowed Amy to get over on him?*

His brow furrowed in deep thought. This was utter humiliation. Never in his life had he felt more like a fool than now. And Courtney...what she must think of him after this. Here she was driving him around trying to fix more problems created by his previous fucked up choices in women. It just wasn't fair to her.

They were headed to meet their new lawyer for the first time. Solomon Benson of Benson &

Krieger Law, PLLC had been referred to them through Diane and Jeffery, who promised that while the lawyer would be *expensive,* he would be "worth every dime."

Only, Brett didn't care how much it cost him. He just wanted someone to tell him that they could protect what was rightfully theirs, which was sole custody of Cameron. *Sole custody* was key. There was no way in hell he was going to share him with anyone other than Courtney. No one else deserved him. No one had put the time in, no one had sacrificed and it would be over his dead body that anyone else would lawfully be able to call Cameron their son.

"We should have left 10 minutes earlier," Courtney said, looking at the clock on the dashboard. "If we hit any traffic when we get to Morehead, we'll be late for our first appointment." She didn't want to be tardy nor do anything that might allow Mr. Benson take their case a little less serious. Plus, this was a friend of her parents, and it was always in the back of her mind *to not embarrass them.* She chided herself quietly about that even entering her mind in the middle of this.

Brett turned from the window and glanced over at Courtney who was a picture of chaos now. Her body language was all wrong. She sat erect, back rigid and pulled away from the seat like at any moment she would catapult out of the windshield.  Her sundress was pushed up over her toned thighs in a pool of fabric draped in between her legs and her face was twisted in deep, agonizing thought.  *This was tearing her apart.*

Slipping a gentle hand over on her bare leg and forgetting about his own concerns, he squeezed her.  "Breathe," he said soothingly. "Everything is going to be okay."  *Possibly a lie, okay.*  But it was worth telling her that to keep her from worrying.

Courtney didn't realize that her feelings where showing again...right there on her sleeve like usual.  Taking a breath, she relaxed her shoulders.  "That obvious, huh?" she asked, sinking back in her seat.  There were times that she could be more like Brett.

Glad that he could hide his angst better, he replied with a calm faux ease, simply for her benefit.  "Oh, yeah.  It's more than obvious.  You need to relax, baby."

"I'm just..." Courtney huffed in frustration. "I'm praying this guy is who we need.  The clock is counting down.  That court date is coming up."

"If he's not who we need, then we'll keep looking until we find the right person," Brett said simply.

Courtney gave a nervous chuckle. "Or we could just run." Her eyes cut his way.

Brett laughed.

"I'm not kidding," Courtney said abruptly. "We have money. Plus, I'm over North Carolina. I want to spread my wings a little. Before this, I was thinking California...maybe Stanford, *if I could get accepted*. But now, I like the idea of Venezuela."

"A non-extradition country," Brett said, shaking his head. "Baby, that's crazy." Unfortunately, it wasn't the craziest idea he had gotten so far. Gavin still wanted to just kill the guy.

"It's nothing that I wouldn't do for Bella," Courtney said honestly. And in her mind, Cameron was just as much hers as her daughter was.

Brett could tell that she had put a lot of thought into Venezuela, and he was honored to have such a committed wife, but there was no way that he could ever leave the country that he had already sacrificed so much for to become a fugitive. If he did, everything would be in vain. Plus, he loved the U.S. of A. far too much to be without her, no matter that she was the craziest bitch he had met. "How about this," Brett said, hand still on her thigh. He bit his lip and paused. "How about we just win this thing?"

Courtney smiled at him. Of course he would say that. Brett didn't run from anything, even when it benefitted him to do so. "That would work too."

*** 

They were right on time without a second to spare. Courtney and Brett exited a bank of gold elevators and entered the posh 12th floor executive suites of Benson & Krieger law firm at 12:59 p.m. The elation while quiet and unspoken was immediate and just short of hearing angels singing in the heavens.

Releasing a sigh of relief, Courtney rubbed Brett's back and smiled at the sign on the door. They had finally arrived, despite all of her unnecessary worry.

Guiding her husband up to the glass-paned doors one step at a time, she held them open for him as he maneuvered on his crutches.

"Got it?" she asked as he passed through the doors.

"I'm fine, baby. Thanks," he answered, ignoring the nagging pain in his leg and the emasculation of her opening the door for him.

To their amazement, although the parking lot was nearly full, in the lobby there were no other clients waiting. The airy modern space was lit up with track lighting and gleaming marble floors and looked more like a museum of art instead of a law firm. Based upon all the glass, wood and leatherwork around the office, Brett could tell that this place was going to be steep, but there were also plenty of awards and placards on display, which meant that they won...a lot.

Walking up to the oval glass reception desk to check in, they were greeted by a slender Asian woman in a simple but elegant peach suit with her hair pulled back in a conservative bun. She was on the phone speaking very angrily to someone in Arabic. It might have been strange in any other place, but so close to a military base, diverse cultures and bilingual people were a norm.

*One should never assume anything.*

Obviously frustrated by the caller on the other end of the line, the receptionist's first glance went to Brett in his drab black Nike jogging suit and battered face. Based on the high and tight haircut, she assumed that he was more than likely military. But still, he didn't look very important to her, *probably one of the firm's indigent cases that they took on from time to time.*

The second, even shorter glance was at Courtney, who looked more polished than her counterpart did. *Probably a case worker.*

Raising her finger to have them wait as she finished the call, she turned her attention back to the phone as if they weren't there. Snarling orders in Arabic, she restrained herself from hitting the desk to make her point.

Courtney was so happy to be there on time that she didn't even notice the woman, but Brett's fine-tuned senses were honed in on her petulance.

For the first couple of moments, Brett waited in understanding that she was preoccupied with the call, and then after the conversation continued into the realm of deliberately awkward disrespect, he glowered at her with enough heat to singe.

"Great," he said aloud, turning away from the woman before he shot her to death with his mind bullets. *Just what he needed- another rude-ass person telling him what to do and at the same time expecting to get paid for it.* He had already gone off on the cable television people that morning for charging him full price for service that seemed to only work half the time. *Everybody wanted something for nothing.*

"You got some gum?" he asked Courtney, leaning against the desk on purpose. He put his crutch up against the side to add symbolic weight to the tense situation.

Clueless, Courtney fished out a stick of spearmint gum from her Michael Kors purse and passed it to him. "What's wrong?" she asked, sensing something had suddenly gone awry. *That seemed to happen to him more and more lately.* "Do you want to sit and wait?" It was her way of suggesting that they move away from the receptionist before he said something offensive.

*Too late.*

Bret hated being ignored but more than that he hated bad customer service. It was simply one of his pet peeves. "No, I don't want to wait. I want her to get off the phone. She could have at least said something to the effect of *I'll be with you in a minute.* Hell, I'd settle for *fuck off,*" Brett said, popping the gum in his mouth. He was certain that the receptionist heard him, and that was his intention. Giving an exaggerated pause, he continued in the same tone, "*Instead,* she's making us wait while she pretends to be on an *important* call."

Courtney looked back at the woman apologetically, embarrassed that her husband was quietly making a scene. This was so unlike him

– the old him.  She put her hand up near her temple. "How do you know it isn't an important call?" she whispered, trying to turn her body away from the woman a little more.

His voice was brittle now.  "Because she's talking to some unlucky character about installing her new in-ground pool," Brett said, raising his voice slightly. "Now she's bitching about the price. Trust me. It's not life or death."

Courtney's expression grew cold. "Not likely." She moved her hand from her face. *To hell with the woman being offended.* "I forgot you speak Arabic."

"I didn't," Brett said turning back around to face the woman, whose mouth had popped open. *"Lugha wāhidah lā takfī."*

Courtney gave a disapproving glare to the woman, who quickly got off the phone once she realized that she no longer had a language barrier to protect her conversation.

"Sorry for that. May I help you?" she asked with a bright, customer service *screw you* smile to match her condescending tone.

"Yes, you can," Courtney said, returning the same smug smile. "Mr. & Mrs. Black. We *had* an appointment for 1:00 p.m." She glanced at the clock on the wall.  It was currently 1:10 p.m. Late, despite all of her damn effort.

Clicking her mouse with her acrylic tipped finger to alert her monitor, which had gone to *sleep mode* because she had been on her private call so long - the receptionist scanned the schedules quickly to see which junior lawyer they were assigned. Probably the new jerkoff junior partner who was intent on calling her darling.

Finally, she found their name, not at the bottom, where she assumed, but at the very top. Her demeanor changed abruptly as if someone had just electrified her seat. They were not *indigent*. They were seeing the founding partner of the law firm. *Shit*.

The receptionist grinned again, this time with a lot less sarcasm and a lot more shit-eating. "Yes, I'll notify Mr. Benson that you arrived."

"On time," Brett added with a carefully neutral expression.

"Of course. If you could have a s..." The receptionist stopped mid-sentence while looking at Brett as she picked up her phone. She had just overheard him say that he didn't want to have a seat. There was no need in offering. Dialing Mr. Benson, she stood up from her seat. "Hello, sir. Your party has arrived." Pausing, she waited for a response. "Yes, sir. I'll bring them back right away." She hung up the phone and stepped around the desk.

"If you will just follow me," the receptionist said, hands now laced together in a servant capacity.

"Lead the way," Brett said, pulling his crutches back under his sore underarms.

"Talk about a 180," Courtney whispered as they walked.

"What was that about?" Brett asked.

Courtney shrugged her shoulders indifferently. "Maybe you scared her."

"How did I scare her?" Brett asked, looking over at his wife.

*Being an asshole,* Courtney thought to herself without answering. She now gave the sarcastic smile to Brett that the receptionist had given her. He immediately recognized the silent implication, but refused to say one more word on it.

Following the woman from the vast lobby through the long corridor of small offices on each side filled with junior lawyers in windowless rooms busily working and talking on their phones, they both figured out why the parking lot was full. Behind the tranquil lobby of calm and serenity, there was a mad house of employees.

Brett knew then that business was good.

They came to a large corner office at the very end of the corridor, where they were met by a tall, African-American man in a dark blue tailored suit and shiny white even teeth. He was in his mid-50's, all polish and class, but something about him seemed down-to-earth at the same time. It was quite a refreshing change from the experience receptionist.

"Can I get you anything to drink?" the receptionist asked nervously as she handed them off to their appointment. She was quietly praying that they wouldn't rat her out to the big boss.

Brett ignored her as if she hadn't said a word, while Courtney simply nodded no.

"Hello," Mr. Benson said, offering his hand to Courtney. "Very nice to meet you. You must be Courtney." His glance lingered for a moment like he knew her, then he turned. "And you must be Brett. Thank you so much for your service." He shook Brett's hand firmly.

"Thanks," Brett said, liking what he saw so far. This guy seemed like he had it together at first impression but now it was time to get down to the brass tacks of it.

Courtney looked around as they entered the massive space. "Nice office." Chandeliers. Bar.

Solid oak furniture. Oriental rugs. An endless library of books. This guy was the real deal.

"Thank you. Please come in and get off those crutches, man," Mr. Benson said, leading them over to the two blue leather seats in front of his enormous wooden desk in front of the panoramic view of the Atlantic Ocean.

The first thing Courtney wondered was how much his retainer actually was. It had to be at least enough to cover the expensive real estate, the suit, the furniture, and that nice diving watch on his wrist. *They were in for a ride.*

"First, thank you so much for considering us. We are honored." He scanned the couple and sensed their nervousness. He had heard that this office could be rather intimidating, but Mr. Benson was good at breaking the ice for his clients. "Courtney, I took the liberty of speaking with your lovely mother for nearly an hour on the phone the other day," he said, having a seat behind the desk. His broad shoulders relaxed as he unbuttoned his suit and pushed up to the desk, exuding old, seasoned confidence that only came with many years of success.

Courtney knew that swagger; her father had it. "Did she talk you to death?"

"No, but she did get me up to speed. At least, from her perspective. In the court of law, it's a third party account but it gave me a good place to start."

"Thank you for seeing us on such short notice," Brett answered.

"It's not a problem at all. As I understand it, we don't have a moment to waste." Mr. Benson, taking cues from Brett, opened up a file and reached for his reading glasses on the table. Shaking his head, he sighed as he looked over the papers. "This is a raw deal, huh?"

"Very raw deal," Brett said, still disgusted by the idea that he had to be here. "I was told that you were the best. And I need that. As you can see." He looked at the file curiously. What did that guy have in there? They had just met. Then he thought about Diane. As much as Courtney and her mother talked, that file probably had every single detail about his entire life in it including his blood type and social security number.

"We don't want to lose our son," Courtney said abruptly. She laced her fingers together in her lap.

"And we don't care how much it costs," Brett added.

Both affirmations were music to Mr. Benson's ears. "Well, we're going to work hard to ensure that that doesn't happen, but first I like to give all my clients background on who I am and who we are as a firm.  To give you a little background on me that's not on Google, I've been a lawyer for over 25 years.  Prior to that I was a Marine with the 2-2 over at Camp Lejeune.  I even had the pleasure of working under Colonel Lawless for a very brief stint."

"Really?" Brett said, seeing that they already had something in common.

"Oh yeah," Mr. Benson said with a grin. "As you know, when you're active duty you have to sign over your legal custodial rights to someone else to ensure that if you need to deploy quickly, there won't be a problem for the child. I did that blindly. I signed over rights to my wife, who decided while I was away, the marriage was over. When I came back and tried to get my rights to see my child back, I ended up with every other weekend, a month during the summer and a portion of the holiday break, even though I was more than a part-time dad.  Now keep in mind this was before the *Servicemembers Civil Relief Act*.  So as soon as I could, I left the Marine Corps and went to law school.  After graduating at the top of my class from UNC Chapel Hill, I started a small law firm with my best friend, Edward Krieger.  It was a studio space in the nastiest office ever about 10 miles from here. I later bought that building and turned into a homeless shelter. Fast-forward 25 years later, we are now the best family law firm in the region, and I am now comfortably retired and a grandfather. I spend my weekends making up for the time I missed with my oldest daughter."

"Retired?" Brett asked. "So this is a what? A special case?"

Mr. Benson was glad that he asked. "Put it like this, at this hour, most days, I'm on the 10th of 18 holes or having lunch at Gramercy Elementary school with my grandbabies. I haven't taken a case in about three and a half years. I leave that to our staff of over 15 junior partners." He laughed. "But Diane and Jeffery are good friends. When Jeffery came to the country club to talk to me about this case and play a little golf, I was happy to be of service," Mr. Benson said proudly. "Plus not only do you not turn down a USMC Colonel, but your story was also something that I could appreciate. No man should be forced to be away from his child."

Brett couldn't agree more.

Courtney was quiet but deeply moved. The other day when she had shown up at her mother's house talking about Sharon Riley, her father was already looking out for them. She had to tell him thank you as soon as she left here.

"We truly appreciate you," Courtney said, clearing her throat.

"Well, we are trial lawyers with over 1500 successful, favorable verdicts. We have a team of highly specialized lawyers, assistants and investigators at your disposal. We belong to only the best associations and have the best affiliations."

"I've got an investigator already," Brett said quickly, circling back to the part of the conversation that caught his attention. "He has a firm out of California and he's a former Marine familiar with the area. He's going to be snooping around for the next couple of weeks, and then he'll get that information to you."

Mr. Benson was impressed. "Great. That's great news. Let's see what he turns up. If you need us, we'll also employ our guys. Does your contact know the laws of North Carolina? I'd hate for any evidence to be considered inadmissible."

"James Gavin is the best," Brett answered with confidence. "I put my life in this guy's hands for years. I trust him and his skills."

Courtney was shocked yet again. She thought Gavin was just visiting, but in fact, her husband had been already laying the foundation for their case. A part of her felt guilty for her haste to believe that he wasn't motivated.

Mr. Benson seemed pleased with Brett's answer. "Great. Now that we have that out of the way, let's start at the very beginning. You tell me what has happened *exactly* as it happened, and I'll take a few notes. Once we're done, I'll ask you a series of questions to get some clarification. And then we'll work out a game plan."

The conversation went on for over 40 minutes. In the quiet office, Brett and Courtney purged, as they never had before about how they had met, how they had worked to ensure Cameron had a good life and how they had been served with papers. Each one gave the other the opportunity to tell their story, which often erupted in tears and frustration. But they made it through and when they were done, they at least knew that they truly loved each other. Only love would cause two people to sacrifice so much.

When it was all done, the lawyer now relaxed with his suit jacket off, hanging behind him on his chair and his sleeves rolled up, took a sip off his second cup of hot coffee and began his questions. "As I understand it Leo Tabor has not had any contact with the child to your knowledge?" Mr. Benson probed.

"Never," Brett said, drinking out of water bottle and wiping sweat from his brow. His face was beet red in anger having relived his entire traumatic experience all over again in this man's office. He would have rather been shot again than dredge all of this up.

"Well, I'm sure during the hearing he'll request temporary visitation." He quickly spoke to calm Brett. "We'll request the judge push that off until a third-party child psychologist of our choosing can explain how that is not in the best interest of Cameron." He looked through his other questions and beat the table with his pen. "And are you going to see someone for the PTSD?"

Brett jerked his head. "What PTSD?"

Mr. Benson laughed. "The obvious PTSD that the plaintiff will use against you." He reached into his drawer and pulled out a card. "This is on my dime and it's completely untraceable and confidential. Go and see her. Dr. Lansing is the best in the business and she produces results."

Brett wanted to turn down the card, but Courtney reached out and took it. "Thank you. We'll call her this afternoon."

"Good. We need to show that you are doing everything to ensure a safe and healthy environment for your son," Mr. Benson reiterated.

Brett looked over at his wife. "Now I have PTSD?"

"Yes, you have PTSD," Courtney confirmed in a stern voice.

"Also, you said that you completed the adoption process on Cameron making Courtney the legal parent before you left for Iraq?" Mr. Benson asked, going down his list.

"Yes," Brett answered.

"I'll need that documentation along with this long list of other items that my assistant will type out and email to you," Mr. Benson said, eyes glued to the paper.

Brett huffed. "Not a problem at all. All I have, at least for the next 27 days, is time."

Mr. Benson frowned as he looked over Brett's statement. "Earlier you said that you actually spoke with a man the day before Amy boarded the plane to leave you. And this is the man you assume that she was going to leave you for? Do you remember his name?"

Brett had avoided earlier saying that the mysterious man was black. It wasn't exactly something that made a difference one way or another. And he didn't want to give his lawyer the feeling that he was racist, which he wasn't, but now the cat had to be let out of the bag. "Yes, it was Jermaine. I didn't get a last name, but I did keep the number...just in case." He reached into his pocket and pushed the number across the table.

"Call the fucker if you want to. I don't care. In fact," Brett stopped and chuckled, "feel free to depose him. I would love for him to explain that to his superiors."

Mr. Benson chuckled. "Oh, we just might," he said, picking up the number. He looked at the number and paused. Wiping his face with his thumb, he bucked his eyes. "Jermaine, you say?"

"Yeah, I would never forget that name. He had a message that said, *Hi, you've reached Jermaine. Leave a message, and I'll hit you back as soon as I can...*"

"*Peace*," Mr. Benson said, indicating that he knew the voice mail. He knew the man.

Brett and Mr. Benson locked eyes in silent hysteria.

"Why do I get the feeling that you know this guy?" Brett asked without blinking.

"Small world," Mr. Benson exhaled, pushing away from the desk. He stood up and walked over to the bookshelf on the far wall. Coming back, he set a silver frame on the table of a young man in uniform. "His name is Captain Jermaine Stanley Benson. He is stationed in Okinawa, has been for the last four years. Damn good officer. Sorry to say, not so good at choosing women."

Courtney put her hand over her mouth. *What in the hell?*

"He's my son," Mr. Benson said, having a seat. His face was colored with disappointment. "I'm very sorry, Brett."

"Does this mean that there is a conflict of interest and we've done this all for nothing? Is it that kind of *sorry*?" Brett asked, feeling the heat begin to prickle the tips of his ears again.

"No," Mr. Benson said coolly. "This means we don't have to dig around looking for your witness in another country, because we already know who he is." His wide masculine jaw clenched wishing that he could get his hands on his son's neck at the moment. "I'll call him myself tonight and get any information that he has, you will have by tomorrow evening. You have my word on it."

Brett released a humorless laugh and wiped his hands over his head. "Do you believe this shit?" he asked, turning to Courtney.

Courtney removed her shaking hand from her mouth and looked at Mr. Benson. "Did you know? Did my mother tell you?" But how could she? Courtney didn't even know about that small detail. Brett had never told her the man's name although he had told her about the incident.

"I had no idea," Mr. Benson said, completely off his game at the moment, and that hadn't happened in 25 years.

"Then it must be true," Courtney said, taking her husband's hand.

"What's that?" Brett asked, looking at her small elegant fingers. At the moment, he really just wanted to go. Get the hell out of there. The room was starting to cave in on him, and he couldn't be responsible for his actions.

"Everything happens for a reason," Courtney said, reassuring the both of them. "We were meant to be here, and you were meant to work this case. Everything is going to be alright."

Brett's eye twitched, but he knew that she was right. Some things went far beyond coincidence. Looking over at Mr. Benson, he smacked his lips. "Where's the contract? I'm ready to sign."

# Chapter 18

"It takes a minute to find a special person, an hour to appreciate them, and a day to love them, but it takes an entire lifetime to forget them."          —Anonymous

A closed casket meant that there would be no viewing of the body. Judy had chosen to forego the wake the night before, and the family had complied with her wishes. Since two Marines in dress blues had shown up at her home almost two weeks ago, no one had seen her outside of her immediate family as she had turned away all callers and visitors.

Instead, she had asked that all money and gifts be sent to the Wounded Warrior Project in Joe's name and that everyone who wanted to pay their respects do so at the funeral only. It was just like her to give everyone marching orders. That was what she had always been good at and what Joe had always chided her about.

But Brett thought that he had a better relationship with Judy than that. He thought that she considered him to be *immediate family* and that sometime before the funeral; he would have been able to simply come over and give her a hug.

But he had been wrong.

Judy didn't want to see anyone at all.

Today, in full dress uniform, adorned in the many service medals he had earned over the years, he loaded in the car with his family and headed to Fayetteville, North Carolina, *where Judy and Joe had grown up, first met, and married*, for the funeral.

Brett wanted to be at the church for the service earlier than everyone else. Not just to spend some time with Joe, but also to hopefully see Judy.

Courtney tried to reason with him for the last two days about Judy's state of mind and why she had felt the need to be so reclusive. Expressing all the things a wife felt after a husband was suddenly plucked out of her life had helped him come to terms with his forced absence from the Mabry family, but he still needed closure. Today, he prayed that he'd get it.

The drive had been a quiet one with the kids napping in the back for most of the trip, and Courtney quietly listening to her new book on tape, *The Lover's Ball*. It wasn't that she was so into the book. It was more to have something to keep her mind off of the funeral and what she needed to get by. And she thought, in her unselfish attempt, that the story might help Brett too.

But Brett hadn't paid attention to the story blasting in the speakers; instead, he was lost in his own tragic opera with five full acts of misery. He was drawn into the story of two best friends who had divulged every fear, hope, dream and disappointment with each other since the day they joined Recon, who had spent most major holidays together and been there at the birth of each other's child, when they weren't deployed. And those last moments together, in the hills of Afghanistan, when even then they had done everything to protect each other and keep each other safe, thinking that tomorrow they would see each other and dissect the entire mission over a beer and barbeque with their wives and kids only to ripped from each other too soon and their families destroyed—that had been the story that he was immersed in now.

The ending was not what he had expected and no matter how badly he tried to tell himself that this was just war, and this was a part of it and no one was exempt, he felt an enormous cloud over his life. His best friend was gone and he was left with survivor's remorse.

How would he handle seeing the people who had entrusted him with Joe's life? How could he explain how he had lived and Joe had not? How could he face Judy?

Even then, Joe's bright smile crossed his mind. He could still hear his voice ringing in his ears. He remembered every single detail of their friendship. Joe never gave him a pass. He always told him what was right and what was wrong. He always pushed him to think and never let him, not even when he wanted to, put his family last.

And now his most trusted confidant was waiting on him an hour away in a box.

Brett pushed a breath out, trying hard not to fidget too much in the passenger seat, although it was nearly impossible to sit still.

The suit was constricting, but it would not have mattered if he had worn jogging pants, nothing would have been comfortable, because it wasn't his suit he wanted to get out of – it was his skin.

As they passed the *Welcome to Fayetteville* sign on the brick wall just inside the city line, Brett felt the heat begin to singe his skin. Sweat formed on his forehead and he noticed that his vision began to blur. *Great, another panic attack.*

Clearing his throat, he turned stoically toward Courtney, trying not to spaz out in front of her.

"Can you pull the car over, please?" he asked in a monotone voice, holding on to the handle of the door.

Courtney pulled herself from her story, now deep into the plot, and looked over at him. "Baby, are you alright?" she asked, brow furrowed.

His voice was strained. "Pull the car over," Brett said, eyes bloodshot red, his mouth beginning to water.

She quickly pulled off the road onto the shoulder, and Brett let himself out. Forgetting his crutches, he threw his legs out the door and yanked himself out of the car in just time enough to throw up on the ground. It was a violent eruption that made his back spasm.

"Mommy, is Daddy okay?" Cameron asked, stirring from his sleep to look out of the window at his father.

"He's fine, baby. His stomach is just upset." Courtney popped the seatbelt and opened the door. Waiting on a car to pass, she closed the door and then made her way to the other side where Brett was bent over.

"Oh, God," she said, under her breath. She hadn't realized how hard this was going to be for him until now. She wondered if he'd make it through this.

Rubbing his back, she gently wiped his face with her other hand.

"I'm okay," he said, feeling the coolness of her skin against his own. He held her hand on his face for a moment, thankful again to have her but still utterly embarrassed by his episode.

The way that he looked up at her, vulnerable and hurting, broke her heart. She wanted at that moment to pick him up and hold him, but she was just a little woman and he was so big. Bigger than life...only he didn't even know it.

Brett quickly regained his composure when he saw the rush of emotion over Courtney's face. He had scared her. He didn't mean to do that. He didn't mean to do *any* of it. It was just hard these days to keep as cool as he wanted. Sometimes, like now, things bubble to the surface despite his most eager attempts.

Courtney wasn't quite sure what to say. She knelt beside him over his vomit in silence as cars zipped past them on the road, nearly blowing up her dress. Helping him up, when he was able to stand, she wiped off his uniform, catching a glimpse of a store in the distance. "We can stop at the gas station. I'll get you cleaned up."

Brett nodded.  That was probably best. "Thanks."

She almost said something to give him encouragement – almost - but she decided not to say another word on the matter.  Sometimes, a man just needed to be left alone, or at least that was what her mother had told her about her father.  This was one of those times she would use her mother's advice.  She could see it in Brett's eyes.  He didn't need to open up right now and pour out all of his emotions the way that he had just released his breakfast.  He needed to hold it down and make it through today without breaking.

***

Only a few people were at Faith Tabernacle Church when Brett, Courtney and the children arrived, but they were all workers getting the Church ready for the larger crowd.  Parking in a spot near the entrance of the Church a few spaces down from the hearse, Brett and Courtney quietly unloaded their family and made their way up the steps and through large white double doors.

The large Church was completely empty inside except for the casket, draped in United

States Flag, at the very front under a large cross draped in purple fabric.

Courtney swallowed hard as she saw it. There was Joe, finally, back with Brett.   The doors of the church closed, echoing throughout the sanctuary and somehow adding more weight to an already heavy situation.

Brett locked eyes on his best friend's casket and took off his cover.  His eyes blinked fast.  "I guess that's him," he said, clenching his jaw tight.

Courtney looked down at Cameron and smiled. "Why don't you help me with Bella? We'll get a seat since no one is here yet."  She bounced the little girl on her hip, grateful that Bella was so quiet.

"Why are we so early?" Cameron asked innocently.  He looked around the Church in awe. He had never been to one so big.

Brett rubbed Cameron's mop of freshly cut curls and smiled at the boy.  "Daddy wanted to have some time to say goodbye to his friend."

They walked slowly down the middle aisle carpeted with a purple stripe that led down past wooden pews to the pulpit. Brett never took his eyes off the casket. Slowly his made his way with his crutches until Courtney veered off to take a seat with the kids.

He made the rest of the walk toward the casket alone.

With every step, he could feel the tears streaming down his face. His breathing became more erratic, catching every once in a while in his dry throat. His vision was clouded by huge tears holding on to the ends of his long eyelashes but he continued his walk until he finally made it to his destination. He stood there in silence for a minute looking at the box like at any moment it would spring open and Joe would pop out and surprise him.

But there would be no such joke today.

Tight-fisted, even with all the pain radiating throughout his body – most of it caused by the emotional anxiety he felt inside – when he arrived at the casket, he dropped his crutches and stood up as straight as an arrow.

Looking straight forward as if addressing an officer with a face of stone, Brett whispered, "It was my truest honor...to serve at your side."

Raising his right gloved hand slowly from his side with careful precision, he saluted his friend.

Courtney watched her husband with tears running down her face. Wiping them as they washed over her cheeks, she looked over at Cameron, who without explanation stood up from the pew and walked toward his father.

"Cameron," Courtney whispered.

But Cameron did not turn around. His little footsteps were so light until Brett did not hear them, but when he looked down to his left side, there his son was, standing as straight as a little Marine with tears running down his red little cheeks. Mimicking his father, he stood stiff as a board and saluted Joe, just like his father.

\*\*\*

After a very emotional Church service, six white-gloved hands gripped the flag-draped casket with the bursting white stars over the left shoulder, bearing one of their own. With ramrod posture and synchronized steps, the Marine Corps Body Bearers ceremoniously carried Staff Sergeant Joe Mabry to his final resting place.

Only a few steps back, Brett walked with tears in his eyes with his wife and children, recounting the service quietly. He had been a few pews back from Judy and the family during the entire ceremony, but she had not looked back once. Instead, she hung her head and dabbed her face with a handkerchief, sobbing quietly throughout the ceremony and staring at the box in which her husband had been laid to rest.

Suddenly, Brett understood why she didn't want to see anyone. While it was hitting him hard, it was hitting her so much harder. She looked thinner, gaunt even. When he caught a glimpse of her face, he saw dark circles under her eyes, more apparent since she had cried her makeup off. Her face had aged since he last saw her, probably aged in two weeks, and she looked as though at any moment, she might just keel over.

He felt bad for being so angry that she didn't want to see him, but he knew that he would never tell her so. He'd never do anything in the world to make that woman any unhappier than she already was. *Joe wouldn't have liked that.*

However, Judy hadn't been the only tearful one. Brett had not cried so much in his entire adult life – not for anything, not for any reason. When his mother passed, he was happy that she was done with her suffering. Cancer had nearly eaten her down to the bone. When Amy died, he shed a few tears but was consumed with pure rage. When he was nearly killed, he didn't recall crying for himself, but he did cry at the thought of finally being home. But this was different.

This was sorrow.

He had nearly fainted as he stood before the congregation to give tribute to his friends. The bright lights glared down on him making him sweat. The sanctuary was packed with people all focused on his every word, despite his hatred for being the center of attention. And at the start, despite his booming Texas baritone, his words had been soft, almost faint.

"There are few men in this world that I consider to be my friends," he said, looking out at Gavin, David and Jeffery.

"But I was blessed to call Joe Mabry my friend. He was a great Marine and an even better father and husband. He showed me how to be a better man, because he was *the* better man."

The tears had nearly drowned him as he tried to smile. He could see Courtney, wiping her face, and nodding at him, encouraging him to continue.

"What we do out there in this world for our country is personal. The medals are appreciated, but that's not why we do it. We do it because we love our country, and we love our family and our way of life. And we'd do anything to protect it. Joe died protecting that ideal and there is no medal that will take away the pain of his sacrifice."

His head dropped.

"For that, I am truly sorry. But we shouldn't remember him as just a patriot. We shouldn't remember him just as a fine Marine. We should remember him as a man who was always trying to be better for his men, for his family, for his country and for God. I think he will be welcomed in the Kingdom of Heaven. I think that the angels will rejoice in his arrival, and in that, in time we too can rejoice at having known him at all. But for now what gives me solace is the fact that he will be missed and remembered and immortalized by his actions and his legacy."

There was more to say, but Brett could not continue. So he nodded towards Joe's widow and simply said, "We love you, Judy. We'll always be there for you. Always."

It had been a struggle to leave that podium because the weight of his convictions and the overwhelming sorrow made it hard to move. But he had pushed past it, just to be strong long enough to get back to his seat. There he had collapsed.

With each memory shared and scripture read, it became more and more apparent that he'd never see his best friend again. He'd never pop open a beer and kick his heels up with him under the North Carolina sun. He'd never complain with him about humping until they were chaffed. He'd never confide in him again and expect some sort of answer. *And that was the hardest part.* Joe had been his compass in many ways.  He had been his big brother, his non-judgmental family.

Up until this point, Brett had avoided the reality that Joe was dead.  Up until the moment that he was forced to stand at the casket, he had been able to push what had happened out of his mind as though it never was.  But there were no more blinders to pull down and no more lies to tell himself.  Joe Mabry was dead.  And somehow, he had to push on.  Life was cruel that way.  In one hand, you were given so many blessing that you could not count them all.  And on the other hand, you were given so much pain that you couldn't carry it.

As he thought about that unfair equation with a certain amount of raw unadulterated cynicism, a strange voice whispered to him. "Give the other hand to God.  Let Him carry your burdens." It wasn't exactly something that Brett would have thought or even said and at that moment, he wondered if Joe wasn't somewhere looking over him, assigned to be his unfortunate guardian angel.

At the burial site, a long processional of people walked through the cemetery to the family plot, holding on to each other and still sobbing. Light rain fell, cooling the hot day and showering the inconsolable.  But Brett was grateful for the rain. The drops of water hid his unrelenting stream of tears, but they did not hide his blood-shot eyes or his inability to control his quivering lips. It did nothing to hide his shame and guilt or the agonizing pain swelling inside of him. But in the smallest of ways, it provided comfort.

*I want closure,* he thought to himself. *I can't live like this forever.* His chest was tight with angst and the more that he tried not to sob outright, the more it hurt inside. But how could he let it go? When? *When could he let it go?*

Standing behind his wife and kids who sat in the back of the group at the gravesite, he watched as the body bearers stood perfectly still, holding the flag taut above the casket while the Chaplain spoke.

In synchronized precision the Honor Guard lifted their rifles, and fired off a three-volley-salute, each one jolting everyone there, ceremoniously indicating the dead had been properly cleared and cared for.

As the sound of Taps was belted out by a talented bugle player, Brett lowered his head, rain falling from his beautiful lips.

*This is it,* he thought.

Then silently they began to fold the crisp, beautiful American flag. Their slow, deliberate motion magnified the honor and appreciation reflected in this final act for Joe Mabry and his tremendous service and sacrifice.

With the folding of the flag, Brett tried to release it. *It was now or never.* Perfectly still, he gritted his teeth and balled up his fist and commanded the sorrow to leave him. *Get out!* He screamed in his mind. Like a mist emanating from deep inside, his energy began to physically pulse through his body. He closed his eyes in the rain, pushed out the tears and quietly screamed until there was nothing left. It was such a physically exhausting and a completely unexplainable action that it left him trembling. But somehow, he just knew he had to let it go. He had to get it out. He had to reach down and pull it from the depths of his soul so it wouldn't ache anymore.

And so, he did.

When he opened his eyes, he hadn't realized that the crowd was dispersing or that his wife and children were standing and looking bemused at him or that his brother-in-law was being held by his father over near the trees where hardly anyone could see. In fact, he wasn't sure how long he had stood there at all. It was as if the world had stopped moving.

All he did know was that *it* was finally gone.

\*\*\*

The repast couldn't be held at Judy's home because the crowd was much too large, so the local community center had opened up its doors and the VFW was catering a world-class BBQ in Joe's honor.

The somber mood had quickly given way to happiness.  People were laughing hugging, talking, eating, and moving on with their lives a little at a time.  And the sun had actually broken from behind the clouds and was shining brighter than ever.

As Courtney fixed the kids a plate at the buffet in the middle of the gym floor, she spotted Judy over in the corner near the pushed back bleachers, wiping food from one of her kids' face. Putting down her plate, she made her way over to her.

"Hey," Courtney said, trying to smile.

Judy looked up, her brown eyes still blood red, and gave a weak smile. "Hey girl," she said, voice hoarse, probably from crying.

Courtney quickly went to her and hugged her. "It's so good to see you."

"You too," Judy said hugging her back.  As Courtney finally released her from a hurt-locker of a hug, Judy patted her daughter before she ran off to play with the other kids.  Judy shrugged. "Normally, I'd check her manners for not speaking to you." She chuckled. "Just not in the mood today. I'll get her later."

Courtney was glad to hear a little banter. "Kids will be kids. Let her slide this time."

"Did you enjoy the service?" Judy asked.

"It was really amazing," Courtney said.

"Well, I thought so too. Momma put everything together with my meddling aunt. Normally, they would make a mess of whatever they touched, but they did a really good job for Joe." Judy smacked her lips and moved past the moment. "How's Brett?"

Courtney frowned a little. "He wants to see you so bad." She knew that she might be overstepping, but what were good wives for, if not to overstep?

Judy ran a nervous hand over her limp, damp hair. "I know. I feel horrible about not seeing him. I just..." Tears started to well up at the corner of her eyes again. "I've just been a damn mess." She confessed. "I lost 15 pounds. Couldn't have done it on purpose if I tried." Smoothing her hands over her simple black dress, she tried to find a positive to dwell on.

"I told him you were just going through it. He thinks you..." Courtney bit her lip. Should she say this? Now? "He thinks you might blame him. Hell, I think he blames himself."

Judy's face was suddenly frowning. "Why would he think that?"

"Guilt," Courtney said with a huff. She looked behind her to make sure that he was not anywhere around. If he had known what she was doing right now, he would have killed her. "He has been weird to say the least, since he came back. I can't make heads or tails of what he's even thinking most of the time, but I do know that he feels guilty, even if he doesn't say it."

Judy shook her head. She wasn't surprised. "Why do men always think everything is about them?"

Courtney laughed. "Because they're idiots."

"Big ones," Judy said, a little more upbeat. She put her hand on her hip. "Well, where is he? I'm going to set him straight right now."

Courtney knew that she was doing her a big favor, after all, she was at her husband's repast playing Dr. Phil. Grateful, Courtney wrapped her arms around her and hugged her tight. "Thank you for this."

Judy held her. "I love you guys. You're my family. I...I just need some time." As Courtney pulled away finally, she huffed. "I promise, once I get myself together, I'll be around more."

"I'm going to hold you to that," Courtney said, wiping tears. "I miss you being around."

"Miss you too, girl." Judy saw Brett on the other side of the room. "Tell him to meet me in that little side room. I'll wait on him. We can talk without the ambiance of a professional basketball game."

"Yeah, it is loud in here." Courtney looked around at all the people who had come out. "Joe was a loveable guy."

"Yes, he was," she said, picking up her purse from the chair beside her. "Go tell him. I'll go on in."

Courtney couldn't make her feet move fast enough. There was a crowd of people between her and Brett, and she damn near dove over the top of them like a running back driving the ball for a fourth quarter touchdown to win the game.

"Excuse me," she said, moving through the crowd. "Coming through!" she said louder as she finally shoved past a group of laughing Marines to get to Brett.

Brett raised a brow as he saw her approaching. "What's got your panties in a bunch?" he asked, shoving a chicken tender into his mouth.

"Judy wants to talk to you," she said, a little out of breath. Wiping her brow, she realized that she had broken a sweat.

Brett's face dropped. "She wants to talk to me now?" he asked.

"Now," she said, a little pushy. She nudged him and pointed toward the small breakout room across the gym. "She's in there waiting for you *alone*."

Brett put the food down. Taking a deep breath, he glared at his wife. "She mad?"

Courtney gave an incredulous stare. "No." She pushed him again. "Go."

"Alright, alright," he said nervously. "I'm going."

***

He could smell Judy's perfume as he entered the room. She had always worn the same perfume, Poison by Dior, for as long as he could remember. Joe used to say that if he smelled that scent, he knew trouble wasn't far behind.

Closing the door behind him, Brett fumbled with his crutches, wanting at that moment to throw them across the room. *Couldn't just one damn thing be simple with these things? Must everything be a fucking hassle?* He caught himself in the middle of going into a rage and turned toward her, forcing himself to smile.

Judy was sitting at a long brown cafeteria-style table, slouched over a little rubbing her feet. She looked up at him and smiled.

"My damn feet are killing me. Momma bought me these new shoes, and they have hurt since about 30 minutes after I put them on. You know I don't like anything but my Crocs."

"Get over here," Brett said, opening his arms.

Standing up, she walked over to him barefoot and gave him a hug.

Brett held on a lot longer than he normally did. "It's so good to see you," he said sincerely.

She patted his back. "It's good to see you." And she meant it. Rubbing her small hand over his face, she looked at the bruises. "You're healing up nice." She wiped a tear. *Damn it,* she had promised herself that she wasn't going to do that when she saw him. "How are you?"

"I can't complain," he said, knowing damn well that that was all he ever did.

"Let's just get down to the brass tacks of it, Marine," Judy said in her North Carolina Southern twang. "Courtney says that you've got an idea of why I didn't want you to come around. And from what she tells me, it's utter bullshit."

Brett couldn't help but laugh. What did he expect from Judy Mabry but brutal honesty? "Eight months in the country made me almost forget what a potty mouth you have." He shook his head.

"Well," Judy said, ignoring his sudden attempt to divert. "Is that what you really thought? That I didn't want to see you because I was mad at you or blaming you?" Her hands were on her hips now as she prepared to give him a good *talking to*.

Brett's head dropped. "I should have been over there, Judy."

Judy curled up her lips. "So what? Courtney could be in the same place I am? And what would that have helped?"

"If I had been there, I could have done something."

Her head snapped. "Yeah, you could have died. *You would have.* My husband was a better Marine than you, Brett," she said in a matter-of-fact tone. "If he got killed, then you didn't have a chance."

Brett was flabbergasted. The look on Judy's face was priceless. She was sure of what she was saying, and there was nothing that he could have said to the contrary that would have changed her mind.

"He got shot trying to save me," Brett said seriously. "Did he tell you that? Did anyone tell you if I hadn't gotten shot, we would have been at full complement?"

"He got *grazed*," Judy said, lips tight. "I talked to him a few days after. He was fine and if he weren't, they would have never released him to go back under the wire." She led him over to the table to take a seat. Taking a deep breath, she put her hand on his chest. "I know that you've always been the type of man who thinks that you're in control of the universe, but you're not. You're not that special, baby. You're a man just like every other."

Brett tried to smile but it quickly turned into tears. He shook his head and dipped it toward her as his words turned sour on his lips. "I love you, and I can't pretend that this isn't my fault. I'm trying to live with it. I really am. I'm trying to accept it." He clenched his jaw. "But I won't deny it, because that ain't right."

Judy slipped her hands around his face. Looking deep into his beautiful blue eyes, she pushed down tears in gulps of breath. "God decides. Not you." She shook her head as though she had told herself this before a thousand times in the last two weeks. "Not you." Her thin lips quivered. "Joe loved you. He would be so happy to know that you're still here."

Brett put his hand on hers and sank into her. "I don't know how strong of a man I'll be without him. I know it sounds pitiful, but it's the truth.

He was all the family I had outside of you and the kids."

"Well, you're going to have to be stronger than you were, *is all*." Judy wiped his tears. "He always believed in you, Brett. He told me that he was on a personal mission to bring you closer to God."

Brett laughed. "Yeah, I know."

"Did he fail?" Judy asked seriously.

Brett moved her hands and looked up at the ceiling of the room, rotating his neck in circles. Finally, he looked at her. "No, he didn't fail," he answered honestly.

That made Judy happy. "I've got some healing to do, but when I come around, *and I will*, I want to be able to call you and come visit without feeling like I'm going to visit *Club Doom*. If I can make it through this, so can you. I mean, you got that beautiful woman out there and your new beautiful baby girl and Cameron..." She smacked her lips. "Well, honey, God must have something else for you to do on this Earth."

Brett rubbed a hand over his head. "I love them so much." He wanted to tell her everything, tell her how he'd come into some money and now Amy's past was haunting him, but there was no way he would burden her with his problems. He simply shook his head. "You're right."

Judy didn't need confirmation. She knew that she was right. "Well, if you love them like you say that you do, then you have to follow that up with some action. Get some help. See someone. Talk to someone. Get things in order. *Fight for your family!* Just because you not over there in that wasteland doesn't mean that you don't have to keep fighting."

Brett felt like she could see right through him. He ducked his head again. "I don't really believe that I've been fighting quite enough since I got back. I've been too busy feeling sorry for myself."

Judy reached into her purse and pulled out a handkerchief to wipe her runny nose. "You and me both, kid." She pushed out a breath and sat up a little taller. "But I think it's high time that now that we've thrown our pity parties, we get back to living. Joe would have wanted that, and whether we admit it or not, we need it."

Brett offered his hand. "No more pity party?"

Judy shook his hand. "No more pity party." She smiled. "You know; I think this was just what I needed." She nodded. "I do." Looking around the room, she smiled like she had just had an epiphany. "This is the first time since those Marines showed up at my front door that I've felt like a real human being. Thank you."

"For what?" Brett asked genuinely confused. How in the hell had he helped?

"For being a bigger pussy than me," Judy said with a wink.

Brett couldn't help but laugh. "I can't believe you go to Church every Sunday with that mouth."

"Well, God knows that I ain't no Saint, but He loves me anyway." She stood up and picked up her shoes. "I'm done wearing these. The guests will just have to excuse me."

"Oh, I think you'll get a pass as long as it doesn't start smelling like corn chips in the gym," Brett joked.

She helped him up and passed him his crutches. "I'm glad that you're my friend, Brett," she said as they walked beside each other to the door.

"I'm glad that you're my friend, Judy," Brett said, looking over at her. He thought it was funny that God would send such an unlikely messenger. Ironically, the person who gave him everything back today was the person who had lost the most.

# Chapter 19

*"A man's wife has more power over him than the state has."*
        *~Ralph Waldo Emerson, Journals*

On the way home from the funeral, Brett had more clarity than he had since this entire situation began. In truth, the closure that he desperately needed, he had received and now he felt dramatically liberated. And while it was sidebar from his original intention on seeing her, during their conversation Judy had been right. He needed to fight back; he needed to fight harder. And he intended to do just that, starting now.

Something had been bothering him for the last few days. It had festered like salt in an open wound, picking at his pride and silently putting his manhood into question. If he was going to start to fix things in his life, he had to start there. He knew that now. Of course, his wife's little voice of reason had crept into his mind trying to stifle the Alpha in him with sensibility, but he knew that if he let this infraction slide, then it would only happen again. And it would be his fault.

When a person allows someone to disrespect them once, they are both put at an awkward crossroad. The person who had presented
the insult is put into a position of control and
power, and the person who received the insult is
put into a position of submission. But if there is
ever a chance to reverse the roles and to reclaim
the pride lost, then it must happen before the
two people can move forward. Or at least, that
was how he had always lived his life.

Now he had to reverse the roles, and he had
to let the person responsible for the insult know
that he had changed them.

Glancing behind him, he saw both children
were asleep again, exhausted from a long day of
sitting, standing, rain, sun and excitement. He
wasn't far behind them in the exhaustion department, but before he left Fayetteville, he had
one final thing to check off his list.

"Hey baby," Brett said, putting his hand on
Courtney's leg.

"Yeah," she said, keeping her eyes on the
road.

"Do me a favor?"

"Anything," she said with a gentle smile, clueless to what he was about to ask.

"Stop by Sharon Riley's place. The kids are
asleep. They won't even know that we were

there. It'll only take a minute. I'll make it quick."
He knew before he even asked that Cameron
would be her main concern. Courtney didn't
want their son anywhere around those people
and he didn't blame her. But today, she'd have to
make an exception.

Courtney's hands gripped the steering wheel
tighter as her heart lurched. "Why do you want
to go there?"

Brett sucked his teeth. "I need to talk to them
face-to-face."

Smelling trouble in his seemingly innocent
request, Courtney scratched her brow in contemplation of how this could play out. *Jail.
Hospital. The news.* Definitely something that
involved breaking the law. "The lawyer gave very
specific instructions on what we need to do until
the case is complete."

Brett expected her to be the voice of reason,
but today he was determined to get closure with
everyone who owed him. Sharon Riley *owed* him.
"Sometimes it's not about what should happen.
Sometimes it's about what needs to happen."

His response did nothing to quell her reservations. "I told her that if she ever came to my
house, it would be the last house that she ever
visited."

Brett was proud that she had stood up for herself, but that wasn't the point for him. "Did she tell you the same?" he asked, already knowing he was being a smart ass.

"I think it was sort of implied," Courtney said, still refusing to look at him.

"Well, I didn't agree to that."

"It's not that I'm afraid of her. I'm not. I just don't want to do anything that could negatively affect this case." Courtney clarified.

Brett knew she wasn't afraid of Sharon Riley, but that wasn't the point either.

Courtney waited for him to say something in response, but he didn't. He simply looked out of the window and listened to the radio.

They drove for a few more blocks without a word between them. The audiobook rotated to the next CD for the second half of the story, and the sun in the rearview mirror slowly began to set.

Quietly, Brett waited for Courtney to accept what he needed to do and Courtney tried to figure out how to beg him not to do this.

But it was apparent that they were at an impasse.

Finally, she turned on her left blinker, made a U-Turn and headed in the direction of the Riley's home. Her body language said that she didn't approve, but she was done telling him what to do. Pushing her foot down on the accelerator, she huffed. It was better that if they just hurry up and get this done and over with.

Brett looked over at her with her beautiful brown face turned down in displeasure and found her anger to be utterly adorable. He loved that she was such a team player, even when she didn't want to be. The soft curves of her lips were poked out and her nostrils slightly flared in agitation. And he was certain that her brain was spinning at 100 miles a minute. He glanced down at the long miles of swan-like elegance of her neck and the small gold necklace dangling just at her throat and felt the need in him began to ignite.

Feeling his grinning stare, she cut her eyes at him. "What?" she asked in a voice filled with faux disgust.

Brett smiled slyly. "Nothing."

*Well that just wasn't good enough for Courtney.* "Had to be something," she prodded.

"I was just thinking that you really are a good woman." His eye twitched. "Maybe too good for me, but I'm not giving you up."

Courtney found that funny. "Defiant until the very end."

"Well, sometimes a man has to recognize when he's lucked out," Brett said, pushing back in his seat and adjusting himself before she even noticed what she was doing to him.

Courtney appreciated the compliment, but there was something else that wouldn't allow her to just leave the subject alone. "Why are you doing this?" she asked, as she drove into the cul-de-sac of the Riley house.

Brett let her pull all the way into the Riley's driveway before he answered. As he opened the door to step out, he paused and glanced over at her. Her hazel eyes were big as melons now, gleaming in confusion and fighting for understanding. "I swore as your husband to never allow anyone to ever hurt you. I promised your father too. Do you remember that?"

Her voice softened. "Yes," she said, lips parted. "Of course I remember that."

Brett reached across the seat and touched her bottom lip with his thumb. Looking at her mouth, he tilted his head. "What kind of man would I be if I didn't keep my promises?"

\*\*\*

Sharon Riley was up to her elbows in folding linen, pulled fresh out of the dryer, when the doorbell rang. Followed by two very hostile knocks on the door, she realized that her husband was waiting on her to get it. *Typical.* Throwing down the Egyptian cotton sheets in a pile on the guest bed, she made her way down the long corridor of shiny hardwood floors and gold framed mirrors to the front door.

As she got closer to the entrance, she could see a large male's silhouette. Half expecting it to be Leo when she pulled the curtain back to look out, she was surprised to find Brett Black in full dress uniform glaring at her like he wanted to chew off her face. But he always looked like that when he talked to her. Evidently, he didn't like her much.

Opening the large wooden door, she cracked open the wrought-iron door just enough to let in a breeze and stared at him. "Can I help you?" she asked, glasses down on her nose.

Brett nodded. Despite his disdain for the woman, he was still a Southern gentleman at heart and could not begin without greeting her. "Hello Sharon."

"Brett," she snarled, pissed that somewhere between being his ex-mother-in-law and a Southern Baptist Pastor's wife; she still could not get enough respect from him to rate being called *Mrs. Riley*. "What are you doing here?"

*I came here to burn your fucking house down,* he thought to himself. Instead, he smiled. "I came here to say something to you that I couldn't say over the phone."

She brushed a strand of hair from her face with her aged finger and pulled her green cardigan into her chest. "I wasn't aware that you were even in the country," she said, noticing the crutches and his bruised face. *He looked like he had been run over by a train*, she thought, *too bad he couldn't have been hit twice.*

"Good thing that I was...back home, huh? I couldn't imagine that summons coming to my front door without me being there to receive it. You could call that a blessing," Brett quipped. He couldn't help but be an asshole even though he had promised himself he would avoid all theatrics.

Sharon rolled her eyes. Something about him referring to the Bible irked her. "If you say so."

Brett continued with poise. "Is your husband here? I'd like to say what I have to say to both of you."

"Bill!" she screamed out, knowing no matter where her husband was in the house, he could hear her shrill voice. Glancing past Brett, she saw Courtney in the car with the children in the back.

"What is it?" William asked, emerging from his study.

"Brett Black wants to see you. He says that he has something to say to both of us," Sharon said sarcastically. She could hear her husband's large padded footsteps as they approached. Folding her arms across her chest, she waited.

William was just as shocked as Sharon to see Brett in the flesh. It was his understanding that he wouldn't be home for another two weeks to a month, but based upon the way that he looked; he must have been injured in combat and sent home early. *That would definitely be a blow to the case.*

"How can we help you?" William asked all but politely. Without intention, he scanned the man's immaculate dress and the colorful, shiny medals on his uniform gleaming in the fading sunlight. The damn boy looked like new money. *No way he wanted him showing up to court like that.*

Brett was neither tense nor nervous about the confrontation. Gripping the handles of the crutches, he stared them both down. It was amazing that at one point in his life, he actually tried to please these hypocrites. "I'm not a man who believes in bullying women no matter how angry they make me. So I wanted to say this in your presence, Bill. Plus, I don't trust her as far as I can throw her. I don't need her trying to say that I did something to her."

Sharon was instantly offended by his snide remark, but William knew Brett was smart for thinking ahead. *Though he'd never tell him that.*

Brett got on with it. "I'm here for two reasons. First off, you are to *never* call my wife again...for any reason. I know how you people are. I've dealt with you long enough to know that when you call, it's to stir up trouble."

Sharon immediately jumped in. "The only time I call is when I want to see my grandson. I don't bother you people for any other reason," she said, shaking her finger at him.

Brett continued as if Sharon hadn't said a word. "*Like I said*, I won't have you harassing her. And we all know damn well what your problem is. You don't like her because she's a black woman."

Sharon was insistent. "We don't like her because she's trying to keep us from our grandson. He *needs* our influence. He needs to be in the church learning scripture, learning how to live with a decent moral upbringing..."

Brett drove the point home. "Dear God. Thumping that Bible on Sunday morning; burning that cross on Sunday night. Keep your attacks on me, *if that makes you feel good about yourself,* but leave her out of it."

"I resent being associated with the Klan," Sharon said, turning up her nose.

"Well if the sheets fit. Oh, I'm sorry, am I striking a nerve with you. Let me tell you what I resent. I resent the trunk upstairs in your attic with his and her hoodies that says otherwise. So don't you dare talk to me about good moral upbringing," Brett said, condescendingly. He winked at William as he adjusted on his crutches. "Yeah, Amy was a talker when she wanted to be."

"Did you come here just to call us racists, son?" William asked, completely unmoved. "We are God-fearing..."

Brett cut him off. "*Secondly!* This court case is going to end badly. Not for me. For you."

"No one keeps us away from our family," Sharon said, happy with herself about the heartache she had caused him. "It's your fault that it had to go this far."

"No one in their right mind gets in the way of a father and his son," Brett snapped. He swallowed hard causing his Adam's apple to bob. "Once, I loved your daughter, but at some point, I stopped being good enough for her. Between her countless affairs and her decision to run off to Japan and leave me and her toddler son, I think it goes without saying that your kin didn't matter very much to Amy Riley."

He saw their faces change as he confirmed their quiet assumptions. "Her choices killed her, not me. You can accept it, or you can't. I don't' care. Doesn't change it from being the truth. You're supposed to be religious, right? *The wages of sin is death.* Well, it's apparent with the paternity case and all of her other indiscretions with anything that had officer insignia on it, that she was *sinning* more than you or I knew." He wanted to say fucking so bad until he literally had to bit his tongue, but he was going to get through this without losing his honor.

"You expect me to believe that my daughter just up and ran off?" Sharon said, defending her dead child. "Amy loved you, even though no one wanted her to. I told her not to marry you. I told her what would happen. I told her that you would make her miserable."

"Well, how does it feel to be right about something that you can do nothing about. Bravo. You were right. But it's not my fault that you chose to spoil her to the point where she could never appreciate anyone or anything, no matter how hard they tried. For her, it was always getting to the next level, but figuring out a way to do it without having to actually work for anything. Well, I pray to God that she found peace in death because she brought me hell in her life."

"I've heard enough from you," William growled. While he was no stranger to his daughter's antics, he was not about to be raked over the coals by a poor bastard kid from the fields of Texas.

"Have you?" Brett asked, completely unmoved by the old man's warning. Maybe 30 years ago this guy was good with his hands but now as a senior citizen, even with one leg, he'd fuck him up. "I don't think you know the half of it. But you will. I'm glad that this case came up truthfully, because now all of those old skeletons are going to be pulled right out of the closet for the world to see. And everyone will know that your daughter was a whore." There he said it. He finally said it, and it felt good.

"Spoken like a true gentleman," Sharon said, gripping the door handle. "You've always been trash, Brett Black. You always will be. Nigger-loving trash."

William looked away.

Brett stood tall on the one good leg while balancing on his crutches, knowing Sharon was trying to bait him. Only, he was not about to let them win. "You know, it didn't dawn on me until right now, but you're right again, Sharon. I did love a nigger once, but then she packed up all of her shit with her shiftless, lazy worthless ass and went officer hunting across the Pacific. Last I heard, it didn't end well.

"I came to this house to tell you that as a man who has survived five tours to Iraq and Afghanistan, gun shots and near death isn't the type of man who is going to give up on his son because some sperm donor shows up and wants to know if his last deposit landed in between your daughter's legs. If you thought that I was scared, then you thought wrong." Brett clenched his square jaw. "I wanted you to look me in my eyes when I told you that you will lose and when you do, you'll never see Cameron again. Never. Not as long as he lives."

"Pride goes before the fall," Sharon snapped, raising her brow at his leg in a cast. "But I don't have to tell you that, do I?"

William felt that this had gone too far. Lightly squeezing her shoulder, he grabbed the door and looked out to see who was outside. He had to end this conversation immediately, just for face sake. The last thing he needed was the neighbors seeing Sharon berate a wounded Marine in uniform under the United Sates flag mounted on the porch or for the world to hear that his precious daughter was in fact the whore of Babylon.

Brett looked at Sharon and smiled. "You know you all make that face."

"You all - who?" Sharon said, pulling away from her husband. She wasn't going anywhere and she wasn't ending this until she had said what was on her mind to this sniveling piece of shit.

"The enemy," Brett said coolly. "You always make that face when you realize that you're defeated. It's the same face all around the world, not that you've ever been anywhere. You'll just have to take my word for it. Evil is evil. You've just proven that."

"We'll see who has the last laugh, Brett. That boy doesn't belong with you and that woman. He's not yours. You have no right!" She looked so much like her daughter when she got angry with her wicked words and high soprano voice until he felt like Amy had been reincarnated as a 60-year-old woman.

Ending the conversation, he licked his lips. "Stay away from my family, Sharon Riley. And do yourself a favor and actually try practicing some of the things in that Bible. It's a good book. You might want to do more than skim it sometime."

Turning away from them, he headed back down the stairs, one step at a time.

"Don't you dare come to our home again," Sharon yelled as neighbors looked on curiously. "Next time, we will call the cops on you!" William held her back by her narrow shoulders. "I hope you burn in hell!"

Brett didn't answer any of her nasty remarks. He didn't have to. He had gotten under her skin the way that she had gotten under Courtney's. Plus, he had called them on it. And no one liked to be called on their shit.

As the door slammed and William's voice rose at Sharon insisting she stop making a fool of herself, Brett knew that they knew they had lost too. The power shift had begun.

Courtney peered out of the window as he approached the car. "What just happened?" she asked, putting down her cell phone. She had recorded the entire thing, just in case, she needed evidence for the police or her attorney, but she couldn't hear what they were saying until Sharon started cursing at him.

Brett got in the car and closed the door. "That's what you ladies call *closure*."

# Chapter 20

"Ask and it will be given to you; seek and you will find; knock and the door will be opened to you."

- Matthew 7:7 (NIV)

With Al Green playing on the surround sound system piped out on the patio to add a little ambience to the already romantic evening, Mr. Benson slipped a hand behind the woman's back and gripped her waist, pulling her closer to him as they sat on the sectional enjoying the gentle breeze and each other's company. A smile crept across his lips as he nuzzled his nose into her hair and breathed down her neck.

*Thank God for Friday night.* He had been waiting all week for this moment.

Mae was the most beautiful woman he had ever laid eyes on, and he knew that he was damn lucky to actually have her in his life. It was just happenstance that he met her at a reception for the Black Lawyers Association in Raleigh a year ago. He knew then, when he saw her standing at the bar alone, ordering a dirty martini as she flipped her natural hair over her shoulders and

killing that navy blue St. John's dress, she was
going to be trouble for him. He had been right.
After introducing himself, she bought him a
drink, and the rest was history. They had slept
together that same night in his hotel room. The
next morning after room service, he had done
the unthinkable for a playboy like him and asked
her on a second date. She accepted, and he
hadn't slept with another woman since then. On
top of that, she was single like him, divorced
twice just like him and wealthy, just like him.
He couldn't have found a better match if he had
tried. Now, every Friday was reserved just for
them – no kids, no grandkids, and no drama.
She drove down from Raleigh, or he drove up
from Atlantic Beach. It didn't matter as long as
they saw each other. Hadn't missed a Friday in
52 weeks, and they both were firmly against
marriage. Third time wasn't necessarily a charm,
and they were now set in their ways. Why mess
up a good thing?

"Damn, you smell good," he growled, wanting
to take her upstairs to the bedroom right then
and make sweet love to her. She was wearing
that dress tonight and keeping his attention. He
liked a woman with a little meat on her bones
and she made the meat on her bones look delec-
table. Size 14-16, with hips and ass like Pam

Grier, a face like Phylicia Rashad, and a mind like Thurgood Marshall. She was superwoman.

Mae smiled. He was always so frisky after a few glasses of cognac. For him to be such a big muscular man, he couldn't hold his liquor at all. Putting down her drink on the table, she turned to him and wrapped her arms around his neck. Face-to-face, she looked him in his big brown eyes, filled with needy seduction, and kissed him slowly.

His wide-set full mouth tasted like cognac and chocolate and was as soft and lush as any bed of petals she had laid in. *Mmm*, she wanted to lay into his mouth tonight, curl up with his spear-like tongue and let him feast on her body for dinner. Melting into his wide chest, she inhaled the fragrance of his cologne and the warmth coming from under his white Armani button down.

"Come closer," he said, pulling her up onto his lap. Making her straddle him in her red silk dress, he set his legs wide and angled his growing erection to play with the center of her damp panties.

"You are something else with yourself, you know that?" she said, feeling his large hands roam down her back with tender restraint.

"I'm normally a very civilized man, baby girl," he joked. "But you bring the animal out of me. I've been thinking about you all day. Now that I have you here, I'm going to do everything that I've been fantasizing about." With his index finger, he pulled at the spaghetti strap of her dress until it was down on her shoulder, and then gently ran that same finger around the low-cut front of her dress.

"What are you doing?" she asked in a raspy voice.

He looked up at her with a devilish grin, eyes twinkling. "I'm hungry for you," he said, easing one of her breasts out of her dress. His thumb stroked her nipple, creating a flame in her loins.

She moved her hair back, arched her back and allowed him to taste her, slow and sweet. His lips attached to her skin and suckled at her brown nipple while his large hands gripped her buttocks.

Mae bit her lip, breathing erratically as he flicked her nipple with his tongue over and over again until it start to make her sex pulse out of control. "We should take this upstairs," she said, hand on his bald head, guiding him.

"Why not make love right here?" he suggested, kissing a trail from her breast to her neck.

She closed her eyes and swallowed her throat dry now from breathing hard. "Because I'm 47 not 27." she whimpered.  It was funny though, even as she said that, she knew that he made her feel young again.

"I've never seen a 20-something woman look as good as you," he said, hand moving further up her dress. "Besides, it's not like anyone will see."

It was tempting for Mae, but she quickly pushed the idea out of her mind. She was a sitting judge, had been an amazing assistant DA, and a damn good trial lawyer, there was no place in her life for this kind of adventure.  All it would take is one extremely powerful lens in front of one extremely ambitious photographer to put all of her work in jeopardy.

"I spent $4,000,000 on this house for absolute privacy.  Out here on this patio, it's just me, you and the Atlantic Ocean.  No one is going to see. Trust me," he said, sucking on her ear.  Mr. Benson's lengthy erection trailed the inside of his pants leg, pressing against her, changing her mind.

*What was life without adventure?*  Mae thought to herself suddenly.

She planted her hands on his large forearms and looked in his eyes. "Complete privacy?" she asked in a high-pitched tone, feeling him slowly undulate under her.

"No one but you...and me," he whispered, knowing he was close to sealing the deal. A smile quirked at the side of his lips. "You can enjoy the breeze. I can lay you down right here on this sofa, strip you down naked, kiss you from your head to your toes..." His husky voice strained as the need grew stronger. "Trust me. You'll love it. I'll make damn sure of it."

Mae was at her wits end. Just the image of them in a naked embrace in front of the bay made her shiver. In all her years, she had never made love on a patio before, and it hadn't been on her bucket list until now. Her lip twisted up in thought and just as her mouth opened to say yes, his phone rang.

The sound of the phone was like an alarm clock sounding after an hour of sleep. Jolting the both of them, Mae's suddenly curiosity wilted.

Mr. Benson threw his head back, defeated by the untimely and unwelcomed interruption. He knew that no one called him on Friday nights unless it was an emergency. So it more than likely was.

Pulling away from his embrace, she exhaled. "You better get that," Mae said, coming back to her senses. The forces of the universe had decided. *Bedroom it was.*

Mr. Benson looked at her and shook his head. "I was so close, wasn't I?" The phone rang again.

Mae grinned. "You have no idea."

"When I get off this phone, we're going to continue this discussion," he said seriously.

Gently lifting her and setting her beside him on the sofa, he stood up, adjusting his rock-hard erection and disappeared behind the glass pane doors that led into the house, leaving Mae to set her gaze panoramic view of the chartreuse marsh grass and blue-gray water of the coastline and fantasize about what might have happened.

Mr. Benson picked up the phone in the den and instantly recognized the number. He answered it quickly and went into his downstairs study. Closing the door, he huffed. "Boy, I left a message for you two days ago," he said, frustrated. He sat down in the corner in an armchair hanging under a picture of the Omega Psi Phi Fraternity Incorporated founders.

Jermaine was immediately apologetic. "Sorry, Pops." He stepped out into his garage and went to the corner where unopened marked boxes were. "I just got your message. I haven't been home in a couple of days."

Mr. Benson knew that his frustration stemmed from his current situation, so he silently excused the boy. Glancing at the door, he wiped his mouth. *He had been so close.* "You know, I know when you were growing up, things weren't easy between me and your mother. Then after that with Linda but still I thought I taught you better than this? A married woman?"

Jermaine took his knife and opened up the top brown box. The sound of it drowned out his father's voice. "I knew Amy was married, but I didn't know that she had a kid. She completely forgot to mention that," he said in his defense. He avoided discussing his upbringing altogether. It was a moot point anyway. "If she had said that, I would have never offered for her to come here." He opened the box and looked inside.

"How did you think you were going to hide a married woman on a military base in the first place?" Mr. Benson was not impressed, but that was nothing new. Jermaine had gone through more women than he could count over the years.

"I wasn't going to hide her anywhere. She was just going to stay here until she figured out her next move. We weren't shacking up like it sounds. She said that she was leaving her husband. Evidently, he was some grunt who always stayed gone and she had had enough."

"How did you even meet this woman?" Mr. Benson asked.

"I met her in the gym while I was at Camp Lejeune. We worked out together a lot," Jermaine said, forgetting to mention that they also had sex a lot too. Amy was great at sex. So great, until he paid for a $2,000 plane ticket to get more.

Mr. Benson knew better than to think that his son was just being a Good Samaritan. "So you mean to tell me that you all were just friends and you were just helping her out? Is that your story?"

"Something like that," Jermaine said, looking through the contents of the box for the first time.

Mr. Benson pushed back in the seat and huffed. "Come on, son. I wasn't born yesterday."

Jermaine pinched the bridge of his nose. "Ok. I was screwing her." He lowered his voice. "She was...*skilled* and interesting, and I was bored as hell when I first got here. I was going stir crazy."

"You better thank God in Heaven that she didn't make it over there," Mr. Benson said sternly. "This could have been a career killer for you." He knew that his son was brilliant and a part of the new world, but in his old world,

Jermaine was a young Black man who was running off with a married White woman. His chain of command would have crucified him.

Jermaine leaned against the garage wall. "Look, Dad. I'm not alone right now," he said, hearing heels tapping on the hardwood floor of his kitchen and echoing out to the garage.

"Neither am I," Mr. Benson said, smoothing a hand down his shirt. "So, it's safe to say that your dick is inconveniencing both of us."

Jermaine rolled his eyes. "What do you want me to do?"

For Mr. Benson, the answer was simple. "Stop screwing married women," he said abruptly.

"No, Dad. What do you want me to do about this case that you're working on?" Jermaine said, holding up his finger as a Japanese woman stuck her head out of the door and smiled at him. "I'll be just a second. I'm talking to my father," he said, bidding her to go back inside.

Mr. Benson rubbed his temples. This wasn't the time for a long, drawn out conversation. There was no way he was going to keep Mae waiting much longer. "Do you have any communication from this woman still in email form or maybe even text or some of those sex pictures?"

"Dad, the girl died in a plane crash. I didn't keep any sex pics. It would have been too weird." The idea of jerking off to a dead woman made him a little sick. "But I do have six big ass boxes in my garage. I'm looking through them right now."

Mr. Benson frowned. "Boxes?"

"Yeah, when she left Camp Lejeune, she couldn't bring all of her stuff on the plane. It would have cost a fortune. So she sent it ahead through FedEx that morning before she boarded the plane." He scratched his neck. "I never opened them until right now. It wasn't like we were that close. Plus, I didn't want to pry."

"You didn't want to pry?" Mr. Benson asked.

Jermaine shrugged his shoulders. "Yeah, I mean. This was *her* stuff. I felt like I'd be invading the privacy of a dead woman by going through it, but also I didn't want to throw it away. That felt disrespectful. So, I put it out in my garage in the corner with her name on it and just left it."

"I need you to send it back to me," Mr. Benson said a little more urgently.

"Okay. I'll send them Monday," Jerome said, glad to get the deceased woman's belongings out of his hair and the conversation over with.

"No, son. You'll put whatever sweet little ass you have there with you in your car, load up those boxes and send them to me right now. It's Saturday morning over there. You don't have anywhere to be."

Jermaine didn't push it. "Okay," he huffed. That totally messed up his plans but there was no way that he was going to defy his father. "Anything else?"

"No," Mr. Benson said. "Normally, I'd want sworn testimony from the lover about what happened, but you are my son. This would taint your career. So, do yourself a favor. First, use a condom...always...even five minutes from now when you get off the phone and go back to whoever is crazy enough to be waiting on you. Second, don't ever sleep with a married woman for any reason. Third, don't ever call me on a Friday night again unless you're near death."

"Understood," Jermaine said, throwing Amy's diary back in the box. "I really didn't know she had a kid."

"Yeah, well, you'll find married women don't exactly tell their lovers everything," Mr. Benson said, standing up. "Good night."

"Night," Jermaine said, hanging up the phone.

# Chapter 21

**"Everything that is hidden will be brought into the light. Everything that is a secret will be made known."   Mark 4:22 (NLV)**

Although the military was vast and its personnel numbered nearly 2,000,000, it hadn't taken much time for Gavin to pull up dirt on Leo Tabor.  In a town as small as Jacksonville, Marines and Navy men not only worked together, they lived among each other, which meant there was a steady flow of gossip.  This came in handy when conducting an unofficial investigation on one of their own.  After a few calls to a couple of Navy men who owed him favors and a few more calls by his team on the West Coast to Annapolis, Gavin had found out everything he could about the man who would be "father."

None of the information that had come back on Leo was favorable, especially in a court of law.  According to records, he was released on an *Other Than Honorable* discharge from the Navy about eight months ago.  But that wasn't the juicy part.  According to another officer who used to work with Leo, he received the discharge for screwing his commanding officer's wife. The relationship had gone on for about six months without being detected by anyone, but the two got sloppy and were caught by accident at a party given by the Admiral, screwing near the 16th hole on the golf course.

Leo had tried to bribe his way out of being turned in by the MPs who found them and would have been let go on a warning, but then one of the guys recognized the woman.

News of the affair traveled fast, and the Navy Command had to act fast to rid themselves of the shame. Lieutenant Commander Leo Tabor was removed from his post at Camp Lejeune's Field Medical Training Battalion and thrown out on his ass by the Navy.

No surprise that divorce papers followed shortly after. Evidently, the ex-wife had been the big bread winner. So proof of his infidelity had cost him his wife, his home and his piggy bank. With no other experience outside of the military in the medical field and no willingness to return as a failure to the upper East Coast blue blood family of doctors who raised him, he had settled down in Wilmington, NC and was living as a reject. Word on the street was that he spent his time at a high-end strip club, pimping out some dancer that he lived with and pretending to be some veteran combat bad ass, when in fact, he had been a dentist by trade.

So the question Gavin couldn't answer was why did Leo want Cameron now after all of this time? Surely he had known about the boy since his birth, maybe even since his conception. However, he had never been in the boy's life. Nothing about his profile said that he cared about being a family man, especially since he didn't see the young daughters he fathered with his ex-wife, who was a lawyer in Wilmington and a partner at a small, family-owned law firm.

Gavin knew it had to be about money. Only Amy didn't have any, and if she did, it would have gone to Brett upon her death. So what was the angle? His investigation had led him to ground zero.

Stepping out of his new car in a pair of well-worn jeans, a gray t-shirt and a Cardinals baseball camp, Gavin passed the keys to the young valet and walked into the lit up front entrance of The Hellhound Strip Club. It was packed to capacity on a Saturday night. The hostess up front greeted him and asked him to take off his hat, but after slipping her a $100 bill, she let him pass.

Music boomed in his ears. Strobe lights danced across the main stage. Drunken men in huddles laughed and drank, while watching the women dance. Women in short skirts and tied up tank tops carried drinks around on trays through the crowds while others danced nearly naked on the poles strategically placed around the building. It was definitely a mad house tonight, perfect for reconnaissance. Glad that he had gotten his PTSD under control before he took this job, he calmly strode through the hordes of people. This shit would have normally made him insane. But he had learned to deal when he had to. Tonight, he had to.

With the photo of Leo memorized, he made his way to the bar in the back, the best vantage point to scan the room, and took a seat. As soon as he did, he caught the attention of Daisy. She had her eyes locked on the six-foot four giant with the Superman smile. Quickly pouring six shots of vodka, she pushed them to the edge of the bar and took a wad of money from a young college boy who was so drunk, he looked like he was going to pass out at any moment. His friends, however, weren't the least bit more sober.

Screaming above the music, she made a motion with her hand under her neck. "I'm going to have to cut you off after this," she said, irritated by having to tend to them for several hours.

College guys were the worst when they were drunk and horny. She had been hit on like a hundred times by them, each time turning them down with a special little fuck-you face that she had adopted only after starting to work here.

"Cut me off for what? I don't even have a buzz yet," the young college guy lied as his friends laughed and bunched around him. They all gawked at her like she was a piece of fresh meat.

"Oh, you've got a buzz," she said, rolling her eyes. Pausing as she counted the money, she looked up at him after realizing he had left a very large tip.

The patron smiled sheepishly. He knew that would get her attention. "Just keep them coming, Daisy, and we'll keep taking care of you."

Daisy needed that tip. Tuition was coming due and rent. And if more tips came from where that last tip came from, then all she had to do was make sure that someone who was less drunk was going to drive the little asshole home.

"Just…" She clenched the money in her hand and denied herself the feelings of guilt or responsibility. "Just slow it down a little okay." She looked around to make sure that no one of importance heard her. She could get yanked for over-serving this little shit, but her boss had never called her on it before. All he cared about was how much money she made at the end of the night.

The patron winked at her. "*Slowing* it down," he said, picking up the shot and downing it as quickly as he could. Hitting the table, he screamed out. "Bros before hoes!" His friends loudly repeated, holding up their drinks.

She rolled her eyes and walked away.

Walking over to Gavin, she threw her towel over her shoulder and pushed up on the bar in front of him. "First time here?" she asked, voice raised to fight the booming music that tried to drown her out. Her eyes traveled the length of his mountainous frame.

"Is it that obvious?" Gavin asked, giving her his charming smile. He saw her breasts before he saw her face, and getting a closer look, he knew that it was one of her better selling points in this place. "Do I stick out or something?"

"No, I just would have remembered your face," Daisy said, flirting. But he did sort of stick out. It was that masculine sensuality that permeated from him like visible pheromones.

"Really?" Gavin leaned forward too, muscles bulging in his arms as he did. His tattoos immediately caught her attention. After working here for a while, she knew military tats when she saw them.  His looked bad ass.  That only made the tall man sexier.

"Marine?" she asked.  "Camp Lejeune?"

Gavin frowned.  "I get that all the time. No, I'm actually a priest," he said, seriously.  His eyes glinted with pure sex appeal.

Daisy laughed. "A priest?"

"Yeah," he nodded, licking his deep red lips. "Want to confess something?  You look like you've been a very naughty bartender."  He refused to look at her breasts.  She'd be expecting that. Instead, he kept his gaze at eye level.

Daisy laughed again, turned on by the lusty arrogance of the man.  "Maybe I'll confess later, Marine."

Gavin sat back on the bar stool. "So you don't like Marines?"

"I didn't say that."  She wiped off the table. Running a finger behind her ear to push her hair out of the way, she grinned at him.  "What are you having tonight?"

Gavin scanned the bottles behind her on the bar.  "How about a shot of scotch."  He watched her as she reached for the shot glasses. *Nice ass*. A bit young for him though.  He liked his women a little more experienced than his kid sister.

She came back and poured the shot.  "This one's on me."  Smiling as she walked away, she helped another patron. Standing there with him gazing at her was starting to make her suddenly self-aware.

Gavin knew that he was in. Tomorrow when he showed up again, *if he had to*, it would be obvious that he was interested in her and not so obvious that he was actually looking for Leo.

Just as he downed the shot, he saw Leo come busting out of the bathroom near the back end of the bar and head his way. *Jackpot.* Gavin looked away from Leo quickly and signaled at Daisy for another one. "Hey, sweetheart, can I get another shot?"

"That quick?" she said, bending over behind the bar. She liked that he called her sweetheart. Southern charm always got points in her book. Just maybe, she'd leave him with her number at the end of the night.

"Yeah, I'm going to need another one. Funny thing. I get nervous when I talk to pretty girls," Gavin lied.

Another man approached the bar and was about to sit in the chair beside him, so he quickly pulled it toward him. Giving the guy a look to go away before Leo approached, he held on to the space territorially until Leo approached. "Make this one a double," he said as Leo walked up to the bar. He pushed the stool away from him.

"Anyone sitting here?" Leo asked Gavin, standing behind the stool.

Gavin looked at the chair and shrugged. "No dude. You're good." He turned his attention back to Daisy, making sure to show special interest now.

Leo sat down on the seat and followed Gavin's gaze to the bartender. "She's hot, right?" he said it like he had already had a piece of her.

Gavin shook his head. "Oh yeah. Smoking."

"Yeah, in this club, they all are." Leo tapped the bar. "Hook me up, Daisy," he said, looking over at Gavin's tats. The one that drew the most attention was the jump wings with an elaborate skull and cross KA-BARs. There were only a few men in the world who could boast that tattoo and unless this guy was a poser, he was a part of a very elite group of Marines. "So you're Force Recon, huh?" He wondered if he was sent by Brett Black to spy on him. *Wouldn't surprise him.* Marines stuck together like flies on shit.

Gavin took his eyes off of Daisy nonchalantly, barely glancing Leo's way. "Used to be. Way back. Got put out for a bum leg before most of these boys in here started puberty." He locked eyes on Leo. "You military? Have to be if you recognize the tats." He smacked his lips. "Unless you're a fuck boy. And let me just say, I'm honored, but not interested."

Leo laughed, knowing that the guy was kidding about the gay joke. "Was Navy. I'm out now," Leo said as Daisy came back to pour both of their drinks. She made them quickly and then moved on to another group of men waiting on the other end of the bar.

Gavin gave a bleak pause and cleared his throat. Leaning into Gavin, he narrowed his cold gaze on the man as if he were going to say something very serious. "Hey. Seriously. You think she has a boyfriend? I mean, she's probably got a boyfriend or something right? Girls like that don't normally just stay single a long time." He looked back over at Daisy and shook his head. "I mean, she can't be single."

Leo was thrown off by the stranger's disinterest in him. He didn't even ask about his MOS, which most guys did. He didn't ask if he was an officer, which most people did. He didn't seem to care about him at all. Maybe he was being a bit paranoid. "Not that I know of. Daisy tends to keep to herself."

Gavin knocked down another shot and growled. The spirits burned as they went down his throat. Slamming the shot glass down on the table, he grinned. "Well, I'm definitely interested in her. Just a little hard to get her attention with all these other *fuckers* in here vying for her attention at every turn."

"It's normally a much better atmosphere for talking if you come back during the day. Plus, they have a buffet," Leo said, relaxing his shoulders. Casually, he sipped his drink and watched as his girlfriend came out on stage.

"Well then, I'll come back again tomorrow," Gavin said following Leo's stare to the main stage.

The DJ reminded the crowd to tip their waitresses before he went into the spiel about the next dancer. Her short, energetic intro made her sound like she was going to come out on the stage to perform a heart transplant.

The blonde busty woman pranced out on stage in gold high heels and a gold metallic T-strap bodysuit. Wiping the pole with a towel before she began, she bent over with her rear end facing the audience and dropped to the floor in a split as her song began.

"Damn," Gavin said, loud enough to get Leo's attention. "Who the fuck is that?" His faux interest came across genuine, but in truth, she wasn't his type. He didn't really do blow up dolls.

Leo felt a tinge of pride by the man's reaction. "That's Amber."

"Does *Amber* have a fucking boyfriend," Gavin asked with a chuckle. "Shit, I'd like to power drive that."

"She's got a boyfriend, alright," Leo said, smiling at Gavin. "And to power drive that pussy will cost you more than a Marine's salary." Just in case Gavin was a cop, he added a little something extra. "Trust me. I know. She's breaking my bank."

"You're the *boyfriend*?" Gavin asked, seeming surprised. He bucked his eyes. "Damn dude."

"I'm the boyfriend," Leo confirmed. He pulled at his perfectly slashed nose as he inhaled and rose up on his seat. His eyes watered. "Trust me. That is grade A ass. She does everything too. *Everything*." His brow rose suggestively.

It was then, as Leo's eyes appeared dilated, that Gavin realized that the Navy boy might also have a little nose candy problem. Taking it down a notch, he threw up his hands. "Hey, man. I ain't got that kind of money. Upscale escorts? Shit, I blew most of my stash on an eight ball before I got here." He watched Leo's face. Would he be shocked by the omission of drug use or interested in partaking?

Leo's smile was wide. "Well, trust me. I understand that. Shit, when a man needs a fix," he picked up his glass and saluted Gavin, "he needs a fucking fix."

"Amen to that," Gavin said, giving him a fist bump. *Great,* now he'd have to figure out how to score some smack just in case this douche bag came asking for some. Inside, he was ready to just follow this Leo character to the bathroom the next time he went and snap his neck in urinal, but he made Brett a promise. No murder. However, he knew some real live dedicated Navy men who might have volunteered to do it. This guy was an embarrassment.

"I think I'm going to like you," Leo said, eyes greedy at the prospect of getting high for free. "What's your name again?"

"Jake," Gavin said, offering his head. He was certain the guy would look him up in the upcoming days, but by then, he'd have what he needed, and it would be too late.

"I'm Leo," Leo said, offering his hand. "Nice to meet you. Let's get another drink."

"Now you're talking," Gavin said, hitting the bar with his balled up fist. "Hey, Daisy. Get your pretty ass over here and get us another round!"

***

Mid-afternoon the next day, Gavin rolled over in his hotel bed completely naked with a raging hard-on and an insatiable need to drink a gallon of water. Flashes of the night before flooded his memory. So many shots. So many girls. So much bullshit. Strip clubs were all the same, and so was everyone in them. Everyone was either there to get laid, get paid or get away from someone at home.

While Gavin had not had that many shots since his last night as a Recon Marine many years ago, the key to the previous evening had been all about alcohol. In order to get close to Leo, Gavin had to first get him drunk and loose so he'd be willing to talk more about his private life. That didn't take long.

The next step was to establish his story as a retired Marine with a disgruntled ex-wife and a small son in the nearby area. A few years back, his team had set up a series of private Facebook and Twitter pages that they maintained on weekly basis. They were so detailed with pictures, places and events until anyone who didn't know him intimately would never know that the profile was a fake. After going through picture after picture with Leo of his children, his renovations of his house in Denver and Christmas parties at his job, Leo was not only convinced but tired of delving into Gavin's fake life.

After all, the man was a narcissist. He relished in talking about himself, not learning about others.

About an hour into drinks at the bar, Gavin made a quick run out to the strip club parking lot to score cocaine off a yuppie banker getting ready to get a blow job from one of the dancers in his Porsche. He came back in and went with Leo to the bathroom several times. The greedy fucker was so *geeked* about getting high; he hadn't noticed that he was doing so alone. Sure Gavin pretended, but he had never done drugs a day in his life and didn't plan on breaking his streak for Leo.

Two hours into a full cocaine and booze bender courtesy of Gavin, Leo was his new best friend. He was blabbing like a baby – not about Cameron or Amy – but about his bitchy ex-wife. Gavin made sure to make plenty of mental notes, especially about the woman's name, job, where she lived and what she did in her free time.

On top of that, the sexy little bartender Daisy was eating right out of the palm of his hand bringing him drink after drink and only charging him half, in hopes that he'd come see her again. He flirted with her all night and as the drinks continued to flow, so did the prospect of seeing past her young age.

However, the true wild card had been Amber who came into the mix three hours into the night. After finishing for the night, she came over to the bar in a scantily clad dress and hoe heels and drank with them, shot for shot. Everything about her screamed gold digger from her acrylic nails to her blinding bleach blonde hair and oversized boobs. However, what was most obvious was Leo's ability to control her. It was obvious to Gavin that she was his present meal ticket, but what wasn't obvious was how he planned to ditch her.

At the end of the night, Leo was high as a kite and wanted to keep the party going, especially the coke. So, he invited Gavin over to their condo for a nightcap, but Gavin was a man of habit and preparation. He had prepared for the meeting with Leo. He had used old habits of collecting information on his mark, but he had done all of that because he was in a controlled environment. Leo's house was out of his territory, and based on how Amber was looking at him by the end of the night, he was certain that Leo was prepared to give him that "free taste" he had suggested earlier.

Instead after giving Leo the last of the coke as a parting gift, he headed back to his hotel. After all, he had a camera attached to his baseball cap that had to be downloaded to his computer and sent over to Brett's lawyer, and there were still a few more things that he needed to do before he headed back to Jacksonville.

The door to the bathroom came open and filled the room with steam. Sitting up in the bed, he watched as Daisy came out with her hair wrapped in a towel and her naked body shimmering with water. She was beautiful naked. Young and flawless, her natural curves looked even better when he wasn't drunk. She kept a little brunette patch of hair on the landing strip between her legs nearly hidden by wide hips. Her large breasts bobbed as she walked and her back naturally arched in before leading out to a wide full ass.

Gavin had enjoyed her last night, all of her, several times. It was evident by his hand print still stamped on her left buttock. But that was nothing in comparison to the scratches he still felt down his back. Showering later would be a bitch.

She stopped in her tracks when she saw him. His brown eyes were locked on her like a predator on his prey. Sandy brown hair sat atop his head all disheveled and his tan long body rippled with taut muscle basking in the sunlight coming from the window. With a knowing smile, she pulled the towel off of her damp hair and threw it in the corner. "You're awake," she said, walking over to the chair to retrieve her clothes.

"Yeah," Gavin said, wiping a hand over his face. "I didn't realize that I'd slept so late." He looked at his watch on his wrist and realized he had missed check out. Not to mention, if he didn't get a move on, he'd miss his other appointment in less than an hour.

Daisy eyed his erection with new interest. "Well, it was a long night." Her insinuation was more so about their time together after they arrived back from the hotel. He had fucked her mercilessly, something she hadn't been prepared for even as he entered her.

"Too long," Gavin said gruffly of Leo. He hadn't realized her meaning or that he had offended her with his statement.

Daisy sighed to herself. Last night he had been charming but today he seemed like a different man. The lust had gone from his eyes and his demeanor had changed. As a sheer defense mechanism, her attitude instantly hardened as she realized what was going on. She had just been a booty call and now it was time for her to go. "It's 12:30. I have to head back to the bar and get ready for the night. So, I'll be out of your hair in a minute." Without meaning to, her attention focused on his prosthetic leg. Turning uncomfortably away, she slipped her black tank top over her head and pulled it down over her breasts.

Gavin looked at his leg and frowned. "Sorry that I didn't mention my leg before." He pushed to the end of the bed and stood up. Stretching his arms out, he popped his neck.

"It's okay," Daisy said quickly.

*But it wasn't.* In truth, seeing the prosthetics he got out of his clothes the night before had scared her but not nearly as much as the two Glocks on the nightstand or the two laptops on the desk. She got the feeling that maybe this guy wasn't who he said he was. *Computer techs didn't carry guns.* Still, despite her reservations, she had slept with him. And that had been her fault.

Gavin walked over to her and wrapped his arms around her waist. His hard body pushed up against her igniting heated arousal. His heart beat against her back, letting her know that whatever he wasn't, he was at least human.

"You don't have to lie about the leg. I'm used to it, so I tend to forget," he said, kissing her shoulder. He looked at her through the reflection of the mirror in front of them. His brown eyes seared through her reservations about having sex with him again. "I should have said something to you beforehand. I'm sure it took you by surprise."

Daisy blinked hard. His voice vibrating against her turned her on more than she cared to say and his hands on her skin clouded all sensibility. She moved her neck for him to kiss her again. He did so immediately. Slowly, he kissed her shoulder until she burned inside for him.

"I was more surprised by other things," she said, still a little sore from the night before.

"Like what?" Gavin asked, moving her hair off her shoulder. He pressed his erection in between her thighs and cupped one of her breasts. Pinching her nipple in between his fingers, he fondled her.

Goosebumps formed on her skin. "Like the size of your cock for starters," she said, remembering how hard it was to adjust to his girth and how powerful her orgasm had been as it rushed over her, sending her into paralyzing scream that ended with her trembling and collapsing on top of him.

Gavin licked his lips. His gaze trailed her backside. "Did you like it deep inside of you,

Daisy?" he asked, voice thick and husky. He removed her tank top again and threw it on the floor.

"Yes," she whispered.

He fisted her hair tightly. "And do you want it again?"

"Yes," she panted, chin up and head back. Her skin had flushed red now at the thought of him taking her.

"Do you want it now?" he asked, voice dark and hot, matching his eyes. All he needed was consent, and he was going to tear her body apart again.

She spread her legs apart and looked at him in the mirror. "Yes," she whimpered. Her sex ached to have him. "I want you now." And she did want him, but she didn't understand why. Something about him was impossible to deny even though at the same time something about him was all wrong.

Her breaths became erratic and her mind scattered into a thousand thoughts. Was she about to do this again? Her mind said no, her body, however, responded by pooling hot liquid between her thighs, and she hated herself for it.

She bent over the dresser and pressed her hands against the wood. Then in some mad hysteria, she spoke. "Will I ever see you again?" she asked, looking back at him.

Gavin's lips quirked as though he'd been asked that a million times before her. "Do you really want to?" He slid his finger into her tight sex and watched her eyes close. Rubbing the hand down her back, he slapped her butt again, this time making her buck.

Biting her lip, she opened her eyes. "I don't know," she said, swallowing hard. "I don't even know how you are." She stared at his reflection.

"Does it matter?" Gavin asked, reaching for a condom on the table. He slipped it between his teeth and tore the gold foil wrapper.

Honestly, Daisy wasn't sure if it did really matter. She wasn't really sure what this even was. He was so mysterious; a man of so few words. For all she knew, she was screwing an assassin.

"At least tell me your *real* name," she said as she watched him roll the condom down his long veiny shaft.

Gavin looked at the woman glaring at him in the mirror, breasts exposed, bent over the dresser, legs spread, ready to be impaled again by him and felt absolutely nothing emotional, only sexual. He smoothed his hand over her clit and made her moan. After all, wasn't that what this was all about? Sex.

"I told you my name. It's Jake," he said, grabbing her waist and pulling her into him as he pushed through the folds of her body.

The lie didn't bother him at all. In fact, it protected him, just like the condom, just like the refusal for real human connection and the inability to receive emotional rejection by one more well-meaning woman who would eventually break his heart.

His pent-up anger reared its head, but not in the way she could detect. It only made him harder, more erect, and more impenetrable.

Her womb contracted as he thrusted deep into her trembling body until he was buried at his hips inside of her. He was almost too much for her, but she wouldn't admit it. Besides, it wasn't like this was going anywhere.

He thrust into her again. This time with more power.

She clawed the dresser with her nails and screamed out.

Pulling out, almost to the very tip of his manhood, he focused on her body. "This is what's real, Daisy," he said, pushing all the way back down inside of her again. The slap of skin against skin echoed through the room and her wetness splashed against his thighs. He groaned as his balls tightened. "This is all that matters," he said, voice strained.

She tossed her head back, black wet hair falling over her shoulders, mouth open in ecstasy and bucked against him, begging for more as he planted his prosthetic leg and good foot firmly in the carpet. Gripping her hips, he gave her what she wanted. Pounding hard into her body, he watched himself in the mirror, pumping deep as he could go, as hard as he could. Her voice vibrated as she moaned. With one arm extended back to brace her hand against his arm, she held on as he unleashed powerful thrusts into her. Over and over again, he pumped into her without a single other thought, until they both reached a violent, loud climax at the exact same time.

Her scream finally ceased, but she was stupefied by the orgasm. That was by far the best that she had ever had in her young age and it was given by a man that she didn't even know.

Daisy fell against the dresser, refusing to look at the mirror or him as he pulled carefully out of her. Her body convulsed and her skin was beet red. Heaving and trying to get her breath, she closed her eyes in embarrassment. *I should have left when I started to*, she thought to herself.

Gavin looked at her, leaning against the dresser in a completely weakened state and bent to kiss her.

"Don't," she said, balling up her fists.

Gavin stepped back. "Did I hurt you?" he asked, concerned.

Daisy rose up and smoothed her hands over her hair. "No," she said, inhaling a breath. In a state of confusion, she scanned the room, grabbed her panties and shorts and went over to the edge of the bed to slip them on.

Gavin blew out a breath. "What then?" he asked, watching her curiously.

Daisy stood up and pulled her shorts all the way up on her thighs. Zipping her pants, she bent down and grabbed her shoes. "I just wonder how that would have felt if you had felt it too," she said, looking over at his guns intentionally. "If you could feel anything."

Gavin stood naked, still wearing his condom, still sweating but did not say a word. Had he just allowed himself to be that transparent?

Daisy waited for an answer; when she saw that he would not give one, she gave a cynical laugh. "Jake?" she said, snatching her keys off the nightstand.

"Yeah," he answered.

"Go fuck yourself," Daisy said, storming out of the door and slamming it behind her.

Gavin scratched his head. Stunned by the woman's outburst, he shook his head and went to the door to make sure it was locked.

*Women.*

Looking at his watch, he grabbed the remote, turned on the television and headed in the shower.

*Great, now he only had 30 minutes to get to his next appointment.*

# Chapter 22

"And like the old soldier in that ballad, I now close my military career and just fade away, an old soldier who tried to do his duty as God gave him the sight to see that duty."
- **General Douglas MacArthur**

Before dusk broke the horizon, David Lawless had already been up for a couple of hours. Only he hadn't been running or working out, watching news or studying. Today, he was doing something much more important. Grasping the top of the headboard with one hand and holding up Kelly's long refined leg with the other, he slammed into her body one slow thrust at a time. Sweat poured from his face down onto her breasts as he bit down on his lip fighting the sincere desire to fill her with his seed. His body glowed against the dim candlelight on the nightstand beside three bottles of champagne. Music played in the background. Soft red rose petals covered the bed. The sound of a woman screaming throughout his loft apartment and beyond the confines of the door were pronounced and undeniable.

But David didn't care. He didn't care if he woke up the entire neighborhood, if the police came knocking, if the fire department kicked down the door, he was going to make love to this woman until he had his fill. Only, so far, even after five times, he couldn't get enough.

Kelly's dark brown skin gave dramatic contrast to his white sheets. He stroked her face, running a finger from her cheek to her mouth, then inserting the digit to watch her suck on it slowly.

The blood raced through his veins as he felt that familiar strain again. Seeing his face tense, Kelly locked her leg around his shoulder and pulled away from his finger. "Don't you dare slow down," she ordered.

"Don't you dare move," he said, eyes blazing with intense seduction.

She held on to him, fighting back her own orgasm, but his beautiful virile body made it difficult to resist. A wave of heat rushed over her body and suddenly shock waves caused her to curl her toes and shake uncontrollably.

"Yes!" she screamed out. "Yes! Yes!"

In her own ecstasy, she had not noticed that the very sight of her pleasure had sent David over the threshold and his seed spewed into the condom.

Breathing hard, he wiped a hand over his high and tight and looked down at her with a loving grin. "What was that? Number four?"

"Number five," Kelly said, pulling him to her to kiss his lips. "I love you."

He studied her face in silence. "I love you," he said, rolling over on his side to look up at the ceiling.

"What's wrong?" she asked, detecting something in his tone.

David reached behind him and tucked his pillow. "I just realized something."

"What's that?" she asked, still too weak to move.

"Tonight's going to be too late," he said, pushing himself up in the elevated queen-sized bed.

Now Kelley was curious. "Too late for what?" she asked, turning toward him on her side.

Reaching over on the nightstand, he pulled open the drawer and pulled out a box. He turned to her with the small blue box in his hand and smiled. "I know how you hate traditional."

She looked at the box without saying a word.

"And you know how I love traditional. I was going to do this in front of my folks at dinner tonight on one knee and flowers, but I know your style. You like privacy. You like intimacy."

He hiked his brows. "In a way, right now at this very moment seems perfect."

Kelley pulled her eyes from the box in shock.

"David," she said speechless. Putting her hand over her mouth, she sat up beside him, resting her back up against the tall headboard.

He sat up in the bed and took her hand. "I'm a man that knows what I want in this world, and I don't settle for anything less. I knew that I wanted to be a Marine from the time that I could pretend. I knew that I wanted to be blessed to have a family like my father and a wife that I could cherish, like he cherishes my mother. But I never imagined that I'd find someone as beautiful and amazing and smart as you." He bit his bottom lip. "This tour was hard for me, but not as hard as it was for others. I made a promise to myself to go after everything that I want and not to stop until I have it. Well, outside of being the Commandant of the Marine Corps, I want you. I only want you. I want a wife that I can come home to every night, raise a family with, someone who will be there by my side from the day that we walk down the aisle to the day that we die, not because it is expected but because it's what we want." His bedroom eyes gazed up at her, expecting for her to be in joyful tears, but he was surprised to see that she was grimacing like she was going to be physically ill.

"David, I can't marry you," Kelly said in a matter-of-fact tone. Gently, she pulled her hand away, but the residue of rejection still permeated the room.

David was confused. "Did I miss something?" he asked, pulling the cover over his exposed lap. There was no way he was going to be rejected butt ass naked.

Kelly shook her head as she tried to put into words what he had just said. "You want a wife that you can come home to *every night*. You want a wife that cooks and cleans and throws elegant parties off the shore and wears fucking Prada suits to pick out groceries." She laughed at the thought. "You want to be the Commandant of the Marine Corps and sit in back rooms of parties smoking cigars with the rest of the Boy's Club in your perfectly squared away dress blues and your chest full of ribbons."

So far David didn't see what the problem was.

Kelly put her hand on her chest. "I want to be Commandant. I want a long, successful career in the Marine Corps. I'm a *lifer*," she said with conviction. "I knew that I wanted to be a Marine when I was five years old. I turned down *I don't know how many* jobs in the civilian world to join the military." Her brows furrowed. "The truth is I'll never be there when you get home. I'll be off on some assignment. The kids, while beautiful, will spend most of their lives with the nanny and eventually you'll divorce me because you'll resent the fact that we're more than just similar like people say, we're the same person, David. Therefore, you'll have no choice but to compete with me, and no matter who wins, we'll both lose."

David held the box in his hands in silence. This wasn't what he had expected. How had he missed all the signs? How had he not known that this wasn't what she wanted? He swallowed hard and took his gaze off the end of the bed. "I'm very sorry that I misread you all this time," he said, clenching his jaw. He looked at her now with a mix of pain and disappointment. "I thought when you said that you loved me..."

Kelly reached over and drew his face in with her hands. Kissing him on his lips, she took a deep breath. "I do love you, very much. And that's why I can't allow myself to let you make this decision. Hearing you profess what you want in a wife makes me understand how much I'm not the one for you." She released him and pushed her head against his. "Please try to understand."

David didn't. He reached back over to the nightstand and put the ring away. Closing the drawer, he realized that she hadn't even asked to look at the two-carat solitaire diamond from Tiffany's. He shook his head. It hurt, but she was right. *She was no housewife.*

Without another word, he jumped out of the bed and slipped on his boxers. With a flick on the computer, he turned off the music and headed toward the bedroom door.

"Where are you going?" she asked, pulling the cover over her body.

David turned to her and smiled. "I'm going to the kitchen to fix us our last breakfast." He winked at her. "I might not know much else, but I know how you like your eggs."

***

Today was turning out to be a pretty shitty day. Brett didn't like hospitals, and he didn't like clinics. Unfortunately, in the last four hours, he had been to both. The appointment with the Navy Hospital on base early that morning hadn't turned out like he expected.

According to the team of doctors who crowded around the room in their white coats and green smocks staring at him like he was a circus freak, he would need an additional surgery to fix his knee and there would still be permanent damage. So the pins that were in there now would be there forever. The good news was that his shoulder had healed up well and so had his broken ribs. But for all the good news that they were spouting off, no one told him, regardless of how many times he asked, if he would be transferred back to Recon out of the Wounded Warrior Battalion after he was healed.

Instead, they all gave the same generic answer with painted on smiles. "Let's just get you healed up first, and we can focus on that after. This is going to be a long process. Blah, blah, blah." He was so sick of hearing that.

For the time being, he was pulled out of his hard plaster cast and given the more manageable walking boot he had been fitted for a week ago. But he still had to use the crutches, at least for a while.

"Stand on the crutches. Put your bad foot on the floor, lightly. Lean your body weight on until it hurts. Then walk like that, partial weight bearing. When this becomes easy, lean on it more, until you can dispense with the crutches," the doctor had ordered while making Brett do it a few times to watch his technique.

Brett thought the entire set up was bullshit. Why did he need a doctor to tell him how to walk when he had been doing it for 35 years just fine? Still, like a good Marine, he practiced a few times, quietly brooding, until they were satisfied with his mobility.

He didn't care. Whatever it took. The point was that he had been in this damn thing for eight weeks and he was more than ready to be on his own two feet and back in the gym.

When he came back out into the waiting room, Courtney had seemed thrilled. She lit up like a Christmas tree when he walked over to her, although when he had left her their earlier, she had sulked. She wanted to hear what the doctors had to say first hand, but he knew that if she came in there with him, she'd be advocating for him to retire.

That simply wasn't happening.

Now after being asked a million questions by his wife in the car about what the doctors had said to him during his visit, he was sitting in a CDX laboratories about to move one step closer in this case to identifying Cameron's biological father.

The original court order had been set for weeks before, but Mr. Benson had filed for a continuance based upon his client's "fragile physical state." He even brought official records and statements from the base to substantiate his claim. The Court had bought the argument hook line and sinker and gave Brett a few more weeks to get the test completed. At the time, that little breathing room seemed like a lifetime away.

Well, a *few weeks* had passed quickly. And here he was. He looked around the clinic at the men and women waiting and felt instantly embarrassed. Ducking his head, he put his elbows on his knees and buried his face in his hands.

*I don't belong here*, he thought to himself. *I never cheated once. I was always a good father and a good husband, and this is what it got me.*

"Black," a woman called out as she stepped out of the door and waved for him to follow her.

He took a deep breath, grabbed his crutches, stuck them under his arms and meandered across the floor for everyone to gawk at before finally disappearing with her behind the large door.

The older black woman in pink flower scrubs walked him to a small room. "If you come in here, Stacey will be right in to see you." She looked up at him with a small ounce of sympathy. "You can have a seat over in the corner."

"I'd rather stand," Brett said, stepping inside of the small room. He looked around nervously.

She had been doing this a long time and picked up on his angst. "Can I get you a cup of water or something, hon?" Stepping in the room with him, she pulled a napkin off the table and handed it to him.

"Thanks," he said, taking it.

"I promise it won't hurt. It's just a quick swab on the inside of the cheek," she explained.

"It's going to hurt more than you know," Brett said, wiping his brow.

\*\*\*

Courtney wanted to scream. She wanted to pull the car over and just fucking scream until there was no more air left in her body. But instead, she kept her eyes on the road and drove to her mother's house in silence, trying not to feed off the negative energy that Brett had been giving off since he rolled out of bed this morning.

Turning up the radio a little louder, she cut her eyes at him once and turned down the street to her parent's house while he sat looking out of the window like he wanted to be anywhere but with her.

Feeling her millisecond glare, he looked over her way just in time to see her turn her head. "What are we going over here again for?" he asked, turning down the radio.

"Mom said that we were all having dinner at David's request. I guess it's his last one for a while since he's back at the base."

"Lucky him," Brett said, wishing that he could snatch his boot off. His toes were itching and all that he could do was wiggle them.

"What's that supposed to mean?" Courtney snapped.

Brett frowned. "It means he's lucky to be back at work," he said, clueless to her chaos. What he really wanted to know was why they had to have *family night* so often? He got that they were tight knit but this was ridiculous. What he really wanted to do was go out and have some real adult time, have a damn beer at a bar and relax without trying to figure out which utensil was the salad fork. *But he'd never say that.*

Realizing that one more word might send his wife over the edge, he bit his tongue and turned back toward the window. He didn't feel like fighting tonight.

When they pulled into the well-lit driveway, they saw that David had already arrived. Pulling up behind his car, Courtney jerked the gear into park and turned off the engine.

"What is wrong with you?" Brett asked, wishing that he hadn't.

"Nothing," she said, snatching her keys out of the ignition and jumping out of the car. Slamming the car door, she pushed her purse up on her shoulder and made her way to the door without bothering to help her husband.

Brett was glad for the small distance between them. She had been bitchy all day, and he didn't understand why. Had he said something? Was she tired of driving him, because he was damn sick of being escorted everywhere. He had been driving himself around since he was 15 years old and now he was relegated to the passenger seat like a five-year-old.

As Courtney walked into the house, she saw Cameron on the other end of the hallway. Running to her, he jumped up in her arms. "Hey Mommy," he said, kissing her cheek.

She embraced him tightly, smelling bubble gum on his breath. "Hey baby," she said, feeling a little better at just seeing his face. "Where's your sister?"

"Already asleep," he said, as though that was uncommon for a baby. He looked passed her to see Brett come in. "Hey Daddy."

"Hey little man," Brett said, closing the door behind him.

"You got a new shoe!" Cameron shimmied down out of Courtney's embrace to get a better look at Brett's walking boot.

Brett picked him up and kissed his head. "I swear you grew today."

"Let me see your boot," Cameron said, hanging out of his daddy's arms.

Brett set him down and showcased it for him. "One step closer to having both of my legs again," he said as Cameron bent down to touch it.

Courtney quickly walked off, leaving the two of them alone. She headed to the dining room where everyone had gathered.

As soon as she hit the corner, she began apologizing. "Sorry we're late," she said, setting her purse down by her normal chair.

"It's fine," Jeffery said, eyeing the chicken parmesan only a few inches away from his plate. His stomach growled angrily. "If you had been a little later, we would have started without you."

David glanced over at Courtney, a glass of wine in his hand already, and sneered at her. "How do you still show up late when Mom and Dad are watching the kids? I mean, isn't that your normal reason? What's your excuse now?"

Courtney cut her eyes at him like she could strangle him at the dinner table. She was really in no mood tonight. "I'm sorry, *your highness*. Have you been waiting long?"

Diane came in through the other door and set down a casserole dish on the table. "He just got here five minutes before you," she said, hitting David on the back of the head. "Behave, you two."

David took another sip of his wine. "I'm just saying, sounds like she needs a new watch."

Diane was finally ready to sit down now that she had put the last dish on the table. Smoothing her hands down her skirt, she looked at the table in complete satisfaction and realized that she was missing one person. "Where's Kelly?"

David set down his glass and chuckled like a mad man. "I honestly have no idea."

The room became silent. *That didn't sound good.*

"What happened?" Diane pried. Taking her seat on the other end of the table, she quickly turned her attention to her son.

David sat back in his seat and rolled his tongue around the roof of his mouth. "Apparently, she wants to be the Commandant of the Marine Corps and our future kids and the idea of cocktails parties and Marine Officer Wives Clubs will get in her way."

Jeffery set down his knife and fork, knowing that the chicken would have to wait just a little longer. "Commandant of the Marine Corps? A woman?" The idea of that was simply preposterous to him.

"Why is that funny?" Courtney asked, snapping at her father.

"Why is that an issue?" Diane followed.

David put up his hand. "We broke up. Okay. We just...broke up." He rolled his eyes. "It's not that complicated. We want different things."

"How can you want different things? You're so much alike? Both officers. Both graduated at the top of your class from college and the academy." Courtney asked flabbergasted. "You make the perfect couple." This had to be just a little bump in the road. They weren't really broken up. It couldn't be.

David appreciated her naiveté. At least, he wasn't alone in his. "Well, that's the problem. We want the same things. Evidently, that was a problem for her." He felt the pain he had worked all day to push to the back of his mind star to propel forward and drown him all over again.

Diane's heart sank into her stomach watching her son go through such heartache. She tried to console him. "Maybe you can work it out."

David immediately responded, elevating his voice to the point of strain, "She doesn't want to work it out," he said, running his hand over his glass. His voice calmed as he felt his father's eyes peering at him. "I think that was pretty evident this morning when I asked her to marry me and she said no."

Everyone looked surprised. Not only did they not see the breakup, they really didn't see the proposal.

Brett reached for the bottle. "Well, better to find out what you both want before you marry." It was the best advice that he could give considering that Amy was still haunting him with her whore antics from the grave.

"What is that supposed to mean?" Courtney asked.

"I wasn't talking about you," Brett said, pouring a hefty glass. He tried to ignore her growing agitation. "I simply meant that it hurts now, but if she's already unhappy, she's not just going to magically become happy after she walks down that aisle." Brett looked over at David and raised his glass. "At least you have your work to return to."

David tilted his head. *Brett had a point.* "I am glad to be back, but it's not the same without you."

"Well, hopefully, I'll be back in a month or two. The doctors are giving me the run around, but trust me before you deploy again, I'll be back 100 percent. We're going to give those bastards hell."

Courtney frowned. "Are you serious?"

Brett shrugged. "Yeah, it won't take that long to heal."

"Brett, you are not going back," Courtney said, unable to hold her tongue. "You almost died over there."

"It's my job, Courtney," Brett said, trying to keep his cool at her father's dinner table.

"You almost *died*," Courtney said, voice rising.

Diane jumped in. "Maybe we should hold off on the fighting until after dessert."

"No," Courtney said, nostrils flared. "Brett," she said, turning to him. "You cannot go back. We have enough money now to start over, do something else. You can't just throw it all to the wind and go back there." Plus, she couldn't take the idea of him coming back more injured.

"It's my life, Courtney. It's what I chose. I'm a lifer. You can't just expect me to give it all up in my prime."

David's head popped up. He had heard that before, as a matter of fact, he had heard that this morning, but it was weird seeing it play out. Suddenly, Kelly's words rang in his head.

Courtney growled. "I don't know if you've noticed but you're not exactly in your prime anymore – not for the Corps."

Brett sneered. "Like you would know." Just because she was a Colonel's daughter didn't mean that she got to act like she'd stood a post.

"I *do* know," Courtney said, pointing at his leg. "When are you going to face the music? This is it. The Marine Corps is over."

Brett stared at her. "Courtney, what is your problem? You've been on me all day."

"My problem?" she said incensed, hand to her chest. "You're the one who's been distant since you left the doctor's office. Did they confirm what I've been trying to say?"

"Trying?" Brett laughed. "You've been doing a lot more than trying to say that I'm a failure. You've been screaming it from the rooftops."

Courtney's mouth popped open. "That's not true. I've never said you were a failure."

"Then what are you trying to say?" Brett asked.

Courtney stood up. "I'm saying that it's either us or the Corps. You can't have us both. Not anymore. Not after burying Joe. Not after the four other funerals that you went to over the last couple of weeks. Not after I almost lost you!" She hit the table as images of the closed casket funeral flooded her mind.

"It's not fair to ask me to choose," Brett said, forgetting that he was at her family's house. He turned his fiery hot gaze on her. "You can't just snatch this from me. Leo can't just snatch my son from me. I get a damn say in my life, too!"

David twisted up his lip. Is this what he had to contend with if he had married Kelly? Would the two of them had this conversation if he had wanted her to quit?

Courtney had heard enough. "What about us? Do we get a say? Your family? Your children? You selfish son of a bitch. We've sacrificed everything for you, and it's still not enough." Tears ran down her face. "Everything is about the Marine Corps. Everything is about your career. What about us, the people that you leave every time you go over there? And then we have to fix you back up when you come home, after you're all broken and twisted?" Looking around the table at her father, her brother and her husband, she threw down her napkin. "You know what? All three of you can *kiss my ass*!" Running out the room, her footsteps echoed as she ran up the staircase to her old bedroom.

Jeffery looked down at the table at his wife without expression. "Is she alright?"

"I don't know," Diane said, standing up. "I'll be back. You all just help yourself to dinner."

David looked over the spread. "Tell you the truth, I'm not really hungry," he said, as Diane left the room. He didn't want her to hear now that she'd gone through all the trouble, but all the talk about Kelly had ruined his appetite.

Jeffery picked up the entire dish of chicken. "Good. More for me."

Brett stood up, deflated from the conversation. "You wanna get out of here and go get a beer?" he asked David.

"Yep," David said, standing up too. He looked at his father. "Dad?"

"I'm starving," Jeffery said, getting two rolls before Diane could catch him. "I'll watch the kids. You two go." He paused and looked up at them both, pointing his finger. "Just don't get into any trouble."

# Chapter 23

"After marriage, a woman's sight becomes so keen that she can see right through her husband without looking at him, and a man's so dull that he can look right through his wife without seeing her."

– Helen Rowland (American Journalist)

Courtney sat curled up in the window seat of her old bedroom window looking out at the sprinklers watering the front lawn while she sobbed quietly in the dark. She was angry with herself, angrier than she had been in a long time. This was not the way things were supposed to go, but the blood had boiled so hot inside of her downstairs until her frustration leapt forward from her diaphragm spewing out of her mouth like hot liquid lava.

And now that she had said what was bothering her, she felt hollow and wished for nothing more than to take it all back.

To her surprise, just a few minutes earlier, she had watched Brett and David leave together, jumping in her brother's car and heading down the drive. Going where? She didn't know, but somehow seeing them pull out onto the street beyond the gate made her feel even more alone and in the wrong.

The truth of the matter was that they didn't need distance right now; they needed answers. And she needed to tell him that it was an honest mistake to handle things the way that she had. Although it was not her intention, she had embarrassed him not only in front of their family but also his superior officers. And she was sorry for that. After all, Brett had never embarrassed her in front of her mother or Cameron.

Wiping her eyes as the light flickered on, she ducked her head when her mother came into the bedroom. Her footsteps were soft as she crossed the hardwood floor.

Courtney braced herself. *Time to face the music.* Her mother had always been a stickler about dinner table outbursts. That room was supposed to be their sanctuary away from the world. But from time to time someone broke her cardinal rule, and then paid the consequences for it.

Diane stood in front of Courtney as she looked at the checkered pink cushions. "I thought you could use this," Diane said, offering a hot towel. She stuck it under Courtney's face.

Courtney took it gratefully. "Thanks," she said, eyes puffy. Wiping her face, she looked at all the makeup that wiped off. God, she must look like a monster right now.

"You're welcome." Diane looked around the room and smiled. "You haven't been up here since the night you moved out. You remember that?"

"Yeah. Daddy and I got into another huge fight about Yale." Courtney remembered like it was yesterday. "I was always disappointing him. I just couldn't take it anymore. I thought at least if I wasn't in his house, my failures wouldn't constantly disappoint him."

Diane remembered something quite different, something that Courtney didn't know, and she'd never bother to tell her until now. "Your father slept in your room that night when you bolted out of here in tears with a bag of clothes and your purse. It was the first time that he had slept anywhere outside of his bed when he was home. *Every other bed and sofa in this house gives him back pain.* He was waiting for you to come home, so he could apologize. In his normal stubborn way, he was determined to believe that you'd come back after you'd cooled off, and he'd be in here to see you when you did. Evidently, he said a lot of things that he didn't mean." Diane knew her daughter would read between the lines. She clasped her hands together and looked at the crown of her daughter's head. "People do that sometimes. They love someone so much until when they see them doing something that could hurt them, they explode...overreact." She nodded. "Sometimes it comes out *all wrong* even when you mean well and you just want the best for them."

Courtney balled the towel up in her hand. "If I had known, I would have come back." She huffed. "I was stupid."

"You weren't stupid," Diane said honestly. "You had to do things your way, is all. And no matter how much you loved your father, you had to make your own choices as an adult."

"Sounds familiar," Courtney whispered.

Diane took a seat beside her and rubbed her back. "Are you going to be alright?"

"No," Courtney said, exhaling defeat. She sniffled. "I'm so sorry for what I said down there. Daddy must be furious with me."

Diane smirked. "Your daddy has heard worse. He'll be fine."

Courtney wasn't sure that he had heard worse from her. She cringed at the thought. "I'm falling apart." It was an obvious admission of guilt, considering everyone had been there to witness her breakdown, but still she said it anyway as a gateway for answers. Her mother had to have answers, because she didn't.

Diane shook her head. "It's not easy. Lord knows that it's not easy." It broke her heart to see her daughter experiencing the same pain that she had so many years ago. "This life that we choose...as wives of military personnel...it is a sacrifice."

Courtney looked up at her.

Diane continued to rub her daughter's back. "I waited for so many years for Jeffery to finally retire. It was on every Christmas list. We had so many conversations just like yours." Glancing off in the distance, she could hear the echo of her memories in her ears. "But he always went back to his mistress. At times, I swore he loved her more. The Marine Corps." She removed her hand and buried it in her lap. "So many fights. So many late night conversations that led right back to his duty to his country."

Courtney frowned. "Mom, I don't want that. Not now. You were at the funeral. You saw what Joe's death did to that family. He's much more likely to be hurt again now that he's hurt. He's going to be off his game and second guessing himself."

Diane smiled. "I've been to so many funerals. Quite honestly, I thought that by now I'd be numb to it." She recalled the many men that they had buried over the years, the continual expression of condolences, and the anguish of carrying the burden of her husband's command, especially those nights when he cried himself to sleep. No, it had not been easy at all. "Joe's was still difficult for me and Jeffery, because he had been under his command once." She lifted a brow. "But men won't stop dying in war because Brett retires or chooses to go back. There is nothing that you can do about it."

Courtney knew that her mother didn't mean to belittle her situation, but somehow hearing her mother's words made her realize that her situation was not unique. And that scared her more.

"So you're telling me that no matter what I feel inside," Courtney wiped another tear, "he's just going to go back?"

"No," Diane said, sure of herself. "I'm telling you that eventually he will realize his walk, and no matter what he chooses, you have to be there with him. You're his wife. The Marine Corps is his career. He shouldn't have to choose because you make him. He should choose because he wants to. That's the only way this game is

played without shared resentment.  *Consent*."
She moved a strand of her hair from her daughter's face and smiled at her.  "Till death do you part?  That's what you vowed.  There was no clause about his job in your marital contract."

Courtney was expecting some other advice.  Her voice croaked.  "I could not handle losing him, Mom.  I just couldn't."  Goose bumps formed on her skin.  Her lip trembled at the thought of burying him in that casket.  "He's my everything.  Am I just supposed to sit quietly by and watch him risk it all again because of pride... a bruised ego?"  Her eyes raced up to her mother's for understanding.

And Diane did understand, but she wasn't sure that they did.  "Brett loves you, and you love him, but you all don't communicate well in crisis.  Have you told him how you truly feel?"

"*Yessss*," Courtney hissed.

"Have you sat down and really told him what you want for your life and what you want for his?  Have you told him what this experience has done to you?  Have you really talked to him about the choices that he has and what you want him to do with those choices?  Have you asked him sincerely to allow you to be a part of this entire process no matter how it turns out?"

Courtney stuttered, "I think so." In her heart, she knew that she had tread lightly on the subject since his return. With the paternity suit, the injuries, his teams' deaths, there was little room to talk about what she wanted out of life or what she expected from him. And maybe there had been time but she felt selfish about bringing up her wants in the midst of everything.

"If you only *think* you have, then you haven't." Diane had hope for them, but she knew that they were young and needed guidance. "You need to talk to your husband. *Not scream at him. Not curse him out.* You need to talk to him and make him understand. Only you can do that. No one else can. And trust me, Brett will listen."

Courtney unfolded her feet from under her and clutched the edge of the seat. "I'm afraid."

"What are you afraid of?" Diane asked.

"I'm afraid that he'll say no." Courtney chuckled as she involuntarily sniffled. "What if he says no?" She looked her mother dead in the eyes. "Right now, I feel like I'm just the wife, just the mother, just the stepmother." She swallowed hard. "I don't feel like Courtney. I don't feel in control of this situation at all."

"Well that's because you're not in control." Diane turned to her and held her hands. "God is in control. He's always been in control. You, however, have the power to speak the blessings that you want in your life, *over* your life. You want this paternity case to come out in your favor? *Speak it.* You want your husband to retire? *Speak it.* You want your husband re-newed and your marriage fixed?" She gripped her daughter's soft hands and said the words firmly and with utter conviction. "*Speak it, Courtney.* Just like you need to talk to your husband, you need to start to speak over your family with authority."

Courtney nodded in understanding.

Diane's face was covered with tears. "I know this is hard on you, little girl. You didn't exactly pick the easiest road in life. Your husband is a Recon Marine hoping to be a lifer with a son that is not biologically his, and now he's injured and you've gone from a carefree existence to a moth-er with two young children and a wounded spouse."

Courtney's tears were infinite now. Hearing someone lay her life out there made her feel even more vulnerable.

"Yeah, it hasn't been easy," Courtney said, re-fusing to sound so glum. After all, they were now a lot wealthier. There was more to be thankful for than not, but somehow, she couldn't keep her normal glass-half-full outlook on this one.

"Your father and I knew that it wouldn't be easy. We worried...quietly. Jeffery especially. I think that's why he was so hard on Brett when he first found out about you guys. It wasn't that he cared about him being enlisted or white. He was worried about the consequence of falling in love with someone so much like him. Jeffery said a special prayer every night that those boys were gone. He didn't want you to be a widow or to spend the rest of your life taking care of someone or missing the special touch of your big brother. He wanted more for you than he had given me, and Jeffery has given me so much." She glanced over at the door and saw her husband's shadow in the hall listening on. Turning back to her daughter, she lifted her chin. "But now that you've taken these vows, now that you've taken on this life, you have to make the most of it. You have to own it. The good and the bad. You can't just run away anymore. People are counting on you."

Courtney reached up and wiped her mother's tear before it could fall from the corner of her eye. "Thank you, Mom." Her voice was as soft as a gentle breeze. "I love you and Daddy so much. You've been so good to me."

"We love you," Diane said, rubbing her daughter's face. "We love all of you."

*\*\**

Sitting like three whipped dogs at the bar of the Devil Dog Tavern, a seedy little pub off Marine Boulevard, Brett, David and Gavin enjoyed the simple pleasure of an ice cold beer and endless shots of Gentleman's Jack.

The bar was a historic cornerstone of the grunt experience complete with a USMC flag that hung above the back of the bar, dated dark wood paneling on the walls, old wooden seats, a 30-year old pool table in the back next to a dart machine and poor overhead lighting. Pictures of Marines down through the decades lined the walls along with medals, news articles and nostalgic recruiting posters. It was like a Marine's tree house. All it was missing was a *No Girls Allowed* sign, or at least *No Good Girls*.

Considering it was the middle of the week, the bar was nearly empty with only a few old vets in the corner sitting quietly, staring into nothingness while they nursed their whiskey and occasionally breaking into conversation, and a young couple hidden in a back booth whispering sweet nothings and kissing excessively.

An old jukebox near the bathrooms played non-stop Stevie Ray Vaughn while the old barkeep, a man in his 60s with a very large gut and a gray beard, stood at the far side of the bar watching television and cleaning glasses.

Brett felt like he was honestly at Disneyland. Every breath he took in smelled like stale cigarettes, greasy cheeseburgers and beer, none of which were acceptable at home. Not to mention that he hadn't been out since he had gotten home. Being pent up in the house for weeks on end had taken a toll on him. He hadn't realized how much until tonight. Everything started to fall apart, including his normally reserved behavior toward his wife. Now, she was pissed at him, and he didn't blame her. *But he couldn't take it back.* Partly because he meant every word he had said to her and partly because he doubted she would forgive him anyway.

Pulling himself away from his thoughts, Brett looked over at the two men beside him. "What a night, huh?"

David just nodded as he took another shot. He really was not interested in talking, just getting as fucked up as humanly possible.

"One night is just like the other," Gavin said, arms leaning on the bar. Exhausted from the drive up from Wilmington, he was about to crash at the hotel when Brett had called him and invited him out for that beer they had previously discussed. In truth, Gavin was tired of being at bars, but he could hear it in Brett's voice that he needed to talk. *Maybe he needed to talk too.*

Brett stared at himself in the mirror on the other side of the bar. He looked a damn mess. The bruises had gone but the scars were permanent. And yet, Courtney still loved him. "Your sister hates me," he said to David.

David downed another shot. "She doesn't hate you. She's just mad at you."

Gavin's head quickly snapped over to Brett. "Why is she mad at you?"

David chuckled. "Because he's stupid."

Brett frowned. "I'm stupid?"

The alcohol burned David's throat as it went down. Swiveling in his chair, he turned his entire body toward Brett. "You're a damn good Marine." He lifted a finger. "You're the best Recon Marine that I've ever met outside of myself and my father. I'll give you that, just man to man."

Gavin raised a brow. This guy must not have seen him back in the day. He made these new guys look like choir boys when he had two legs.

Brett was taken aback by David's compliment. He glanced at the shot glass. "Maybe you've had one too many of those, man."

David rolled his eyes. "I'm not just blowing smoke up your ass, and unfortunately, I don't even have a buzz yet. I'm just putting it out there." He shrugged. "But you're stupid because you don't see that this transfer over to Wounded Warrior Battalion isn't temporary." He picked up another one of the shots lined up in front of him and downed it, then pushed the empty glass down the bar. He looked Brett in the eyes. "You're not coming back."

"You don't know that," Brett growled.

"I know it," David said, putting his arm on the bar. "I'm your superior officer. You don't think I know? Everyone knows."

Brett shook his head. "I can beat this fucking injury."

"Yeah, you can. You can beat it just enough to be transferred to an admin position. Your MOS has to change. You cannot continue with a..." David pointed at Brett's leg. "You got shot by a fucking AK-47 in the leg!" he said in a strained voice, unable to understand how Brett didn't get why returning was an option. "You should be glad that you didn't get shot in the face."

Gavin nodded in agreement. "Or in the balls."

David motioned toward Gavin. *He had a point.* "Or in the balls," he repeated.

Brett wiped a hand over his face. "No. I'm a fucking United States Marine..."

David cut him off. "So is everyone at the fucking bar. So are hundreds of thousands of other men and women. What is your point?" He frowned at Brett. "What? You think you're special or something?"

"No, I don't think I'm special," Brett barked. Anger overwhelmed him. He hit the bar. "But what the fuck am I if I don't have it? What the fuck am I supposed to do, if I'm not doing the job that I signed up to do, that I was willing to die to do? Who am I?" His voice rose.

David blinked and shook his head. "You're still Brett Black...a fucking Marine."

Brett bit his lip and inhaled a breath so vast until it nearly popped his lungs. "I'm not ready to retire."

"And Joe wasn't ready to die. Just be glad that you didn't make that call. Be glad that you didn't cost four men their lives because you said go right when you should have said go left." David clenched his wide jaw. Remorse darkened his bright brown eyes.

Gavin put down his beer. "You can't possibly be serious?" he said to David. "You give him this big speech just to sound just as stupid at the end."

Both Brett and David turned to Gavin.

Gavin raised his boot cut pant leg past the gun holster and hit the prosthetic leg to make his point a little clearer. He locked eyes with Brett. "Here's a wakeup call for both of you. You get shot...you get FUBAR, there is no other recourse when you're a Recon Marine and you end up lucky enough not to get killed but not lucky enough not to get injured. You end up either transferred or stepped out medically."

Turning his fiery gaze to David, he tilted his head. "Someone has to make the call during an Op. Someone *always* has to make the call. If it hadn't been you, it would have been someone else with your rank. That's your job as an officer. But once you make the call, the rest is not up to you. What happens out there once we do what we're supposed to do is not up to you." He pulled down his pants leg. "Sometimes you're victorious, and we get to go back home happy. Sometimes, someone gets shot or runs over an IED." His voiced lowered. "And sometimes you don't get to come home at all, except in a body bag on ice." Gavin rested his forearms on the bar and took his eyes off of both of them. "But it's not your call who gets to do any of it. And it's not

our call either. Otherwise, we'd win every battle...every war; we'd never have funerals; we'd
never need prosthetic limbs or wheel chairs or
crutches or surgery or therapy or psychotropic
drugs or any other bullshit. But you're not in
control of that."

David needed to hear that, whether he knew
it or not. He sat there staring at Gavin for a
minute before he straightened up in his chair.

Brett picked up his beer and took a sip. *What
did they know?* Rolling his eyes, he pulled out his
phone and checked it. *Not one damn call from
her.*

"Courtney is my sister, and I love her," David
said, moving the attention off of him. "Her
happiness should mean more to you than the
Corps."

"Who says it doesn't?" Brett asked defensively.

David laughed. "You've been walked out on,
right?"

"Yeah, so what?"

"So, what did she leave you for?" David asked.

Gavin sucked in a breath. *Low blow.*

Brett didn't respond. He knew that David
knew the answer to his question.

"Exactly. Don't make the mistake of losing a
second woman." David thought of Kelly and

sneered. "It's really hard to find someone who not only makes you happy but tries to support you. You have to support her back. If you don't...someone else will."

Brett threw his phone on the table. "I love her. I do, but I worry that she doesn't want me. Not like this."

"Cop out," David said, unwilling to hear excuses.

Brett sucked his teeth. "It's not a cop out. It's the truth."

"Dude, you got shot. That handsome pretty boy mug got scarred. So what. Chicks dig that shit," Gavin joked.

"I've known my sister for a lot longer than you, and she's never given a man what she's given you...which is everything by the way." David watched Brett's facial expression change from anger to sadness.

"She told me to kiss her ass," Brett said, still blown away by that. "She's fed up with my shit."

"Correction. She told all of us to kiss her ass," David chuckled. Now that had been actually funny and very much out of character for Courtney. It would definitely go down in Lawless history.

Gavin chimed in. "I'm sure I would have been the only one at the table to oblige her, but for the team I would have literally kissed her ass."

Brett looked down the bar at him. "And that would have been the last ass you would have ever kissed."

"It would have been worth it," Gavin said with a wide grin and wink. Brett's wife was super fine. *Too fine* for him in his opinion. Although, he'd never even pictured that scenario of kissing her ass. Brett was his friend, therefore, Courtney was family, just like Judy.

All three men laughed, breaking the tension in the conversation and giving them a chance to relax.    Finally, levity.   It was a hard thing to come by these days.

"She just wants you to put her first," David reiterated. "Like she's been doing for you."

Brett knew that David was right.   "Yeah. She's been definitely putting me first.   It's so uncomfortable." He rubbed the back of his neck. "She's the glue in my life. She keeps all of us together."   But it was more than that. "I can't live without her, but I know she'd do just fine without me. I mean, she's unstoppable," he said thinking about all she had accomplished for them in just a short period of time.

David wished that Kelly had felt that way about him, but obviously not. What was obvious was that his old flame had serious ambition, but that only gave him more fuel for his career fire. If it was the last thing that he did, he would make Commandant of the Marine Corps, just so he could rub it in her damn face.

Gavin picked up another shot. "Hey, do you think a woman can tell that you can't feel anything?"

David looked over at him and frowned. "Can't *feel* anything?"

Gavin blinked slowly, head still facing forward. "Yeah," he said, recalling the conversation with Daisy.

"What do you mean, *like*, you can't feel her when you are inside of her?" Brett asked confused by Gavin's question. *Where the hell had that come from?*

"That sounds like a medical problem. You should have that checked out," David said, suddenly not feeling so bad about his situation.

Gavin rolled his eyes. "I can feel my *dick*." The words blurted out a little louder than he intended. The bartender took his eyes slowly off the game and looked over at Gavin disapprovingly.

Gavin lowered his voice and looked at his open palms. "I mean, I can't...fall in love with a woman anymore." His confession was hard for him to admit. "I can't feel anything. I just know what to say and know what to do to get what I want and make them feel like they want to give me what I want, but inside...nothing."

David laughed cynically. This guy was complaining about not being able to feel love when his heart was breaking into pieces. The irony of it..."It's overrated. Trust me," he said, picking up his beer again.

"I wouldn't say it's overrated." Brett raised a brow. "It is complicated though."

"Well, which one is it?" Gavin asked sincerely. "Complicated or overrated?"

David shrugged. "Both," he said, taking another swig of his beer. His thoughts were still with Kelly. "It's like this. As long as you act like you don't care where the relationship is going, they're attentive." His eyes narrowed as he tried to make sense of the situation. "They set up all these parameters, make you jump through all these hoops and lay down all the rules." He took in a deep breath. "As soon as you comply," he slammed his closed fist in hand. "Bam! They don't want you anymore."

Brett twisted up his lips. He didn't agree with David, but he understood his frustration. Being rejected wasn't exactly the type of thing that a man took well from his girlfriend. "You'll have to excuse him. His girlfriend of over a year just broke up with him after he proposed to her."

Gavin bucked his eyes. "*Damn!* Talk about #wastinghistime." And that was why he doubted he'd ever get married. Women were too much of a mystery. He licked his lips. "Still doesn't answer my question though."

"You don't feel anything, because you don't love the woman." Brett raised his finger for another whiskey. "And if you don't love her, she can't feel anything, because there is nothing there to feel."

David thought that they were getting ahead of themselves with the bar diagnosis. "Wait. Do you love her? Do you like her? Do you want to love her?" David asked, just for clarification.

The idea was preposterous to Gavin. Did he want to love the bartender at the strip club? "No," Gavin answered. "I just want to be able to love when I meet the right woman."

Brett downed another shot. "Well, then, there you go. You'll know it when you feel it."

"Not true. I felt it. And she...didn't." The men were silent at his response and at that moment, David suddenly felt like he had shared too much, allowed himself to be too vulnerable. So he shut it all off. He looked down at all the empty shot glasses in front of them and pulled out his keys from his pocket. Setting them on the bar, he reached out his right hand to Gavin. "Keys, please."

"For what?" Gavin asked. He didn't have the least bit of a buzz right now, and he didn't need a babysitter.

"Because we're not drinking and driving." David took Gavin's keys and pushed both sets up to the top of the bar. "Until you get a DD-214, I'm still your superior officer, Brett, and after that, I'll just be your pain-in-the-ass brother-in-law. Either way, I have a responsibility to look out for you. I'll call Uber and have them pick us up once we're done.

"Uber?" Gavin rolled his eyes. He was more accustomed to having the girl he meets at the bar take him home. And there is always a girl, no matter what. He skimmed the empty bar. *Usually*, there was always a girl.

"Yes, Uber," David said, pulling out his phone from his wallet. "I have the app downloaded. I always keep it on me."

"Funny, I always have a condom on me," Gavin said, eyeing a woman as she walked into the bar. They made eye contact immediately. Giving a small grin, he winked at her, letting her know that if she wanted, she could have his complete attention tonight.

Brett followed Gavin's gaze to the redhead with the wide hips and big breasts as she came over and sat at the corner of the bar. He turned to Gavin. "Not tonight, dude. Give your dick a rest."

"You need to go home to your wife and make up before there is no one at home waiting for you or *your dick*," Gavin said, motioning for the bartender. He perked up a little. "Excuse me, kind sir. Can I get a drink for the lady?"

David looked over at Brett and hit him on the shoulder. "One more round on me and then you go home?" It sounded like a question, but it was an order.

"I'm not drunk yet," Brett said, words slurring.

"That's the point," David answered. "While you're still in shape to talk to her, go home and make up with your wife. Put her first. Talk to her. Reassure her. Do whatever married men do to stay married." He shrugged and looked when the bar door opened. This time a Black woman entered wearing jeans and a Cardinals t-shirt, cut into a V-shape in the front. With long braids pulled back from her face and a pie face complete with big brown eyes and a dimple in her chin, she strutted over to the bar and sat beside the redhead.

"Do you feel like suddenly hanging out for a few more hours?" Gavin asked David under his breath.

"On it," David said as the woman looked over at him and grinned. He hit Brett on the arm. "Go home or you can break my baby sister's heart and I can shoot you in the other leg. Then you'll definitely be retired out."

Gavin laughed and turned to Brett. "I think he's serious. He's got that whole Captain America thing going on." It was time to get rid of the dead weight. Brett would only dampen the mood, and these girls looked like all they wanted to do was have fun.

Brett laughed. "Alright. Alright. Call me a cab or an Uber or *whatever*. I'll go home and figure this out." He knew exactly what they were up to, and he didn't want to be around to witness it. If he were going to spend time talking to any woman, it would be Courtney.

\*\*\*

Brett had never used Uber before, but it was quite a handy little service. A young man, using this job as second income for his new little family, picked him up in a Toyota Prius right outside of the bar a few minutes after David reserved the ride, and then drove him home with almost no conversation and music from a peaceful jazz station on the radio.

When they pulled up outside of the house a half an hour later in the rain, he was glad to see Courtney's car in the driveway, but he was nervous too. How would he handle this? What would he say? What wouldn't he say? He had a knack lately for putting his foot in his mouth. He'd have to work harder on that. He'd have to work harder on everything.

Closing the passenger door to the driver's car, Brett limped slowly up to the door. Being bull-headed, he had left his crutches at the Lawless' house earlier when they went to the bar. So now, he was only using the boot, which was sort of uncomfortable after such a long day.

The rain washed over his face and body, making his cotton t-shirt cling to his taut lean muscles and highlight the dog tags under his shirt in between his wide well-formed pecs. As he approached, the front porch light came on.

Courtney opened the door and stepped out on the porch in her nightclothes, wearing his favorite shirt and with her hair in a flirty pony-tail.

Brett walked slowly, keeping his eyes on her, like she was the prize he would win if he could just make it. Holding on to the rail, he moved up each step until he was up on the porch. Just a few more steps. Making his way over to her, he stood at her feet, his large frame looming over her petite body as he breathed hard.

Courtney lightly touched his chest.

"I'm sorry," he said quickly. It was better to get that out of the way first. "I was wrong."

Courtney looked up at him. Her hazel brown eyes were still red and puffy from crying. "I'm sorry too." She grabbed his large hand and looked at his wedding ring. "I know it's late, but can I talk to you?" She restated that question. It needed more authority. "I need to talk to you tonight."

Brett touched her face, looking at her full lips, the adorable curve of her nose and the determination of her small chin. "Of course, we can talk."

"I don't want you to say anything tonight. I just want you to hear me out. I want you to hear what I want, not just for you but for us and for me." She didn't blink.

Brett was just glad she was giving him another chance. On top of that she didn't want him to do all the talking, which meant he'd be less likely to fuck it up. His voice broke through the silence of the night and sound of rain hitting the ground. "Whatever you want, baby. We can talk all night if that's what it takes."

Courtney was glad to hear him say that. Leading him into the house, she closed the door behind her and locked it. "I put on some coffee."

Brett looked down at her in her night shirt and tall socks and felt desire start to rear its head. Maybe it was the whiskey or the sight of her nearly naked but he wanted to take her right then and there in the living room on the floor.

Inhaling the scent of strong Columbian coffee, he quickly pushed away his aching desire. Tonight, there would be no distractions, at least, not until she had said what she had to say. Then he would have her.

"Where do you want to do this, baby?" he said, hearing the television going in the den. He walked toward it, hearing Joe's voice. "What's that? What are you watching?" He stopped in the doorway and looked across the room at the television. She had been watching their wedding video while he was away. Joe was giving his Best Man speech. He stood there and watched it for a moment and actually smiled. That had been a good day for everyone, especially for him.

Looking over at her, Brett reached his hand out for her, dripping water in a pool around his feet on the hardwood floor in the hallway. "Come here."

Courtney walked up to him and hugged him tight, ignoring his sogginess. She closed her eyes tight. "I don't want to ever forget why we did this," she said, voice quivering. "I don't want to forget that feeling that I felt the day I married you."

Brett ran a hand down the back of her head as he held her in his tight embrace. "I don't either, baby. I promise you," Brett kissed her shoulder, glad that he had taken David's advice and come home. "We'll fix this together."

# Chapter 24

"I selected an enormous Marine Corps emblem to be tattooed across my chest. It required several sittings and hurt me like the devil, but the finished product was worth the pain. I blazed triumphantly forth, a Marine from throat to waist. The emblem is still with me. Nothing on Earth but skinning will remove it."

—Major General Smedley D. Butler

When Mr. Benson's office called, Brett and Courtney were out shopping for food and enjoying the day with Bella. After hearing the news, they had dropped everything immediately and hightailed it to his office.

"The test came back. There is a 99 percent chance that Cameron is Leo's biological child." Mr. Benson threw the results on his desk and walked over to the window. "We have to get you ready for the trial. Leo Tabor's lawyer filed for temporary visitation, but I was able to get that thrown out."

"How?" Courtney asked.

"Cameron has never been around Leo. Even though we have established Leo as the biological father, a judge still needs to decide custody. For now, considering Brett has been the presumed father and has cared for him his entire life, it is better for things not to change until the trial." Mr. Benson pushed another file over to Brett. "Your friend was very helpful in me making my case early this morning. These pictures of Leo in the bathroom getting high may have persuaded the judge a little more than normal."

Brett looked at the black and white still shots from the video Gavin had recorded with his baseball cap and felt himself turning red. "This piece of shit wants custody of my son?" He pursed his lips together. "Over my dead body."

Mr. Benson noted Brett's rage. They'd need to make sure that during the next few months, it didn't get the best of him.

Brett felt like he was going to throw up. "I guess I had been hoping even if he weren't mine biologically that he wasn't Leo's either." He raked a hand over his face. "Okay," he said, taking in a deep breath and trying to find his center. "How do we get ready for trial?"

"I've set a date, 60 days from today. A couple of my junior partners will meet with you each week to help get you ready with answering

questions and outlining any additional information that you need to provide. We've also
submitted our first set of interrogatories to the
other side. He has to have them back within 30
days from today. If you look at that combined
with the evidence compiled by your friend Gavin
and the sworn testimony he's been able to secure, then we are looking good. We have a
chance."

Courtney looked at Brett. "What evidence?"

"Gavin's been snooping around. Leo's got a
past. He's a coke head, a philanderer, a disgrace
to the Navy." Brett just didn't understand. "It
just doesn't make sense. Why does he think that
he'll get Cameron considering how fucked up he
is?"

Mr. Benson had asked the same question. "It
has to be financially driven. Maybe Amy's parents are paying him, but I doubt it. They would
have come for you much sooner than this, unless
they didn't know where he was and just now
located him. There could be many different
ways he's being paid." Mr. Benson took a seat.
"If we can find out what his motive is, then we
will do better in court."

"You can't let me lose my son," Brett said seriously. He gripped Courtney's hand.

Mr. Benson hated to make promises. "I have two boxes of Amy's belongings in the back office with our team combing through everything, hoping we can use something else as evidence. Right now, we have a diary with detailed accounts of affairs with men on base and her acknowledgement that she was keeping Cameron's paternity a secret from you."

Courtney looked over at Brett, expecting him to get angry at the news of Amy's deception, but he barely blinked. He was over her, over everything that she had done and glad to be rid of her.

Brett pushed up to the end of the chair, focused on something far more important than his late wife's previous lovers. "What else do we need to seal the fate of this case? What ensures me a win?"

Mr. Benson looked over at Courtney and then to Brett. They were good kids. It truly was a pity that they were forced to go through this, but he had seen many couples like them over the years. "Patience. In my experience, at the very end of a case because of stress and other things, people get impatient, and they start to make stupid mistakes. Do yourself a favor, don't be one of them. If you come into contact with Leo, do not engage him. You and I both know that this situation is so tense, you'll end up in jail, and that won't look good to a judge."

Brett laced his fingers together. "What else?"

"You've done everything you can do. Now, you have to let me do everything that I can do. I'll make sure that Cameron doesn't have to be exposed to the man before the trial. If needed, I'll get continuances if we get on the scent of his true motivation behind this and need more time to compile evidence."

Courtney was outraged. "This could take years, couldn't it?"

Mr. Benson couldn't lie. "Unfortunately, yes it could."

"Whatever it takes," Brett said, standing up.

***

"How long is this going to fucking take?" Leo screamed into his cell phone as he sat outside the lawyer's office. The lawyer that the Reilys had hired called him just before his appointment with the lawyer holding Amy's money and told him that while paternity had been established, the judge had decided against allowing temporary visitation.

"You said temporary visitation upon establishing paternity would help this case?" Leo said, hitting the dashboard. "Now you're telling me that I can't see him until after the trial?" His brow furrowed. "What kind of Mickey Mouse bullshit is this?"

If Leo had just given the lawyer time to answer, he would have told him three minutes ago "They've got evidence on you, Leo. The judge felt like you could potentially be bad for the boy. He won't know until the trial. Now I've got 25 pages of questions that you need to get on right now and get answered. You know the drill. I need your tax returns, your DD-214, and your bank statements. Everything."

"Why do I need to turn that in? It's not like I'm divorcing the kid." He had all of it, but it wasn't exactly stellar. He was in the red for his checking and savings. His DD-214 said that he had been discharged Other Than Honorably and his tax returns told the story of his two daughters that he hadn't seen in two months."

"No, but you are petitioning for full custody of this young boy. And if you fall short of that, you may end up with joint custody or visitation. Either way, you're going to have to start paying child support and they need to review your entire life and make sure that they are not snatching a child out of a perfectly good home and giving him to a deviant."

"Are you calling me a deviant?" Leo snapped.

"No, I'm saying that's what the courts don't want to happen. I'm calling you to tell you what happened with the case."

Leo didn't want to hear anymore. "When is the trial set for?"

"In 60 days," the lawyer said, tired of dealing with the man. He was not the guy that Rev. Riley had made him out to be, but attorney-client confidentiality made certain parts of his knowledge on Leo privileged.

Leo gripped the steering wheel and shook it. "That's too far out."

"It's the soonest we can do this." The lawyer was confused. "Why are you rushing this? As I explained to you, this isn't something that can happen overnight. This man was raising this boy as his own and has been for the last five years."

Leo moved the vents so the air would hit him dead smack in the face. "If we get to trial in 60 days and the judge says that he's mine, will he be mine that day or that week?"

"Once the judge makes the ruling, it immediately goes into effect. But the trial more than likely won't be just one day. It could be two days. It could be two weeks."

Leo didn't want to hear the negativity. "Can it be done it two days?"

"If everything is in order, I suppose."

Leo shook his head. "Then get it in order. I know that the Riley's are paying your bill, but if you can get it done in two days and I can get my son with paperwork proving that he's my son, then I'll make it worth your fucking while in less than a week. I'll double what they are paying you."

"Leo, I set my fee and that's what I expect to get paid. I don't provide service any differently to my clients. I'll give you the best I've got to give. But we're facing an uphill battle and you doing coke in the bathroom of a strip club doesn't help your case."

Leo paused. "What?"

"They have photos of you doing what appears to be cocaine in a strip club," the lawyer said, disgusted. "That's why you don't have visitation right now. And don't be surprised if a part of the process before going to court includes you submitting to a drug test. I can almost guarantee that order will be coming next."

Leo had done coke with a couple of guys over the last few weeks, but only one had come around recently. It had to be that fucker, Jake.

"You're my lawyer. What happens if it was coke," he said, looking at his watch. He was going to be late in two minutes.

"If it was coke, then your case just became that much weaker, Mr. Tabor," the lawyer said rolling his eyes. "Was it coke?"

Leo knew that it was quite possible that his lawyer would report all of this back to the Rileys. And he couldn't afford that. "No, it wasn't coke. It was Adderall. I snort it to make it take effect quicker. I've been on ADD meds for years."

The lawyer knew it was a very good possibility that he was lying. "Even if that were the case, you were still abusing a controlled substance in the bathroom of a strip club."

"If I had to choose between cocaine and Adderall as a story, I'd pick the fucking Adderall," Leo said to the lawyer. "I've never had a DUI. I've never been admitted to any facility for drug use. Get creative and I'll focus on how to handle the drug test."

"If there is something that you need to tell me, Leo, now's the time," the lawyer said, hitting his pen on his desk.

"As a matter of fact there is. I'm late, so I need to talk to you later. Just have your secretary send me the email of whatever questions I have to fill out."

"I need them back in 30 days to get what you want done."

"You'll have them," Leo said, hanging up the phone. What a joke.

*\*\**

Richard Clemmons had been a lawyer for over 20 years. And while his small firm had only been marginally successful, he never had come to work one day and not felt like he had done at least one thing to make the world a better place and he'd never seen anyone as slimy as Leo Tabor.

He sat in his office now, looking like a Ken doll, perfectly squared away but a complete mess on the inside. Pushing his tuna sandwich away from him on the desk, he plopped down the other file on Amy Black.

"I've looked through everything, Mr. Tabor. It clearly says that you have a certain amount of time to secure full custody of Cameron Black and legitimize him as your rightful son before I can release these funds to you."

Leo felt like the man was speaking gibberish to him. So many words, but not saying shit. He threw up his hand. "How much time?"

Mr. Clemmons looked the paperwork. "From the time of the death, you have exactly 30 months. You are at exactly 27 months and 15 days as of today." He closed the file. "She made this very simple, sir. And we notified you upon her death per her final wishes that also detailed in this document. If she were to accidentally die, you were to be notified. You would have 30 months or 2 and half years to secure custody. Has this custody battle been going on for two and a half years?"

"No," Leo said, throwing his head back. "I was married okay. What am I supposed to do? Go home and tell my wife that my fuck buddy died in a plane crash and I need to stop by Jacksonville and pick up our kid?" He laughed hysterically. "Then my bitch of an ex-wife serves me with papers out of the blue. So, I had no choice. I had to try to seek custody."

"For the money," Mr. Clemmons said, narrowing his gaze on Leo.

Leo didn't answer that. "I have two and a half months to secure full custody. If I don't, what happens to the money?"

"Quite simply, it goes to someone else." *He didn't know how much clearer he could be.*

"Who?" Leo asked, sitting up as far as he could in the chair. "The Rileys? Brett Black? Who?"

"I'm not at liberty to tell you that," the lawyer said calmly.

"Can you give me a fucking hint?" Leo pushed out of the seat and stood up. He paced the room. "How would you feel, Counselor, if $750,000 was at your fingertips and there was nothing you could do about it because of a time crunch from hell?"

Mr. Clemmons rested his elbows on his desk and looked up at Leo. "I think I would be more concerned about my son." He motioned over at the photo of his four grown boys and their mother in the frame next to the lamp. Even after being married 22 years to the same woman, he had never cheated, and he never would.

"Well, if I'm flat broke, I can't very well take care of him, now can I?" Leo said, rolling his eyes. "I'll be back here in 75 days for that money."

"If you bring me what I need to fulfill the requirements of this document, I will make sure that check is made out for you in the amount of $735,000."

Leo's eyebrows rose. His mouth popped open. "I'm sorry. Did I miss something? What happened to the rest of the money? Did she donate it to charity, request that it be piled up and burned during the next full moon? What? What now?"

"Surely a man like you understands that I'm not doing this for free. My fee is $15,000 to make sure that Mrs. Black's demands are met before anyone gets this money." And after meeting Leo Tabor it was abundantly clear why Amy had gone through all the trouble of making sure some safe guards were in place. This guy was a real piece of work. And in his opinion, he had no business with an impressionable child.

"Why not get creative and pay yourself a fee of..." Leo shrugged his shoulders as the thought of a number that might change the man's mind. "...$25,000 to just sign the check over with a copy of the paternity, which already has been established. I'm a match. 99 percent. I'm the father of the fucking kid. What more do you want from me?"

Mr. Clemmons huffed. "Congratulations, sir. But I won't be making any other arrangements with Mrs. Black's money outside of the one that she set up when she came into my office when the child was born." He pushed back in his old leather chair. "I need a court-ordered judgment identifying you as the father and the primary custodian, guardian, responsible party for Cameron. If I don't have that in 80 days, I cut a check to someone else." He raised his hand in protest of any additional outbursts from Leo. "Again, I cannot and will not disclose who the secondary party is. You can assume all you'd like but I won't help with that. I have a job to do and you are not my client. Amy Black is my client."

"And she's dead!" Leo said, throwing up his hands. "So who cares what she wants?"

"Well, she paid me $15,000 to care," Mr. Clemmons said, glad that he could tell this man to screw himself without actually saying the words.

Leo shook his head in disgust. "You lawyers are blood suckers, you know that?"

"So I've heard, Mr. Tabor." Mr. Clemmons pointed his pen. "The door is behind you, sir. Have a good day."

***

Early in the afternoon, Gavin walked into the Hellhound to find it nearly empty. Music boomed and the strobe lights were on as normal but there were very few patrons. Scanning the room, he saw Amber in the corner on some old horny guy's lap rubbing in his hair and whispering in his ear. The bouncer was by the door looking around the room making sure there was no trouble brewing, and Daisy was at the bar cleaning up and getting ready for tonight.

As soon as she saw him, her shoulders slumped. Trying to look busy, she went to the other side as he took a seat by three men who were laughing and talking. He nodded at them. "How are you doing?" he asked them.

"Good. How about you?" one of the men said, finding it odd that the guy went out of his way to speak.

"Doing good." Gavin eyed their tattoos and their dress. They were military. Good.

"What are you having?" Daisy asked mechanically.

Gavin didn't expect much more from her. He hadn't called Daisy once since they had hooked up, even though she had called him.

"Can I talk to you?" he asked, biting his lip. He watched her move in jerky motions, obviously uncomfortable by his presence.

"I'm working," she said, bending down to tend to the back of the bar. "Do you want a drink or what?"

"I want to talk to you," Gavin said in an even tone. "Please."

She rose up and looked at him. "Do you want a drink or not?"

"Give me a Jack and Coke," he said, pulling out his wallet.

She fixed the drink quickly, without her normal flair or flirting. Bringing the drink over to him, she slammed it on the bar. "Are you starting a tab?"

Gavin reached out for her hand. "I just want to talk to you."

"About what?" she asked, heart pounding in her chest. He looked even better today than he had looked the night that she met him. *Was that even possible? How was that fair?*

He looked around the club. "Is there somewhere we can go privately for just a moment?"

"No," she said emphatically.

"This is a strip club. There has to be somewhere *private*." He scrubbed a hand across his face. It was hard enough to come here, but he didn't know if he could beg her all day. This was either going to happen or not. His eyes pleaded with her to try to be reasonable but he was seconds away from turning around and leaving out the door. "I'm not trying to waste your time. I'll be brief."

Daisy's angry glare cooled a bit. "You've got five minutes."

"That's all I need," he said, getting up from the bar.

"Leann, watch the bar for me," Daisy said to the waitress who was passing by. She threw the towel over her shoulder and motioned for him.

Gavin followed Daisy into the private rooms illuminated by red lights in the back of the club.

Music was piped into the rooms over a sound system, but it was still low enough to talk.

Pulling the black sheer curtains to one of the smaller rooms with a love seat and ottoman, she turned to him with folded arms. "Hurry up, I don't want to get in trouble."

Gavin stepped closer to her. "My name is James Gavin. I'm a private detective. I'm here on a case investigating Leo Tabor in a paternity suit where he's trying to take one of my friend's son away from him."

Daisy unfolded her arms. "Okay. So what does that have to do with me?"

"Nothing," Gavin said honestly. "But you wanted to know who I was, and I felt like I owed you that."

Daisy looked down at the floor. "Do you live here? Will I ever see you again?"

"Probably not." Gavin grabbed her arm and pulled her closer to him.

She inhaled the sexy scent of his cologne and thought about their night together. Wanting to melt into his chest, she looked up at him with watery eyes. "Then what is this about?"

"*This* is about me not being an asshole. You shared your body with me, and you didn't even get a *nice meeting you*." He felt horrible about that, or at least he wanted to. "But it wasn't you."

"It's not you, it's me? Really, Gavin?" She couldn't believe he was about to use that excuse.

"It's not you; it's everything. It's PTSD. It's my affinity for an allusive lifestyle. It's my way of not getting hurt, but whatever it is, it's not you."

Daisy knew that he wasn't lying about himself. This time, she could feel something between them, though it felt awfully like a final separation. Still, she appreciated it. "Do you live here?"

"No," he said, rubbing her arm. "I live on the West Coast."

"And did you get what you came for?" Her lips pursed together like she wanted to cry.

"I got as much as I could." He smiled. "You know, you're the first woman to ever really call me on my shit. And that was scary for me. But it was sobering at the same time. I never meant to hurt you, and I know that I did. So I came here to say that I'm sorry. I came here for you. This is not about me."

Daisy nodded. "You wanted to give me closure."

"Yeah," he said in a near whisper. "Someone should have it. Right?"

Daisy tried to brush off the crazy idea she had in her head that maybe they could have something special. She'd have to chalk this one up to a lesson learned. Still, she knew that Gavin didn't have to come clean with her. "I'm glad you came here to see me and do this. It doesn't stop you from being an asshole, but it's redeeming."

He chuckled. "I'm glad I came too. Trust me, a few years from now when you're big and successful, you'll be glad that things didn't work out between us. I'm a mess."

She doubted it. "Is Leo going to get this kid?" God, she couldn't imagine that mind shaping a young child's life. He was a horrible person.

"Not if I can help it, but I need who I really am to stay between us. I'm trusting you with that. And I don't know what you'll do with that trust, but a lot of people are depending on it."

Daisy rolled her shoulders. "Wow. I was so determined to be angry with you for the rest of my life. It's sort of disappointing."

Gavin smiled. "Well, you are one of the few people that I've managed to disappoint by doing the right thing."

Daisy moved in closer. "One last kiss."

Gavin pulled her chin up. "I thought you'd never ask."

As he grazed her lips with his own, he wrapped his arms around her and kissed her deeply, feeling even more aroused by the fact that for once, he didn't have to lie about who he was or for that matter omit who he was to be intimate with a woman.

"That fucking guy!" a male voice boomed as the door slammed to the entry way of the private rooms.

"Lower your voice," Amber warned. "People are working in here." Her heels clicked on the floor as she followed behind him.

Gavin stopped kissing Daisy and put his finger over her mouth. "Shh," he whispered.

Leo stormed into the room beside them while Amber pulled the curtain. She turned to him and put her hands on her hips. "Now calm down and tell me what's going on."

"What's going on? That fucking snake attorney Richard Clemmons said that establishing paternity isn't enough. I have to actually get full custody of the kid before he'll give me the money."

Amber shrugged her shoulders, pulling at her G-string as she did. "Well, you're one step closer then. That's supposed to be good news."

"No, it's not good news. I have 75 days. The trial is in 60 days. One continuance could fuck us," Leo said, sitting on the sectional sofa. "If I don't have Cameron in my custody on the 75th day then all this shit is for nothing. I will lose that money no matter what.  $735,000 minus his *fuck-me* fee."

"So are you going to drop the case?" Amber asked. "What about our plans?"

Leo rolled his eyes.  It was pathetic that she actually thought that he was going to take her with him, but for now, he needed to continue the façade.  "Your plans. My plans.  None of it matters if I don't get this kid.  The family lawyer says that the case could go on for months. So potentially, I could end up with this kid and no money." That was something he just couldn't do. Hell, he didn't want the kids that he already had.

"So are you just going to quit?" Amber didn't know how long she could support him.  It was breaking her financially and physically. She had to work double shifts now to keep him and his lifestyle going, but he had promised he would pay her back every penny plus a brand new life.

"No, of course not, I'm not just going to quit. I have to see this through until the 75$^{th}$ day.  I also have to quit coke completely.  He says there might be a drug test because of the pictures." He growled and slammed his fist into his hands. "If I get my hands on that motherfucker, Jake, I'm going to rip his soul from his useless body."

"What does Jake have to do with anything?" Amber asked confused.

"He's a plant. I knew it. I should have gone with my gut. He turned in photos of me doing lines in the bathroom. There is no telling what else he has." Throwing his head back on the sofa, he covered his eyes with his hands. "That crazy bitch Sharon is intent on seeing this thing through. She's willing to pay for a lawyer for months *or years*, if that's what it takes. I mean, do I look like I need a fucking kid right now?"

Gavin looked down at Daisy as they listened on. "Go back to the bar," he whispered to her. There was no way that he wanted her caught up in this. So, no matter what he had to ensure that Leo could never come back here to this place. It was the only way Daisy would be safe.

"What about you?" she mouthed.

"Go," he said, pulling the curtain open. "Be quiet." He pushed her out of the door.

Amber sat down beside Leo. "You just have to try as long as you can. At least until the 75 days are over." She rubbed his back, her shiny fake bracelets jingled as she did. "Baby, we can do this." *They had to do this, or he had to go.*

"Can we?" Leo moved his hands and looked at her. "If you see that motherfucker around here. You let me know."

"Jake? He's here," Amber said, head tilted. "Or at least he was here."

"Here in the club?" Leo asked, sitting up. *Was she the dumbest woman on the Earth or did she just try to pretend to be?*

"Yeah, I saw him talking to Daisy, but I think they left."

Leo jumped up. "Are you sure that they left?"

"I don't know."

*Of course, she didn't know. She didn't know anything but how to shake her ass and give blow jobs.* Leo snatched open the curtain. "If he's here, I'm going to fuck him up." Stepping out in the hallway, he was met by Gavin who was standing in the middle of the hall.

"Looking for me?" Gavin asked, sucking his teeth.

"You picked the wrong one," Leo said, charging for him.

As Leo charged full speed into him, Gavin grabbed Leo by the shirt and they both flew in the air several feet forward. Barreling through the entryway of the private rooms back out into the club, the dancers screamed when the men landed on the floor, trying to move out of their way.

The air flew out of Leo's lungs and he was paralyzed for a moment.

Gavin quickly rolled on top of Leo and pinned him down to the ground. Reaching back, he punched Leo square in the jaw, knocking out one of his pearly white teeth while still holding on to his polo.

Leo face slammed into the concrete floor and blood flew everywhere. *So much for the flawless Ken doll look.*

Gavin hit him again and again, each time harder. "You say something about kicking my ass, you piece of shit!" Gavin screamed as he leaned forward, spitting in Leo's face. "Let me know when you want to begin."

In nothing but a purple G-string, a bikini top and heels, Amber ran from the private rooms and jumped on Gavin's back, clawing at his face. "Get off of him!" she screamed.

Gavin reached back behind him with one arm and grabbed her by her hair. Throwing her across the room, he felt Leo's hands reach for his neck and choke him. His fingers gripped his throat, nails dug into his skin. Leo screamed out as he tried to choke the life from Gavin.

Slipping his muscular arms in between Leo's iron grip, Gavin balled up his fist and then pushed his arms apart, breaking Leo's hold on him. Grabbing him by his collar again, Gavin pulled Leo up and head-butted him. His head flew back and his neck jerked.

By then the bouncers were on top of both of them, separating the fight. As they yanked Gavin up forcibly by his arms and head, he managed to get one last kick to Leo's exposed ribs. The sound echoed around the building.

Leo rolled over on his side in the fetal position.

"I thought you were bad? My grandmother can fight better than you and she's 80!" Gavin screamed.

He managed to catch his breath. "You better be glad they broke this up. I was going to fuck you up!" Leo screamed, praying that the men didn't let him go.

Gavin laughed as the two muscular men in black shirts dragged him across the room. "I thought you were a Special Ops Navy man!" He made sure to scream it loud enough that the men at the bar could hear him. "You aren't shit, Leo Tabor. You're a poser. A fucking dentist thrown out on your ass by the Navy for fucking a superior officer's wife. They don't' give medals for that and it's not considered a fucking tour of duty!"

Amber gasped, trying to straighten her hair up as she cowered in the corner. "Wait. I thought you said you were a Navy SEAL?" This was the first time she'd heard anything about

Leo being a dentist. *What about all those sto-ries?    Were they all lies?    Had she been duped...again?*

Daisy looked on from behind the bar with a grin on her face. This was absolutely priceless. She just wished that the bouncers hadn't broken the fight up. Leo deserved a good ass-beating.

"You don't know shit about me!" Leo said, spitting blood as one of the bouncers helped him up. He grabbed his ribs, feeling as though one of them might be broken. Gawking at his tooth still on the floor, he coughed up more blood.

"Yeah, I know you're not a Navy SEAL," Gavin said, laughing. He knew the guys were looking. "I know your service jacket doesn't have any combat action medals. I know the only hand-to-hand combat you've had was in the academy. And I know that you don't have the fucking right to pretend to be Special Ops. I hope you run up on one that kicks the dog shit out of you though."

Leo couldn't afford to lose any more credibil-ity in this place, but he could feel the slow changing of the tide. People glared at him suspiciously awaiting an explanation not only for the lies but for the ass beating he had taken from the stranger. Plus, Leo had told stories or allud-ed to his fake service with most of the locals in this place. It was only because of his bizarre stories that no one fucked with him.

He looked around at all the people who stood staring at him, judging him. "Ask any Navy man. They will fucking tell you. I earned my right. Did you?"

Gavin lifted his pant leg. "I earned every single solitary piece of it. Marine Recon, bitch! Did you tell Amber that you got an Other Than Honorable Discharge from the Navy and you have no retirement, no benefits, and no money? And you can't be a dentist right now because it would require you to lay off the coke and you can't get a recommendation from the Naval Hospital." Gavin laughed. He snatched away from the men as they let him go. Shocked at the new information, they weren't sure what to make of Leo anymore. "You're a joke," Gavin said, shaking his head. "You got your ass handed to you by a one-legged Vet, but you're supposed to be a SEAL."

"Regardless, you have to go, dude," one of the men said to Gavin. "And don't come back."

Gavin straightened his shirt. "I'm going. But your boy is a liar and a cheat. And if a real Navy man runs up on him in here this won't be the last time that someone kicks his ass. That's a promise. Your best bet is to bounce his ass out too...for good." He looked over at Daisy, feeling better that she was safer now.

The three men at the bar that Gavin had spoken to when he first arrived, looked on and listened to the squabble whispering among each other. When Gavin walked out of the door, they followed.

"Hey," one of them screamed as Gavin headed for his car.

Gavin turned around, half expecting them to follow. "What's up?"

"By the look of you, I'd say you're 0311," the man said, pulling up the sleeve of his shirt to reveal a SEAL tattoo.

Gavin shook his head. "I was, once upon a time. Then I went 0321 until I medically retired." He hit his leg. "Left one of my limbs in the shit."

The man nodded. "And that dude back there? Is he what you say he is? A poser?"

Gavin walked back up to the young man, who appeared to be in his late 20s and completely gung-ho. "Worse. But who am I to get involved. Marines are just a department of the Navy. One of you boys should teach him a lesson."

The guy looked back at the club and then at his two friends. "We'll get down to the bottom of this for you.  If he's a poser, he won't be for much longer. You've got to earn the right to claim that title."

"Damn right." Gavin offered his hand. "Appreciate it."

The guy shook his hand. "Sure thing."

Gavin watched the three men go back inside with a smile on his face. He knew that Leo was in for the night of his life, and after tonight, he'd never be able to show his face at this strip club again. Jumping in to his car, he threw on his shades and turned on his engine. As he pulled out into the street, he dialed a number on his cell.

"Hello," Mr. Benson said, answering on the first ring.

"It's Gavin," he said, checking his rearview mirror.

"Got any good news for me?" Mr. Benson had been thoroughly impressed with James Gavin and his ability to gather information. Hopefully, he could put him on retainer in the future.

"Well, I know that you guys are looking for a link to the money and this case. I have one. There is an attorney, Richard Clemmons, who is the trustee over $735,000 that Leo's looking to get if he can not only establish paternity but also get full custody."

Mr. Benson cracked a smile. "Excuse me for a minute," he said as he got up from the table and went to the restaurant's bathroom. He shut the door and pressed the phone to his ear. "You sure about that?"

"Yeah. I heard it all. Didn't get it recorded, but here's the deal. Leo only wants to pursue this case for another 75 days, so if you can get a continuance past that, you win automatically. He's not going to fight for this a day longer than he can use it to get the money."

Mr. Benson had something better in mind. "These two have been through hell. We're going to push for the first part of this trial and expose Leo Tabor for what he is to the judge and to the Riley's. That way if he ever gets brave enough to go after Brett Black again, he'll think twice. Plus, all of this will be on record. We're going to destroy him once and for all."

"Great, but I can't testify now."

"Why?"

Gavin smiled. "I just beat the shit out of him at the strip club."

"Plead self-defense. I need you."

"What about the money? Can you get a summons for the information from the lawyer?"

Mr. Benson racked his brain. "Clemmons won't just hand it over to us. I know him. He does everything by the book. Let me work on it. I'll let you know."

Gavin put his foot down on the accelerator and changed gears. "Let me worry about getting the documents from Clemmons. You just focus on getting the case together. After all, what you needed to win was motive. Well, I just gave you that. Now, give my friend a winning case so he can move on with his life."

Mr. Benson chuckled. "Done."

# Chapter 25

"Boredom is the biggest problem. The same position. Same day of the week. It becomes boring when you don't bring any added flowers home."

– Dr. Ruth

The alarm clock blasted loud beside Courtney's head on the nightstand, indicating it was 5:30 a.m. Reaching over without opening her eyes, she slammed her hand on top of it and hit the snooze button, then snuggled back into soft warmness of her pillow. *Just a few more minutes.*

Wiggling her butt into what should have been Brett's body, she realized that she was in the bed alone. Most unusual. Raising up, she looked toward the bathroom to see if the light was on, but it was off. *So where was he?*

She laid her head back down on the pillow and closed her eyes, but her nagging curiosity refused to let her procrastinate. Getting up, she slipped on her bunny slippers and made her way out of the dark bedroom.

Down the hall, the kids' bedroom light was on and the television was already playing Disney.

"Daddy, she likes pink shirts," Cameron said, pulling out another outfit from the dresser. "Bella doesn't like green."

"How do you know?" Brett asked, changing Bella's diaper. He bent down and kissed her face. "Hey baby. Hey," he cooed as she held on to his face and giggled.

"Bella likes pink," Cameron said, handing his father the outfit. "She likes this one best. Grandma bought it."

Brett took the little dress without protest. Slipping it over her head, he pulled it down the length of her little chubby body and gazed at her with approval. "She looks cute."

"Don't forget the bow," Cameron said, walking back over to retrieve one from the top of the dresser.

"Let me guess. Pink," Brett said, looking at Cameron's clothes. "Are you going to wear that to class?"

"Yes," Cameron said more as a question than an answer.

Brett looked at how tight it was around his collar. "You might need to change your shirt. That one looks a little snug on you."

"It's my favorite," Cameron said, huffing.

"I promise I'll buy you another one in a bigger size next week. Okay, big guy? Just work with me for now." Brett slipped on Bella's socks and debated if she could go without her little booties. Besides, she always lost them by the end of the day.

Courtney stood in the doorway watching them in quiet delight. Brett looked so sexy in his black boxer briefs and dog tags. Plus, since he started aquatic therapy, his body had toned up even more, making her want him even more, if that was remotely possible.

After they talked for hours that rainy night, he changed and so did their life. She was no longer a single mother and he had opened up a little more.

In the last month, Brett had turned into a completely new man. He cooked. He cleaned. He ran errands via Uber. He made appointments himself. And he included her more in his decisions about work. They were moving toward the life that she told him she wanted and nothing could make her happier.

"Can I help?" she asked, finally walking into the bedroom.

Brett picked up Bella and bounced her in his arms. "Nope. We've got it." He walked over and bent to kiss her lips. Lingering there, he kissed her again, this time slower. Pulling regretfully away from her sweet mouth, his blue eyes flashed open and locked on her. "Why don't you go and get back in the bed. I'm going to finish getting them ready."

"Them?" Courtney asked. "Where is Bella going?"

"Yeah, them," Brett said with a twinkle in his eye. "You and I have plans today after I get back from my physical therapy and PTSD session. So, you can sleep in until nine and then you have to get up, get showered, eat some breakfast and get ready to go have some fun by 11:00."

"What are we doing?" Courtney asked, looking at Cameron. He always spilled the beans. All he needed was a little prompting.

"Don't tell her," Brett said quickly to Cameron. He winked at Courtney. "It's a surprise. You'll have to wait and see."

Cameron grinned at Courtney. "Mommy wants to know, but I can keep a secret."

"Since when?" Courtney joked.

Brett picked up the baby powder and put it into the baby bag. "Go! Get out of here." Nudging Courtney along, "I've got this."

"You sure?" she asked, heading out the door. She couldn't believe he was taking care of them, but she wouldn't protest any longer. She didn't want him to change his mind.

"I'm sure," Brett said, swatting her bottom. "Now go." Watching her backside as she walked out of the room, he made a mental note of what he wanted from her later.

\*\*\*

Courtney did exactly like Brett told her. At eleven o'clock sharp, she was dressed in jeans and a t-shirt ready to go on their mystery morning excursion. She had to admit, being allowed to sleep in before going out on a surprise date was hot and completely unexpected. But it would have been even better if he told her where they were going. She couldn't help but wonder if she was dressed appropriately.

A few minutes later, Brett returned home whistling cheerfully and then smiled at her.

"Where's Bella?" she asked, hoping it would tell her something about what was going on today.

Brett didn't bite. "She's with your Dad. And before you ask, your mom is going to pick up Cameron when he gets out of school."

That had been Courtney's next question. Now she had to think of another.

"I bet its killing you not to know," Brett joked, enjoying her displeasure.

"It is," she said, closing the magazine. Standing up from the sofa, she picked up her purse. "You could at least give me a clue."

"No clues," he said heading upstairs.

"Where are you going?" She said, holding on to the staircase banister, watching him hopping up the stairs. How did he move that fast in that boot thing?

His voice echoed as he disappeared down the hall. "I've gotta grab one thing and then we can go."

"Go where?" Walking over to the window, she saw her mother's car in the driveway. Squinting, she pushed up against the window. "Is that my mother out there?"

Brett came back with an extra baby bag. "Yeah," she's giving us a ride."

Courtney folded her arms. "What is going on?"

"Wouldn't you like to know?" Brett said, extending his arm. "Stop being stubborn and let's go."

Getting in the car, Courtney looked over at her mother and sneered. "He's got you involved in this little scheme too?"

Diane smiled back at her daughter and slipped on her shades to hide her eyes from the bright sunny skies. "Are we all set?" she asked Brett.

Brett closed the back door and set the bag on the seat. "Now we are all set."

"Great," Diane said, looking back as she pulled out of the driveway.

Courtney was going crazy as they headed toward Jacksonville. Every single time that she opened her mouth to speak, her conversation circled back to the date. "Where are we going? So what are we doing?"

But both Diane and Brett were completely quiet. They drove relaxed in her mother's big-body Mercedes straight through town and headed toward Highway 24. As they pulled on to the road headed toward the airport, Courtney exploded.

"Okay, now this has gone on long enough. What is going on? Where are we going?

Brett grinned sheepishly. "We're almost there."

"Is someone coming here?" Courtney asked, looking over at her mother.

Diane smiled but didn't say a word. There was no way that she was going to give this surprise up. Brett had been working on it for nearly two weeks.

When they pulled up to the front of the airport, Brett got out and grabbed his backpack. "Okay, this is our stop," he said, opening Courtney's door. "Let's go, baby."

Courtney looked between them confused. "Go where?  What's going on?"

Diane leaned over and kissed her daughter's cheek. "Enjoy your trip.  Now goodbye," she said, pointing at the door. "Get out."

Courtney took her husband's hand as he helped her out of the car.  Closing the door behind her, they watched as Diane quickly pulled off.

"Brett, I have to know what is going on," Courtney said wanting the surprise to end.

Brett moved her off the curb and escorted her inside. "Remember the last time we spoke when I was in Afghanistan?  We were making plans for a trip."

"Yeah," Courtney said with a crooked smile.

"Well, I figured that I still owed you one and I'll be laid up for a few weeks after the surgery so now is the best time," he said, cracking a smile.

"What?" Courtney put her hands on her head. "Where are we going?"

"New Orleans."

Courtney screamed. "I love New Orleans."

He laughed. "I know."

"What about clothes? I have a stick of gum, some perfume and some hand sanitizer in my purse."

"I've already made arrangements," Brett said, walking with her to the line to check in.

"I don't understand," Courtney said, looking at his backpack.

"I called ahead and had the Manager of the hotel make arrangements for clothes, lingerie, personal hygiene products, shoes and most importantly...reservations."

"How long will we be gone?" Courtney stuttered.

Brett loved to see her so speechless. Finally, he had gotten one over on her nosy butt. "Five days," he answered.

Another question. "How long have you been planning this?"

He laughed and wrapped his arm around her. "Two weeks."

She was about to ask another question, but he covered her mouth. "Baby, relax and enjoy this. Trust me."

The excitement got the better of her. Wrapping her arms around him, she kissed his lips and hugged him. "Oh my gracious. I can't believe that you're doing this!"

\*\*\*

The city of New Orleans was beautiful from the moment that they got off the plane. They were greeted by the sound of Creole music and the upbeat tempo of a busy bustling crowd. Exiting out of the airport, a driver in a black Mercedes was waiting to whisk them off to the French Quarter. When they arrived at the Bourbon Orleans, a historic and elegant hotel right off of Bourbon Street, they checked in and went up to the Governor's Suite.

As soon as Courtney opened the door, she screamed. The suite was old world Southern charm at its finest from the gleaming black marble floors to the Provence-style décor and three-pronged brass candelabras strategically placed around the spacious living room and seating area among hundreds of red roses and gift boxes full of treats that Brett had arranged.

He'd also made sure to have them stock the refrigerator, set the dining table for a formal five-course meal and lay out exactly what he wanted her to wear tonight which was really close to nothing.

The plantation shutters overlooking the lush greenery of the courtyard and saltwater pool had been pulled to make the room dark and candles glow, adding ambience to the already romantic setting.

"Oh my goodness, Brett," she said, smelling the roses on the wet bar.  Two bottles of champagne chilled beside the roses with a box of chocolate strawberries ready for her to open.

Brett closed the door behind them and watched her as she took in the opulence of the space.

Courtney opened the card addressed to her and read it aloud.  "Words cannot express how grateful I am for all that you've done and all that you are in my life.  I'm hoping that this small vacation will be the relaxing break that you need and deserve.  Love always. Your husband, Brett." Closing the card, she wiped a tear.

Brett walked up behind her and massaged her shoulders. Kissing the column of her neck, he whispered in her ear. "I love you, baby."

She turned to face him.  "I love you too," she said, raising up on her tiptoes to kiss his lips. "I love you so much."  Her hand trembled as they cupped his face. "I can't even explain how I feel right now."

"Are you happy?" he asked, loving how excited she seemed.  It made him feel good to be able to do this, to be able to afford this, without worrying how it would affect them later.

"I'm beyond happy," she said, looking around the room.

Brett stepped away and put his backpack on the sofa. "Well, there should be a hot bath drawn in the bathroom. Why don't you slip into it while I pour you a glass of champagne?"

Courtney put down her purse and made her way through the living room and seating area to the large bedroom. A king-size bed was surrounded by more candles and roses and in the middle of the bed was a pair of low cut French lace panties and matching bra.

She bit her lip. Tonight, she felt like getting absolutely crazy.

Brett opened his backpack and pulled out the files. Looking through each one to make sure that they were all there, he went to the bar and poured two glasses of the bubbly. According to the manager, this stuff was not only expensive, it was also supposed to put you on your ass. Good. He wanted her loose and pliable tonight. With no kids, no appointments and no interruptions, he felt incredibly free.

Brett found her in the bathroom, in the sunken Jacuzzi bathtub, hidden under a ton of bubbles. She had pulled her hair up in a ponytail and relaxed back with her eyes closed.

He sat on the edge of the tub and passed her a glass. "Here you go, baby," he said, eyeing a pebbled nipple as she reached for the champagne.

"I wish you could get in with me," she asked, moving around in the water. "There's plenty of space."

"This foot would probably ruin the experience. I'll just jump in later," Brett said, holding up the files in his hand. "Soooo, the trip was just one part of the surprise. This is the other part."

Courtney took a sip of the champagne and rested back in the tub. "What is that?"

He opened the file and pulled out a piece of paper. Setting it on the edge so she could see it, he waited with bated breath.

Reading carefully, she finally looked up at him. Her mouth dropped open. "Brett, I don't understand."

"It's an agreement with a local realtor. I put our house up for sale. According to her, the market is hot for our area, and considering all the upgrades we made on it, we should make a killing." Brett pulled out another piece of paper. "And I bought this." He put a picture of a 4-bedroom cottage style house by the bay in Palo Alto, California.

Licking his lips, he raised an arched brow at her. "According to Gavin, this type of property, especially on the bay, is really hard to come by, and he would know...it's his old house. We got it a little under market value because he doesn't really need the cash."

"What are you saying, Brett?" Courtney said, tears falling down her face.

He reached over and wiped them gently. "You mean everything to me, and I didn't realize that we live in the same house that Amy and I lived in, because I was so wrapped up in my shit, but your talk with me that night made me see life through your eyes."  He cleared his throat. "Also, I know you want to go to Stanford. I know you want to start over. I know you need me to be on board with it.  So, I made the first steps."

"Stanford." She shook her head. "It was just a dream until now.  I guess I can actually apply." The thought blew her mind. "I never thought I'd even get the opportunity to consider it seriously."  Courtney's body trembled in shock. Selling her old house.  Buying her a new one. Her mouth quivered as she tried to speak.  This was all too much for her.

Brett pulled out a letter and set it on top of the picture of the house. "Mr. Benson's friend is a former judge. She's also some big alum at Stanford.  Your mother and I sent her your information and transcripts, basically your mom did, and this lady got you an informal acceptance into Stanford. I mean, informal in the sense that you can go, but you're going to have to officially accept and I have to send them a check, but I called ahead and told them to expect it soon."

Courtney put her hand over her mouth. The diamonds in her ring sparkled in his eyes. "Is this real?" she asked, setting the glass of champagne down.

Brett knew that Courtney was on the verge of an explosion. Her bright eyes and shallow breaths almost frightened him. "Baby, I want us to be together for the rest of our lives. You were right. I needed to put my life into a new context. I needed to see what's best for all of us, and that's not the Marine Corps. Not anymore." He rubbed her chin.

"Nothing is more important than you and our kids. That's why I'm medically retiring out and accepting a job offer with Gavin in San Francisco at his private security firm. That way the next baby we have, I can be there from start to finish and not miss whole portions of this life we're trying to build together." He smiled at her. "You wanted me. Well, you've got me."

Courtney's face was unreadable. "Could you move the papers, please?" she asked.

"Sure." Brett put them back into the folder and then stood up and placed them on the vanity. This wasn't exactly the reaction he was...

When he turned around, Courtney had stood up in the tub. Her body glistened with water and bubbles stuck to her sweet frame. "Take your clothes off," she said, eyes blazing. She stepped out of the tub covered in suds as he pulled off his shirt and wrapped her arms around him.

Pulling him into her kiss, she passionately tasted his mouth. She was so forceful, so dominant, until Brett immediately got hard.

Picking her up, he put her on the vanity and yanked his pants open. Courtney breathed hard. Spreading her legs wide, she ran a hand from her side up to her breasts and pinched her nipple.

Brett pulled off his pants and underwear, then immediately went to her. His penis was rock hard, aching to be buried deep inside of her.

Her hands roamed over his stomach, caressing deeply crevassed muscle as he grabbed her by her buttocks and pulled her to edge of the vanity. Trailing a kiss down her shoulder, he slipped one of her eager nipples into his mouth and watched as she laid back, head against the mirror.

Her moans were sweet, soft. As her hips rose up, her sex pushed against his lower abdomen.

Throwing one smooth leg over his shoulder, he rubbed his knuckle over her clit then slipped a digit into her wet sex. She moaned louder and her back arched. Slipping a second finger into her, he growled. Water and soap trailed into her belly button as she pushed her hands against the mirror. She wanted him inside of her so badly.

Without warning she felt his velvety tongue in between her thighs, spearing in between the folds of her swollen flesh. In and out he went until he felt her hands move from the mirror to his head, gripping his dirty blonde hair as she guided him. He pinned her thighs down and lapped at her, drinking in her wetness, sucking at her over and over again until audible sound of his mouth and her wetness combined with his rhythm made her cry out.

"I'm close," she said, holding his head. Her mouth refused to close as she watched.

He pulled her closer to him, kissing her deep, licking her from her throbbing clit all the way down to the end of her labia then spearing inside of her.

"Yes," she screamed.

He moved faster and faster, held her tighter until finally he pushed her over the edge and her orgasm sent her spiraling into a paralyzing ecstasy. As her vagina pulsed, he rose up, eyes hooded with dark eroticism.

Grabbing her little body by her waist, he pulled her down off the vanity, flipped her over and pushed her breasts up against the cool marble counter.

Courtney opened her legs wider. "Fuck me," she begged.

Her words made him mad with need. His large hands reached in front of her and rested on her stomach. Pulling her closer to him, he pressed his erection against her. "Fuck you?" he asked, voice husky.

"Yes," she panted.

Brett slapped his rock-hard penis against her sex. "Fuck you hard?" he asked, slipping a finger inside of her just to make her scream.

"Please," she begged. "I need you so bad."

With his hard sex fisted in his hand, he ran it over her sensitive flesh. The tease was agonizing for her. "Ask again?" he said, rubbing it over her clit.

"Please," she cried out. Slipping her fingers in between her thighs, she made him watch. "Take me."

The sight of her playing with herself pushed him past a tease. He released a hissing archaic growl before pummeling mercilessly into her body. His smooth steely penis ached as he filled her with each thick heavy inch until he was at her hips. With one hand, his fingers dug into the sides of her hips as he thrust in and out, holding her body down with the other hand against the vanity.

Each stroke was harder than the next. Making her body jerk, he stretched her sensitive skin, pushing his chest up against her back.

His arm came around her and he nibbled at her ear as he felt her body start to tremble. "Yes," she screamed.

"Come for me," he said, standing back up. He spread her cheeks open to get a better view of her. Slapping harder and harder against her, he played with her clit as he destroyed her.

"Brett!" Courtney screamed, her voice hoarse. The sound of his body slapping against her own echoed throughout the bathroom.

"Give it to me," he said, grabbing her by her hair and raising up on his heel.

She backed into him, pushing harder and harder and he went deeper and deeper. Reaching back, he smacked her left cheek then smoothed his hand over it.

The sensation of pain and pleasure again sent her over into a spiral and her orgasm pulsated throughout her body.

Brett could feel her contractions. Hard and fast, he bent over her back and gripped her shoulders, pulling her closer to him as he felt himself explode inside of her.

His loud roar spilled out into the living room and hallway. Shaking, he held on to her, digging his nails into her flesh, he released every ounce of himself before he let her go.

Courtney nearly collapsed. Standing up, she turned and looked at him with amazement. "Care to take this into the bedroom?" she asked, throat dry.

Brett grabbed the champagne. "You read my mind."

She went to step back in the tub to wash off but Brett stopped her. "No," he said, looking at her body. "I want you just like that."

"No washing off?" she asked, threatening to stick a toe into the water.

Brett licked his lips. "I'm just going to get you dirty all over again."

# Chapter 26

"It is God who avenges me, and subdues the peoples under me; He delivers me from my enemies. You also lift me up above those who rise against me; You have delivered me from the violent man."

- Psalm 18:47

Parking among the litter of cars in the crowded lot, Brett and Courtney arrived at the Onslow County Courthouse early on Tuesday morning to go through the clearance process and meet with Mr. Benson, who was there nearly an hour before with his three-man wrecking ball team making sure that everything was ready.

With a charismatic, million dollar smile, he met them just past security in a sharp tailored blue suit cut to fit his NFL linebacker frame.

"Brett, Courtney," he said, shaking their hands. "Nice day for a trial, huh?" He winked at them both.

"If you say so," Brett said under his breath.

With a quick glance, Mr. Benson scanned their appearance individually and as a couple. Standing as straight as an arrow, Brett was wearing his Marine Corps issued Alpha uniform that fit his tall wide frame to perfection, boasting a green coat with his staff sergeant rank, green trousers, khaki long-sleeve button-up shirt, khaki tie, tie clasp, and black shiny shoes. On his coat, a host of ribbons and marksmanship badges brandished the left chest. His dirty blonde high and tight had been shaped the night before and his face was shaved as smooth as a baby. While mostly healed, his face still carried a large scar across his eye lid to the side of his temple and a scar across his wide mouth. However, Mr. Benson was pleased. Brett looked like the new poster child of the Marine Corps, plus the boot on his foot didn't hurt.

Courtney had been dressed by her mother for the day to appear more of a Stepford mom than the rabble-rouser she was. Her feathery hair was styled in a classic wrap. Her make-up was simple and soft, only designed to bring out her natural features. She wore a lively pink V-neck shapely sheath St. John dress with matching pink heels and pearls as accessories and a simple gold wedding band instead of her normal huge diamond. Mr. Benson was impressed. She looked like a First Lady, and in a trial, it would be hard to attack her without violating someone's fragile sensibilities.

"Well, how are you both?" Mr. Benson asked, ushering them down the halls past other people who waited impatiently for their appearances, argued with their court-appointed lawyers and talked on their cell phones. Some of them wore jeans and stretched out cotton t-shirts, others wore worse, making Brett, Courtney and their dream team of lawyers stick out like a sore thumb.

"Fine," Courtney lied with a shaky smile.

"Nervous as a whore in church," Brett said honestly. He hadn't slept a wink the night before and based upon how much tossing and turning Courtney had done, neither had she. Still, this morning they were up at the crack of dawn running off of pure adrenaline.

Mr. Benson laughed as though their worry was completely unnecessary. "Don't be nervous. *Be sad, shocked and hurt*, like we practiced. That goes over better. Remember you're the victims here." He raised his thick dark brows at Courtney. "You let me be nervous for you."

"You nervous?" Courtney doubted it.

"Well, one can pretend," Mr. Benson said with a twinkle in his eye.

Today, more than ever before, Mr. Benson exuded a certain bright-eyed confidence that most people had only after they won a case.

As they made their way to the courtroom where the trial would take place, they saw a bench full of familiar and not-so familiar faces and just a few feet down, the plaintiff and his one lonely attorney sat with Sharon and William Riley.

Mr. Benson waved down to them sardonically. "This trial is going to be like slaughtering pigs." He turned to Courtney and Brett. "Okay, you know your Mom and Dad, of course. You know James Gavin. You know Judy Mabry." He paused at the other group of people. "But here's some folks that you don't know. This is Mrs. Catherine Tabor, Leo's ex-wife. She's going to be a character witness for you today, and she's also one hell of a lawyer in Wilmington."

Courtney's eyes bucked as she offered her hand. "Thanks so much for doing this," she said sincerely.

"Glad to," Catherine said, feeling her ex-husband glare at her from the next bench over. He'd never understand how much she was going to enjoy this.

Mr. Benson tried to control his laugh. "This is Lance Corporal Mark Sheer. He was one of the Military Police who arrested Leo Tabor on the golf course the night that he was caught with his commanding officer's wife."

"Nice to meet you," Brett said, shaking his hand firmly. "Appreciate you for doing this."

"My pleasure," Mark said, looking at Brett's medals.

"And I want you two to sit here, right between Gavin and Catherine," Mr. Benson said, motioning toward the bench. "Let me huddle with my team for a second and then I'll be right back."

When they sat down, Mr. Benson and his team gathered in the corner in clear view of Leo and his attorney. He was internally trying to intimidate them and whether he knew it or not, it was working.

Brett and Courtney had worked with Benson's dream team for a month to get ready, every day for an hour, Monday through Friday. One Black woman, one Black man and white man all under the age of 30 with plenty of energy and clinging to Mr. Benson's every word, the lawyers had combed through every piece of the case and prepared an ironclad defense for the Black family. Now it was time to execute their master plan.

Gavin scooted over as Brett sat beside him.

"Hey," Brett said, removing his cover. Already he had started to sweat in all the layers of clothes.

"What's up," Gavin said, wiping his tired eyes. In a sleek black Michael Kors suit and shaven face, he looked like a different person than his normal rugged self. And his presence continued to grab the attention of Catherine, who was glad that Benson had given some space between her and the sexy private investigator or she might have just reached over and attacked him.

"Late night?" Brett asked, looking over at his friend.

Gavin's voice was low and brittle like he was battling a hangover. "Oh yeah. Spent most of it at a fucking golf course last night." He huffed and rubbed a hand over his head. "I hate golf."

"Some girl you chasing got a father with some money or influence you need?" Brett asked, scared to hear the answer.

Gavin looked over at Brett and smiled. "I'll tell you later."

"Alright, let me give you guys and gals an update," Mr. Benson said, clasping his hands together as he returned to them. He heaved a deep breath. "We have had a slight change in today's events. The judge who was assigned to hear the case, Barrington, got really sick yesterday at the golf course and was rushed to the hospital." He raised his palms. "Don't worry. *He's alright*. Just really bad food poisoning.

Something tropical and very nasty, but he'll survive. He's going to be out for a few weeks recovering, but we have a very capable judge taking his place. Her name is Ellen Warford. You may have heard of her before. She has a twin sister, Mae Warford, in Raleigh, NC who is a judge also. They're like royalty around these parts and from what I've seen she's a very fair and balanced judge. *Anyhow,* she'll be hearing the case and hopefully helping us reach a verdict."

Diane had heard of the fabulous Warford sisters. They had made all the social papers for the last decade. Smiling, she leaned into Jeffery. "Ellen Warford is a Black woman married to a white retired Marine," she said, astonished at Mr. Benson's skill. "This is a perfect match for the kids."

"Too perfect," Jeffery said, shaking his head. He wasn't sure what had happened, but he did know that it was no coincidence. "As long as it plays in our favor, I won't complain."

Brett turned to Gavin and frowned. "How much of this were you responsible for?"

Gavin yawned. "Leo's ex-wife was easy to find and eager to burn him at the stake. The MP was happy to help after he found out you were a Marine." He shrugged like it was no big deal.

"And the golf course?" Brett asked.

"*Plausible deniability*, bro," Gavin said, pushing back on the bench. "Learn it and love it."

Brett looked down at the bench about 20-feet down from them. "Is that Leo?" he asked, eyeing the man like he wanted to kill him.

Gavin didn't bother looking over at the guy. "Yep, that's him."

"What happened to him? Was that you, too?" Brett asked as he sat back.

"I can truly say that I didn't do that," Gavin laughed. "Evidently, the guy ran into a few Navy SEALs who were not too happy that he was a poser." Though he was responsible for the introduction he wasn't responsible for the outcome. Pity.

"Well they fucked him up," Brett smirked. "Damn, I wish I could have been there."

Courtney grabbed Judy's hand and held it in her own. "You're a life saver," she said, smiling at her. "Thank you for this."

Judy cracked a wide smile. "Your attorney offered me the opportunity to sit on a stand and call Amy Black's narrow ass a whore." She chuckled. "I wouldn't miss it for the world."

Courtney suddenly understood why Mr. Benson was so incredibly confident. He had assembled a group of people that would not only

vindicate her husband and vouch for his character but also help crucify Leo Tabor and Amy
Black posthumously.

"Okay," she said, releasing her anxiety. "This
is going to work out."

***

Leo pulled at his restricting neck brace and
tried to ignore the aching pain shooting up his
knee to his groin and the dull ache in his lower
back as he tried to get comfortable on the hard
bench. *But there was no hope.* Wearing a full
cast on his left leg, a less-than-attractive back
brace and a neck brace, he sat beside Sharon and
William Riley, while the lawyer looked over the
files one last time as if he would discover some
miracle that hadn't sprung forth since they
started this shit.

It occurred to Leo as he lay in the hospital
alone for those weeks that this had been a bad
idea. In fact, it ranked as the worst idea of his
life. If he had just stayed away from the Rileys
and Brett Black, he would have still had a perfect
nose, a bright smile and some sex appeal that
might have landed him an old cougar to mooch
off of until he got back up on his feet, but in his
current condition, no one wanted any part of
him.

That was something he wasn't used to. He had been beautiful his entire life and now he was just handicapped.

Leo had been sulking about his pathetic situation for weeks. After being jumped by three Navy SEALs in the bathroom of the strip club the same night of the fight with Gavin, he had been hospitalized for weeks and left with an enormous doctor's bill. To make things worse, things were now very shaky with Amber, who promised to put him out on his ass if he didn't win this case. He knew she was a gold digger but he thought she would at least keep her cool until after the trial, but after being found out about being a defunct Navy dentist with a missing tooth he couldn't afford to replace, she treated him like pure concentrated shit.

Damn, he hoped to win just so he could rub it in Amber's face before he hobbled his ass on a plane and said goodbye to the United States.

"This isn't good," the lawyer said, shaking his head. Benson was going to make him into his bitch in that courtroom today with what they had and he knew it. He had begged Leo to walk away, but the man wouldn't, and so he had to proceed.

"What isn't good?" Sharon asked, trying not to look down at all the people who had come to

Brett's defense. She didn't even know he had that many friends. Now she wished that William had allowed her to bring some of the congregation from the Church, but he had insisted that this was a personal matter that would not be discussed outside of the home.

"We have a new judge." The lawyer closed his files and shoved them back in his briefcase. "Barrington is sick. Word is that he's got some kind of food poisoning you can only get from India."

"What's wrong with having a new judge?" Sharon asked, wishing William would have a little more buy in to this trial. He had checked out of the entire process since Brett Black showed up at their door nearly three months ago. It was like he didn't even care anymore.

The lawyer lowered his voice and turned to her. "She's a Black woman."

Sharon's eyes grew big. Even though she knew what the lawyer was implying, she still prodded. "That's not supposed to matter. The judge is supposed to be impartial."

"They are going to call you to the stand and make you confirm the fact that you used racial slurs about Courtney Black." The lawyer rolled his eyes. He wasn't too keen on what Brett had asserted in the briefs. Evidently, the First Lady of their church was a racist.

Sharon swallowed hard. "Well, I will just say that I was angry."

The lawyer was not impressed with her answer. "Brett is also accusing you both of being a part of the Klan. He's saying that Amy told him very proudly before offering to take him to a rally herself."

"We can deny that." Sharon blinked fast like the lawyer had just slapped her.

"You won't say anything at all," William finally said to Sharon. He turned to the lawyer. "I'm seriously considering leaving here with my wife before this begins."

"Sir, if you leave, this case will bomb for sure," the lawyer threatened.

Leo smacked his lips. And he thought he was a piece of work. These people were just as disgusting. No wonder Amy was such a fuck up.

"William, we are not leaving." Sharon sat back and crossed her arms. "And what about that woman over there. Who is that?"

"Which one," the lawyer said, refusing to make eye contact with Mr. Benson. Everyone knew he was a bully both in the courtroom and outside of it. Plus, the Rileys had said Brett Black was broke, but he knew that Benson's retainer started at $200,000, so there had to be a lot of money somewhere.

"The well-dressed white woman in the black suit sitting by Judy Mabry," Sharon said. "Who is that?"

The lawyer didn't respond. Instead he waited on Leo to give the Rileys an explanation.

Leo finally piped up. "She's my ex-wife."

"That's your ex-wife?" Sharon said flabbergasted. She made Amy look like a second class citizen with all her poise and elegance.

"I thought you said she was a horror," Sharon hissed glibly.

"She *is* a horror," Leo said, wishing that this day was over. "Just wait and see. She'll say anything to destroy me."

It was more like *anything she said would destroy him*. For everything that these people knew, Catherine knew more and a lot worse. Now, she'd finally be able to use it all against him, just like she had promised a hundred times before.

After much contemplation, he had started to throw in the towel when the lawyer prepped him the week before. After Benson submitted their interrogatories and listed evidence, witnesses and a boat load of requests including a drug test, he wanted nothing more than to walk away. But if he did, he would also be walking away from the money. So, he had to suffer through the extreme embarrassment in the hope of winning. If he lost, however, he would just have to change his number and move, which was a very real possibility anyway.

"Our best bet is to rely on the expert witness who should be here in just a little bit. With her testimony about children doing better with their biological parents, it's very possible that we can still win this," the lawyer said, trying to be up-beat.

"Well, at least if it looks like we are losing, we can request a continuance to another date," Sharon said, rubbing Leo's back.

Leo grinned at her, but he knew better. After today, he had 15 days and then it was off to a new game plan.

William stood up. Throwing his suit jacket over his arm, he nodded at Leo. "Son, I wish you well, but I'm not going to stay here and be embarrassed before the entire community."

Sharon looked up at him in shock. "Bill, sit down."

"No," he said, offering his hand to the lawyer. "Good luck. Send us the bill and we'll settle."

"You can't be serious? I'm not going any-where," Sharon insisted.

William kept his voice low. "Then don't go anywhere, Sharon. But I'm leaving. I haven't worked this hard to have my reputation snatched from under me. I'll pick you up after the trial." Turning away from her, he walked away leaving her on the bench between the lawyer and Leo. As he passed by Brett and Courtney's bench, he kept his nose up and his eyes on the end of the hallway.

"Where's he going?" Brett asked.

"I have no clue," Gavin said, standing up. "Let me check on this and I'll be back."

Mr. Benson looked at his watch and then went to the courtroom door. Opening it, he motioned inside. "Everyone, come on inside. Let's get ready to rumble."

As Brett and Courtney took a seat at the table beside Mr. Benson and his team, who were given extra chairs, the rest of the folks filed in behind them quietly.

In a black robe with her hair pulled back in a bun, Judge Warford stepped out of her chamber and headed for her seat. She sat down and immediately began to speak under her breath to the clerk before nodding and raising her eyes to the people in the room.

The bailiff, a heavy-set older man with a gut, finally stood beside the side of the elevated platform and the stenographer. "All rise." He paused as everyone jumped back to their feet. "This court is now in session. The honorable Judge Warford presiding. Please take your seats."

Judge Warford smiled. "Good morning ladies and gentlemen. Calling the case of Tabor versus Black. Are both sides ready?"

"Ready for the plaintiff, your Honor," Leo's lawyer said, still standing.

"Ready for the defendants, your Honor," Mr. Benson answered.

***

Opening statements from both sides were powerful, but Benson clearly overpowered the room using buzz words like adultery, conspiracy, dishonor and bigotry. It didn't help that the pain on Brett and Courtney's face as he explained what had happened to them made them look like saints.

Round two was witness calling. Sharon went first. Making sure to seem as meek and humble as possible, she barely raised her voice as she was sworn in. Sitting on the stand, she continued to smile at the judge, hoping to butter her up, but based upon the concrete glare of the woman, the trick wasn't working.

"I loved my daughter and I love my grandson. All we want is for him to be closer to his biological family," she said, answering one of many of pre-rehearsed questions by Leo's lawyer. "It was so hard to lose her." Tears fell. "It was even harder to be denied our grandson by Brett and Courtney. But after hearing that Cameron wasn't even his biologically, it became abundantly clear that we had to fight for our grandson."

"Thank you. I have no further questions," Leo's lawyer said, glad that she hadn't fumbled. However, when he saw Mr. Benson smirk and close his leather bound notebook, his heart skipped a beat.

"Does the defense have any questions?" the judge asked.

"Yes, your honor." Mr. Benson walked from behind the table and pulled at his suit jacket. "Mrs. Riley you say that you only want what's best for your grandson, Cameron Black. Is that correct?"

"Yes," Sharon said flatly.

"Do you think the Black family is what's best for Cameron?"

"No," she said, looking at Courtney.

Mr. Benson slipped his hands in his pocket. "Do you plan to be a part of Cameron's life in the event that the plaintiff is granted custody?"

"Yes. We've already talked about it. We want to be there to help him raise Cameron and give him a strong upbringing, good morals and values."

Mr. Benson didn't waste any time. "Have you ever called Courtney Black a nigger?"

Sharon paused. "I might have when I was angry. I lost my cool."

"Is that a yes or no?" Mr. Benson asked. He gave Sharon a *fuck-you* smile.

Sharon hesitated and the judge quickly jumped in.

"Answer the question Mrs. Riley."

"Yes," Sharon said, putting her hands on her knees.

"Do you use that language often?" Mr. Benson asked, walking closer to the stand.

"No." Sharon tried to redeem herself. "I lost my head when Brett Black called my daughter a whore."

"That must have hurt. Why did he call your daughter a whore?"

"Because he found out that Cameron was not his biological son. My daughter had an affair. But it only happened once and from what I am told, it was brief."

"If it pleases the Court, I'd like to submit exhibit A and have it admitted as evidence," Mr.

Benson said, going to his table to pick up a note from Amy to Brett about picking up laundry. After the clerk slapped a sticker on it and passed it back to him, he eyed Sharon's discomfort.

"Does the Plaintiff have any objection?" The judge asked.

"No, your honor," Leo's lawyer answered.

"Would you be able to recognize your daughter's handwriting, Mrs. Riley?"

"Yes, anywhere," Sharon said, nostrils flared.

"Permission to approach the witness," Mr. Benson said.

"Permission granted," the judge said, looking over at Sharon.

"Can you verify that this is Amy Black's writing?" He walked back over to Sharon and handed it to her. "Is that her writing?"

Sharon rubbed the paper as though it was her only link to Amy. "Yes, it is," she said, starting to cry again.

Mr. Benson went back to the table. "Exhibit B, your Honor, for admittance into evidence. Mrs. Amy Black's personal diary." He went back to the table and picked up Amy's diary. Walking back to Sharon, he sucked his teeth.

"Can you open the diary to the first tab and read aloud the highlighted portion into the microphone, Mrs. Riley?"

Sharon opened the diary and took a deep breath. "I wish that I could just move back in with Mom and start my life over sometimes."

"Is that your daughter's handwriting?" Mr. Benson asked.

"Yes, it is." Sharon said, taking the Kleenex provided by the bailiff.

"Will you please open the diary to the purple tab and read the highlighted portion, please." Mr. Benson stood in front of her.

Sharon re-opened the diary. "Mom says that if I want to be happy, I had better start to look at other options because Brett Black ain't it. After I told her about my relationship with..." she paused. "with Leo, she was extremely upset that we broke it off and that I had started a new relationship with Jermaine instead of some of the other men that I had been screwing around the base. There is only one reason she doesn't like Jermaine even though he's an officer. She doesn't like niggers. She has told me over and over again that mixing with them will end the world as we know it. But Jermaine is not a nigger, he's a real man and we're going to be happy together. One thing for sure though. I can't tell mom about the baby and I can't tell Jermaine about Cameron. I'm just going to have to start all the way over and go from there."

There was a gasp in the room and suddenly Sharon wanted to stand up and leave. *Damn Amy for writing this shit down.* She turned her chair slightly away from the glaring judge and cleared her throat.

Mr. Benson tread carefully. "That is your daughter's personal diary. Is it your position that you didn't know about Leo?"

"I don't recall any of this," Sharon said, closing the diary. "I don't recall talking to my daughter about any affair or saying those disgusting words."

"Remember, Mrs. Riley that you are under oath. Do you recall this conversation with your daughter?"

"No. I've never heard of any Jermaine and I never knew about Leo until he showed up at my door," Sharon said, wiping her tears.

"So you didn't know a name. Alright. Did you know that Amy had plans to abandon Cameron, leaving him with her husband Brett Black, to attempt to run off with *another man* who was an officer in the Marine Corps?"

Sharon twisted up her mouth. "No."

"At any point, did Brett Black tell you that this had occurred?" Mr. Benson had her right where he wanted her.

"He said it on the porch when he came to my house three months ago." Sharon eyed Brett. "That's when he told us that Amy had left him."

"Is that when Brett called Amy a whore?" Mr. Benson asked.

"Yes."

"Do you think that Amy's decision to abandon Cameron was in his best interest?" Mr. Benson asked.

"No," Sharon said without emotion.

"Would you consider yourself a racist, Mrs. Riley?" Mr. Benson asked compassionately.

"No," Sharon answered emphatically. "My husband and I are Christians. He's the head of a church in Fayetteville and our doors are open to everyone."

"Do you think it would be in the best interest for Cameron to be around hate mongers or hate groups?" Mr. Benson went in for the kill.

"Absolutely not."

Mr. Benson turned away from Sharon and looked over at Leo. "Can you open the diary again, this time to the bright green tab and read the highlighted portion of the text for the court, Mrs. Riley."

Sharon's voice trembled. "I ran up on some awesome old people artifacts in the attic of my parent's home today looking for pictures from high school. There in the corner, folded neatly in a box was my parents matching Klan robes from when Daddy was a young man. LOL. There was a picture in there of them from before I was born in their get-ups looking like complete rebels. They are so cheesy. I had to take a keepsake."

Mr. Benson winked at Leo's lawyer then turned on his heels to Mr. Riley. "Were you ever a member of the Ku Klux Klan, Mrs. Riley?"

"No," she said, eyes lowered.

"To your knowledge was your husband a member of the Klan?"

"No."

"So what did Amy find up in the attic? And what picture is she referring to?"

"I have no idea." Sharon looked up at the ceiling.

Mr. Benson went back to his table. "Your Honor, the defense would like to submit exhibit C." He picked up an old photo and walked it back over to Sharon. With each of his steps, her heart pounded in her chest. Mr. Benson slowly laid the picture in front of her and quirked up the side of his lips. "Is that you in the white Klan robe beside your husband?" He pointed at the picture.

Sharon's eyes pulled slowly away from the photo. "Yes."

"So I'll ask you again. Do you think it's in Cameron's best interest to be around hate groups or hate mongers?" Mr. Benson asked, waiting for the plaintiff's lawyer to...

"Objection," Leo's lawyer said, jumping up from his seat. "The defense is badgering the witness. She has already answered that question."

"Sustained," the judge answered mechanically.

"No further questions for this witness your Honor," Mr. Benson said, taking a seat. He rested his forearms on the table and got ready for the next round. "That is how it's done," he said under his breath to Brett.

As the rest of the witnesses were called, Mr. Benson provided more and more evidence that supported his argument that Amy had been a bad person. Judy spoke to how disrespectful and lazy Amy had been during the entire course of the marriage. Gavin spoke to how many fights he witnessed where she was loud and belligerent. But then he moved his attention to Leo Tabor.

As Catherine sat down and swore in, Leo felt the brace around his neck grow a little tighter, nearly cutting off his air way. Mr. Benson went through a series of questions to verify who she was, where she worked and why she had divorced Leo, but then the juicy questions came.

"Where you aware that Leo Tabor was, to use your term, a serial philanderer," Mr. Benson asked.

Catherine looked over at Leo and sneered. "Not until I went to the doctor for my annual exam and found out that I had an abnormal pap. It was the first in 20 years."

"Why did you have an abnormal pap?" Mr. Benson asked.

"He had given me HPV," Catherine said, gripping the stand with her nails. "After that I had him followed to get solid proof. The detective found out he was sleeping with four women at a time. The evidence came in to me around the same time that he got in trouble for sleeping with his commanding officer's wife during some party. They were found on a golf course having sex by two Military Police officers. I wasn't there. I had refused to attend after I found out about my condition and his cheating."

Sharon shot mind bullets into the back of Leo's head as she soaked in the embarrassment for him. This information would have been very helpful to know before she went to bat for him.

"What about the kids?" Mr. Benson said, moving on. "Would you classify him as a dutiful father?"

"No," Catherine said firmly. "He's behind on child support. He misses most of his allotted time to see the children and when he does seem them, he seems to only do it because he has to. There is no excitement."

Leo wouldn't' look at Catherine. Instead, he looked past her, directly at the wall and prayed for it to be over soon. He tuned out the rest of her testimony and refused to pay attention until Mr. Benson stopped his line of questioning.

The MP gave more of the same confirmation about Leo getting caught with his testimony detailing how the couple were found on the golf course that night. "Naked in the 69 position on top of a blanket with a bottle of champagne and a small dildo."

Leo could have done without the dildo portion, considering they had already bust his balls wide open.

When Gavin was called, Leo was ready to throw in the towel and go. "How much more of this do I have to bear?" Leo asked the attorney. "We can regroup when she calls a recess."

"It's been hours," Leo complained.

The lawyer huffed under his breath. "She'll call a recess soon."

After Gavin swore in, he detailed the strip club, the coke, the fight, Amber, the pimping and lastly, the posing.

"Do you think that based upon your experiences with Leo that he truly cares about his grandson?" Mr. Benson asked, setting Gavin up for the free throw.

"No. I overheard him say that Amy Black had a life insurance policy for $750,000 that would be given to him only if he established paternity and full custody." Gavin winked at Leo. "If he doesn't get the boy, he doesn't get the money and he's flat broke."

Mr. Benson was getting a work out today. Walking back to his table, he retrieved a copy of the life insurance policy that Amy took out and the instructions to the trustee on how to carry out her last wishes.

Leo sat up. "How in the hell did they get a hold of that?" he asked in a strained voice.

After getting it admitted as evidence to the court, he knew that he was done with Gavin. "No further questions."

The judge had heard enough and she had not even gotten to the testimony of Brett and Courtney Black or Leo Tabor. Taking a sip of her water, she looked out at the exhausted room and decided. "I'm calling a one hour recess. Both parties return back here at 1:30 p.m." Slamming the gavel, she stood up and disappeared into her chambers.

The defense was exhausted but feeling good. They shook the hands of the witnesses and let them know that they could leave and move on with their day while at the same time speaking to Brett and Courtney under his breath about what was going to happen next.

"Let's get out of here," Mr. Benson said, walking with the large party out of the doors, leaving Sharon and Leo to lick their wounds.

Sharon quickly stood up and leaned over the partition. "I need to talk to you right now," she ordered Leo. "Right now."

Leo held up a hand to dismiss her as he went over what would happen next. "Not right now, I need to talk to my lawyer, Sharon. This is a trial if you haven't noticed."

"I'm paying for the lawyer and I say now," she snapped.

"Not now!" he growled, voice echoing in the nearly empty room.

The bailiff walked back into the court from the private chambers and looked over at Leo.

"Sorry," the lawyer said. "We're getting ready to leave." He gathered up his things.

Sharon stepped back and grabbed her purse, appalled that Leo had just screamed at her. "You've cost us this case, but you won't cost us another dime. As of 1:30 this afternoon, we are no longer paying for your lawyer." Throwing her purse over her shoulder, she strode out of the court room and let the door slam behind her.

Leo rubbed his head. "Can today get any fucking worse?"

"Do you have money to pay for your trial?" the lawyer asked.

"It depends," Leo said, sitting back down. "Do we have a chance in hell of winning this case?"

"I'm just going to level with you. No. Even though Cameron is your biological son, your lifestyle, your history, your finances, your military record all count against you. And no judge in her right mind is going to take that boy from two parents who love him and care for him and give that child to you." The lawyer didn't blink. Instead, he sat there glaring at Leo with his arms folded over his suit waiting for the truth to finally sink in. "If this is about money, you're not going to get it."

"Then what am I doing this for?" Leo asked, standing up.

"You tell me."

Leo looked up at the seal over the judge's chair. "I gave it a good try, but it's time I got on a plane and head back to Rochester to make amends with my father." In other words, he was going to tuck his tail between his legs and run back to safe quarters like he always did when things got tough.

"I'll tell the defense and close the case when the session reconvenes."

"Thanks," Leo said, resting his head on the table. "Can you just leave me here for a minute?"

"Sure. No problem," the lawyer said, grabbing his things, glad it was finally over.

***

Out in the hall, the entire defense team, along with Brett, Courtney and the family all stood talking and debating where to go for lunch when Sharon burst through the doors.

Walking up to Brett, she swallowed down her pride. "Brett, can I have a word with you, please?"

Courtney looked at the side of Sharon's head, then rolled her eyes. "I'll be over here, honey."

"No," Brett said, holding Courtney's hand. "You can say whatever you have to say in front of my wife."

"Very well," Sharon said, trying to focus. "Even though the judge has not yet ruled, it's obvious that Leo Tabor won't be getting Cameron. And I know that this will leave a scar on our relationship for years, but I'm hoping you will still allow Cameron to be in our lives. He's all we have left." Sharon wiped real tears. "This was a mistake. I admit that. But I am begging for your mercy."

Brett licked his lips. After so many hours in the Court, his mouth was parched. "Whose fault is that, Sharon?"

"It's ours," she eked out. "And I'm truly sorry. But I love my grandson. Please don't take him away from us."

Brett had no pity. Had this trial gone differently, she would have gladly taken him away. "Allow him to see you so you can turn him against Courtney? So you can turn him against me? So you can turn him into a racist? *I don't think so.* I'm a man of my word, Sharon. I told you that I would be there for your daughter until death do us part. And I did. I told you that you'd never see Cameron again after you tried to ruin my entire family and you won't." His voice was calm and quiet. "This is the end of the line, Sharon. There is no going back from here."

The hallway was silent, all watching as Sharon was forced to take her medicine. Unable to even think of a cruel response, she turned on her heels and headed down the hall in the same manner that her husband had.

Gavin walked over to Brett and hit his shoulder. "She'll be okay."

Brett honestly felt sorry for her. He never wanted it to come down to this but they had chosen the outcome for him by trying to take his son. "I doubt she will be okay, man. But what can I do?"

"Well, I followed Old Man Riley from the court house this morning and evidently, he's got another kid here in Jacksonville that he went to see while Sharon was being put through the ringer by Benson." Gavin laughed. "Cameron's not the only grandchild she has. Well, if you count step-children. He's just got to tell her about them. Pretty ironic, don't you think?"

Brett's mouth flew open. He turned to Gavin and frowned. "You can't be serious?"

"Yeah, I am." Gavin pulled out the address he had written on a piece of paper. "I bet if I slip this to the lawyer in there, he'd make sure she got it."

"I tell you, the Rileys are just full of surprises," Brett said flabbergasted.

Gavin watched as she finally disappeared down the hall. "That's probably why the Reverend didn't want to get on the stand. He wasn't sure what we had on him. It wasn't even about Sharon and her shit. He just didn't want to get busted."

"Runs in the family, I guess," Brett said, turning his attention away from her. "I appreciate you man." He offered his hand and Gavin took it. Reaching in, they gave each other a hug. "Hey, you're my brother."

Mr. Benson walked back over. "So far, so good. Let's head out and get something to eat at Chili's. We can go over what's coming for you one last time."

"Not so fast," Leo's lawyer said coming out of the courtroom, looking like he had just been dragged over the coals. He walked over to Mr. Benson and whispered in his ear. "Mr. Tabor is dropping the case." He raised his hands. "Let me correct that. Leo has dropped the case. You and I both know he's getting pummeled in there. It's time to throw in the towel."

Mr. Benson looked over at Brett and smiled. "I'm going to talk to this good gentleman alone, and I guess if what he says checks out then I'll meet you at Chili's for a celebration lunch."

Brett ran a hand over his head in disbelief. "Wow," he said realizing his cover was still inside of the court room. "I'll be right back," he said, disappearing back behind the door.

When he came into the courtroom, the lights had been turned off. In darkness, Leo sat in the same place, staring blankly into nothingness.

Brett pushed open the partition that separated the back of the courtroom from the tables and went over to the table where his cover still sat where he left it.

Leo looked over at Brett and rolled his eyes. "I guess you've already heard, huh?"

Brett put his cover back on and turned to Leo. "Yeah. I heard."

Leo had never felt so humbled and beaten before in his life. The experience had left him hollow. "I guess you and I both know that I deserved it...all of it."

Brett was surprised at how the anger had just dissipated inside of him. He no longer felt the need to beat Leo within an inch of life, not to mention that someone had already beat him to it. "I wouldn't say that you deserved all of it. It's abundantly clear that you had help."

Leo tapped his fingers on the table. "I'm sure you'll take good care of Cameron."

Brett didn't hesitate. "I will."

Remorse darkened Leo's face. "Do me a favor? When you finally have to tell him about me, don't tell him everything. I don't want him to know that his old man was a piece of shit."

"I've always taught my son to come to his own conclusions about people. I'm sure with this, he'll do the same," Brett said, unsure of exactly how he'd really handle telling Cameron the truth when the time came. No matter how it played out, he'd do it with honor and love. "You know, when I came back stateside, I didn't understand why I was spared. I remember one of the nurses telling me at Bethesda hospital that God must have had something important for me to do. But I just brushed it off. Until today, after hearing the testimony of people that you and Sharon Riley had influenced or impacted, I realized that if I had not come back alive, my son would have been subjected to a world where honor, pride and loyalty would have never truly been a part of his life. He would have turned out like...you. So thank you, for helping me realize, more clearly, my purpose. Because while I had an idea, I didn't know for sure until today."

That was a low blow. Leo would have honestly preferred a left hook to the cold hard truth. "I'm sure you have at least one question you want to ask me. Now's the time," Leo said with a deflated huff. He knew that once he left out of these doors, no one here would ever see him again. *He'd make damn sure of it.*

"About Amy?" He rolled his eyes. "No questions," Brett said, walking away. "She wasn't that important."

"I have one," Leo said before Brett could leave.

Brett stopped and turned around. "What's that?"

"How did you find out about the life insurance policy? I mean, the lawyer wasn't exactly forthcoming with information on it. Amy designed it that way."

Brett thought about it and smiled. "I'm going to have to plead plausible deniability on that one." In truth, he didn't know. Gavin just showed up with it one day.

"So is the money coming to you? Because I never saw who the secondary beneficiary was." Leo couldn't help it. He had to know after all of this.

"Yeah. I should get it in about 20 days." Brett smiled. "But I will tell you this." He chuckled and wiped a hand over his face. He folded his arm across his chest. "And it's going to fuck you up, *but* if you had just come to me *like a man*, instead of trying to snatch my son out of my life, and told me what you wanted, I would have gladly given it to you. Cameron is worth a lot more than $735,000. But if you ever knew him, then you'd know that already."

Leo glared at Brett. He *had* met Cameron once in Wilmington in a Mexican bar, but he'd never tell anyone that. "You would have just given it to me?" He said the words like he couldn't comprehend such a thing.

"Yeah. All I would have asked is that you never seek custody or visitation, which I'm sure you wouldn't have been interested anyway. And it would have been a win-win situation for both of us. You would have gotten your money and I would have gotten peace of mind." Brett shrugged. "But now, I'm just going to use $250,000 for legal fees and put the rest up for my son."

Leo shook his head. *This guy was unbelievable.* "Just that easy, huh?"

"Yeah, it would have been just that easy," Brett said, turning back around and walking out of the door. He didn't want to give Leo any more of his time, any more of his life, any more of his thought. When he walked out of this room, it would be as if Leo Tabor had never existed.

As the door to the courtroom slammed behind him and with it the last link to his sordid past with Amy Riley, Brett was met in the hallway by his family and friends who cheered him on and hugged him as they prepared to go out and celebrate their victory. The trial was over and so were their worries.

This had been the longest few months of Brett's life, but he had survived. In truth, it was the hardest battle of his life, the hardest lessons learned, the hardest glories earned and he was damn proud to be standing her with everyone who meant anything to him celebrating that fact.

Locking eyes on his beautiful wife, he grabbed her by her hand and pulled her into him. Kissing Courtney on her full lips, Brett hugged her tight. "I couldn't have done this without you," he said sincerely. "Thank you, baby."

Courtney wiped her happy tears. "I love you so much. There is nowhere else I'd rather be then right here with my family."

"I love you," he said, wiping her face. He turned to his group of friends and raised his hand to the air. "Now, let's get out of here and have some fun!"

# Epilogue

Six months after the court case ended, Brett and Courtney Black moved away from the sunny shores, mossy lakes and pine trees of Camp Lejeune and re-rooted their little family in Palo Alto, California to start their new life together. Gavin's cottage home was spectacular – modern and roomy, it was already large enough to consider adding yet another family member in the very near future.

A great little extra surprise was that the property on the beach came complete with an awesome boat and peaceful dock that Brett immediately took a liking to and claimed as his own. Finally, he'd have a hobby when he found time. For now, he was starting the certification process to become an official new member of Gavin's security firm.

Courtney was accepted into Stanford and was already taking classes both on campus and online, so she could still spend plenty of time with Cameron and Bella. Plus, she had joined a female surfing team that loved the water as much as she did.

Life was coming together for them finally, and they were moving forward and never looking back.

Back on the East Coast, Gavin made a beeline down the coast to Atlantic City. As he entered into Mr. Benson's empty office on an early Saturday morning, he found him sitting at his desk in a Cowboy's t-shirt and jeans, most unlike the man who seemed to love a good suit.

"Thanks for coming on such short notice," Mr. Benson said, wiping his tired eyes. He hadn't slept a wink in 24 hours.

"Don't mention it," Gavin said, closing the door. "It sounded pretty urgent."

"It is." Benson motioned at the chair. "Have a seat." Turning around his computer, he showed Gavin a photo of Mae Warford on his monitor. "Recognize her?"

"Yeah, she's the female judge that heard Brett's case," Gavin said, scooting his chair up closer to the desk.

"No, this is her twin sister, Judge *Mae* Warford, my girlfriend." He met Gavin's shocked eyes.

"Explains why you wanted Barrington out of the way."

Benson put up his finger in protest. "I said out of the way. I never said poisoned. That was your call."

Gavin shrugged. "It didn't kill him, just slowed him down and helped him lose about ten pounds with his fat ass. It was just a little *Delhi Tummy*. Anyway, what's going on with your girlfriend?"

"Mae has been receiving death threats from a neo-Nazi group near Raleigh, North Carolina. The threats have come over the phone, via email and then yesterday, she walked out and found that they had a swastika spray painted on the front door of her house. This has gotten out of control. If they know where she lives, it's because they are following her." He gritted his teeth.

"FBI on it yet?" Gavin asked, pulling out his notepad. He wrote down a few notes.

Benson was not about to put all his faith in the FBI. "Yeah, of course."

"I'll need the FBI contact she's working with," Gavin said, scribbling fast.

"I need someone who can be with her all the time. Someone who knows trouble when they see it and can be creative when they need to be. I need a grunt on this one, Gavin. Nothing less." Benson turned the monitor back around. "I have to warn you. She's bullheaded, but it's only because she's a Black woman in a white male dominated profession. But that still doesn't mean she should be subjected to this shit. And I have to do something about it."

"Why does this neo-Nazi group want to kill her?"

Benson sat back in his chair. "She's hearing a very important case. It's making national news. They want to put pressure on her so that she'll go easy on their leader." He threw the USA Today on the table in front of Gavin.

"Okay, I remember this guy. He's responsible for a string of church burnings and vandalisms and the murder of a community activist," Gavin said coolly. "What do you want from me on this?"

"I need you to be her security until this case is over," Mr. Benson said, reaching behind his desk and picking up a small overnight bag. He threw it on the table. "That's $200,000 cash, completely untraceable and non-taxable if you don't report it. If you do, just let me know, so I can get my paperwork straight."

Gavin took the bag and opened it. Looking at the bands of cash, he raised a brow. "How long do I need to be there?"

"As long as it takes," Mr. Benson said. "And there's more where that came from. Just make sure that no one hurts a hair on her head."

"Does she know that I'm coming?" Gavin asked, putting the bag beside him.

"I told her that you'd be there tomorrow," Mr. Benson said, knowing the sudden move might inconvenience him, but hopefully the money would change his mind.

Gavin sucked in a breath. "Tomorrow?" That was sort of pushing it.

"I'll owe you," Benson said, desperately. "And that's always a good thing. I have resources that would be beneficial to a man like you."

"No shit." Everyone knew that Benson was someone you wanted on your side when things got strange, and for him, things always got strange. Gavin rubbed his temples. "Okay. Yeah, I'll do it."

"Good." Mr. Benson stood up and offered his hand. "I truly appreciate you."

"Don't mention it," Gavin said, throwing the bag over his shoulder. "I'll touch base with you once I get to Raleigh. For now, don't tell her anything about me over the phone. I'll call back and get with my guys to come up with a plan tonight."

"Keep her safe, Gavin," Benson said seriously. "I think she might be my wife."

"Don't worry. I'll watch out for her," Gavin assured. "For now, just get some rest."

## The End.

# About the Author

**Latrivia Welch** (formerly Latrivia Nelson) is a USA TODAY, Amazon and National Bestselling Author of interracial romance and interracial romantic suspense novels. She divides her life into three professions: author, women's reproductive rights advocate and CEO of RiverHouse Publishing, LLC. Based out of Memphis, TN, she is considered one of the founders of the bw/wm romantic suspense genre. Latrivia is married to the love of her life, Bruce Welch, and is the mother of 2.5 beautiful children. She has penned over 20 novels under the Latrivia Nelson brand. This is her last book under that brand.

Books from now on will be under Latrivia Welch.

Visit her website at www.latriviawelch.com to learn more.

# Latrivia's Charities of Choice

There are so many worthy charities that need your help. Please consider making a contribution to the following charities to help military men and women and their families in their time of need.

**Semper Fi Fund**
http://semperfifund.org/

**Soldier's Angels**
http://www.soldiersangels.org/

**Wounded Warrior Project**
http://www.woundedwarriorproject.org/

**Whether time or money, consider giving back to the people who have already given so much.**

# STAY IN TOUCH

**Official Author Website**
www.latriviawelch.com

**Official Email**
Latrivia@LatriviaWelch.com

**Official Twitter**
www.twitter.com/LatriviaWelch

**Official Blog**
www.latriviawelchblog.com

**Please "Like" Latrivia on Facebook**
www.facebook.com/LatriviaWelch

# CURRENT BOOKS

**The Lonely Heart Series**

- **The Ugly Girlfriend (2010)**
- **Finding Opa (2010)**
- **The Grunt 1 (2011)**
- **The Contingency Plan (2012)**
- **Highness 1 (2015)**
- **The Grunt 2 (2015)**

**The Medlov Crime Family Series**
- **Dmitry's Closet (2010)**
- **Dmitry's Royal Flush: Rise of the Queen (2010)**
- **Anatoly Medlov: Complete Reign (2011)**
- **Saving Anya (2012)**

**The Agosto Family Series**
- **Ivy's Twisted Vine (2008)**
- **The World in Reverse (2013)**

**The Chronicles of Young Dmitry Medlov:**
- **Volume 1-7 (separate short stories**

**Seeking Santa (Short Story)**

# UPCOMING BOOKS
(Under Latrivia Welch)

## The Lonely Heart Series:
- Highness 2
- Red & Blu
- Gracie's Dirty Little Secret

## The Chronicles of Young Dmitry Medlov:
- Volume 8-12

## The Agosto Series:
- Wicker Men

## The Medlov Men Series:
- Gabriel's Regret
- Anatoly's Retribution
- Dmitry's Redemption